FROM HELL, WITH LOVE

BRYCE OAKLEY

No AI has been used in the making of this book.

Edited by Heather Flournoy

Cover Art and Design by @artful.sasha

CONTENTS

For the disasters who figured it out anyway.

CHAPTER ONE

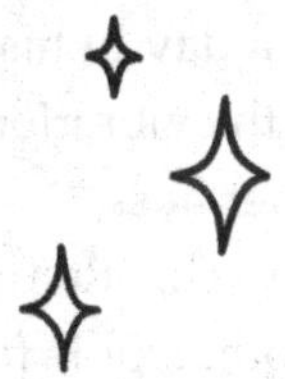

RAMONA GREENBRIAR HAD ALWAYS BEEN GOOD AT FINDING THINGS THAT were lost, just never the things she was actually looking for.

Case in point: the sandwich.

She stared into the donation bin with the kind of resigned horror that came from two years of working retail. She'd seen a lot of things show up in these boxes — dog-eared romance novels, self-help books with suspiciously specific margin notes… Once, the bin box had been filled to the brim with an entire collection of VHS tapes about competitive bird watching.

But this was a new low.

Someone had donated their lunch.

She snapped on a pair of latex gloves that she kept for donation-bin excavation and gingerly lifted out what had once been turkey and swiss on whole wheat. The smell hit her immediately — something between decay and despair. She gagged, arm outstretched as she speed-walked to the dumpster out back.

Late January in Fernwick was the kind of cold that made her nostrils stick together when she breathed in. Her breath fogged in front of her face as she tossed the bready biohazard into the trash. The metal lid clanged shut. She stood there for a moment, hands on her knees, breathing in the slightly less offensive smell of dumpster and dead leaves buried under dirty snow.

The universe had a sick sense of humor.

"You good out here?"

Ramona straightened to find Marcus leaning against the doorframe, vaping something that smelled like artificial mango and broken dreams. He was twenty-three, exclusively wore black turtlenecks, and had never done actual magic a day in his life but burned palo santo in the shop because it "elevated the vibration."

He was also, annoyingly, her boss.

"Someone donated a sandwich," Ramona said.

"Gross." Marcus took another pull from his vape pen, shrugging his shoulders. "Don't forget to sanitize your hands before touching inventory."

He disappeared back inside, and Ramona stood there in the cold, staring at the dumpster. The metal was rusted at the corners, peeling paint like dead skin.

Thirty-five years old. An advanced degree from Thornwood Academy. A handful of years of published research on medieval spellwork translation that people still cited at conferences she was no longer invited to.

And she was throwing away strangers' lunches behind a bookshop that sold fifteen-dollar bundles of sage.

Her phone buzzed in her back pocket, the vibration sharp against her hip. A text from her sister.

Iris: *Mom keeps asking about Imbolc. What should I tell her?*

Ramona's thumbs moved on autopilot: *Tell her work is great. Super busy. Can't make it.*

The lie came easy. Too easy. Work was busy — her mother just didn't need to know that "work" meant alphabetizing crystals and pretending tarot cards were an actual product worth $65. That her "research sabbatical" had turned into two years of retail purgatory.

She shoved her phone back in her pocket and headed inside, grateful for the blast of overheated air from the ancient radiator. The shop smelled like incense and dust and the faint chemical tang of Marcus's stupid vape pen.

The donation box awaited. She used hand sanitizer on top of her gloves, then returned to sort through the rest. Most of it was the usual — three copies of *The Secret*, a book about essential oils that smelled like it had been stored in a gym bag, outdated advice guides with titles like *The Cabbage Soup Cleanse.*

She was about to declare the whole box a loss when her fingers brushed something at the very bottom.

A book.

But not just any book.

The cover was water-stained leather, cracked with age, with hand-drawn sigils that had faded to barely visible. The spine was broken in three places. No title on the outside, but when Ramona carefully opened it, the first page read in elaborate calligraphy: *Summonings and Bindings: A Practical Guide.*

Her heart stumbled in her chest. Now, this. *This* was a find.

This was a real grimoire. She could *feel* its magic. An actual, legitimate, old-as-hell grimoire, the kind with handwritten spells and ingredients that included things like "grave dirt" and "moonlight captured in silver." The kind she used to study in candlelit libraries, feeling very important and very scholarly. The kind of book that had always called to her.

She caught sight of herself in the mirror near the affirmation card decks. Purple hair sticking up at odd angles, the result of a glamour spell gone wrong back in high school that she'd decided to just live with. Dark circles under her eyes. The Mystic Moon Books shirt hanging off her shoulders like a costume she couldn't quite pull off.

She looked away.

Marcus was helping a customer select a "manifestation journal" — really just a fifty-dollar notebook with moon phases printed on it. Her boss wasn't magical, and probably didn't even know witches and magical beings were real, and that Fernwick was one of the largest magical cities in the country.

She had maybe five minutes before Marcus would be on her to stock something for him.

Ramona turned the pages of the grimoire carefully, the old paper crackling under her fingertips. Some of the spells were standard fare —

protection wards, attraction charms, the usual. Others were more esoteric. More powerful.

More interesting.

A spell to summon your heart's desire.

Another to call forth prosperity and good fortune.

One that claimed to "reveal your truest path when all seems lost."

The academic in her — the part that wasn't quite dead yet — recognized the linguistic patterns, the symbolic frameworks. This was old magic. Pre-standardization, working on intent rather than precision, which meant it was either incredibly powerful or incredibly dangerous, depending on who was casting.

Most likely it was a mix of both powerful and dangerous for *anyone*.

Ramona should have put it on the clearance shelf. Should have priced it at $5.99 and let some college kid buy it for the aesthetic.

Instead, she slipped it into her canvas tote bag. The leather was cool against her palm. It felt like something.

It felt like possibility.

Or maybe just stupidity. Hard to tell the difference these days.

The rest of the shift crawled by with the speed of continental drift. A woman spent an hour asking about crystal energies before leaving empty-handed. A man tried to convince Ramona that the $42 oracle deck should really be $28 because "Mercury is in retrograde and money is just energy anyway."

The urge to explain that Mercury retrograde was an optical illusion and had nothing to do with cosmic commerce died in her throat. She smiled. She nodded. She ran his credit card for the full amount.

Marcus took a two-hour lunch and returned with a green juice that cost more than Ramona made in three hours. When five o'clock finally arrived, Ramona was grabbing her coat when Marcus's voice stopped her.

"Hey, Ramona? Got a sec?"

Everything inside her went cold.

Those three words — *got a sec* — never preceded good news. They preceded conversations about "productivity" and "company direction" and "unfortunately, we have to make some changes."

She turned, coat half on, clearing her throat and forcing her voice into a casual, feminine pitch. "What's up?"

Marcus pressed his lips together and tilted his head, the expression he probably thought looked sympathetic. "So, uh, I wanted to give you a heads-up. We should probably talk tomorrow. About where things are going. Your role here, that kind of thing."

"My… role?" Ramona asked, a tiny squeak in the words.

"Yeah, just… let's touch base in the morning, okay?" He was already looking back at his phone, dismissing her. "Have a good night."

Ramona stepped out into the January cold. Her breath fogged. Her fingers were numb. *Let's touch base* was corporate-speak for *You're fucked*.

Two years she'd been working here.

Two years, and apparently that earned you a firing delivered in startup-bro language.

Her phone buzzed. A text to the family group chat from Iris with a photo attached: Iris and her husband at some Italian restaurant, everyone's teeth unnaturally white in the dim lighting. The caption: *First Mommy and Daddy date night in months!* 🍷

Iris, with her thriving curse-breaking business and her perfect family and her complete lack of understanding about why Ramona couldn't just "bounce back" from a divorce and a career implosion.

The photo made something twist in Ramona's stomach. Not jealousy, exactly. More like grief for a version of herself that used to exist. The one who had dinner reservations and date nights and a wife who looked at her like she mattered.

She shoved her phone in her pocket and headed for her car — a rusty sedan old enough to vote that made an ominous rattling sound whenever she went above forty-five miles per hour. Once upon a time, she'd driven a sensible Subaru. Had a parking spot with her name on it at the academy. Had a future.

The grimoire sat inside her bag on her passenger seat the entire drive home, a presence in her peripheral vision. She didn't look at it directly. If she looked at it, she'd have to decide what it meant that she'd taken it.

• • •

THE SMOKE ALARM was going off when she opened the door to the apartment.

The building was the kind of place where the radiator clanked all night and the landlord responded to maintenance requests with "I'll get to it" and then didn't. But rent was cheap, and her Croneslist roommates were — well, they were something. Three other witches and one accidental human who'd moved in via a "roommate needed" ad in a major miscommunication.

"I know!" Kashvi shrieked from the kitchen. "I know it's smoking!" She seemed to be yelling at the alarm, not a person.

Ramona found Kashvi brandishing a spatula at a pan that was producing alarming amounts of smoke, sparklers shooting from her fingertips in agitated bursts. Whatever had been cooking was now a blackened hockey puck that might have been a grilled cheese in a past life.

Felix emerged from his room, Gerald the pigeon perched on his shoulder like some kind of deranged parrot. Felix calmly reached up to silence the alarm. "You're officially forbidden from using the stove."

"It's my kitchen, too!"

"And yet somehow you're the only one who consistently summons the fire department." Felix looked at Ramona, his expression somewhere between sympathy and exhaustion. "Thai leftovers in the fridge if you want them."

Her other two roommates, Cammie and Posey, sat on the couch watching *Love Potion*, their current favorite reality dating show.

Ramona mumbled something noncommittal and headed straight for her room, shutting the door on the sounds of Kashvi arguing that the grilled cheese "wasn't even that burnt."

Her room was small. A bed held together mostly by duct tape and hope, a dresser she'd found on the curb, a bookshelf sagging under romance novels and magical theory textbooks she couldn't quite throw away. The window looked out on an alley where someone's cat held screaming concerts at three a.m.

She sat on her bed. The springs creaked.

She pulled the grimoire out of her bag. The leather was still cool under her fingers, worn smooth by decades — maybe centuries — of hands. She wondered who'd owned it before. Another desperate witch? Someone who'd succeeded where she'd failed? Or someone who'd ended up worse off than her, donating their most precious possession alongside a moldy sandwich?

She'd stopped doing magic. Really stopped, not just "taking a break" like she told people. Two years since the incident, since she'd decided her magic was more liability than asset.

The grimoire fell open to page forty-seven, like it wanted her to see it. Written in faded ink:

To Summon Success and Fortune

When darkness descends and all paths seem barred, call upon those who dwell beyond to light your way. Speak the words thrice and offer what you hold most dear. Aid will come, though perhaps not as expected.

The ingredients were simple. White candles. Salt. A personal item of value. The incantation was only four lines.

Ramona read it three times, her academic brain automatically parsing the structure. Basic summoning framework, standard protective elements, reasonable power requirements. The kind of spell she would have assigned to undergrads to translate.

The kind of spell that shouldn't work on someone whose magic consistently did the opposite of what she intended.

She closed the grimoire and set it on her nightstand. This was stupid. She was thirty-five years old, possibly about to be fired from a job she'd taken as a temporary stopgap, living in an apartment with roommates like she was still in her twenties, and lying to her parents about everything that mattered.

Her sister was thirty-seven with two kids, a thriving business, and a husband who actually showed up to family dinners, even if he had the personality of a damp napkin. Most of her grad school cohort was tenured by now. Her ex-wife had already replaced her on every level — new relationship, new house, new life.

And Ramona was here.

Stuck.

Her phone lit up with her mom's contact photo.

She'd arrived in Fernwick with the hope that an entirely new city meant a fresh start. And it did offer anonymity, but apparently two hours wasn't far enough away to entirely escape her past.

RAMONA WATCHED IT RING. Once, twice, three times. She sighed and answered on the fourth ring, already grimacing.

"Hi, Mom."

"Ramona! Finally. I was starting to worry." Her mother's voice was formal and precise, just as it had always been. "Iris mentioned you've been busy."

"Yeah, really busy. We're doing inventory this week."

It wasn't technically a lie. Marcus had mentioned inventory. Sometime back in September.

"That's wonderful, honey. I wanted to call about Imbolc dinner and give your apparently very busy schedule a chance to remember your dear family on one of our sacred days." She really had to give credit to her mom's ability to make a dinner invitation sound disappointed. "Iris will be there, and your father and I would love to have you there."

Ramona tugged at a loose thread on the edge of her skirt, realizing her tights had a run. She traced her finger along the ladder of threads. Damn. These were her last good pair of tights. "I'll try. Work's been really demanding."

They talked for another five minutes, her mother filling her in on her father's latest chess tournament and the new expansion at her apothecary. Ramona made the appropriate interested noises, gave vague updates about her "career," and promised to try harder to make it to Imbolc dinner.

When she finally hung up, she stared at the grimoire on her nightstand.

She stood up, swaying slightly, and crossed to her dresser. She glanced toward the grimoire, but something inside of her gave a sharp tug. *Don't.*

Ramona instead pointed her finger at her reflection in the mirror above her dresser. A simple Level I spell. Just a minor color correction, take the purple back to her natural brown.

She spoke the incantation clearly, deliberately, pouring what little sober concentration she had left into the spell.

Nothing happened.

Her reflection stared back at her, purple hair and all. Mocking.

She tried again, enunciating each syllable like her old professor had taught her. Intent and precision. Will and focus.

Nothing.

One more time, adding more intent, more focus, more desperation—

Her hair flickered for half a second to a shade of purple so dark it was almost black, then snapped back to the faded mess.

She turned back to the grimoire on her nightstand. If she couldn't even manage a basic glamour spell most witches knew at thirteen, what made her think she could successfully cast a summoning from a donation-bin grimoire?

The book sat there, innocuous. Just leather and paper and someone else's desperation, donated alongside a turkey sandwich.

Ramona picked it up, feeling the weight of it. For a moment — just a moment — she imagined it. Lighting the candles. Speaking the words. Something, *anything*, changing.

Then she set the book back on the nightstand and turned off the light.

The spell wouldn't work anyway. Nothing ever did.

She climbed into bed and pulled the blanket up to her chin, ignoring the hunger pang in her stomach. Through the window, she could hear the alley cat starting its nightly concert. The radiator clanked. Somewhere down the hall, Kashvi was still arguing with Felix about the stove's sensitivity.

Tomorrow she'd go back to Mystic Moon Books. Marcus would have his talk. She'd probably get fired from a fake magic shop run by a twenty-three-year-old who thought crystals were a personality trait.

And the grimoire would sit on her nightstand, gathering dust.

CHAPTER TWO

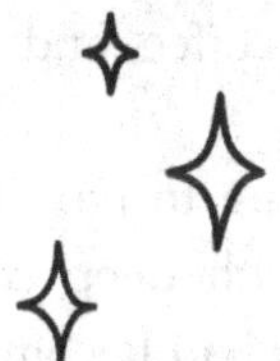

RAMONA WOKE UP TO THE SOUND OF SOMEONE SCREAMING.

She bolted upright, heart pounding, before realizing it was just the cat in the alley. Again. She lay back onto her pillow and stared at the water stain on her ceiling that looked vaguely like a duck.

The duck seemed to judge her silently.

Her phone buzzed on her nightstand. A calendar reminder: Rent due in one week.

She closed her eyes. Right.

Ramona opened her banking app and immediately wished she hadn't. Between groceries, her car insurance, and the fact that she'd been low on hours this month, she was exactly $442 short.

The number sat there on her screen, accusatory.

She lay there for a moment, doing mental math that refused to work in her favor. Her next paycheck wasn't until after the due date, and she'd been late almost every month for the past six months. She could ask her parents, but that would require explaining why she needed money, which would lead to questions about her job, which would unravel the entire lie she'd been maintaining for two years.

"Fuck," she whispered to the duck-shaped water stain.

She dragged herself out of bed and shuffled to the kitchen, where

Felix was making coffee and Gerald was perched on the back of a chair, watching with his judgmental pigeon eyes. The morning light coming through the kitchen window was gray and weak. The weather outside had all the charm of a wet paper bag.

"Morning," Felix said, not looking up from his French press. He was wearing a sweater with a cat on it, which Gerald seemed to take as a personal insult based on his agitated cooing.

Ramona poured herself coffee and gave a sideways glance at Gerald.

"Hey, about rent, I'm going to be a tiny bit late again," Ramona said, not looking at Felix with deep concentration. As the longest tenant of the apartment, Felix had become the rent collector, a job that meant Ramona had to apologize to him near the end of every month.

Felix shrugged. "Okay. Get it to me when you can."

THE BOOKSHOP FELT SMALLER than usual. Or maybe Ramona just felt like the walls were closing in.

She'd arrived ten minutes late, and Marcus was already there, reorganizing the crystal display in a way that made absolutely no sense. Rose quartz next to obsidian? The man had no understanding of basic energetic principles.

"Morning, Ramona," he said without looking at her.

"Morning."

She busied herself with opening the register, counting bills with numb fingers, anything to avoid the inevitable conversation. Maybe if she looked busy enough, he'd forget. Maybe a meteor would hit the shop. Maybe she'd spontaneously combust.

Unfortunately, none of those things happened.

At 10:47 a.m., Marcus found her restocking the Occult section in the back corner — the small, dark area filled with books that no witch worth her wand would ever touch. *Wicca for Dummies*. *How to Talk to Your Spirit Guides*. A book called *Crystals and Cryptocurrency* that seemed to fundamentally misunderstand both concepts.

"Hey, so." Marcus leaned against the bookshelf, vape pen in hand. The artificial mango smell made her stomach turn. "About that talk."

Ramona set down a copy of *Moon Magic Made Easy* and turned to face him. Her pulse kicked up. "Right."

"So, the shop's been doing really well. Like, really well."

For one wild, impossible second, Ramona's heart lifted. They were doing well. He was going to give her a raise. Maybe even make her assistant manager. She'd been here two years, she knew every corner of this place, she could—

"We're opening a second location," Marcus continued, grinning like he'd just announced world peace. "Downtown. Bigger space, better foot traffic. It's gonna be huge."

"That's… great," Ramona said carefully. The hope in her chest continued to bloom.

"Yeah, and I've been thinking about who should run it." He paused, and Ramona held her breath. The moment stretched.

Ramona saw the meaning of his pause. He was trying to tell her he wanted her to run the new shop. She smiled, almost blushing at the idea. "I'd—"

"My brother's perfect for it. He just graduated, super business-savvy, you know how it is."

The breath left her lungs. The smile left her face. She blinked in surprise. "Your… brother," she repeated slowly, as if maybe he just needed to hear it said back to realize what kind of an idea that was.

"Yeah! Dylan. He was in Sigma Nu, so he's got great people skills. He's gonna crush it."

Ramona stared at Marcus. At his stupid turtleneck and his stupid vape pen and his stupid, oblivious face. The entire shop was funded by his rich parents — of *course* he'd hire his brother. Her hands were shaking. She shoved them in her pockets. "And what about… here? The original location?"

"Oh, you'll keep doing what you're doing. You're great at it." He said it like he was giving her a gift. Like she should be grateful. "I mean, someone's gotta hold down the fort, right?"

"Right. Like… a manager here?" Ramona said, not exactly proud of the embarrassingly high octave her voice her had reached.

"Uh, hmm. We'll figure that out."

That did not sound promising. She gave a curt nod anyway. It wasn't a no, at least. And with a second location, that meant Marcus would be away from this store more.

"When does it open?" Ramona asked. "The new store."

"Dylan's already there, getting things set up. We're really building it from the ground up together," Marcus said, looking pleased.

"Oh, okay. Congrats on a second location. That's super exciting."

"Yeah, I'm getting some signage installed here so I needed to have you up to speed when customers are asking about it."

"Right. Yeah. Consider me sped up," Ramona said, mentally cringing at herself while she surreptitiously brushed her clammy hands on the sides of her skirt.

"Cool. Glad we're on the same page." He pushed off the bookshelf. "Oh, and can you work on stocking more of those manifestation journals? They're selling like crazy."

He walked away, leaving Ramona surrounded by books about chakras and auras and finding your inner goddess.

The injustice of it sat in her throat like broken glass.

She made it through the rest of her shift on autopilot. Rang up customers. Smiled. The manifestation journals felt heavier with each one she restocked, like the universe was fucking with her specifically. A woman asked if maybe Saturn in Scorpio was affecting her love life. A man wanted to know which crystal would make him better at day trading.

Ramona answered their questions with the same tired, upbeat script she'd used for two years.

At 5:03 p.m., she clocked out, walked to her car, sat in the driver's seat, and started crying.

Not pretty crying. The ugly kind, where her face got blotchy and her nose ran and she couldn't catch her breath. She cried until her eyes hurt and her throat was raw and she'd gone through an entire travel pack of tissues from her glove compartment.

Two fucking years and Marcus's frat boy brother was going to run the new location.

She caught sight of herself in the rearview mirror. Her hair was a mess. Mascara streaked down her cheeks. The face of a full adult woman crying in a shitty car in a strip mall parking lot because she didn't get promoted at a fake magic shop.

This was rock bottom.

Or at least, she *hoped* it was rock bottom. Because if there *was* further to fall, she didn't want to know about it.

THE GRIMALKIN WAS three blocks from the apartment, which was exactly the right distance for a bad day. Close enough to walk to without thinking about it. Far enough that going there felt like a decision.

Ramona had not made a decision. She had just started walking and ended up there, which was how The Grimalkin worked.

It was on a block that didn't quite make sense geographically — a narrow door the color of charcoal, set between two buildings that shouldn't have had space for it, marked by a wooden sign in the shape of a cat with the paint half gone, swinging on a single chain in a nonexistent breeze. If she didn't know to look for it, she could walk past it every day for years and see nothing but wall. Ramona had been coming here since moving into the apartment.

She pushed the door open. It swung inward, as it always did, regardless of which side she pushed from.

Inside, The Grimalkin had low ceilings, dark wood, candles burning at a color that was almost but not quite orange — something closer to an golden-violet that made everyone look like they were lit from the inside. Every table and counter had mismatched chairs that were all, somehow, comfortable. A long bar made of something that might have been reclaimed church pew. The jukebox in the corner, an old Wurlitzer in iridescent green, playing something slow and slightly accusatory that Ramona felt was directed at her specifically.

Odette was already there.

Odette was always there. The Grimalkin's owner and usual bartender, she was ageless in the specific way of certain women and certain bars — not young, not old, but permanent, like the building had grown up around her. Maybe it had. She had dark hair pinned back with something that might have been a bone hairpin. Eyes that had seen everything and filed it away without judgment. She had never, in all the years Ramona had been coming here, asked a single intrusive question. She had also never failed to pour the right thing.

The Grimalkin's regulars were the kind of magical community that had fallen through the cracks of respectable coven life — hedge witches who would never be accepted to Thornwood Academy; a pair of elderly sisters who came every Thursday and had been coming every Thursday since before anyone could remember and ordered the same thing and never spoke to anyone else; a water witch who tended bar sometimes and could make a cocktail that tasted exactly like whatever you were grieving. Most importantly, there was a three-legged cat named Parliamentarian who belonged to no one and accepted tribute from everyone. A warlock named Dennis who claimed to be retired, which nobody believed. People who had left their covens and people who had been asked to leave their covens and people who had never wanted a coven in the first place — the self-taught, the lapsed, the quietly powerful, the catastrophically mediocre. It was not a place where anyone came to be impressive.

As for the non-witches: There was a corner booth that two orcs had been occupying for what seemed like decades, running what appeared to be an extremely informal mediation practice for other supernatural beings. A banshee Ramona had talked to once who only came in on nights when she wasn't working, just to sit somewhere loud enough to drown out the noise in her own head. Something in the back that Odette acknowledged with a nod and nobody else looked directly at. The fae, when they came, were obvious immediately — too beautiful, too careful with their words, ordering drinks they'd nurse for hours while watching everything. Odette charged them double, and they paid without comment.

The Grimalkin had a policy that was never written down anywhere: Everyone was welcome as long as they kept their business off the tables, settled their own debts before they walked out, and didn't make the cat uncomfortable. It was a remarkably effective policy.

Parliamentarian was currently occupying the stool next to Ramona's preferred spot at the bar. He looked at her when she sat down. She looked back. He moved one stool over with the dignity of someone making a deliberate choice rather than a concession.

Odette set something dark and warm in front of Ramona before Ramona had fully settled onto the stool. Ramona didn't ask what it was. She drank it. It tasted like the specific exhaustion of being exactly who she didn't plan to be.

Odette moved away. Parliamentarian stared at her. The jukebox changed its mind and put on a song featuring jaunty piano.

Ramona stared at the bar top and let the ambient noise of other people's problems wash over her.

She was on her second whatever-it-was when the stool beside her filled up. She didn't look. Then it filled up on the other side. Then a third time, the scrape of a chair pulled up behind her.

She looked.

Felix. Posey. Kashvi, already unwinding her scarf. Gerald, on Felix's shoulder, watching her with the solemn attention he brought to most situations.

"Hi," Ramona said.

"Thought you might be here," Posey said simply, settling her coat over the back of her chair. She had soil on her left sleeve.

Kashvi's fingers sparked once, briefly, gold. "Your spiritual energy was very loud."

"My energy—"

"*Very* loud," Kashvi repeated and flagged down Odette.

Ramona looked at them. All of them, here, on a Tuesday, because apparently her emotional state had broadcast itself across three city blocks. She opened her mouth to say she was fine, she was just having a drink, she didn't need—

"Marcus is opening a second Mystic Moon location," she said instead. "And giving it to his brother, Dylan."

"Dylan? The frat guy?" Felix said.

"That's the one."

"What a dick," Kashvi said. A particularly aggressive sparkler shot sideways and narrowly missed the person on the next stool, who didn't flinch, because this was The Grimalkin and people minded their own business.

Odette replaced Ramona's drink without being asked. Ramona took it as the gift it was.

Cammie arrived twenty minutes later, pulling her café apron over her head as she walked in the door. She took one look at the situation, sat down, and said "okay" in the tone of someone who had assessed the damage and was prepared to stay until it was dealt with. She'd been their roommate for eight months.

Ramona still wasn't entirely sure how Cammie had answered the Croneslist ad — Felix and Kashvi had been living together when Posey and Ramona had joined, and none of them had thought to question how a thoroughly non-magical woman had found a listing on a thoroughly magical classifieds board. Cammie had never explained and they had never asked, because Cammie had a quality of existing exactly where she was supposed to be that made questions feel unnecessary.

She sat down, pushed her red hair back from her ear — the one with the dozen piercings, each one slightly different, a collection with no apparent system — and looked at Ramona expectantly.

Somewhere around the third drink, Ramona found herself giving a speech.

"Assistant Professor," Ramona said. The words came out slurred at the edges. She gestured with her glass, nearly sloshing it. "Published researcher. Office with a window. And a wife." She paused. The word sat there. "I had a fucking wife."

The table went quiet. Even Gerald went still.

Cammie tilted her head. Her red hair slid over her shoulder. "I didn't know you were married."

Right. Because Ramona didn't talk about that. Didn't talk about much, actually. Kept to her room, paid her rent when she could, shared the kitchen in shifts. When she moved to a new city to start a new life, she focused on not bringing too much of the old one with her. That was the arrangement.

"Simone." Ramona took another sip. The drink had given up tasting like anything. "So fucking pretty. Everyone loved her. Everyone." She paused. "Especially Kate Stone."

The group got quieter. Even the jukebox seemed to hold.

"Six months they were sleeping together. Six months." Her voice cracked on it. "And everyone in the coven knew. Everyone in my department. Every single person." She pressed her thumb against the base of her glass. "And no one told me."

"Fuck," Posey said quietly.

Kashvi's sparklers had gone completely dark. She reached over and put her hand over Ramona's on the bar. Didn't say anything.

"It's not forever," Cammie said finally. She sounded like she was trying to mean it and wasn't quite sure she did.

"Isn't it, though?" Ramona's vision blurred. The candlelight smeared at the edges. "Two years and I'm going backwards. Marcus's frat brother is going to run a store and I'm going to keep pretending Mercury retrograde is real and—" She pressed her palms against her eyes. Everyone was giving her that look. That careful, pitying look she'd been getting for two years. "I should go home."

"Ramona—" Felix started.

"I'm fine." The lie came easily. "Just a bad day. Thank you for—" She gestured vaguely at the drinks, at them, at the whole situation.

She slid off the stool. The room tilted slightly. Parliamentarian watched her go with an expression of three-legged dignity. Odette said nothing, which was its own kind of kindness.

She managed three blocks.

The apartment building came into view with the particular relief of a place that was hers even when nothing else was. She got the door open. Got up the stairs. Got into the apartment and stood in the dark hallway for a moment, just breathing.

They were nice people. Good roommates. They weren't her friends. She'd learned the hard way what happened when she let people get too close. It was safer to keep the walls up.

Even if the walls were starting to feel less like protection and more like a very small room she'd been standing in for two years.

She changed into the thrifted novelty T-shirt that said *Witch Happens* and sat on her bed. The springs creaked. The room was quiet.

The grimoire was still on her nightstand, exactly where she'd left it.

Ramona picked it up, her thumb caressing the smooth leather. The pages were brittle with age, crackling softly as she turned them.

She flipped to page forty-seven.

To Summon Success and Fortune.

Right. Because that had worked out so well for everyone in the history of magical disasters.

But.

But what did she have to lose at this point?

Her job was a dead end. Her sister was thriving. Her parents thought she had a career when really she had a name tag and a slowly dying sedan. She was thirty-five years old and drunk on cheap liquor and she couldn't even fix her own hair and she was so, *so* tired of pretending everything was fine.

Maybe the universe owed her one. Maybe after everything was taken from her — her marriage, her career, her dignity — maybe it was time for something to finally go right.

"Fuck it," she said to her empty room.

The words hung in the air. No one answered.

The living room had gone mercifully quiet as she stepped out to gather the ingredients with the methodical focus of someone who'd given up on hope but hadn't quite given up on spite. White candles courtesy of Felix's stress-shopping habit. They smelled like "Autumnal Harvest" and had probably cost more than they should have. Salt from the kitchen, the cheap kind in the cardboard container that left her fingers gritty. A personal item of value.

She stared at her jewelry box. Most of it was costume jewelry, things she'd picked up at thrift stores or received as forgettable gifts. But there, tucked in the corner, was a silver ring her dead grandmother had given her when she graduated from Thornwood. The metal was tarnished, the small stone — some kind of quartz — cloudy with age.

Her grandmother had pressed it into her palm at the ceremony, her papery fingers warm. "For when you need to remember who you are," she'd said.

Ramona picked it up. The silver was cold. Heavy.

She placed it in the center of her floor.

The candles went around it in a circle, their flames casting shadows that seemed too large for her small room. The salt formed the barrier.

She lit the candles one by one. The flames flickered, casting strange shadows on her walls that seemed to move independent of the light source. Probably just the draft from the window.

Her hands were shaking. Whether that was from the wine or the nerves or the sheer stupidity of what she was about to do, it was impossible to tell.

Then she read the words. They felt strange in her mouth, not quite Latincane or the ancient tongues she'd studied.

Once. Her voice cracked on the second syllable.

Twice. Clearer now, more confident, more defiant.

Three times. The final repetition came out steady, almost aggressive. Like a dare.

Nothing happened.

Ramona sat there on her floor, surrounded by candles that smelled like a sad beige catalog, feeling ridiculous. Of course nothing happened. This was a spell from a donation-bin grimoire donated alongside someone's turkey sandwich. What had she expected? A lightning bolt? A choir of angels? A fucking sign from the universe that her life wasn't a complete—

The candles went out.

All of them. All at once.

No wind. No reason. Just sudden darkness.

The temperature in the room dropped so fast, Ramona could feel it bite at her throat as she breathed. Her heart kicked against her ribs. The air smelled like sulfur and something else — expensive perfume. Bergamot and something darker, heavier. Oud, perhaps. Like smoke and crushed flowers.

The shadows in the corners of her room seemed to deepen, to move, to coalesce into something solid. Something with weight and presence and intention.

And then there was a silhouette.

Standing in the center of her salt circle, backlit by the streetlight coming through her window. Tall. Broad-shouldered. The outline of a person, maybe, but the edges seemed wrong somehow. Too sharp. Too still. Like someone had cut a hole in reality and something had stepped through.

Ramona's heart was trying to exit her body through her throat. Her hands were frozen on her knees. She couldn't move. Couldn't breathe. Couldn't think beyond the single, screaming thought: *Oh fuck oh fuck oh fuck.*

The figure shifted, and then…

A long-suffering sigh. A whispered, "Oh, you've got to be fucking kidding me."

A woman's voice. Low and rough with an accent that seemed from somewhere far away, with a quality that made Ramona's bones vibrate. Not loud, but everywhere at once, like it was coming from inside her own skull.

The streetlight caught the edge of a face. Sharp cheekbones. A jaw that could cut glass. Eyes that reflected the dim light like an animal's.

And Ramona, drunk and terrified and so far past the point of rational thought, could only think one thing:

The spell actually fucking worked.

CHAPTER THREE

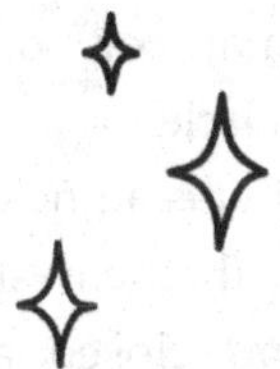

RAMONA'S FIRST THOUGHT WAS: I'M GOING TO DIE IN AN OVERSIZED T-shirt that says *Witch Happens*.

Her second thought was: That voice is really attractive, which is inappropriate given the circumstances.

Her third thought was: Run, idiot.

She scrambled backward, her back hitting the bed frame hard enough to bruise. The grimoire fell from her lap with a thud that sounded too loud in the sudden silence.

"Stay there." Ramona's voice came out steadier than she expected or felt. "Don't move."

The figure in the darkness tilted its head. The movement was slow, deliberate. Predatory.

"Or what?"

Two words. Just two words, but they made Ramona's bones vibrate like a tuning fork. Her heart kicked against her ribs.

"Or…" Ramona looked around. The candles were out. All of them. The salt circle was intact, the white line still perfect on her floor. That should hold. Basic magical theory, the first thing they taught at Thornwood. Even if she'd never actually successfully completed a summoning before. Even if she was drunk and this was clearly going sideways. "The salt will hold you," Ramona said. "You can't cross it."

There was a pause. The silence stretched. Then a sound that might have been a laugh. Low and dark.

"Is that right?"

The figure took a step forward.

Ramona's stomach dropped. The woman — and she could see now that it was definitely a woman, or something shaped like one — walked right through the salt circle.

Just stepped over it. Like it was a line drawn in chalk.

"Shit." Ramona lunged for the nearest thing that could possibly be used as a weapon. Her hand closed around one of Felix's pillar candles, as though Autumnal Harvest could save her now.

She held it up. Not quite brandishing. Just… holding it. Like that would help.

The woman paused. Looked at the candle. Then at Ramona.

"Are you threatening me with a *candle,* Mortal?"

"It's solid wax," Ramona said. Her voice had taken on a panicked edge. "And I'm not scared to use it."

"Noted."

The woman's eyes — and Ramona could see them now, dark and unsettlingly steady in the dim light — tracked the candle with something that might have been amusement. The streetlight from the window caught her face properly for the first time.

The woman had dark hair that fell just past her ears in waves, slightly mussed like she'd been running her hands through it. Or like she'd just been yanked through a dimensional portal mid-conversation. And she was wearing a suit — black, well-tailored, expensive, though slightly singed at the cuffs. It probably cost more than Ramona's car. The white shirt underneath was open at the collar, showing the hollow of her throat and the gleam of silver chains layered at her neck. Rings glinted on her fingers. A metal watch caught the light at her wrist.

"Who are you?" Ramona asked. "What are you?"

"*You* summoned me." The woman's voice was flat. Bored, almost. "You tell me."

"I was trying to summon success. Fortune. A better job." Ramona gestured vaguely with the candle. "Not whatever this is."

The woman crossed her arms. The movement made her jacket pull tight across her shoulders. "Whatever this is?"

"You know what I mean."

"I really don't."

They stared at each other. Ramona was acutely aware that she was wearing an old T-shirt and no pants, holding an autumnal candle, while a strange woman in an expensive suit stood in her bedroom.

This was worse than the incident. Worse than everything.

"Let's start over." Ramona lowered the candle slightly. Her arm was getting tired. It really was quite heavy. "Who are you?"

The woman sighed. It was the kind of sigh that suggested she'd had a very long day and this was just making it longer.

"My name is Azareth," she said. Each syllable was crisp, precise. "Duchess of the Third Circle. Keeper of the Endless Ledger. Vice President of Temptation and Minor Inconveniences, Hell's Southeastern Division." She paused, running a hand through her already-disheveled hair in a gesture that looked habitual. Frustrated. "And you just dragged me out of a performance review."

Ramona blinked. "Hell has a Southeastern Division?"

"We reorganized in the nineties. Corporate structure." Azareth looked around the room, taking in the duct-taped bed frame, the pile of laundry, the water-stain duck on the ceiling. "Mandatory sensitivity training. Quarterly reports. Team-building exercises." Another sigh. "This is what I was summoned for? *This*?"

Ramona scoffed in offense.

"Your bed is held together with tape." Azareth pointed a dark-tipped nail toward the furniture item in question.

"It's vintage."

"It's a fire hazard."

"You're one to talk. You're literally from Hell." Ramona was unsure exactly why she needed to defend her bed from judgment, but it felt necessary in the moment.

"That's different."

"How?"

"Hell has better infrastructure." Azareth's gaze dropped. "And you're not wearing pants."

Ramona's face went hot. She grabbed a throw blanket off the bed and wrapped it around her waist. "Listen, *Azareth—*"

"You're not pronouncing that correctly."

"I don't care." Ramona stood up, blanket-dignity and all. "You need to leave. Now. Back to Hell, back to wherever you came from."

Azareth stared at her. "That's not how this works."

"I summoned you. I can unsummon you."

"Can you?" Azareth's eyebrow raised. "Because from where I'm standing, you have no idea what you're doing."

Ramona opened her mouth. Closed it. Damn, this demon was quite rude and quite observant. "I know plenty about magic."

"You're threatening me with a candle."

"It's a very heavy candle."

"And you're drunk."

"That's none of your business." Ramona set the candle down on her nightstand. This was pointless. "Look. I don't know what spell I screwed up, but you can't stay here. If the Thornwood Coven finds out I summoned a demon—" She stopped. Took a breath. "I got expelled once already. They'd love an excuse to finish the job. Strip my magic. Report me to the Council."

"Sounds dramatic."

"I'm being practical." Ramona's voice came out flat. "So you need to leave. Please."

Azareth didn't move. "I can't."

The words landed wrong. "What do you mean you can't?"

"You bound me here." Azareth's voice was patient now. Too patient. "The spell you cast created a tether. I'm bound to you until the spell's conditions are met."

Ramona's head was pounding. "A tether?"

"Yes, in a way. A magical bond." Azareth paused, squinting at something past Ramona's shoulder. "Is that the grimoire you used?"

Ramona glanced back at where the book had fallen. "Maybe. What conditions have to be met?"

Azareth crossed the room — Ramona didn't bother brandishing the candle this time — and picked up the grimoire. She flipped through the pages, her expression growing darker with each turn.

"This is a real shitty grimoire," Azareth said flatly.

Ramona had the strange urge to defensively cradle the grimoire in her arms. Instead, she set her jaw and clenched her hands.

"Most of these spells are written by amateurs." Azareth held up a page. "You *really* didn't notice how bad these spells are? This protection ward is missing at least three key ingredients. This love spell would give someone hives. And this—" She turned to page forty-seven. "This summoning spell is supposed to call a minor spirit of fortune. Instead, it called me."

"Why?"

"Someone altered it." Azareth examined the page more closely. "See these symbols? In the margin?" She tilted the book toward Ramona. Strange markings caught the candlelight, drawn in different ink. "Someone added an amplification charm. Which means instead of a fortune spirit, you got me."

"A demon." Ramona gulped down her mortification for a moment. Wasn't this precisely what she'd spent her career decoding? And then she'd gone completely smooth-brained about the mechanics the moment she had a glass of wine?

"A very busy demon who is now bound to a drunk disaster witch and is going to have to file *so* much paperwork." Azareth pulled a small leather-bound book from her jacket pocket. She flipped through pages covered in tiny handwriting.

Ramona stared. "What's that?"

"The manual."

"Like, a demon manual?" Ramona asked, peering.

Azareth tilted the book away from Ramona's stare. "Just the standard issue. Ah. Here. Section 8633, subsection 12, line 734." Azareth didn't look up. "'In the event of an unauthorized summoning resulting in a binding tether, the summoned entity must remain within sixty-six feet of the summoner until such time as the original spell conditions are met or the bond is ritually severed.'" She snapped the book shut. "Sixty-six feet."

Ramona's brain was working through the implications. Slowly. "Sixty-six feet."

"If I go farther than that from you, we both experience excruciating pain. The manual describes it as 'like being torn apart from the inside.'" Azareth tucked the manual back into her pocket. "Very poetic."

"I have a job." Ramona's voice came out quiet. "I have roommates. What am I supposed to tell people?"

"That's not my problem."

Ramona scoffed. "It *is* your problem. You're here."

"Only because you summoned me."

"By accident."

"Intent is irrelevant to magical law." Azareth glanced at her watch. "I have approximately sixteen hours before Hell's HR department notices I'm missing. Which means I need to figure out how to break this bond before I'm AWOL and they dock my PTO."

Ramona rubbed her temples. The wine headache was setting in. "If you're bound to me, does that mean you can't hurt me?"

Azareth's expression shifted slightly. Something that might have been surprise. "That's actually a smart question."

"I'm drunk, not stupid."

"Debatable, Mortal." Azareth pulled out the manual again, flipping to a different section. "Section 8634, line 892. 'A binding tether prevents the summoned entity from causing direct physical harm to the summoner.' So yes. I can't hurt you. Even if I wanted to."

Ramona paused, looking Azareth up and down. "Do you want to?"

Azareth smiled, and Ramona's heart gave a distinctly prey-like squeeze. Were those fangs? Did this demon have *fangs*? "Ask me again in the morning," Azareth said.

"Good enough." Ramona reached for the grimoire, pulling it into her lap. The pages crackled under her fingers. "How do we meet the conditions of the spell? Do you know how to undo this? The tether?"

Azareth was quiet for a moment. Then she sighed. "In theory, yes."

"In theory?"

"The spell has conditions. You summoned aid for success and fortune. The tether breaks when those conditions are met — when you achieve what you were asking for. Or…" She paused. "There's a ritual severance. But it requires specific components. Rare ones. And it has to be performed at a convergence point during a new moon."

Ramona did a mental calculation. "Three weeks." Three weeks would be mid-February. After Imbolc, which she would surely be skipping now. But before Ostara — the Spring Equinox Gala — which was toward the end of March.

The Ostara Gala was the magical community's most important event of the year. More significant than Imbolc, more formal than the Harvest Ball. It celebrated the spring equinox, the balance of light and dark, renewal and rebirth. Every coven in the greater Thornwood area attended. The Thornwood Coven hosted a table. The High Priestess would be sitting with the Magical Council — the five most elite, powerful witches from Thornwood, Fernwick, and the surrounding areas. It was the kind of event where you wore your best dress, your most elaborate glamours, and smiled while pretending your life wasn't falling apart.

Kate and Simone would be there.

Ramona had skipped the last two years, citing work obligations that didn't exist. Her mother had been "understanding" the first year. Disappointed the second. This year, she'd been clear: "You're coming to Ostara, Ramona. People are starting to talk."

But if she couldn't break the tether at the new moon in three weeks…

"The night before Ostara," Ramona said slowly. "There's another new moon the night before Ostara."

"March twentieth," Azareth confirmed, pulling out her phone.

Ramona blinked. The phone was sleek, matte black, but something about it was… off. The screen had a faint red tint that made her eyes hurt to look at directly. And were those flame patterns moving along the edges?

Azareth tapped at the screen. When the interface loaded, Ramona caught a glimpse of app icons that looked wrong. Way too corporate. Was that one called "BrimstoneBox"?

"Looks like there's a rather close convergence point close to downtown Fernwick. And another two hours north. In the mountains," Azareth said, still scrolling.

"What kind of phone is that?" Ramona asked, leaning in again.

"HellBerry." Azareth didn't look up. "Nothing fancy. Runs on 666G."

Ramona stared, unable to tell if this demon was telling a joke. "That's not a real thing."

"Works better than whatever mortal service you're using." Azareth's thumbs moved across the screen with practiced efficiency. "Though the autocorrect is terrible. Last week it changed 'quarterly reports' to 'quarterly blood sacrifices,' and I had to explain that to three different departments. The disappointment was palpable."

"That's..." Ramona didn't know what to say. "Does it actually get reception in Hell?"

"Gets reception everywhere. Underground, underwater, through magical wards." Azareth finally looked up. "Powered by ambient suffering. Very efficient."

"That's horrifying."

"That's good infrastructure."

The phone buzzed. The notification sound was... Was that screaming? Very faint, very distant, but definitely screaming.

"You have got to change that ringtone," Ramona said.

"Can't. IT disabled custom settings after someone set theirs to 'Never Gonna Give You Up' and it caused a building-wide incident." Azareth glanced at the notification, frowned, and tucked the phone back in her jacket pocket. "I'll deal with that Monday."

"So, having two new moons before Ostara should work perfectly." Ramona wiped her sweaty palms on her T-shirt.

"Is that significant?" Azareth asked, clearly meaning the Ostara date. "The March new moon?"

"No, it's perfect." Something lifted in Ramona's chest. Not quite hope, but close. "We do the first ritual in three weeks. If it works, great. If it doesn't — we have another chance the night before Ostara. Either way, I can send you back to Hell before the gala. No one has to know any of this happened."

Azareth was quiet for a moment. "Assuming we can get the

components for the ritual. And get to the convergence point. And perform it correctly."

"Easy enough." Ramona felt herself relax slightly. Just a few weeks. She could hide a demon for a few weeks. She'd survived two years at Mystic Moon Books. She'd survived finding Simone and Kate together. She'd survived the incident.

She could survive seven weeks. Ramona considered for a moment, then pressed on to ask, "You said until the conditions of the spell are met?"

Azareth nodded, not looking up from her HellBerry. "Mm-hmm."

"And how can we do that?" Ramona asked. "You can bring me success and fortune?"

Azareth glanced up, tilting her head. "Is that what you want?"

This felt like a trick. The predatory stillness of Azareth's body unnerved her.

"I think let's focus on the ritual. It's far more likely to work."

Azareth nodded, looking back to her phone.

"So I just have to keep you hidden until then," Ramona said. "That's manageable. A few weeks. Seven, at most."

"And this Ostara event?"

"A gala. Very formal. Very public. Every witch in Fernwick attends." Ramona shook her head. "But you'll be back in Hell by then. This will all be over."

"You seem confident."

"I have to be." Ramona pulled the grimoire into her lap, flipping through pages with renewed focus. "Do you know what components we need? For the ritual?"

Azareth rattled off a list that made Ramona's stomach sink. "Moonstone dust. Blessed salt from a convergence point. Hawthorn branches cut at midnight. A drop of blood from both the summoner and the summoned." She paused. "A willing severance. Both parties have to want the bond broken."

Ramona nodded. "Perfect. Ideal. Easy."

Azareth raised one dark brow. "Easy."

Ramona looked up sharply. "You want to go back to Hell."

"Of course," Azareth agreed. "But the magic will know if either of us hesitates. Even for a second."

"I won't hesitate."

They stared at each other for a moment. Then Ramona went back to the grimoire, squinting at the cramped handwriting in the dim light. If she could just find something — anything — that might help. A counter-spell. A loophole. Some way to speed up the timeline.

"You should sleep," Azareth said.

"I'm fine."

"You're yawning."

Ramona was, in fact, yawning. She covered her mouth with the back of her hand. "I need to understand what I did. How the spell works. Maybe there's something in here that can help us break it faster."

"There isn't."

"You don't know that." Ramona turned another page. Her eyes were struggling to focus on the text. "There has to be something." She glanced toward her bookshelf, toward the books she hadn't touched in two years. Maybe there was something in there.

Azareth was quiet for a moment. Then, softer: "There isn't. I already checked."

But Ramona wasn't listening. She was turning pages, scanning spells, her exhausted brain trying to parse magical theory while running on cheap wine and desperation.

A Spell for Finding Lost Objects. No.

To Summon Rain During Drought. Useless.

For the Removal of Unwanted Facial Hair. She paused on that one, intrigued for a moment, then kept going.

"You should sleep, Mortal," Azareth said again.

"I'm reading."

But her eyes were getting heavier. The words were swimming on the page. Something about… lunar phases… and… binding rituals… and…

A Spell for the Permanent Freshness of Baked Goods.

Ramona's eyes slid closed. The grimoire was still open in her lap, her finger marking a page about keeping bread from going stale.

CHAPTER FOUR

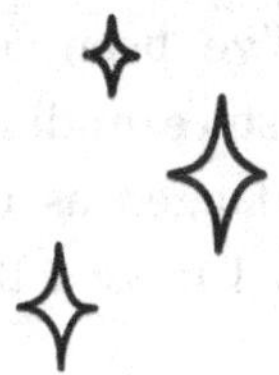

RAMONA KEPT HER EYES CLOSED. IF SHE DIDN'T OPEN THEM, IF SHE STAYED very still, maybe she could pretend last night hadn't happened. Maybe she could pretend she hadn't tried a summoning spell from a donation-bin grimoire. Maybe she could pretend there wasn't a demon in her bedroom.

"Oh good, you're awake."

Ramona's eyes snapped open.

Azareth was still sitting in the desk chair. Still wearing that expensive suit, though it looked slightly more rumpled now. Her dark hair was tousled, a few strands framing her face. She was holding that unsettling HellBerry and looked like she hadn't slept at all.

"You're still here," Ramona said. Her voice came out rough, scratchy.

"Unfortunately."

"I was hoping you were a nightmare."

Azareth raised a dark eyebrow. "Oh, I am, but again, a very tangible one stuck with you thanks to the world's worst grimoire spell."

They stared at each other. Morning light made everything worse. In the dark, Ramona could almost convince herself this was all some wine-induced hallucination. But in daylight, Azareth was undeniably real. Solid. Taking up space in Ramona's shabby bedroom like she belonged there.

She didn't belong there.

"What have you been doing all night?" Ramona asked, sitting up slowly. Her head throbbed in protest.

"Working." Azareth held up her phone. "Hell's email system doesn't stop just because I've been accidentally summoned. I've received forty-seven emails since midnight. Twelve required immediate response. Three were flagged as urgent. And one is from my direct supervisor asking why I missed the second half of my performance review."

"What did you tell her?"

"That I had a personal emergency." Azareth's expression was flat. "Which is technically true."

"I'm a personal emergency?"

Azareth touched the bridge of her nose as though she might let out another long-suffering sigh. "You're certainly something."

Ramona swung her legs out of bed and immediately regretted it. The room tilted. Her mouth tasted like something had died in it. She pressed her fingers to her temples. "I need coffee."

"You need water, Mortal. And aspirin. You drank an entire bottle of wine."

The word hit her like a small slap. "Did you just call me 'Mortal'?"

"That's what you are."

"I have a name," Ramona said, her tongue feeling like sandpaper inside her mouth.

"You haven't told me what it is."

"Am I supposed to tell a demon my name, or is that how you own my soul?" Ramona asked.

Azareth rolled her eyes. "That's for the fae, Mortal."

Ramona opened her mouth. Closed it. "It's Ramona."

"Ramona," Azareth repeated, like she was testing how it sounded. "Noted."

"Are you going to use it?"

"Probably not."

Ramona wanted to argue, but her head hurt too much and she was pretty sure arguing with a demon before coffee was a losing battle. "Fine. Whatever."

Azareth stood up, and the cheap chair creaked in relief. "The kitchen is down the hall?"

"I can get my own water," Ramona protested. "I don't need my roommates knowing I've let a demon into the apartment."

Azareth eyed her critically. "You know demons pass undetected all the time, right? Your roommates won't know the difference between me and a witch."

Ramona furrowed her brow, skeptical. "I don't believe that for one moment."

"You don't think that if any of them had detected a demon for the last twelve hours, they'd have at least knocked?" Azareth said, gesturing to the door. "Besides, you look like you might fall over."

Ramona stood up to prove a point. The room swayed. She sat back down. "Fine. Yes. Kitchen is down the hall. Second doorway on the left."

Azareth moved toward the door, then paused. "How far is it?"

"What?"

"The kitchen. How far down the hall?"

Understanding hit Ramona like cold water. "Oh. Right. The sixty-six-feet thing."

"Yes, the sixty-six-feet thing," Azareth repeated with a small nod.

"I don't know. Maybe thirty feet?"

"Then you're fine. Stay here." Azareth opened the door and stepped into the hallway.

Ramona sat on her bed, feeling ridiculous, listening as hard as she could for anyone screaming. A demon was getting her water. A demon from Hell's corporate structure was fetching her hangover supplies like some kind of evil assistant.

Her life had officially become a joke.

Ramona felt a strange tug in her ribs as the demon left her sight, but Azareth returned a minute later with a glass of water and two aspirin she'd apparently found in the bathroom cabinet. She set them on the nightstand. "Drink, Mortal. All of it."

"Did anyone see you?"

"No, Mortal."

"Stop calling me that."

"No."

Ramona sighed. "Why not?"

"Because it annoys you." A mischievous light seemed to glint in Azareth's eye. "And I have very little entertainment at the moment."

Ramona took the aspirin and drank half the glass. The water was cold and delicious. "Thank you."

"Don't thank me. This is self-preservation. If you're incapacitated, I'm stuck sitting in that terrible chair indefinitely."

Ramona rolled her eyes but finished the water. "I need to shower. I have work."

"Work?"

"Yes. Work. The place where I exchange my time and dignity for money." Ramona stood up again, slower this time. The aspirin hadn't kicked in yet, but at least the room wasn't spinning. "I'm going to be late. Again. Marcus is going to—" She halted. "Wait. Can you…?"

"Can I what?"

"The shower. The bathroom. It's farther than the kitchen." Ramona's brain was trying to do math through the hangover fog. "How far is sixty-six feet in a straight line?"

"Approximately sixty-six feet, Mortal."

"That's not what I… You know what? Never mind." Ramona thought that perhaps this *was* Hell, and the spell *had* killed her, and now she was doomed to a lifetime of domestic torture.

Azareth smirked. "You're asking if I need to be in the bathroom while you shower."

"Yes."

THE DEMON RAISED one perfectly sculpted eyebrow, a grin pulling the edge of her mouth to reveal one of her fangs. "Would you *like* me to be in the bathroom while you shower?"

Ramona glared.

Azareth pulled out her phone and tapped at the screen. "Bathroom is forty-two feet from your bedroom door. You should be fine. I can stay here."

"How do you—"

Azareth showed her phone screen in answer. "I have an app."

"Of course you do."

Ramona grabbed clothes from her dresser. Clean underwear. Jeans. A sweater that didn't have any obvious stains. "If I start to feel pain from the tether… what do I…" She saw the unimpressed look on the demon's face. "I guess I'll just come back."

Azareth's eyes grazed her bare legs, and Ramona felt heat in her cheeks and… other places she was not going to think about. Wow, she'd been single for far too long if demonic judgment was having such an effect on her.

Azareth blinked. "Or you could just scream. That works, too." Again with that slow, catlike grin.

Ramona arched a brow. "You're enjoying this."

"I'm absolutely *not* enjoying this." But there was something in Azareth's eye that was sparkling. "Go shower. You smell terrible and this room is very small."

"Those are strong words coming from someone who lives in brimstone," Ramona muttered.

The hallway felt longer than usual.

Ramona walked slowly, paying attention to how her body felt against the tether, counting each step. At first, nothing. Just the normal sensation of being hungover and exhausted and questioning every life choice that had led her to this moment.

But around thirty feet from her bedroom door, something changed. A tightness in her chest. Like a rubber band being stretched.

At forty feet, the tightness became uncomfortable. Not painful, not yet, but wrong. Like her body knew she was going too far.

At fifty feet, it felt like someone had wrapped a hand around her ribs and was squeezing.

She paused. Turned around. The sensation immediately eased.

Sixty-six feet was not a lot of space.

The bathroom was within range, but she could feel the tether pulling, that uncomfortable tightness that suggested if she went much farther, it would start to hurt.

But she could shower. She could use the bathroom. She had that much.

Small mercies.

Ramona locked the bathroom door behind her and turned on the shower as hot as it would go. Steam filled the small space, fogging up the mirror. She stripped off her T-shirt and yesterday's underwear and stepped under the spray.

The hot water felt heavenly.

She stood there for a long moment, letting it run over her face, her hair, washing away the night's mistakes. Or at least the physical evidence of them. The existential mistakes — like summoning a demon — were going to be much harder to rinse away.

It was only for three weeks.

She shampooed her hair, worked conditioner through the tangles. She should try the glamour spell again. Maybe sober, in daylight, with actual focus, she could fix her hair. Make herself look professional. Make herself look like someone who had their life together.

But that seemed like a lot of effort for a lie no one would believe.

When she finally turned off the water, she felt almost human again. The pain meds had kicked in. The shower had washed away the worst of the hangover fog. She could do this. She could go to work, pretend everything was fine.

She just had to figure out what to do with the demon in her bedroom first.

After her shower, she emerged from the bathroom dressed and feeling marginally more functional to find Cammie in the kitchen making tea.

"Morning," Cammie said without looking up. She was wearing her café uniform — black pants, obscure band T-shirt. Her dark hair was pulled back in a neat ponytail, her multiple earrings themed in celestial symbols of suns and moons for the day. She glanced toward Ramona and nearly startled. "You look like death."

"Thanks, Cam. You're not opening today?" Ramona asked, leaning on the kitchen island.

"Nah. I get to go in when it's not vampire o'clock. What a treat," Cammie joked, pouring a cup of coffee and sliding it across the counter to Ramona. "You feeling okay?"

Ramona mumbled a thanks and clutched the mug gratefully. "Couldn't sleep."

"Mm." Cammie took a sip of her own coffee, not pushing further.

Before the silence could stretch too long, Ramona's bedroom door opened. Azareth emerged, looking somehow more put together than she had any right to after sitting in a chair all night. She'd smoothed her hair back, the dark waves tamed and slick and perfect. The suit was still rumpled, the shirt buttoned higher to her throat, but on her, every detail looked intentional. Expensive casual.

She didn't say anything. Just stood in the doorway to the kitchen, surveying with dark, unreadable eyes.

The temperature seemed to drop.

Cammie glanced up, then did a double take. "Oh. Hi." She looked to Ramona with wide-eyed amusement, like she'd just caught Ramona sneaking out a lover.

"Good morning," Azareth said. Her voice was polite. Distant. The kind of tone that discouraged follow-up questions.

"This is my friend," Ramona said quickly, before the silence could get weirder. "From out of town. She's going to be here for a few days."

"Cool." Cammie waved. "I'm Cammie. One of the roommates."

"I see." Azareth didn't offer her name. Didn't move from the doorway. Just stood there like a particularly well-dressed statue.

Cammie looked at Ramona with wide eyes, then at Azareth, then back at her coffee. "Right. Well. I have to get to work." She grabbed her to-go mug from the counter. "Nice to meet you."

Azareth made a noncommittal hum in her throat, like she wasn't quite sure the sentiment could be returned. Ramona shot her a glare and mouthed, *Be nice.*

Cammie left without lingering. The front door clicked shut behind her.

The moment she was gone, some of the tension in the kitchen eased. Not all of it. But enough that Ramona could breathe again.

"Could you be a little less… demonic, possibly?" Ramona muttered.

Felix's door opened. He emerged with Gerald on his shoulder, already mid-sentence. "Did Kashvi burn something again? I swear I smell—" His voice broke off as he stared at Azareth with his mouth slightly open. "Oh. That's not burnt toast."

"What?" Ramona said.

"That smell." Felix gestured vaguely at the room. "Like… someone just lit a match?" He glanced around.

Ramona hadn't been able to put her finger on it, but Azareth *did* have a particular scent — like someone had just blown out a candle. Not unpleasant, just smoky and rich.

Something demonic. There was no way her roommates were buying that this *wasn't* a demon.

Felix adjusted Gerald on his shoulder. The pigeon was staring at Azareth with unusual intensity. "I'm Felix. And this is Gerald."

For the first time since entering the kitchen, something shifted in Azareth's face. Not quite softening, but… changing. Her attention focused entirely on the pigeon. "Gerald," she repeated quietly.

"Yeah. Found him with a broken wing a few years back." Felix scratched Gerald's head. "He's kind of an asshole to most people, but—"

Gerald cooed. A soft, curious sound that Ramona had never heard him make before.

Azareth took a single step forward. Stopped. "May I approach?"

Felix blinked. "Uh. Sure?"

"I wasn't asking you." Azareth crossed the kitchen slowly, deliberately. She slowed at an appropriate distance away — close enough to see Gerald properly, far enough to not invade Felix's space. Her movements were careful. Respectful.

"Good morning, sir," she said to the pigeon. Her voice had gone quiet. Reverent, almost.

Gerald tilted his head, studying her with one bright eye.

Azareth reached to slide one dark-tipped nail down Gerald's chest. Ramona had never seen anyone but Felix touch Gerald before. "*Columba livia.* Descendant of birds that carried messages for emperors.

Navigated by the stars. Genius little creatures." Azareth paused. "Wow, you're so beautiful."

Gerald puffed up slightly.

"He likes compliments," Felix said, glancing between Azareth and Ramona with a bit of amusement in his confused look.

Azareth kept her eyes on Gerald. "May I?"

Felix raised an eyebrow. "May you…?"

Gerald bowed — *bowed!* — his head and stepped onto Azareth's outstretched hand. Her eyes were wide with wonder as she stared down at him.

Azareth held very still, letting the pigeon settle on her palm. She didn't coo at him or speak in baby talk. Just regarded him with something that looked like utmost respect.

"You've seen a great deal," she said quietly, as if Gerald could understand her. Perhaps he could. Her eyes seemed unfocused. "Survived what should have broken you. That takes strength."

Gerald cooed again, softer this time.

The moment stretched, Azareth standing in the middle of a shabby kitchen, holding a rescue pigeon with the same care most people reserved for religious artifacts.

"Okay," Ramona said slowly. "Well. This is Felix, and Felix, this is —" She paused. She couldn't just introduce this demon as Azareth. She needed some kind of undercover persona. Something distinctly more human. "This is my friend Zara."

Azareth's gaze snapped to her. Something flickered across her face. Surprise, maybe.

Azareth — Zara — was very still. Just staring at Ramona with an expression that was hard to read. Then, quietly: "Zara."

"Yeah. She's from out of town," Ramona began explaining, giving the same excuse to Felix as she had to Cammie. "She's crashing in my room for a bit."

"A friend." Felix gave her a small, knowing grin. "Hmm. Bit of a small room to be crashing in."

Ramona resisted the urge to stomp on his toes.

Zara gently transferred Gerald back to Felix's shoulder. The pigeon cooed mournfully, staring back at the demon.

"You can visit him whenever," Felix said. "He's clearly smitten."

"It would be my honor," Zara said with solemnity.

Felix looked just as puffed up as Gerald by the compliment.

Posey emerged from her plant room, soil under her fingernails as always. "Did someone say we have a guest?"

"This is Zara," Ramona said. "She's visiting for a few days. Weeks. She's from…" Ramona waved uselessly in the air, noticing that no one was really paying her much attention in light of the gorgeous woman standing in the room.

"Nice to meet you. I'm Posey." She smiled, warm and genuine. "Any friend of Ramona's is welcome. There are vegan muffins on the counter if you're hungry."

Zara glanced at the muffins, then back to Posey, making a noncommittal sound.

"Well, if you change your mind." Posey grabbed one for herself, retreating. "Here's hoping Princess Buttercup doesn't try to steal my second breakfast, too."

"Princess Buttercup is a plant." Ramona shook her head as Zara's mouth opened, then closed. "It's better we don't get into all the lore just yet."

Posey disappeared back into her plant room, leaving Ramona, Felix, Zara, and Gerald standing in the kitchen.

"Well," Felix said. "Nice meeting you. See you around." He gave an unabashed wink to Ramona, then a thumbs-up, and mouthed, *She's hot. Good job.*

Ramona briefly considered if dying from embarrassment would be enough to break the tether, or if they'd just become tethered in Hell. Did Zara have roommates? Surely Hell would be an improvement.

Once the room was empty, Ramona lowered her voice. "Okay, you may have been right. They might not have noticed the whole demon thing immediately."

"Mortal, are you trying to apologize for doubting me?"

"Definitely not." Ramona rubbed at the bridge of her nose. "I have to go to work," she said.

"Yes, Mortal. I'm aware." Zara was already straightening her jacket. "Which means I'm coming with you."

"You can't just—"

"The tether." Zara said it like she was explaining basic math to a child. "Unless your workplace is in this apartment, I'll need to accompany you."

"Right. Of course." Ramona rubbed her temples as they returned to Ramona's room. "Marcus isn't in on Mondays, so you should be fine. If he does come in, just… browse. Look at books. Don't talk to Marcus. Don't mention Hell. And for the love of any shred of sanity left in this world, don't tell anyone who you really are."

"I'm a demon, not an idiot."

"Don't…" Ramona quickly glanced over her shoulder. She turned back to Zara and scolded in a whisper. "Stop saying the word demon. You're from across the pond, not across the realm. Got it? No demon talk." Ramona grabbed her bag, started shoving things into it. Wallet. Keys. Phone charger. The grimoire, because she didn't trust leaving it where someone might find it. "This is going to be a disaster."

"Likely."

Ramona glared at Zara. "You could try to be more reassuring."

"I could," Zara agreed. "But that would be dishonest."

Ramona sighed, pulling on her coat. "Come on. We're already late."

CHAPTER FIVE

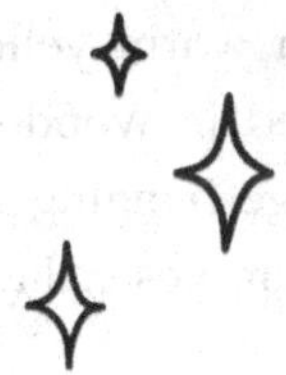

The morning air was cold enough to sting. Ramona pulled her coat tighter as they walked the three blocks from her parking spot to Mystic Moon Books, very aware of Zara walking beside her with a swagger like she belonged on a magazine cover instead of the cracked sidewalks of downtown Fernwick. Zara had gotten a lot of delight out of her car, opening the glove box several times, asking what every dial was for, even tuning the radio to the sad country station as some woman crooned out a mournful plea for her lover to return.

"You're going to freeze," Ramona said.

"I don't get cold."

"That's weird."

"Perks of being from Hell, Mortal. The temperature regulation is excellent."

Ramona didn't have the energy to argue. Her head still ached despite the aspirin, and the morning sunlight felt personally aggressive. She just needed to get through today. And tomorrow. And Wednesday. Then she'd have Thursday and Friday off, except she wouldn't really have them off because Zara would still be tethered to her, which meant—

She stopped thinking about it. One problem at a time.

Mystic Moon Books sat on a corner between a coffee shop and a vintage clothing store, its purple-painted facade and hand-lettered sign designed to look whimsical and mystical. Ramona had always thought it looked like someone's first attempt at a witchy Pinterest board brought to life.

She unlocked the front door and flipped on the lights. The store materialized around them in warm yellow tones — shelves packed with books, crystals displayed in wooden bowls, tarot decks fanned out on velvet, bundles of sage hanging from exposed ceiling beams. Incense lingered in the air from yesterday, mixing with old paper and dust.

It *looked* magical.

It wasn't.

"So this is it," Ramona said, dropping her bag behind the counter. "Welcome to my personal hell. Which is ironic, given present company."

Zara stood in the doorway, surveying the space with an expression Ramona couldn't quite read. Her dark eyes moved methodically across the shelves, the displays, the layout. Like she was cataloging everything.

"It's…" Zara paused. "Charming."

"That's one word for it."

"I was being polite. The actual word is 'chaotic.'" Zara reached out to touch a crystal, switching its place as she muttered something about selenite.

"Yeah, well." Ramona started the register, the ancient machine whirring to life with a sound like grinding teeth. "Marcus prices things based on vibes and organizes based on whatever makes sense to him in the moment. Which is to say, nothing makes sense."

"I noticed." Zara stepped farther inside, her gaze landing on a shelf where protection crystals sat next to romance novels. "Why are the black tourmalines shelved with books about finding your soulmate?"

Ramona sighed, counting money into her drawer. "I'm pretty sure my boss thinks 'protection' and 'love' are 'thematically connected.'"

"That's not how organizational systems work." Zara's tone was bored, but her eyes were wide with interest.

"I'm aware."

Zara moved to another shelf, frowning at the tarot decks mixed in with cookbooks. "And these?"

"He said something about 'kitchen witches' and thought it was clever."

Zara huffed. "It's not."

"Also aware."

Ramona pulled out the day's checklist — a laminated card Marcus had made with tasks like "Sage the corners!" and "Greet customers with warmth!" complete with hand-drawn smiley faces. She resisted the urge to hold it over the nearest candle.

"Okay," Ramona said, turning to Zara. "Remember. You're a customer. Just browsing. Don't talk to anyone who comes in. Don't touch the register. Don't mention Hell. Don't—"

"Mortal."

"What?"

"I've existed for three hundred years. I think I can manage pretending to browse a bookshop."

"Fine. Great. Just…" Ramona gestured vaguely. "Stay out of trouble. Light the candles." She handed a lighter to Zara, but Zara raised one eyebrow. She flicked her wrist, and all of the display candles in the store lit at once.

Ramona opened her mouth to say something but paused, shaking her head instead.

Zara's expression might have been amused. "I'll do my best." She drifted toward the back of the store, hands clasped behind her back, examining books with the focused intensity of someone conducting an audit. Which, Ramona realized, she probably was. A demon from Hell's corporate structure had just been unleashed in Mystic Moon Books.

This was going to be a long day.

• • •

THE FIRST HOUR PASSED QUIETLY. A tourist couple came in, buying a book about manifesting abundance. An older woman browsed the tarot section for twenty minutes before leaving empty-handed. A college student asked if they had "anything real," and Ramona had to give her standard response about "helping people connect with their spiritual practice" while internally screaming.

Through it all, Zara browsed. She moved through the store with methodical precision, occasionally picking up a book, reading the back, setting it down. Clearly making mental notes. During a lull, she approached the counter.

"Question," Zara said, leaning back against the counter as she gestured toward the store. "*Why* do you sell fake magic?"

Ramona glanced toward the door with a surge of anxiety. She lowered her voice. "We don't sell fake magic. We sell… spirituality-adjacent products to non-magical people."

"Non-magical people." Zara tested the phrase.

"Non-mages." Ramona straightened a display of amethyst clusters that didn't need straightening. "The human witching community decided a long time ago it was best if the non-mages don't have to interact with what they don't understand. When we tried, it resulted in, well, a lot of burnt stakes."

"So you hide."

"We coexist. Separately." Ramona moved to restock some candles. "Some covens have a trusted few who know — family members, close friends. But mostly we keep our worlds apart. It's safer for everyone."

"Safer," Zara repeated. "That's kind of sad, Mortal."

"Yeah, well." Ramona didn't want to get into the politics of it. The debates at Thornwood Coven meetings about exposure versus secrecy, tradition versus progress. "The non-mages get their crystals and tarot cards and books about manifesting. We get to practice actual magic without being killed or studied in a lab."

"And where do actual witches get their supplies?"

"There used to be a few shops. But most closed." Ramona shrugged. "It's mostly online these days. There's still one that I know of in Thornwood near the academy. And you can get anything shipped if you know where to look."

Something shifted in Zara's expression. Her eyes lit up — actually lit up, with a gleam that made Ramona nervous. "A business opportunity," Zara said.

Ramona raised an eyebrow.

"But the demand clearly exists—"

The bell above the door chimed. A middle-aged man in loose linen capris entered, heading straight for the essential oils. Ramona gave Zara a pointed look that said *this conversation is over* and went to help the customer.

But as she explained the properties of lavender versus eucalyptus, she could feel Zara watching her. Assessing. Cataloging.

It made her skin prickle.

Around eleven, during another quiet stretch, Ramona found Zara standing in front of another display, staring at it with the expression of someone witnessing a crime.

"Problem?" Ramona asked.

"This sage bundle," Zara said slowly, holding up a small bundle of white sage tied with purple string, "costs twelve dollars."

"Yeah?"

"And this book"—she picked up a paperback about crystal healing —"costs eight dollars."

"Okay?"

"The sage bundle is three plant stems tied together. The book is two hundred pages of printed information." Zara looked at Ramona. "Your pricing structure makes no sense."

"My boss prices things based on what he thinks people will pay."

Zara looked personally affronted by that philosophy. "That's not a pricing structure. That's chaos with a cash register."

"Welcome to my life."

Zara set down the sage and the book, shaking her head. "And the inventory system is… Do you even have one?"

Ramona glanced back toward the register. "There's a spreadsheet. Somewhere."

"Somewhere?" Zara looked like she might launch into a panic attack at any moment.

"Marcus updates it occasionally. When he remembers. Which is never."

"How do you know what needs restocking?"

Ramona shrugged. "I look at the shelves. If they're empty, I restock them. If we don't have it, I make a note of it."

Zara stared at her. "That's not a system."

"I'm aware."

"This place shouldn't function." Zara ran a hand hastily through her hair, clearly stressed.

"And yet here we are. Functioning." Ramona moved past her to help a customer who'd just walked in — a young woman looking for birthday candles, the regular kind, because apparently Mystic Moon Books was now also a place people came for emergency party supplies.

When the customer left with the same candles Ramona usually recommended for cord cutting, Ramona turned back to find Zara examining the discount bin with a look of pure horror.

"These books aren't even organized by category," Zara said.

"They're five dollars each. People dig."

"But if you organized them — by genre, or author, or even just alphabetically — people would buy more because they could actually find what they're looking for."

"Probably."

Zara pinched the bridge of her nose — a gesture that looked eerily similar to what Ramona did when dealing with Marcus. "We have one hundred and seventeen different departments just for processing soul contracts. And somehow, this"—she gestured at the store—"is more chaotic than Hell."

"I'll take that as a compliment."

"It's not."

The bell chimed again. This time, Ramona's stomach dropped.

Marcus.

He pushed through the door in his usual outfit — a turtleneck and approximately forty necklaces layered over each other. His hair was pulled back in a ponytail, and he had that serene smile that meant he was about to ask Ramona to do something very annoying.

"Ramona!" he said, arms spread wide like he hadn't seen her in years instead of one day. "Beautiful day, isn't it?"

"Hey, Marcus." Ramona's brain scrambled. Zara was right there, standing by the discount bin, very obviously not a normal customer. "I thought you weren't in until Thursday?"

"I'm not. Just swinging by to grab the deposit bag. Left it in the office yesterday." He glanced past her, noticed Zara. "Oh! A customer. Wonderful."

Zara had gone very still. Her expression was perfectly neutral — the kind of neutral that screamed *I am pretending to be human* but achieved more of a mannequin quality.

"She's just browsing," Ramona said quickly.

"Take your time!" Marcus called to Zara, his voice too loud for the small space. "Let me know if you need any guidance on your spiritual journey."

Zara nodded once, silent.

Marcus headed toward the back office, weaving through the displays. "How's the morning been? Any interesting customers?"

"Just the usual." Ramona followed him, positioning herself between Marcus and Zara. "Tourists. A few locals."

"Wonderful, wonderful." He disappeared into the office — really just a converted storage closet with a desk and a filing cabinet that hadn't been opened in the two years Ramona had been here.

Ramona caught Zara's eye and jerked her head toward the back, trying to signal to the demon that her mannequin moment should turn into casual browsing.

Zara, blessedly, understood. She drifted toward the back of store, picking up books one at a time.

Ramona exhaled.

"Found it!" Marcus emerged with a blue bank bag. "You know, Ramona, I've been thinking we should host regular events at the new place. It's so much bigger. Maybe a new moon circle? Or a crystal renewal workshop?"

"That all sounds great," Ramona said, only half paying attention as she watched Zara robotically lift books off the shelf without even looking at them.

"Exactly! Which is why you'd be perfect for planning it for Dylan." He patted her shoulder. "Think about it. I'll check in Wednesday."

He was gone before Ramona could argue, the bell chiming his exit.

She waited thirty seconds. Then she walked to the back of the shop. Zara was holding a book in one hand and had apparently been in the process of placing it back on the shelf when she'd frozen.

"Coast is clear," Ramona said.

Zara set down the book. Carefully. On a shelf that Ramona now realized was organized alphabetically by author.

"Are you—" Ramona looked closer. "Are you alphabetizing the romance novels?"

"I was browsing."

"You're literally organizing the books."

"Your system is inefficient, Mortal."

"There is no system. That's the point."

"Exactly." Zara picked up another book, checked the author, slid it into place between two others. "Which is why I'm creating one."

Ramona stared at her. At the demon from Hell who had apparently decided that the most pressing issue in her life was the organizational structure of Mystic Moon Books's romance novel section.

"You just can't help yourself, can you?"

"I've been doing inventory management for nearly three centuries." Zara didn't look up from the books. "This is painful to witness."

"So you're just… fixing it?"

"I'm browsing in an organized fashion."

Despite herself, despite everything, Ramona felt a laugh bubble up. It came out slightly hysterical. "You've been here three hours and you're already reorganizing."

"*Someone* should." Zara didn't even glance her way, but her tone seemed to imply Ramona was helpless, which made Ramona cross her arms in frustration, defensive and ready to argue.

"I didn't ask for your help."

"You didn't have to." Zara finally looked at her. "Your system — or lack thereof — was making my skin crawl. And I don't even have conventional skin."

Ramona stepped closer, examining the shelves in every direction. Zara had made it through about a quarter of the stock, organizing books by author within genre categories. It was… actually much better. She could actually find things now.

"You're good at this," Ramona said quietly.

"I'm good at many things."

"Wow, and so humble."

"That's not one of them," Zara said with a quirk of a smile.

The moment stretched. Standing among bookshelves with a demon who was reorganizing the shop one paperback at a time. It should have felt invasive. It should have felt wrong.

Instead, it felt… nice? To have someone care about the details. To have someone see the chaos and want to fix it instead of just shrugging and saying "Ramona is a lost cause."

"Thank you," Ramona said.

Zara's expression shifted. She seemed slightly embarrassed, eyes wide and blinking. "You're welcome, Mortal."

Ramona took a moment to look at Zara up close, examining how her skin had a reddish quality, how her dark hair waved. How full her dark lips were. She was alluring in a way that made Ramona want to lean closer.

The front bell chimed — another customer.

"I should—" Ramona gestured toward the door.

"Go. I'll continue browsing." Zara picked up another book. "Alphabetically."

Ramona left her there, organizing shelves that hadn't been organized since the store opened. And as she helped a customer find meditation cushions, she caught herself thinking about how Zara was a demon. She was meant to be alluring. She was meant to draw in unsuspecting and desperate humans just like herself. And yet, Zara didn't seem to see Ramona's world as a lost cause just yet. She probably would. Give Zara three weeks and she'd probably be running, not caring about the pain of the tether.

• • •

By five o'clock, Ramona's feet hurt and her headache had returned with a vengeance. She flipped the sign to "Closed," locked the door, and found Zara sitting cross-legged on the floor of the back room, surrounded by perfectly organized stacks of books.

"We're done for the day," Ramona said.

For a moment, Ramona just stood there. The demon who'd arrived in an expensive suit looking like she'd stepped out of a boardroom was now covered in dust, hair falling loose, completely absorbed in alphabetizing paperbacks about crystals and moon phases. It was ridiculous.

"I finished the fiction section," Zara said quickly.

"I can see that."

"Tomorrow I'll start on the reference books."

"You don't have to—"

"I want to." Zara stood up, brushing dust from her pants. "It's satisfying. Seeing order emerge from chaos."

They walked back through the empty store together. Zara snapped her fingers, and every candle in the shop extinguished at once.

Ramona turned off the lights and set the alarm, her hands moving through the familiar routine while her brain tried to catch up. "You know, I've been manually blowing out those candles for two years. Marcus insists on 'ambiance.' There are thirty-seven of them."

"That's inefficient."

"That's... all I can do," Ramona said quietly.

They stepped outside. The afternoon sun was already sinking low, winter days too short for comfort. Ramona locked the door and tried not to think about how she'd just watched actual magic happen in Mystic Moon Books. The irony was almost funny. Almost.

"At least Marcus won't be in until Thursday," Ramona said as they headed back toward her car. The cold bit at her face, making her eyes water. Or maybe that was just exhaustion. "I have Thursday and Friday off, so the next two days should be fairly easy and Marcus-free, and then we have a bit of time to figure out how we're going to get through the weekend shifts."

"I'll stay undercover," Zara said. "Continue organizing."

Ramona should have been annoyed. Should have told Zara to stop, that it wasn't her problem, that Ramona could handle her own mess.

That's what Simone would have said — *Stop trying to fix everything, Ramona. Some things are meant to be messy.*

But the books really did look better organized. And Ramona was so tired of messy.

"Fine," Ramona said. "Organize away."

They walked in silence for a block. Then Zara said, quietly: "You would be good at it, you know."

"At what?"

"Running a magical supply business." Zara didn't look at her. "You have a way with customers."

"It'd be a waste of my education," Ramona said, sniffling in the cold.

"And this isn't?"

"This isn't a career like opening my own shop would be. This is temporary," Ramona insisted. She said it with conviction, even though she'd been saying *temporary* for two years now.

"Well, I'm sure we'll have plenty of time to talk about that with your therapist," Zara said, wrenching open the stuck passenger door of Ramona's car.

"How do you know about therapists?" Ramona asked, grateful for the subject change. "Does Hell have therapists?"

"Of course Hell has therapists." Zara folded herself into the passenger seat with more grace than the car deserved — which wasn't hard, since the car was held together mostly by audacity. "Mandatory after your first century. The emotional burnout rate among temptation specialists is alarming."

"You're joking."

"I'm not." Zara pulled the seat belt across her chest, examining the frayed edge with the expression of someone reconsidering their life choices. "Hell's HR department implemented a comprehensive mental health program in 1997. Weekly sessions, quarterly wellness checks, annual retreats."

Ramona braced herself, hoping the car would start on the first try. The engine coughed, protested, then grudgingly turned over. "Demons do therapy retreats?"

"*Everyone* in hell does therapy retreats, Mortal. Even the damned."

Zara tried to adjust the seat, which didn't adjust, and gave up. "Though I'll admit the trust falls are deeply awkward."

"I cannot picture demons doing trust falls."

"No one can. That's why they're mandatory." Zara looked out the window as Ramona pulled into traffic. "Character building, apparently."

Ramona glanced at her, trying to read her expression. But Zara's face had gone neutral again — that carefully blank look that gave nothing away. The same look Ramona had perfected during the last year of her marriage. The *I'm fine, everything's fine* face.

"Do you actually go?" Ramona asked. "To therapy?"

"That's a personal question."

"You're literally tethered to me. I think we're past personal boundaries."

Zara was quiet for a long moment. Long enough that Ramona thought she wasn't going to answer. Then: "Sometimes."

"Does it help?"

"Sometimes," Zara repeated. Her tone made it clear the subject was closed.

They drove in silence for another block. Ramona counted the traffic lights — three until the turn, then two more until the apartment. Numbers were easier than thinking about how a demon somehow understood personal boundaries better than her ex-wife had.

"You should consider it, though," Zara said without looking at her.

"Therapy?"

"And the business idea." Zara's voice was casual. Too casual, the kind of casual that meant she'd been thinking about it. "When we break this tether, you should think about it. The magical supply shop."

"I'm not—" Ramona stopped. What was she going to say? *I'm not capable? I'm not brave enough? I'm not anything except a witch working retail in a store that sells lies to non-mages?*

"I'm just stating facts, Mortal." Zara finally looked at her. "You're very competent. You seem to be good with customer-facing interactions. And you clearly hate working for Marcus."

Ramona's throat tightened. The compliment felt too big, too real.

Like Zara had seen something Ramona had been carefully hiding. "Thanks."

"Don't thank me. I'm simply making an observation."

But the way she said it — matter-of-fact, certain, like she hadn't just casually dismantled every excuse Ramona had been telling herself for two years — made Ramona wonder what else Zara had observed about her in just one day.

That was somehow the most unsettling thought she'd had all day.

CHAPTER SIX

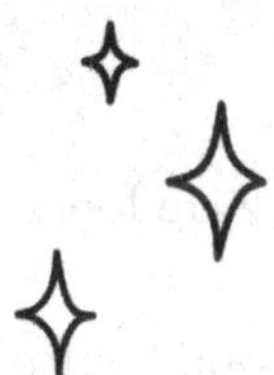

"We're stopping somewhere on the way home," Ramona announced, pulling onto a street a few blocks from the apartment.

Zara smoothed the front of her jacket with both hands and said "very well" in the tone of someone being gracious about an invitation they hadn't technically received.

When they parked, Ramona turned to look at the demon in her front seat. "Can you—" Ramona gestured vaguely at Zara. At all of Zara. The suit. The posture. The quality of presence that had made her car feel unreasonably small. "Try not to look like you're about to conduct a meeting."

Zara looked at her. "I always look like this."

"I know. That's what I said."

"You want me to do something about my face."

"I want you to do something about your entire—" Ramona stopped. Made a gesture that encompassed the situation. "Never mind. Just don't make anyone feel damned."

"I make no promises," Zara said.

Ramona pushed The Grimalkin's doors open without breaking stride. Zara paused on the threshold.

Ramona glanced back. "What." It was not a real question.

Zara was looking at the door with an expression she hadn't worn all day — not the cataloging attention she'd given the crystal display, not the professional assessment she'd applied to the customers. Something more careful. More alert. "This establishment has significant magical shielding."

"Yep."

"The kind that makes it invisible to those who don't know it's here."

"Yep."

"And you know it's here." Zara looked at her. "You've been coming here for some time."

"Yep." Ramona held the door. "Since I moved in. Are you coming in, or are you going to do a structural analysis on the doorframe?"

Zara stepped inside.

She stopped again just inside the entrance, and Ramona let the door swing shut and watched her take it in the way she'd once watched a first-year student encounter a genuinely old text for the first time — that specific quality of attention that meant something had landed.

She watched Zara clock it systematically — the hedge witches arguing in the corner, the elderly sisters at their Thursday table, Dennis the allegedly retired warlock at the far end of the bar — was like seeing it fresh, which she found mildly irritating.

"The fae," Zara said quietly, nodding almost imperceptibly toward a far table. Two figures, drinks barely touched, too beautiful, too still, watching everything with the patient attention of beings who measured time differently. "They're gathering information."

"They always are." Ramona steered them toward the bar. "Odette charges them double."

Parliamentarian sat in Ramona's usual spot, glancing toward her with an air of indifference as if to say: *I won't be moving.*

Ramona, recognizing her place in the grand Grimalkin hierarchy, slid into the stool next to him.

Zara took the adjacent stool with the precise, deliberate movement she brought to all physical actions, as if posture was a professional obligation even in a bar. She was still doing her inventory of the room in her peripheral vision. Ramona could tell.

Odette appeared, turning to Zara. A pause. Brief, almost imperceptible, which meant she'd clocked exactly what Zara was and made a quiet professional note of it.

She set a second glass down. Dark, slightly iridescent, a small curl of smoke rising from the surface.

Zara looked at it. "What is this?"

"Borrowed Time" Odette said and moved away.

Zara regarded the glass for a moment. Then picked it up and took a careful, considered sip. Something moved through her expression — not quite surprise, but close. "Well," she said.

"Well, what?" Ramona asked, sipping her own drink.

"It tastes like the first year I worked in Temptation." She set the glass down and looked at it with an expression Ramona couldn't entirely read. "I haven't thought about that in quite some time."

"The drinks do that here."

"How?"

"Nobody knows. Odette doesn't explain herself."

Zara looked toward the bar, where Odette had already materialized somewhere else. "I respect that enormously."

Parliamentarian meowed at Zara, his eyes narrowing. He watched her for a long moment, then leaned forward to sniff the air. His whiskers pulled forward, and he sat, his tail wrapping around his front feet. He closed his eyes.

"You passed," Ramona said.

"I gathered." Something in Zara's expression had eased, almost imperceptibly.

They stayed for two drinks. The Grimalkin did what it always did around the second — softened the edges of things, made the ambient noise of other people's problems feel companionable rather than intrusive. The jukebox shifted from the torch song into something with a low piano, then into something with no identifiable era, just a feeling.

Zara asked questions, as she had all day. About the sisters who came every Thursday. About Dennis and his suspicious retirement. About the orcs in the corner booth — she had opinions about supernatural mediation practices, and they were detailed and professionally informed and mildly disparaging about the methodology.

"They've been here longer than the furniture," Ramona said. "Nobody knows if they came with the bar or the bar came with them."

"Like Odette."

"Like Odette."

Zara turned her glass slowly on the bar. Something in her had settled in a way it hadn't all day — the professional tension she carried like a second suit jacket slightly loosened, just around the edges. "You said since you moved in," she said.

"What?"

"That you've been coming here since you moved in." She wasn't looking at Ramona, still doing her slow survey of the room. "You said it like somewhere that helped with something."

Ramona looked at her drink. "It was a bad year. I found this place and it—" She paused. "It helped."

Zara nodded. Didn't push. Filed it away wherever she filed the things Ramona told her, which seemed more careful than expected.

Parliamentarian had migrated fully onto the stool beside Zara and was leaning against her arm with the boneless commitment of a cat who had made a permanent decision. Zara's hand rested near him in a way that wasn't quite petting but wasn't not petting either.

"We should test the tether," Ramona said. "Properly. While the apartment's empty."

Zara straightened slightly. Back to business. "Empty?"

"Tuesdays are usually pretty empty at home. Felix's Crypts and Covens game usually runs until ten."

"Then we have time." Zara finished her drink, set the glass down with her customary precision. Odette appeared, glanced at both glasses, raised an eyebrow.

"We're good," Ramona said. "Thank you."

Odette inclined her head. The almost imperceptible acknowledgment that meant *you're welcome* and *come back* and *I have noted that you brought a demon to my bar and have filed this information away for another time* all at once.

They got their coats. Parliamentarian watched them leave from his stool with an expression of dignified regret.

At the door, Zara paused.

"This place," she said.

"I know."

"I'd like to come back."

Ramona pushed the door open into the January cold. "I figured."

THE APARTMENT WAS dark when they got back, which meant Felix was at his Tuesday night Crypts and Covens game. Posey would be at the community garden until sunset. Kashvi was probably at the library. Cammie would be closing at the café.

Privacy. Finally.

Ramona unlocked the door and immediately kicked off her shoes, leaving them in the pile by the entrance that Felix kept trying to organize into a "mindful shoe meditation space." Her feet ached. Her head ached. Everything ached in that specific way that came from standing on concrete floors for eight hours while pretending to be enthusiastic about rose quartz.

"I'm going to make dinner," Ramona announced, dropping her bag on the counter. "You hungry?" Zara had refused breakfast and lunch, and Ramona was beginning to question whether demons even ate food.

Zara had followed her inside, pausing near the shoe pile. "Yes."

Ramona pulled open the fridge, surveying the contents with the grim determination of someone who'd been putting off grocery shopping. Eggs. Half a block of cheese with a questionable expiration date. Some wilted spinach. In the back of the freezer, buried behind one of Posey's elaborate fermentation projects, she found pasta sauce that Felix had made last month.

"Spaghetti okay?" Ramona asked. She glanced toward Zara. "You can come in, you know. Sit on the couch. Or at the table. You're going to be here for a few weeks, you might as well get comfortable."

Zara tilted her head with an assessing expression. "Do you need help making it?"

"It's just boiled water. I can manage," Ramona said with a reflexive snark in her tone. She filled a pot with water and set it on the stove, then rummaged through the cabinet for pasta. She found a box of spaghetti, half empty, that had probably been there since she'd moved in. Good enough.

She wasn't a great cook. Simone had done most of the cooking when they were together — had enjoyed it, even, turning their tiny kitchen into some kind of experimental culinary lab. Ramona had been the one who did dishes, who cleaned up when Simone had used every dish possible. A fair division of labor, she'd thought at the time.

The water took forever to boil. Ramona leaned against the counter, watching Zara walk carefully into the kitchen, examining the room with that same cataloging intensity she brought to everything. Taking in the mismatched mugs, the flourishing herb garden on the windowsill, the collection of takeout menus held to the fridge with magnets from exotic places none of them had ever been.

"Your roommates are all witches?" Zara asked.

"All of them but Cammie," Ramona answered, adding salt to the water.

Zara nodded slowly, reaching to touch her hand to the edge of the saucepan. The water began to boil instantly. "But you're not an official coven?"

Ramona shook her head and added the pasta. "No, not even close."

"Don't witches usually live with their covens?" Zara asked, handing Ramona a wooden spoon from the utensil holder.

"Well, not us. Felix left his old conservative coven after he transitioned. I don't think Posey ever had a coven, and Kashvi doesn't talk much about hers. We all kind of ended up here after—" She stopped and shrugged. "After things didn't work out the way we planned."

"You're kind of a coven of misfits."

"We're just roommates who happen to share a kitchen and occasionally help each other with spellwork." Ramona stirred the pasta more aggressively than necessary. "And Cammie."

"Hmm, and Cammie. Of course," Zara said. "Sounds suspiciously like a coven."

"Had no idea demons had such romantic notions of roommate dynamics," Ramona joked.

"What do your roommates do for work?" Zara asked.

"Kashvi is a librarian, Posey works at a plant nursery, Cammie works at a café, and Felix works at some tech company but I'm not exactly sure what he does. Some kind of coding?" Ramona said.

"You've lived with these people for years and you don't know what they do all day at work?" Zara asked. She muttered something about unfeeling mortals under her breath.

Ramona raised an eyebrow. "Okay, first of all, not everyone lives to work like the demonic realm. Second, we are roommates out of desperation, not best friendship. In case you didn't realize, this group is surviving, not thriving."

Zara's eyebrows raised in surprise, but she didn't press further.

The pasta cooked. Ramona heated up the sauce in the microwave, found two clean bowls in the cabinet, served them both portions that were definitely too large. She set the bowls on the small kitchen table and grabbed forks from the drawer.

Zara sat, summoning a spoon out of thin air, and proceeded to eat spaghetti with the most formal, precise table manners Ramona had ever witnessed.

She twirled exactly three strands of pasta at a time around her fork. Cut nothing. Made no sound while chewing. Dabbed at her mouth with a napkin after every third bite, even though there was nothing to dab. Kept her left hand in her lap when not in use. Sat with perfect posture.

It was deeply unsettling.

"You eat like you're at a state dinner," Ramona said.

"I've been to several state dinners." Zara took another perfect bite. "This is how one eats pasta."

"This is how the Queen eats pasta."

"I wouldn't know. I've never dined with royalty." Zara paused. "Politicians, yes. Plenty of them. But royalty is far above my pay grade."

Ramona snorted in amusement, then watched as Zara's mouth quirked in a small smile, too.

They ate in silence for a moment. Ramona watched Zara navigate the spaghetti with the kind of precision usually reserved for surgical procedures. Three strands. Twist. Lift. Chew. Dab.

"Does Hell have etiquette classes?" Ramona asked.

"Mandatory. First decade of service." Zara twirled another perfect forkful. "Dining, dancing, diplomatic protocol. You never know when you'll be required to attend a formal function in your role as a representative of the Infernal Bureaucracy."

"Representative of the Infernal Bureaucracy." Ramona shook her head.

"It's a very important position."

Ramona tried to emulate the way Zara spun her fork, her own pasta flopping in general disagreement. She slurped her spaghetti, wiping at her mouth with her fingers. "And you're in Temptation and Minor Inconveniences."

"Which occasionally requires formal representation." Zara took a sip of water with the same deliberate precision. "Last year I attended a conference on ethical soul-collection practices that had a black-tie gala to close. Very tedious."

"What do demons wear to black-tie galas? Ball gowns?" Ramona asked.

Zara looked at her flatly, blinking twice. "Tuxedos, Mortal."

Ramona tried to picture it — Zara in a neatly pressed tux, networking with other demons over canapés and existential dread. The image was both absurd and somehow entirely believable.

"Was there at least an open bar?" Ramona asked.

Zara nodded. "Obviously. How else would anyone survive four days of PowerPoint presentations on damnation reform?"

Despite everything, Ramona laughed. Actual laughter, surprising herself. Zara's expression shifted — something that might have been pleasure, or satisfaction, or just acknowledgment that she'd made a joke and it had landed.

They finished eating. Ramona cleared the bowls, washing them hastily in the sink. Zara stood by the table, clearly uncertain whether to help or stay out of the way.

"You can just—" Ramona gestured vaguely. "Sit. I've got it."

"I could assist."

"You're a guest. Or, like a guest-prisoner, I guess." Ramona grimaced.

"Maybe we could just say I'm here for a while," Zara said, wiping the table with a napkin.

Ramona washed the bowls, the forks, the pot. Simple, mindless tasks. The kitchen was quiet except for the sound of running water and the distant hum of traffic outside. Zara had moved to the window, looking out at the street below.

It felt almost normal to have a meal together, talking and laughing. Almost domestic.

Ramona shoved that thought away so hard it probably bruised.

"We should test the tether," Ramona said, drying her hands on a dish towel that had seen better days. "Properly. While no one's home."

"Good idea." Zara turned from the window. "Where do you want to start?"

"The living room?" Ramona gestured to the couch and TV area across the open-concept great room. "Then we'll try the other rooms, see how far we can push it."

They started in the living room, Zara standing by the front door with her phone out, that red glow illuminating her face as she pulled up some kind of measuring app on her HellBerry. Ramona walked backward toward the hallway, counting her steps.

"Tell me when you feel it," Zara said.

At twenty feet, nothing. At forty feet, a slight tightness in her chest like she'd taken a breath and held it too long. At fifty feet, the tightness became uncomfortable.

"It's pretty strong right now," Ramona said, stopping.

"Fifty-two feet." Zara made a note. "Keep going."

Ramona took another step. The discomfort increased, a pressure building behind her ribs. Another step. The pressure turned sharp, insistent.

"Fifty-nine feet," she said, her voice strained.

"Farther," Zara said.

Ramona grimaced, rubbing at her sternum. "Do I have to?"

"We need to know the limits."

Ramona took two more steps, and suddenly it wasn't just discomfort — it was pain. Real, visceral pain, like someone had wrapped a cord around her lungs and was pulling it tight. Her vision blurred at the edges.

She stumbled back, and immediately the pain eased. Zara was moving toward her, crossing the distance in a few long strides.

"Mortal—"

"I'm fine." Ramona caught her breath, leaning against the wall. "Just… I guess that's the limit before it really hurts."

"Noted." Zara's hand was on her elbow, steadying. "We'll try other directions."

Ramona glanced down to Zara's hand on her arm. Her touch was blazing hot, her skin soft. Her black nails were trimmed short, but some kind of illusion darkened the tips of her fingers, like she'd wrapped her hand in shadows.

Zara let go of Ramona, taking a step back, and Ramona stared at the invisible demonic handprint on her arm where Zara had touched her. She hadn't expected Zara to feel so hot to the touch, but perhaps that was just a demon thing? Her eyes flicked up to meet Zara's, finding an expectant and impatient expression there. Ramona straightened, focusing.

They mapped it out systematically, seeing if varying angles or paths changed anything. Each time, Ramona pushed until she felt the pain, and each time, Zara was there with her phone, noting measurements with clinical precision. It should have felt invasive — being studied like a lab experiment, her discomfort quantified and recorded.

Instead, it felt like Zara was trying to understand. Trying to help.

Which was somehow worse.

They were in the hallway, testing the distance to the front door, when they heard footsteps on the stairs outside.

Zara's expression shifted immediately, careful neutrality sliding into place like a mask. "Cammie."

Ramona looked at Zara with a frown of confusion. "How do you—"

The key turned in the lock. The door opened.

Cammie stepped inside, still in her café uniform, her hair pulled back, her face tired. She halted when she saw them standing in the hallway, Zara holding her phone, Ramona leaning against the wall like she'd just run a marathon.

"Hey," Cammie said slowly. Her gaze moved between them, clearly trying to figure out what she'd just walked into.

"Hey," Ramona said, too brightly. "How was work?"

"Long." Cammie set her bag down by the door. "How was yours?"

Cammie looked at Zara. Zara looked back, her expression dark and guarded in a way that Ramona hadn't seen with anyone else.

"Yeah, same." Ramona said, anxious to break whatever awkward feeling had settled over them. "There's a bit of leftover spaghetti on the stove if you're hungry."

"Thanks," Cammie said. "I'll eat it after I shower. Hey, Zara, do you watch *Love Potion?*""

"No," Zara said flatly, then took a few steps, disappearing into Ramona's bedroom, closing the door behind her.

Ramona stood in the hallway, staring at the closed door, then glanced back at Cammie. "Sorry. Jet lag is making her grumpy," she said by way of excuse for Zara's odd behavior.

Cammie shrugged. "No worries." She disappeared into the bathroom.

Ramona took a breath, counted to five, and opened her bedroom door.

Zara was standing by the window, arms crossed, staring out at the alley below. She didn't turn when Ramona entered.

"Are you okay?" Ramona asked, closing the door behind her.

Zara turned. Her expression was carefully blank. "It's been a long day." There was something in her voice — something Ramona couldn't quite identify but could *feel* in her own body. Discomfort? Anxiety?

"Okay," Ramona said slowly. "We don't have to talk about it."

They stood there in silence. The room felt smaller than usual, more crowded. Outside, Ramona could hear the shower running, the pipes groaning. The building settling into its evening routine.

"So," Ramona said. "As far as the bed tonight—"

Zara sat down in the creaking chair, the seat groaning in surrender as it slowly lowered. "This is fine."

"You can't sleep in that chair every night," Ramona protested.

"I don't require as much sleep as humans." Zara made a show of stretching and settling her body. "I'll be fine, Mortal." She said the name slowly, emphasizing their difference in that moment.

"That's—" Ramona began, then paused. Took a breath. "Look, *Demon*. That chair is terrible. You're going to destroy your back."

Zara sniffed in annoyance. "I don't have a conventional spine."

Ramona paused. "What holds up your… most of you, then?" She gestured toward Zara's torso region.

Zara shrugged. "Mine is more of a *conceptual* spine."

"That doesn't make it better!" Ramona rubbed her temples. This conversation was giving her a headache. "I'm going to go get a water for bed. Do you need one?"

Zara tilted her head. "A water? For… bed?"

Ramona scrubbed a hand down her face. "Just… stay here. I'll be right back."

CHAPTER SEVEN

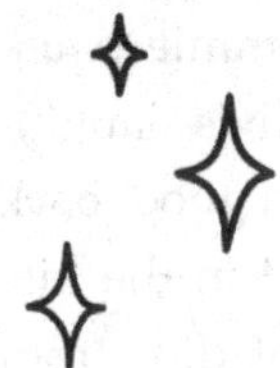

RAMONA WALKED DOWN THE HALL TOWARD THE KITCHEN, ALREADY planning her route: get water, drink it fast, go back to her room where a demon was currently arranging herself in a chair that looked like it was designed by someone who hates comfort.

She rounded the corner into the kitchen and stopped.

Cammie was sitting at the table, eating the leftover spaghetti straight from the sauce pot, wearing her pajamas with damp hair. She looked up when Ramona entered, fork halfway to her mouth, and grinned.

"So," Cammie said, waggling her eyebrows. "Zara."

Ramona moved to the sink, filling a glass with water. "What about her?"

"Oh, come on. Don't play coy." Cammie leaned forward conspiratorially. "She's gorgeous. That suit? The way she talks? Felix said Gerald literally *bowed* to her."

"Gerald is just getting soft in his old age," Ramona tried.

Cammie balked. "Gerald bit the mailman last week."

Fair point. Ramona drank half the glass in one go, buying time.

"How long have you been seeing her?" Cammie asked.

Ramona paused, blinking. "Oh, we're not — she's just a friend."

"Uh-huh. A friend who's sleeping in your room." Cammie giggled — *giggled!* Ramona clearly needed to get the situation under control, fast.

"Just friends, I swear," Ramona said. The idea of being Zara's friend was bizarre. Did demons have friends in Hell? She'd never even asked if Zara had a family. Maybe she had a demon husband or wife or… partner-something.

"Well, I think she's—" Cammie paused as the front door opened. Voices in the entryway: Felix's laugh, loud and caffeinated, and Kashvi's quieter response. "Oh good, backup."

Felix and Kashvi appeared in the kitchen doorway together, Felix still holding a gigantic bag of dice from his game, Kashvi with her library tote slung over one shoulder. Gerald was nestled inside Felix's shirt pocket, tiny pigeon eyes closed.

"Ramona!" Felix's face lit up. "Perfect. We need details."

Ramona held up her hands like she was being held at wand-point. "There are no details."

"There are *always* details." Felix dropped into a chair, gesturing dramatically. Gerald bristled in Felix's pocket, his eyes opening as he scanned the room. "Zara knew the Latincane name for Gerald. The *scientific classification*. She treated him like royalty. I'm obsessed with her and also slightly afraid."

"She's very polite," Ramona said carefully. "And smart."

"She's *intense*," Cammie corrected. "In a hot way. But also in a 'might be secretly a vampire' way."

Ramona choked. "She's not a vampire."

"That's exactly what someone dating a vampire would say," Felix pointed out. Gerald gave an annoyed coo in apparent agreement.

"I'm not dating her."

"But you want to," Kashvi said quietly, setting her bag down. It wasn't a question.

Ramona felt her face heat. "I… That's not—"

"Your magical signature changed," Kashvi continued, studying Ramona with calm curiosity. "I felt it last night. There's something threaded through it now. Like a connection."

"What kind of connection?" Felix asked, delighted. He was one step away from tapping his fingertips together like an excited movie villain.

"I'm not sure. It's..." Kashvi tilted her head. "Unusual. Old magic, maybe? But active. Like it's still forming."

"That's so romantic," Cammie sighed. "Like a soulmate bond or something."

"Okay, all right, that's..." Ramona paused, because if Kashvi was picking up on the tether, she needed a cover. What could she say? *No, it's not a soulmate bond, I've accidentally bound a demon to me until we can figure out how to ritually sever our tie?* It seemed that leaning into the facade was the only way to get them to stop considering it. "It's just new, okay? And I don't want to freak her out. So I need everyone to play it cool while we... you know, figure it out." It wasn't entirely a lie.

Felix's grin widened. "Oh, you're blushing."

"I'm not blushing." Ramona held her palms over her cheeks to hide any evidence that may be lurking.

Cammie grinned. "You're *definitely* blushing."

Before Ramona could defend herself, Posey appeared in the doorway, covered in soil and holding a wilting potted plant that looked like it had one leaf in the grave already.

"Are we talking about Ramona's girlfriend?" Posey asked brightly.

"Kashvi says there's a magical connection," Cammie supplied helpfully.

"Ooh, what kind?" Posey asked, her eyes widening.

"We're trying to figure that out," Felix said, stroking Gerald's head gently with a knuckle. "But Ramona won't give us any details."

"Because it's new and I don't want to jinx it." Ramona tried her best to blush, which wasn't hard, considering how deeply embarrassed she was already. "We're taking things slow."

"Ah yes. Slow with someone who sleeps in your tiny room," Posey pointed out.

"And who Gerald likes," Felix said with a coo of agreement from the pigeon in question.

"And she's already magically connected to you," Kashvi finished.

"How'd you meet?" Cammie asked, leaning forward like she was watching an episode of *Love Potion*. "Is she a witch?"

"She's definitely a witch," Felix said. "She's definitely magical."

Kashvi tilted her head. "How *did* you meet?"

They all looked at Ramona expectantly.

"Hey, darling," Zara's voice called out, and Ramona watched Posey *swoon*. "Are you coming to bed?"

Four sets of expectant eyes — five, counting Gerald — swung to her with interest.

"Uh, yes. I'm coming," Ramona said, and she thought she heard one of her roommates make a vulgar joke as she hurried down the hallway.

Ramona closed her bedroom door behind her, muffling their voices.

Zara was sitting on the edge of the bed.

Not in the chair. On the bed. Hands folded in her lap, posture perfect, expression carefully neutral in the dim light from the streetlamp outside.

"Please tell me demons have terrible hearing," Ramona asked with an embarrassed grimace.

"I heard," Zara said quietly. "That's why I saved you."

Ramona closed the door behind her, leaning against it. "Thank you."

Zara's voice was careful. "You seemed… distressed."

"Distressed?" Ramona crossed to the bed, sitting down with more space between them than was probably necessary. "Try complete and total mortification."

"They seem… enthusiastic." Zara's conceptual spine was ramrod straight, her tone careful.

"I let them think we're dating. To explain your presence."

"Yes. I gathered that."

"And Kashvi—"

"Kashvi is perceptive," Zara said, her eyes focusing on something far away as she considered. "The tether does create a magical signature. It's understandable she would notice."

"They're going to keep asking questions."

"Probably."

"And I can't exactly tell them you're a demon from Hell."

"That would be inadvisable," Zara agreed, nodding.

They sat in silence for a moment. Ramona could hear her roommates still talking in the kitchen — muffled voices, occasional laughter.

"They're just being overbearing. Don't worry about any of that. I'm not..." Ramona awkwardly waved her hand between them. "I don't mean to make you feel uncomfortable."

"They're just concerned about you," Zara said, her voice softer now. "They want you to be happy. It's... nice, actually. That you have people who care."

Ramona looked at her. Zara was still sitting very straight, hands folded, carefully not looking at Ramona. But there was something in her expression — something almost wistful.

"Do you have people like that?" Ramona asked. "In Hell? A family? Friends?"

"Not really." Zara stood up, moving back toward the chair. "Demons don't typically form those kinds of bonds."

"Do you have a family?"

Zara shook her head. "I don't think so."

"Aren't demons born, like humans?" Ramona asked.

Zara shook her head. "No, we're created through energy transfiguration. We don't have parents in the same way a mortal would. We just... are, I suppose."

Ramona tried to read Zara's hardened expression. "That sounds lonely."

"It's efficient." Zara stood and sat back down in the chair, the wood and plastic creaking under her. "You should sleep, Mortal. Tomorrow is another workday." She pulled out her phone as if to signal that the conversation was over.

Ramona grabbed her spare pillow and the throw blanket from the end of her bed. She handed them to Zara, who accepted them with the same polite resignation as before.

"Thank you, Mortal."

"You're welcome."

Ramona awkwardly hid in her closet as she changed into her pajamas — sweatpants and an oversized T-shirt from a marathon Simone had run years before.

She climbed into bed, pulling the covers up. The room felt strange with Zara in it. More crowded. The air seemed different, charged with something Ramona didn't want to name. Like a tentative understanding was beginning to weave between them.

"Lights?" Zara asked.

"Oh, sure." Ramona reached for the lamp on her nightstand. "Hey, can demons see in the dark?"

"Yes."

"Of course you can." Ramona turned off the light.

Darkness settled over the room like a blanket. Ramona lay there, staring at the ceiling, hyperaware of every sound. Her own breathing. The creak of the chair as Zara shifted. The distant hum of traffic outside. The building's old pipes groaning.

This was fine. Totally normal. Just a regular Tuesday night with a demon in her bedroom.

She closed her eyes. Tried to relax. Counted backwards from one hundred.

At seventy-three, she heard it.

A sound from outside. High-pitched, eerie. Like a scream, but not quite. It started low and climbed, wavering at the end.

Ramona's eyes snapped open. "That fucking cat."

"You mean the fox?" Zara asked from the darkness. Her voice was calm.

"It's just a cat." Ramona had lived in this apartment for two years. She knew the neighborhood sounds. "There's one that battles with the raccoons behind the building."

"That's not a cat."

"I'm pretty sure I know what a cat sounds like."

"And I've been alive for three hundred years, Mortal. I know a fox when I hear one." There was a pause. "And it's calling your name, Ramona. Specifically."

Ramona sat up, the covers pooling around her waist. "What? You speak fox?"

"Are all mortals this dense?" Zara huffed in annoyance.

The sound came again. Closer this time. Ramona got out of bed and went to the window, pulling back the curtain. The alley behind the building was lit by a single streetlight, casting everything in sickly yellow. And there, sitting on top of the dumpster, was a fox.

It was small, red-furred, with a white-tipped tail and dark legs. Its ears were pricked forward, pointed directly at Ramona's window. As she watched, it opened its mouth and made that sound again — that eerie, climbing cry that definitely wasn't a cat.

And she felt something.

A pull. A recognition. Like a string tied around her ribs, tugging gently.

Ramona sighed. "I guess it could have been that fox."

Behind her, she heard Zara stand up. Heard her cross the room. Felt her presence at her shoulder, warm and solid.

"You feel something," Zara said. It wasn't a question.

"I don't—" Ramona stopped. "I don't know. I never had a familiar."

"I thought all witches had one. Felix has Gerald, Posey has that plant, even Kashvi has the—" Zara's voice broke off, as if she was trying to stop herself from revealing something.

"Kashvi has what?" Ramona pressed.

"Never mind. Where's *your* familiar?" Zara asked.

"I've just never had one. We had a cat growing up that I used to pretend was my familiar, and Simone's hare was sweet, but I've just never… found one."

"Who is Simone?" Zara asked.

"My ex-wife," Ramona explained, shutting the curtain.

Zara nodded, glancing back to the window where the fox was staring up at them with an intensity Ramona didn't appreciate.

"Do demons have spouses?" Ramona asked, going very still.

"No," Zara said.

"Oh," Ramona said, and she didn't know why she felt a pang of disappointment. Maybe it was just the intense and stoic loneliness that Zara exuded when talking about the demon realm. "Demons don't have any romantic connections?"

Zara raised one eyebrow. "Mortal, are you asking me if demons fuck?"

Ramona nearly laughed from surprise at Zara's bluntness. She shifted her weight and attempted something eloquent. Instead, what came out of her mouth was, "Oh, uh, I mean, that's none of my business, I'm just curious, I only—"

"Of course we fuck. Such things don't require romantic connection, though," Zara said as formally as if she were explaining Hell's highway system.

Ramona turned back to the window, pulling the curtain open again and setting her jaw in an attempt not to combust in mortification.

The fox was still there. Still watching.

Ramona cleared her throat, trying to steer the conversation back to safer waters. "Why is this thing screaming my name, then?" she asked.

"As far as I know, that's how it starts." Zara moved closer to the window, studying the fox with careful intensity. "A familiar choosing you. You're being called, Mortal."

"I don't want it." The words came out sharper than intended.

"That's not really how it works. When you're chosen, you're chosen."

"Well, I'm un-choosing." Ramona let the curtain fall, cutting off the fox's unblinking stare. "I'm good. I don't need a familiar."

"Every witch needs a familiar."

"I'm not a—"

"You *are* a witch," Zara repeated, like Ramona hadn't heard her.

"I'm really not. I'm a retail worker." Ramona crossed back to her bed, climbing under the covers with more force than necessary. "I sell fake sage to tourists. I don't need a magical companion for that. And certainly not a fucking fox. Why can it never be something easy to explain to the non-mages, like a purse Pomeranian?"

Zara was quiet for a long moment. Then she returned to her chair, the springs creaking under her weight. "He'll keep coming."

"Can we not talk about this?" Ramona pulled the covers up to her chin. "Please?"

Another pause. Longer this time. "Of course."

Silence settled over the room again. Ramona closed her eyes, but she could still feel it — that pull. That recognition. The sense that something outside was waiting for her, patient and persistent.

She tried to ignore it. Tried to focus on her breathing, on the exhaustion in her bones, on anything except the image of that fox sitting on the dumpster, calling her name.

Minutes passed. Maybe hours. Time felt strange in the dark, elastic and uncertain.

"Mortal?" Zara's voice was quiet.

"What?"

"Thank you."

"For what?"

"For the pillow." A pause. "And the blanket."

Ramona opened her eyes, staring at the dark ceiling. "You're welcome."

More silence. The building settled around them, groaning and creaking. Outside, the fox had ceased calling. In the quiet, Ramona could feel the different ways her soul was pulled, tethered to Zara in a constant, insistent whisper. The strange tug toward the window, toward the fox.

Ramona closed her eyes again. The exhaustion was finally catching up to her, pulling her down into something that might actually be sleep.

Her last conscious thought was that the chair springs had gone quiet. That Zara had stopped shifting, stopped adjusting.

Like maybe she was actually sleeping, too.

exhausted in her bones. [illegible] anything except the image of that fox sitting on the dumpster, calling her name.

Minutes passed. Maybe hours. Time felt strange, [illegible] and uncertain.

"Mama?" Zara's voice was quiet.

"What?"

"Thank you."

"For what?"

"For the pillow." A pause. "And the blanket."

[illegible] "You're welcome."

More silence. The building settled around them, groaning and [illegible]. Outside, the fox had ceased calling. In the quiet [illegible] different way [illegible] to Zara [illegible] the fox [illegible]

[illegible] again. [illegible]

[illegible] conscious thought was that [illegible] stopped [illegible]

[illegible] she was [illegible]

CHAPTER EIGHT

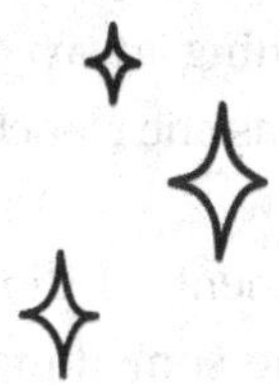

DARK-TIPPED NAILS DRAGGED ALONG THE BARE SKIN OF HER ABDOMEN, gently at first, then growing in insistence. She writhed under the touch, burning up from the inside. Molten heat between her thighs made her impatient, and she lifted her hips — hoping, begging.

"Not yet, little Mortal," the honeyed voice in her ear crooned.

Zara.

Zara above her, the weight of the demon's body on top of hers, pressing her down into the bed.

Oh. *Oh*.

Dark hair fell about Zara's face as she looked down at Ramona, those smoky eyes staring into her own, into her soul, knowing exactly what she needed. Zara's hands, her slightly elongated canines, her tongue, her entirety.

She reached up and touched Zara's cheek, the skin under her hand impossibly hot and soft at the same time. A moment passed between them. Trust, perhaps? Permission.

Light flooded her senses, and Ramona jerked awake, immediately pressing her thighs together to dampen the throbbing ache between them. She looked around the room to get her bearings, finding Zara standing at the window, her hand on the cool glass. Tiny frost designs spiraled out from where her hand touched the window, as if the merging of heat and ice sparked a bit of winter magic.

Ramona's cheeks warmed, embarrassed by the fact that she was just having a sex dream about the demon she'd accidentally bound to her. She scrubbed a hand over her face. "Um, good morning."

Zara was breathing fast. "Yes."

Ramona eyed her. "Are you all right?"

Zara nodded quickly, turning away. "Of course." She cleared her throat, and Ramona watched as she clenched and unclenched the hand that wasn't against the window.

Was it just her embarrassment, or did Zara know what she'd been dreaming? Had Ramona done something like moan her name in her sleep? She bit her lip, unsure whether to ask or completely leave the topic alone.

"Shower, Mortal. We're late for work," Zara said. Her voice was still strained, but surely Ramona was reading into things. "I'll enlist Felix to make you a cup of coffee to go."

Ramona did as she was told, turning the hot water up higher than she normally did, scalding her skin to wash off the embarrassment and any lingering truths about just exactly what she'd been dreaming about.

THE NEXT TWO days of work went by quickly, with Zara creating a long list of inventory, suggesting organizational changes, and putting forth three ideas for pivoting the self-help section into something that would get them a better ROI, whatever that meant.

The only moment of pause was when Iris texted her, asking her to bring bread rolls to her family's Imbolc dinner the following week. Ramona had stared down at her phone, and with Zara's help, had worded a careful response to let Iris and her mother know that she'd be officially missing Imbolc dinner this year.

Iris had sent back seventeen questions within a span of thirty seconds, but her mother had simply given Ramona's message a quick thumbs-up. She'd silenced her phone for the rest of the day, not ready to come up with a response for Iris.

A sharp stab of guilt stayed under her sternum for hours, annoying and insistent, but how could she bring Zara to her family's manor? To dinner? There was no way.

Both evenings were spent sitting on the couch with Posey and Cammie, watching new episodes of *Love Potion*. Zara joined in only from the distance of the kitchen table, asking questions no self-respecting witch ever would about the magical world's most popular dating show.

"You're telling me all of these gorgeous, intelligent witches are trying to get this man to fall in love with them? Why?" Zara asked.

Posey sighed dreamily. "Because it's true love."

Zara snorted. "But he's not even that powerful. He's really got nothing other than his mother's impressive ancestry to lean on."

Cammie glanced toward Zara. "And he's hot. Isn't that enough?"

Zara openly grimaced and Ramona couldn't help but grin, hiding her smile behind her hand.

"Yeah, it's all bullshit," Felix said from the kitchen counter, where he was finishing up a batch of dark chocolate and cherry brownies. "But aren't most things?"

RAMONA'S two days off were a chance to take a breath. Zara had asked to visit the library, and so they'd walked to the Fernwick Public Library. Upon Zara's request, Ramona had taken her to the floor reserved for magical literature that was off-limits to non-mages, where Zara had spent hours looking through literature that might help with their severing. Ramona had passed the time browsing the romance section, then settling into a comfy chair and enjoying a little escapism about hot vampires.

On her other day off, while snow blanketed Fernwick in crisp white, Ramona did laundry and tidied her room while Zara pored over the books she'd checked out, cross-referencing *A Comprehensive Guide to Magical Contracts and Their Dissolution* with *Infernal Agreements: Legal Precedents and Loopholes*.

Back at work the next day, she and Zara had tested the tether by having Zara sit in the café next door to the shop for most of the day while Marcus was around, strategically positioned in one of the booths against the wall shared between the businesses. It had worked well enough, and Ramona had loaned Zara her laptop, where Zara caught up on the latest season of *Love Potion*, all thirty-four episodes of the season so far.

On Sunday evening, Zara used the toe of her shoe to sweep away a few discarded T-shirts and dresses and knelt in front of Ramona's bookshelf, pulling out one of the old academic tomes.

"You were a professor, right?" Zara asked casually.

Ramona tried to shove down the queasy feeling that word inspired. She forced a casual nod, keeping her hands busy by loosely braiding her hair for bed. "In another life."

Zara glanced up, tilting her head. "Humans remember reincarnation?"

Ramona rolled her eyes. "It's just a saying. I mean, I was a professor, and now I'm not… anything."

"Dr. Greenbriar," Zara said, her thumb trailing over the gilded spine of another book she lifted.

Ramona grimaced.

"Tongues of Power: The Strategic Use of Multilingual Construction in Medieval Magical Texts," Zara read aloud. "Wow, riveting stuff."

Ramona scoffed. "Don't make fun of my dissertation. I spent many, many years writing that—"

Zara blinked. "Mortal, I'm not… making fun. I honestly find it very interesting." She sat back on her heels, flipping open the book. "What kinds of courses did you teach?"

"I had two sections of Intro to Magical Languages, and Reading Medieval Grimoires in the spring with History of European Magic, 1200-1600, in alternating years. I was developing this graduate seminar on code-switching that would have been incredible, though, and the dean had talked to me about an advanced paleography course."

It felt like a full lifetime ago that her life had been in the wood-paneled halls of Thornwood. She remembered her first day in her office, the terribly small one too close to the furnace room, sitting at her desk and feeling like she'd really made it.

But the worst part wasn't losing the job. The worst part was losing the students.

The grad student who'd wanted Ramona to chair her dissertation committee. The undergrad who'd finally understood why magical Latincane mattered. The teaching assistant she'd been training. They'd all found other advisors. Other mentors. Other professors who could actually do magic. Because what use was a magical languages professor who couldn't cast a basic spell? What use was expertise without execution? None. No use at all.

So now Ramona sold crystals to non-mages and tried not to think about the students who'd once waited after class to ask questions. Who'd gotten excited about grimoire paleography. Who'd wanted to be like her. She hoped they'd found better role models. They deserved better than a washed-up academic who couldn't even reheat her tea without catastrophe.

Zara was looking at her, watching. "What made you leave?"

"It's a long story."

"I've got a few weeks without much else going on, Mortal," Zara said with a sardonic smile, leaning back against the wall, Ramona's dissertation still in her lap.

"Not tonight." Ramona sighed, and thankfully, Zara didn't press.

Zara gestured toward the bottom row of the bookshelf where all the textbooks were gathering dust. "Maybe there's something that can help us in all of these books, something that only your expertise would be able to find."

"Well, it's a good thing demons don't need much sleep, because that's all you," Ramona said. "I hung up my academic robes a long time ago."

"If you taught a course about medieval grimoires, why didn't the grimoire you used to summon me strike an odd chord with you?" Zara asked.

Ramona wrinkled her nose. She'd been asking herself the same thing. The text had seemed clear to her upon its first reading, and she'd missed so much. She cleared her throat. "Well, first of all, that wasn't a medieval grimoire. That was a more modern text. Second, it's one thing to critically study a spell, and another altogether to perform a spell. Think of it like analyzing a contract versus writing one."

"I do love writing them," Zara mused.

"And let's just say my head's been out of the game for a minute, you know? I wasn't looking at that grimoire like Dr. Greenbriar. I was looking at it as sad sack Ramona," she said.

Zara frowned. "That's..." Her voice faded, but Ramona looked away before the inevitable pity could reach Zara's face.

Ramona chewed on her thumbnail out of nervous habit.

"What about the Thornwood Academy library? Would you be able to get us in there?" Zara asked, tapping the cover of the book in her lap. "Surely there are some books that are more specific than what I could find at the Fernwick library and the online databases."

"No," Ramona said firmly. "There's no way in... any realm that I'd set foot back on that campus. My ex-wife and her girlfriend both work there, and I can't risk it."

"Is it not one of the largest witching academies in the world?" Zara asked. "Surely the odds of running into one another are..." She paused as if doing the mental calculation.

"I'm not going back there," Ramona said, finding her jaw uncomfortably clenched as she bit out the words.

"But you're an academic. You love libraries and research."

"And I value my sanity more than something I once loved years ago," Ramona said. "End of discussion. We're not going."

Zara raised her brows. "We can talk more about it later."

"No."

Zara had a distinctly *we'll see* look on her irritatingly attractive face. She flipped open Ramona's dissertation once again and pulled a pair of reading glasses out of her suit pocket, settling them on her nose.

"You wear glasses?" Ramona tried to hide her amusement at the sight of Zara sitting in her expensive suit on the hardwood floor, wearing oversized glasses and peering down at Dr. Greenbriar's dissertation.

"Only when I'm reading at night," Zara said.

"Those three hundred years are catching up with you, I guess," Ramona teased, crawling under the covers of her bed.

"You bite your tongue, Mortal. In demon years, I'm still in my prime," Zara hissed.

"At least one of us is. I think I'm well past my sell-by date," Ramona half joked.

Zara raised one single, sharp brow. "Well, that's just factually inaccurate."

Ramona felt her cheeks heat, her phone's ringtone disturbing the moment. She fumbled for her phone, hitting the call button with the kind of desperate haste typically reserved for a jailbreak.

"Ramona, I know you don't want to drive that terrible car all the way home, so Bradford has agreed that we will simply pick you up and drive you ourselves," Iris said, not pausing for a moment of polite nicety before her demand. Classic Iris.

Ramona rubbed at her eyes. "Iris, I really can't make it."

"Nonsense. We're thinking four p.m. should be plenty of time, but perhaps should we do three p.m. just to be on the safe side?" Iris, Ramona knew, was only talking to herself.

"My girlfriend is visiting from out of town," Ramona said quickly and firmly, committing herself to the lie yet again, her eyes flicking up to where Zara was blatantly watching, listening. "Mom would panic—"

"Girlfriend?" Iris's voice lifted at least four octaves in interest.

"All right, let's take a deep breath," Ramona said, her own voice lowering in reply.

"You should bring her." Was Iris *clapping* on the other end of the line?

"She's not..." Ramona fumbled for the right word. "Social."

Zara held a hand to her chest in mock offense.

"We can fit her in the van, too," Iris said, her voice still rivaling a mouse's squeak in pitch.

Ramona sighed. She imagined cramming into the minivan with Iris, her husband Bradford, and squeezing in next to the booster seats of her nieces, who historically did not love road trips. It was a two-hour drive, but nothing could make it feel longer than a toddler screaming in her ear the entire time. "My car can make it." She hoped.

"Fantastic. Then, bring the rolls. What's your girlfriend's name? Mom will want to make the seating chart reflect—"

"Zara," Ramona interrupted. Seating chart. There were only six of them — why did they need place cards? The kids would be at a small table surrounded by enough plastic to impress a serial killer. "Her name is Zara."

Iris's tone was now verging on glass-breaking in its high register. "Fantastic. We'll see you there, then. I'll let Mom know."

Ramona said her goodbyes and hung up, only to meet Zara's raised eyebrows.

"We need to work on you maintaining boundaries," Zara said with a deep sigh. "That was honestly shocking in how quickly she was able to manipulate you into agreement."

"She's never met a hill she wouldn't die on," Ramona said, rolling her eyes. "It's like she's always had a way of dominating everything around her. It's probably why she's such a good curse-breaker." She paused, then pointed at Zara. "But we're not asking for her help. Yet. We can figure this out ourselves."

Zara blinked, silent for a moment as though trying to come up with a cautious way to respond. "Well, I'm excited to meet such a master manipulator in the flesh. Maybe I'll find some new inspiration."

"You're not going to, like, steal her soul, right?" Ramona asked, flopping back down against her pillows. "Or Bradford's?"

"Honestly, any man who goes by the entirety of Bradford is kind of asking for his soul to be stolen, but no, I do not intend to do any physical work on this trip," Zara said.

Ramona buried her smile in the pillow. "Will you turn out the light, please?" She watched as Zara flicked her wrist and the lights went out. "Don't stay up too late with that *riveting* dissertation."

Zara made a dismissive hum of non-agreement, and Ramona closed her eyes.

SHE HAD no idea how long she'd been sleeping when the screaming fox woke her up.

No, it wasn't the fox. Something closer. Something wrong. It was *Zara.*

Her eyes snapped open in the darkness, heart already racing. The sound was coming from across the room — raw, anguished, a sound she'd never heard a person make before.

Then the pain hit.

It slammed into her like a physical blow. Her chest seized, her lungs burned, every nerve in her body lit up with agony that wasn't hers. The tether. She could feel it through the tether — Zara's pain, Zara's terror, flooding through the connection between them like poison in shared veins.

Ramona threw off the covers and stumbled across the room, nearly tripping over her own feet. In the chair, Zara was thrashing, caught in the grip of something Ramona couldn't see. Her face was twisted, a sheen of sweat on her forehead catching the streetlight. Her hands gripped the armrests hard enough that the cheap plastic was cracking.

Another scream tore from her throat, and Ramona felt it — felt the echo of whatever was happening in that dream. Fire. Or something like it. Something worse.

"Zara." Ramona dropped to her knees beside the chair, hands hovering uselessly. She didn't know if touching would make it worse. "Zara, wake up."

Nothing. Just another choked sound of pain.

Ramona grabbed her shoulders. "Zara!"

Zara's eyes flew open — wild, unseeing, reflecting the dim light like an animal's. For half a second, she didn't seem to recognize where she was. Her hand shot out, fingers closing around Ramona's wrist with enough force to bruise.

Then she focused. Saw Ramona. The grip loosened slightly but she didn't let go.

"Ramona." Her voice was hoarse, broken. She was breathing too fast, chest heaving like she'd been running. Or drowning.

"I'm here. You're here. You're safe." Ramona kept her voice steady even though her own heart was hammering. The pain was already fading from the tether, but she could still feel the aftershocks of Zara's panic, sharp and overwhelming.

Zara looked around the room like she was cataloging it. Her dark eyes flicked to the water-stained ceiling. The duct-taped bed frame. The grimoire on the nightstand.

"It was a dream," Ramona said quietly. "Just a dream."

"I know." But Zara's breathing hadn't slowed. She was still holding Ramona's wrist, fingers trembling slightly.

"Come here." Ramona stood, tugging gently. "Come on. The bed is more comfortable than that terrible chair."

For once, Zara didn't argue. She let Ramona guide her to the bed, moving like she wasn't quite back in her body yet. When she sat down on the edge, Ramona could see her hands were shaking.

"Lie down," Ramona said. "I'll get you some water—"

Zara's grip tightened on her wrist. Not painful, but insistent. Desperate. "Don't." The word came out rough. "Don't leave. Please."

Ramona's chest constricted. She'd never heard Zara say please like that, like she was asking for something she needed but couldn't name.

"Okay." Ramona sat down beside her, close enough that their shoulders touched. "I'm not going anywhere."

A knock sounded on the door. "Ramona, you guys okay?" Kashvi sounded worried.

"Yeah, sorry, I had a nightmare," Ramona called out. "Thanks for checking on us."

"Let us know if you need anything," Posey said through the door, and Ramona thanked them again, then heard their footsteps down the hall. She almost smiled at the idea that her roommates had both come to her apparent rescue.

Zara lay back slowly, still holding Ramona's wrist like a lifeline. She pulled Ramona's arm across her chest, fingers wrapped around her forearm now, gentler but no less insistent. Like she needed the weight of it. The proof that someone was there. Or that she was here.

"How can I help?" Ramona asked quietly.

Zara's eyes were fixed on the ceiling, on that duck-shaped water stain. "Just keep breathing."

"What?"

"Your breathing. I like the sound." Zara's voice was barely above a whisper. "It helps."

Something in Ramona's chest felt heavy with the weight of melancholy. She let her breathing stay audible, steady and even. In and out. A rhythm for Zara to follow.

They lay there in the darkness, Zara's fingers wrapped around Ramona's wrist, neither of them speaking. Gradually, Ramona felt Zara's breathing start to match hers. Felt the tension in her body begin to ease, degree by degree.

"Do you want to talk about it?" Ramona whispered after a long moment.

Zara shook her head once, sharp. Her jaw was set, that careful control sliding back into place even as her hand stayed locked around Ramona's arm.

Ramona didn't push. She just lay there beside her, breathing, being present in the only way Zara seemed able to accept.

And for the first time since the summoning, Ramona saw it — saw past the expensive suits and the corporate efficiency and the three-hundred-year-old demon who organized bookshops for fun. Saw the soul underneath. Someone who had nightmares. Someone who needed comfort but didn't know how to ask for it. Someone who was scared.

Someone who was lonely.

A sound broke the silence. Scratching. Frantic and insistent.

Ramona turned her head toward the window and her breath caught.

The fox was there, perched on the fire escape. Its front paws were against the glass, claws scraping, its pointed face pressed close. Its eyes were wide, almost panicked, reflecting the streetlight in twin points of gold. It was making small, distressed sounds — half whine, half keen — that Ramona could barely hear through the glass.

"It's okay," Ramona said quietly, not sure if she was talking to the fox or to Zara or to herself. "We're okay."

The fox stopped scratching. It stayed there, pressed against the window, but the frantic energy drained from its posture. It settled onto its haunches, head tilted, watching them with unblinking intensity.

Ramona felt that pull again — that recognition, that string around her ribs. The fox had felt something through whatever connection was trying to form. Had felt her fear. Had come.

They both watched the fox, which watched them right back. Standing guard. Or maybe just refusing to leave.

"It's worried about you," Zara said.

"Or it just wants food," Ramona said, though she didn't truly believe that.

Outside, the fox curled into itself slightly but didn't close its eyes. Just kept watching through the window like it would stay there all night if necessary.

Ramona turned back to Zara and found her staring at the ceiling again, but her breathing was almost normal now. The trembling had ended. Her fingers had loosened their death grip on Ramona's wrist into something closer to holding.

"Thank you," Zara whispered. So quiet Ramona almost missed it.

"For what?"

"For waking me up. For being here."

Ramona's throat tightened. "Sure," she said with an unfortunate lack of eloquence.

Zara's eyes closed. For a long time, neither of them moved. Ramona could feel Zara's pulse through the grip on her wrist — still racing at first, then gradually slowing. Could feel the exact moment Zara's body started to relax, inch by inch, into something that might eventually become sleep.

Outside, the fox remained at its post.

Inside, Ramona lay very still, her arm held across Zara's chest like an anchor, and watched the demon beside her finally let her guard down.

Neither of them mentioned it when they woke up hours later, tangled together, Zara's face buried against Ramona's shoulder and Ramona's other hand somehow wound in Zara's hair.

Neither of them mentioned that the fox was still there, asleep on the fire escape.

Neither of them mentioned that Zara had been crying in her sleep — silent tears that had soaked into Ramona's T-shirt.

But when Zara finally pulled away, sitting up and running her hands through her disheveled hair, and Ramona said "Good morning" like nothing had happened, Zara looked at her with something that might have been gratitude for only a moment before her expression settled back into a familiar bored, assessing look.

"Good morning, Mortal."

It hit Ramona then, that if she'd felt every knife-slice of terror of Zara's nightmare because of the tether, that Zara had probably also felt every moment of the explicit dreams she'd been having almost every night, too.

Oh no.

Oh no.

Her face went hot. Then hotter. Those dreams — the ones where Zara pushed her against the bookshelf wall, the ones in her childhood bedroom, the particularly vivid one from two nights ago involving a desk and significantly fewer clothes...

Zara had felt all of it.

Her cheeks flushed, and she sat up abruptly, desperate for a little distance between them.

"What's wrong?" Zara asked, standing and stretching. Her button-up pulled up over her stomach, revealing a delicious peek of skin. She caught Ramona staring and her mouth curved — knowing.

Ramona made a strangled sound, then cleared her throat. "I'm going to go take a shower." She stood and hurried toward the door, practically fleeing.

"Take your time," Zara called after her, and there was definite amusement in her voice now. "Have a nice shower, Mortal."

Ramona fled. She swore she could hear a low, knowing chuckle as the door clicked shut behind her.

CHAPTER NINE

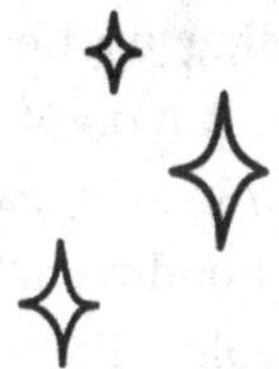

The drive up to Greenbriar Manor was lined with arching, ancient oak trees that formed a tunnel with their branches. In the spring and summer, they turned into a verdant canopy, and in the fall, oranges and yellows and reds greeted guests. Today, gnarled branches reached toward the car like outstretched claws. The effect was as unsettling as the manor that loomed far down the drive. The residence stood like a brick fortress, a horseshoe driveway in front leading straight to a staircase up to the massive and intricately carved front door. What the manor lacked in frill, it made up for in size. Though they'd only been a family of four, the Greenbriars also had a house manager and a cook, which left nearly fifteen more empty bedrooms.

Zara whistled, craning her head to see out the car window. "This is where you grew up?"

Ramona nodded, a lump forming in her throat, constricting her ability to speak.

"This kind of privilege usually makes people monsters. You should be *way* bitchier," Zara commented.

"Ah, the demon has jokes," Ramona said, putting the car in park near the old carriage house. The fact that the car had made it was a bit surprising, but she'd have rather ridden a bicycle all the way here than be crammed in a car with Iris and Zara. Just the thought of them at the dining table together was enough to make her palms feel sweaty again.

"No need to be nervous," Zara said. "I can burn down the house at any moment."

Ramona huffed a small laugh despite her growing unease, glancing sideways at Zara. "I want them to *not* know you're a demon, preferably. Remember—"

Zara rolled her eyes, holding up her fingers as if using them to count the rules. "No stealing anyone's souls, no entering into any bargains that are solely for my own gain, no corporate-speak, and I'm… not a demon. I am from Londoven."

"Okay, but make it believable," Ramona said. "No one says 'I am from Londoven.' You're not a robot."

"Why can't I be Rushen? I could do such a good Rushen accent," Zara said, smoothing the lapels of her jacket. "You know, I'm actually fluent."

"Londoven is the furthest I'm willing to push it." Ramona rifled through her bag, applying a tinted lip balm in her visor's cracked mirror. "You're *positive* my family won't be able to tell you're a demon?"

Zara shrugged. "Your mom and sister sound like gifted witches, especially Iris with the whole curse-breaking business, but I'm fairly confident I'll be undetectable."

Ramona blinked in alarm. "*Fairly* confident? Fairly?"

"Incoming," Zara whispered only one moment before a tap sounded on Ramona's window.

Ramona jumped, despite the warning, and turned to find Iris standing beside her car door, waving. Iris's familiar, a raven, flew from Iris's shoulder down to the ground.

Ramona took a breath and opened the door, stepping out onto the gravel drive. The cold bit at her face immediately. Iris was already moving in for an enthusiastic hug, and Ramona found herself caught in her sister's embrace before she could prepare for it.

Iris was everything that Ramona was not. Iris was tall, slender, elegant. Her shiny, dark brown hair was smooth and coiffed, falling just past her shoulders.

"You made it!" Iris pulled back, her hands on Ramona's shoulders, studying her face like she was looking for evidence. "And you brought your girlfriend!"

Zara emerged from the passenger side, smoothing down her jacket with practiced precision. She'd glamoured her suit for the occasion — a dark blazer over a crisp white shirt, tailored pants that looked bespoke and expensive. She looked like she belonged at a state dinner, not an awkward family Imbolc gathering.

"Iris," Ramona said, her voice tight. "This is Zara. Zara, this is my sister."

"Enchantée," Zara said, offering her hand. Ramona wondered if it was too late to get back in the car and leave.

Iris shook her hand, eyes wide. "Wow. Hi. It's so nice to meet you. Ramona has told me absolutely nothing about you."

"I'm very private," Zara said smoothly. Her accent had shifted ever so slightly, and Ramona wondered if she was really trying for Rushen.

"Okay." Iris looped her arm through Ramona's, already pulling her toward the house. "Come on. Mom's been panicking about the dinner all day. Dad's in the study pretending to read but actually just napping. Same as always. Bradford and the girls are already inside."

Ramona let herself be dragged along, hyperaware of Zara walking behind them, taking in the grounds with that trademark intense focus. The front stairs. The carved door. The entryway with its vaulted ceilings and chandelier that was larger than Ramona's car.

Her two nieces came barreling down the hall in a tornado of ruffles and limbs. The oldest, five-year-old Daphne, hugged Ramona first, launching into her with enough force to make them both take several steps back. "Auntie Mona!" Three-year-old Poppy howled, wrapping her arms around Ramona. Ramona hugged them both fiercely, then introduced them to Zara.

"Nice to meet you, Miss Zara," Daphne said, standing a bit shyly behind Ramona. Poppy was staring up at Zara skeptically.

"Nice to meet you… young… ones," Zara said slowly, as if she wasn't sure how to properly address a child.

Ramona bit the inside of her cheek to hide a grin. The girls ran off, and Iris ushered them inside as if it was her own home. After all, it was her birthright to inherit Greenbriar Manor, as all eldest Greenbriar daughters had before her.

"This is quite the home," Zara said quietly.

"It's been in the family for generations," Iris said proudly. "The Greenbriars have owned this land since the sixteen hundreds."

"Impressive." Zara's gaze swept the portraits lining the hallway— stern-faced witches in elaborate gowns and suits, each one more intimidating than the last. "And these are your ancestors?"

"Every single one," Iris confirmed. "All the way back to Constance Greenbriar, one of the founders of Thornwood Academy."

Ramona felt Zara's attention shift to her. She didn't look back.

They found Ramona's mother in the kitchen, directing the cook with the kind of precision usually reserved for complex spellwork. Eleanor Greenbriar was tall, elegant, her dark hair pulled back in an intricate braid threaded with silver. She wore a dark green dress, formal even for Imbolc, and when she turned to greet them, her smile was warm but didn't quite reach her eyes.

"Ramona." She crossed the kitchen and pressed a kiss to Ramona's cheek. "You look well."

"Thanks, Mom." Ramona's throat was tight. "This is my… Zara. Zara, this is my mother, Eleanor."

"A pleasure, Mrs. Greenbriar." Zara offered her hand.

Eleanor studied her for a moment, assessing, calculating, then accepted the handshake. "Welcome to our home. Any friend of Ramona's is welcome here."

The words were kind. The delivery was coolly polite. Ramona looked between the two of them. If anyone Ramona knew could clock a demon upon first sight, it was Eleanor. Instead, Eleanor dipped her head in greeting.

"Thank you for having me," Zara said.

"Ramona, why don't you show Zara around?" Eleanor turned back to the stove. "Dinner will be ready in an hour. Your father should be awake by then."

Dismissed.

Ramona led Zara through the house, pointing out rooms without much enthusiasm. The library. The drawing room. The conservatory, where her mother grew her magical herbs. Each room was immaculate, perfectly maintained, utterly cold.

"Your mother seems nice," Zara said carefully.

"She can be, sometimes. In her way." Ramona paused at the back door. "Do you want to see the garden?"

"Of course."

The garden was dormant for winter, but even now it was beautiful — structured beds, stone pathways, a fountain at the center that had frozen over. And at the far end, standing alone in what should have been a rose garden, was a tree.

Zara stopped walking, staring at it from a distance. "What's that?"

The tree was ancient — gnarled, twisted, its bark blackened in places like it had been struck by lightning. Its branches reached up and out at unnatural angles, creating shadows even in the pale winter sun. No leaves. No life. Just dead wood that somehow still stood.

"Oh, just some nuisance tree. Iris accidentally killed it with a spell when she was eleven, and nothing can cut it down. It grows back the next morning, no matter what. It's such an eyesore and such a pain in my mom's ass that I secretly kind of love it," Ramona said with a grin.

Two lines appeared between Zara's eyebrows as she stared at the tree for a long moment, then pulled out her phone and took a picture. She turned back to Ramona, gave one last glance at the tree, and turned back toward the house. "Interesting," she was mumbling as Ramona walked past her back inside.

DINNER WAS EXACTLY as awkward as Ramona had feared.

The dining room was formal — long table, high ceilings, another chandelier that cast everything in dim candlelight. The table was decorated in dozens of flickering white pillar candles and woven crosses that she was sure her mom had been making for days.

Ramona's father, Thomas, had finally emerged from his study, looking distinguished and distant in his gray suit jacket. He shook Zara's hand with the same assessing coolness as Eleanor, then took his seat next to Eleanor, who was positioned at the head of the table.

Ramona sat across from Iris and Bradford, with Zara beside her.

Zara watched the raven sitting on a perch beside her mother's owl. Ramona had mentally prepared a dozen excuses for the close distance to Zara all night, but no one seemed to notice that Zara never strayed more than a few feet from Ramona's side.

The food, luckily, was excellent. Roasted vegetables from the garden's stores, fresh bread, a mushroom soup that steamed in ceramic bowls. The Greenbriars' cook had always had an exceptional talent, even without magic. Conversation, however, was stilted.

"So, Zara," Eleanor said after several minutes of silence broken only by the clink of silverware. "What do you do for work?"

"Corporate consulting," Zara said smoothly. "I work remotely."

"How modern." Eleanor's smile was thin. "And how did you and Ramona meet?"

"Through work, actually." Zara didn't miss a beat. "I was consulting for the shop's parent company."

Ramona nearly choked on her soup. Mystic Moon Books didn't have a parent company. Marcus owned it outright, funded by his parents. But her mother was nodding, accepting the lie.

"And you're originally from… Londoven?" Thomas asked. His voice was deep, measured.

"Do we need to interview her so intensely?" Ramona interrupted, wary that Zara would try out a Rushen accent.

"Your English is excellent," Bradford commented, glancing to Iris as if for approval. She gave him a tight smile in return. Ramona snorted into her wineglass.

"Thank you." Zara took a sip of wine.

"How accomplished." Eleanor turned her attention to Ramona. "And how is your work, dear? Still at the shop?"

The question sounded innocent. It wasn't.

"Yes," Ramona said carefully. "Still there."

"Busy season?"

"Always busy."

"I'm sure." Eleanor cut a piece of bread with precise movements. "Though I imagine it must be quite different from your previous position."

There it was, like a knife, slipped between Ramona's ribs with practiced ease.

Ramona's hands tightened on her fork. "Yep," she said, popping the P.

"Still," Eleanor continued, her tone light, "I suppose retail has its own merits. Certainly more stable than academia these days. Less... demanding. As I've always told you, the academy isn't for everyone. I did thrive there, of course, but you never quite did." She sighed, swirling the wine in her glass.

Zara cast a sidelong glance toward Ramona, then looked toward her mother. Iris was staring at her plate. Bradford was methodically eating his soup. Thomas looked up toward Ramona, as if expecting her to say something. As Ramona stole a look at Zara, she noticed the demon was staring directly at Eleanor, her eyes dark.

"And you don't have to worry much about the incident, since you're all the way away in Fernwick," Eleanor added. "Much safer for everyone involved."

The room went very quiet.

Ramona felt like she couldn't breathe. Something came over her when she was with her parents, like she was a weak child again. She wanted to defend herself, wanted to explain, wanted to scream that she'd been trying, that she'd been doing her best, that retail wasn't a failure, it was just —

A chill seemed to fall on the room, the candles in the middle of the table flickering as if in a breeze. "I'm sorry," Zara said. Her voice cut through the silence like a blade. "I don't understand what you could possibly mean by saying that. Could you explain it to me in detail?"

Everyone turned to look at her.

Eleanor's eyebrows raised slightly. "I simply meant —"

"Because from where I'm sitting," Zara continued, her tone still perfectly polite but with an edge underneath that made Ramona's pulse quicken. "It would seem you're implying you're not proud of the path your daughter has chosen."

"Zara—" Ramona whispered.

"No." Zara didn't look at her. Her eyes were fixed on Eleanor. "We gather for Imbolc to celebrate the halfway point between the winter and spring, right? Tonight is a promise of renewal, of rebirth, of fertility. It's meant to be a cleansing date, where you light candles against the darkness and cleanse your home of negativity. And yet, I'm shocked to find that despite the crosses and the candles and the feast, the negativity clearly remains among us."

The silence was deafening. Ramona's mouth fell open in surprise.

Eleanor had gone very still. Thomas set down his spoon.

Ramona couldn't speak. Her throat had closed up completely. Hot, urgent, embarrassed, and grateful tears were building behind her eyes.

No one had ever—

In two years, no one had—

"Well," Eleanor said eventually. Her voice was tight. "That's certainly an interesting opinion."

Zara smiled, her expression almost serene and pleasant. "I would hope that perhaps we can all choose to focus on the brighter days ahead instead of the darkness of the past."

Iris was staring between them with her mouth slightly open. Bradford was pale. Thomas cleared his throat awkwardly.

"Perhaps we *should* look ahead and discuss Ostara," Eleanor said, clearly desperate to change the subject. "The Spring Equinox Gala is in six weeks. The whole family will be attending, of course."

"Of course," Iris echoed quickly.

"Ramona." Eleanor's gaze fixed on her daughter. "You'll be there this year. No excuses."

It wasn't a question. It was a command.

Ramona found her voice. "I'll try—"

"You'll be there," Eleanor repeated. "The Greenbriar family will be hosting a table. Your absence has been noted. People are asking questions."

"What kind of questions?" Ramona asked, though she knew the answer.

"The kind we'd rather not answer." Thomas spoke for the first time since the meal began. "You're a Greenbriar, Ramona. Act like it."

Zara cleared her throat, and Thomas added, "Please."

The hot feeling behind Ramona's eyes intensified. Under the table, she felt Zara's foot find hers, the toes of their shoes touching like an immediate reminder that Ramona wasn't alone.

"We'll be there," Zara said calmly.

Something passed across Eleanor's face — surprise, maybe, or assessment. She looked between Zara and Ramona, clearly calculating something. "How lovely," she said finally. "It will be nice to have you both there."

The rest of the dinner passed in awkward small talk. Iris asked questions about Londoven that Zara answered with alarming specificity. Eleanor discussed the latest Magical Council's ineptitude in elaborate detail — she wasn't a member, but an inner circle of well-connected and wealthy witches were always somehow involved in Council business. Thomas described a scandal at a recent chess tournament he'd attended.

Ramona barely heard any of it. She was too focused on Zara's foot against hers, steady and grounding.

When dinner finally ended, Eleanor suggested coffee in the drawing room before lighting the bonfire in the back paddock. Ramona excused herself for a moment, barely remembering that would mean Zara had to come with her.

Ramona headed upstairs without really thinking about where she was going, Zara following silently behind. Her feet knew the path — second floor, third door on the right, past the portrait of her grandmother that always seemed to be watching.

Her childhood bedroom.

She pushed open the door and stepped inside, and it was like stepping back in time.

The room was exactly as she'd left it when she moved out for graduate school. Twin bed with a faded blue quilt. Desk covered in old notebooks and dried-out pens. Bookshelf sagging under the weight of medieval grimoires, linguistic theory textbooks, and young adult novels she'd never thrown away. The walls were covered in posters — the witch band she'd been obsessed with at sixteen, a map of constellations, a chart of runic alphabets.

And the trophies. So many trophies.

Awards from academic competitions lined the top of her bookshelf.

Spelling bees, language competitions, essay contests. A plaque from her undergraduate thesis defense. Her diploma from Thornwood's doctoral program, framed on the wall like it was something to be proud of.

It had been, once.

The bedroom felt less like a sanctuary and more like a shrine to what Ramona could have been, if only she had lived up to those expectations.

Ramona sat down on the bed, the springs creaking under her weight. The mattress was too soft, the same one she'd had since she was twelve. She stared at the diploma, at the careful calligraphy spelling out her name and achievements.

"May I sit?" Zara gestured to the bed.

Ramona nodded, not trusting her voice.

Zara sat down beside her. The twin bed wasn't made for two people — their thighs pressed together, shoulders touching. Ramona could feel the warmth of her through the fabric of their clothes.

"You kept everything," Zara said quietly, looking around the room.

"My mother kept everything. I haven't been back here since—" Ramona stopped. "Since before the divorce."

Her gaze landed on a photo on the nightstand. Ramona at her dissertation defense, ecstatic, holding up her bound thesis like a trophy. Simone was beside her, arm around her waist, smiling politely.

That version of Ramona looked so happy. So hopeful. So completely unaware that in a few years, everything would fall apart.

"You were brilliant," Zara said. Her voice was soft, but certain. She reached and took the photo frame in her hand, glanced at it, and then set it face down.

Ramona huffed out a bitter laugh. "Past tense."

"You still are."

Ramona groaned. "You don't have to do that."

"I never say anything I don't mean."

Something in Zara's tone made Ramona turn to look at her. Zara was watching her with an intensity that made her breath catch.

"I've read your dissertation," Zara said. "I even found your published papers on code-switching in grimoires — it's extraordinary work, Ramona."

Ramona's throat tightened. "How did you—"

"Hell has an excellent archival library. And I was curious." Zara's expression was serious. "Your research on how medieval witches deliberately mixed languages to control who could access their spells — it could fundamentally change how witches understand magical text preservation."

Ramona shifted her weight on the bed, the springs creaking. "Well, it doesn't matter that I studied dead languages now, since it's all dead to me anyway."

Zara's thumb traced absent patterns on the quilt between them. "You didn't just study dead languages. You proved they were strategic choices. Power moves."

"Really, it doesn't matter."

"Of course it matters." Zara's hand found hers, warmer than Ramona had imagined. Her grip was firm, and Ramona felt a tightening of the tether between them, a taut bowstring of tension. "That doesn't disappear because you can't teach anymore."

Ramona stared at their joined hands. "What use is a magical languages professor who can't cast spells?" Ramona's laugh was bitter. "What use is expertise without execution?"

"The same use as any scholar, any subject-matter expert." Zara squeezed her hand. "Knowledge doesn't require performance. Understanding doesn't require demonstration. You taught them how to read power. How to see strategy in syntax. That's not less valuable because your own magic is…" She paused, choosing her words carefully. "Difficult."

Ramona's eyes were burning. "You don't understand. The theories needed practical applications. My students needed someone who could show them the spells, not just explain the grammar."

"They needed someone who could teach them to think critically about magical texts. And you did that." Zara turned to face her fully. "Do you think all the archivists citing your work care that you can't cast? They care that you can read a thirteenth-century grimoire and explain exactly why the author switched languages mid-incantation. That's rare, Ramona. That's valuable."

They sat there for a moment, hands joined, shoulders pressed together on the too-small bed. The room felt smaller than it had when Ramona was young. Or maybe she just felt bigger — older, sadder, carrying years of weight that teenage Ramona never could have imagined.

"Thank you," Ramona said quietly. "For what you said downstairs. You didn't have to do that."

"Yes, I did." Zara shifted slightly, and suddenly they were very close. Close enough that Ramona could see the exact shade of Zara's eyes — she'd once thought they were black with red speckles, but now she could make out that they were a very deep brown with flecks of gold and orange and red, like trees in fall. Her dark eyelashes were long and thick. "Your mother was being cruel. Someone needed to say something."

Ramona's heart was doing a tap routine in her chest. She had to remind herself that every feeling was the magical bond between them, the tether creating a false intimate knowledge of one another. They were both vulnerable because of it, but Zara was a demon, and a damn powerful one at that. A demon of temptation. A shiver ran down Ramona's spine.

Zara's gaze dropped to Ramona's mouth, just for a second, then back up. Like she felt it, too. Of course she felt it. Ramona couldn't feel a hunger pang without Zara immediately asking her if she wanted to eat. It wasn't a real emotional connection. It was magical duress.

And yet it felt so real in this moment.

The air between them felt charged. Electric. Ramona was acutely aware of every point of contact — their hands, their shoulders, their knees. The way Zara's breathing had changed, gone slightly uneven. The way her own pulse was racing.

Ramona didn't have words for what she wanted. Couldn't form them past the tightness in her throat, the worry and rationale racing through her mind. She just leaned forward, drawn by something magnetic, irresistible.

Zara met her halfway.

Their lips were a breath apart. Ramona could feel the warmth of Zara's exhale against her mouth. Could see her eyes starting to close. Could feel her own heart trying to break out of her chest.

"Auntie Mona!" Daphne's voice rang up the stairs, cheerful and oblivious. "We're lighting the bonfire! Come on!"

They jerked apart like they'd been electrocuted.

Ramona's face went hot immediately. Zara had gone very still beside her, her expression carefully neutral except a darkening color on her cheeks.

"We should—" Ramona started.

"Yes." Zara stood up, putting distance between them. "The bonfire. We should go."

They didn't look at each other as they left the room. Didn't speak as they descended the stairs. But Ramona could feel it — the almost kiss hanging between them like unfinished business. The want that hadn't gone anywhere, just been postponed.

Her hand was still warm where Zara had held it, and the pull of the tether felt sharper, more insistent than ever.

Their lips were a breath apart. Ramona could feel the warmth of Zara's cheek against her mouth. Could see her eyes starting to close. Could feel her own heart trying to break out of her chest.

“Autre Monde!” Daphne's voice rang [illegible] [illegible] obvious [illegible] we're fighting the [illegible]!”

They pulled apart [illegible] [illegible].

[illegible] moments, it [illegible] [illegible] Zara had [illegible] [illegible] [illegible] [illegible] her neck.

“We should,” Ramona [illegible].

“Yes,” Zara [illegible], putting distance between them. “[illegible].”

Ramona [illegible] [illegible] descended the stairs [illegible] [illegible] [illegible].

[illegible]

CHAPTER TEN

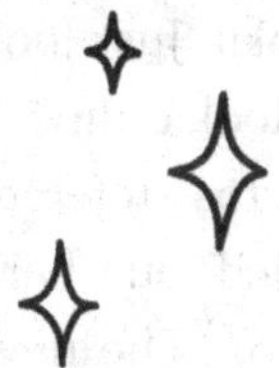

The apartment was quiet when they got back. It seemed all of her roommates were either out or in their rooms. It was customary to leave the lights off, lighting only candles on Imbolc, so the apartment was dark save for one of Felix's Autumnal Harvest pillars sitting on the stove, casting the apartment in a spooky glow.

Ramona dropped her bag by the door and immediately headed for her bedroom, desperate to change out of the nice clothes she'd worn to impress her parents. Clothes that had done absolutely nothing to soften Eleanor's passive-aggressive commentary or make Thomas acknowledge her existence beyond basic pleasantries.

She flipped on her overhead light with rebellious fervor and was halfway through pulling on sweatpants in the closet when she heard a thud.

Then another.

And another.

Ramona emerged from the closet to find Zara unpacking books from her pockets onto the floor. A lot of books. An alarming number of books, actually, considering Zara didn't carry a purse.

"Where did those come from?" Ramona asked, approaching slowly.

"Your childhood bedroom." Zara set down another stack —

medieval grimoires, linguistic theory texts, a few worn paperbacks that Ramona recognized from her graduate seminars. "You left quite the collection."

"I didn't say you could take those."

"You didn't say I couldn't." Zara arranged them with methodical precision, organizing by subject matter. "We need to research the severance ritual. These will help."

Ramona stared at the books. Just looking at them made her chest tight. "I already told you, I'll look online. There are databases—"

"Excellent. Then we can cross-reference what you find with these primary sources." Zara pulled out her HellBerry, already opening some kind of note-taking app. "The new moon is in two weeks. We should start tonight."

"Tonight?" Ramona's voice came out higher than intended. "I just survived dinner with my parents. I just… I need a mental break."

Zara gave her a long stare, then her expression softened slightly. "Tomorrow, then?"

The placating look on Zara's face made a pang of guilt stab into Ramona's chest. She grabbed her laptop from her bag. It had been so long since she'd done any kind of research, interacted with any magical texts. The donation-bin grimoire had been a curiosity, but this research? This research felt heavy. Felt too close to what she'd been doing an entire lifetime ago. She cleared her throat, clicking open her web browser. "I'll start looking some stuff up now. Just… basic searches. To get a sense of what we're working with."

Zara straightened her posture, just slightly, but didn't say anything further than, "That would be helpful. Thank you."

Ramona settled on the bed, laptop balanced on her knees, very deliberately not looking at the stacks of books Zara had arranged on the floor. She opened a browser and typed: *new moon severance ritual.*

The first few results were exactly what she'd expected — neopagan websites with vague instructions about "releasing what no longer serves you" and lots of purple prose about lunar energy. Nothing useful. She bookmarked them anyway.

She clicked on another link. This one was more promising — an academic database article about lunar magic in medieval grimoires, but it required a login: her old university credentials.

Which she no longer had.

Ramona closed the tab.

"Finding anything?" Zara asked. She'd settled into the squeaking desk chair with one of the grimoires, reading with focused intensity.

"Just getting oriented," Ramona said. "It's a process."

She opened a new tab. Typed: *demonic binding severance*

A forum thread popped up. She clicked it before she could stop herself.

Has anyone successfully broken a demonic tether? Need advice ASAP.

The comments were a disaster. Half of them were obvious jokes. The other half were people insisting demons weren't real. One person had written a three-paragraph response about energy work and chakra cleansing that made Ramona want to throw her laptop across the room.

She kept scrolling anyway.

Twenty minutes later, she realized she'd somehow ended up on an article about Mercury retrograde and whether it was a good time to start new projects.

"How's the research going?" Zara asked, not looking up from her grimoire.

"Great. Very productive." Ramona shifted her mouse and quickly closed the tab.

"Mmm." Zara's tone suggested she knew exactly what Ramona had been doing. "Find anything useful?"

"Lots of things. Very useful things." Ramona opened a new tab with renewed determination. "I'll compile my findings tomorrow."

"Of course."

They sat in silence for another ten minutes. Ramona stared at her screen, trying not to get distracted. But the words kept blurring together. Her head was starting to hurt.

"I think I'm done for tonight," Ramona announced, closing her laptop. "My brain is fried."

"Understandable." Zara finally looked up. "We can start fresh tomorrow."

"Definitely. Tomorrow."

RAMONA WOKE to the smell of coffee and the sound of pages turning.

She turned to find Zara at the desk, surrounded by even more books than yesterday. The grimoires were arranged in neat stacks, sticky notes protruding from various pages. Zara's notebook was filled with dense handwriting in what looked to be three different languages, two of which Ramona didn't recognize.

Zara had pushed her sleeves up to her elbows at some point — probably hours ago, given the meticulous organization spread across the desk. The morning light caught on her forearms, illuminating the fine dark hair there, the elegant bones of her wrists as she turned another page, the faint glow of red under her skin. She was wearing her reading glasses, the thin silver frames that made her look like a scholar. A brilliant researcher. Someone who belonged in a university library at three in the morning, lost in primary sources and terrible coffee.

Someone devastatingly attractive.

Ramona's mouth went dry.

It was unfair, really. Zara had no right to look that attractive, completely absorbed in medieval grimoires, one hand absently pushing her hair back from her face, the other making precise notes in margins. The glasses had slipped down slightly on her nose. She pushed them back up without looking away from the text, a gesture so… human.

"Good morning," Zara said without looking up, though she had to have felt Ramona awaken through the tether. "Coffee's fresh. I made enough for both of us."

She turned then, finally meeting Ramona's eyes over the rim of those disconcertingly attractive glasses, and held out a steaming mug.

Ramona's brain short-circuited somewhere between the glasses and the forearms and the casual domesticity of Zara making her coffee at whatever terrible hour she'd woken up to do research.

"Thanks." Ramona took the warm mug and eyed the research setup warily. "You've been busy."

"I told you, demons don't need much sleep." Zara made another note. "I've been cross-referencing binding magic across different time periods. The medieval approaches are fascinating, but the contemporary texts have more detail on severance rituals specifically."

"That's... great." Ramona sat down across from her, wrapping her hands around the warm mug. "Very thorough."

"I found three different versions of the ritual we need. They have slight variations in the incantation, but the core components are consistent." Zara pushed a piece of paper across the table. "I made a list. Could you help me understand this? Some of these phrases are ambiguous."

Ramona glanced at the list. Her chest tightened immediately.

Verra vincarae disruptara...

Sicrae erata principarum...

Lybrae nostara veris...

These weren't just random Latincane phrases. These were complex grammatical constructions that required understanding of magical theory, historical context, subjunctive mood, ablative absolutes...

"I think those are pretty straightforward," Ramona said, pushing the paper back. "Just standard incantation structure."

"But this one here"—Zara pointed—"switches to Old Vallone mid-phrase. Doesn't that suggest something significant? Like what you were explaining about power markers?"

"Maybe. Hard to say without more context."

"The context is in this grimoire." Zara tapped one of the books. "Pages forty-seven through fifty-two. I marked the relevant sections."

Ramona did not reach for the grimoire. "I'm sure you've got it covered. I bet your Old Vallone is excellent."

"I'm *fluent,* but I don't understand the magical significance of the code-switching." Zara's gaze was steady. "That's your expertise, not mine."

Ramona sipped her coffee, grateful for its warmth and for a moment to pause in thought before speaking. "I'll look at it later. After I do some more online research."

"You haven't opened your laptop yet."

"I just woke up."

Zara returned to her reading. "Whenever you're ready."

Ramona sat back on her bed. She did open her laptop eventually, around eleven, but somehow she ended up reading an article about the different personality traits of air signs versus fire signs, and then a quiz about which celestial body she was most aligned with (Jupiter, apparently, which felt wrong), and then…

"Lunch?" Zara appeared in the doorway. "Felix is making sandwiches."

"Sure." Ramona closed her laptop quickly. "That sounds good."

After lunch, Zara tried again. "I've been thinking about the timing. The new moon is on the twenty-eighth. But we need to gather the materials before then — moonstone dust, blessed salt, hawthorn branches."

"Right. We should make a shopping list."

"I started one." Zara pulled out her notebook. "But I'm not sure where to source some of these items. The moonstone needs to be charged at a convergence point. Do you know where we could find that? I know you said most of the shops have closed down, but…"

Ramona shrugged. "There are still specialty shops over near Thornwood. I can look some up."

"That would be helpful. And the hawthorn branches have to be cut at midnight. Do you know where hawthorn trees grow around here?"

"Not off the top of my head. But I'm sure the internet knows."

Zara's patience was starting to fray, just slightly. "We need trees that are magically active. Which requires actual botanical knowledge, not internet searches. We need to ask Posey."

"We can figure it out without dragging my poor roommates any further into it than we need to." Ramona stood up, clearing her plate. "I need to get ready for work anyway. My shift starts at two."

Zara didn't say anything. But Ramona could feel her disappointment through the tether.

"Oh, I almost forgot. I talked to Marcus today," Ramona said as she and Zara walked into the bedroom later that evening. "Told him I need the twenty-eighth off. He was surprisingly cool about it."

"Good." Zara sat at the desk again. She pulled some books out of the pockets of her suit again. She'd insisted on taking five or six to the coffee shop with her. Apparently she'd told the baristas she was studying for the bar, and they'd given her free coffee all day. "Did you have time to look up those supply shops?"

"Not yet. It was busy at work," Ramona lied, trying to conceal it by keeping her heart rate even and her emotions neutral.

"Of course." Zara's tone was careful as well. "Maybe this weekend?"

"Maybe."

Before the awkward silence could settle too heavily, Felix knocked on the open door with Gerald on his shoulder and a bag of microwave popcorn in each hand.

"Movie night!" he announced. "Mandatory fun time. Everyone's been too serious lately and it's killing the vibe."

"I should really—" Ramona started.

"Nope. No excuses." Felix was already setting up the TV. "Kashvi's bringing candy. Posey's making her special brownies — the regular kind, not the fun kind, before anyone asks. Cammie's closing tonight but she'll be here by eight. We're watching the worst horror movie I could find, and I will not be taking questions. It's called *Hex of Kin*."

"I've never heard of it," Zara said from the dining table.

Felix's eyes lit up. "Even better. It's fantastic. You're going to hate it."

Ramona sighed, but she could feel the tension in her shoulders loosening slightly. Maybe a break would be good. Maybe they both needed to stop thinking about severance rituals and medieval languages for a few hours.

"Fine," Ramona said. "But I'm not sitting through any torture porn."

"It's a classic family haunted house movie. Very respectable." Felix dumped popcorn into a bowl. "Now, get comfortable. Gerald has strong opinions about seating arrangements."

Somehow, through a combination of Felix's orchestration and Gerald's insistent cooing, Ramona and Zara ended up on the couch together. Not touching, but close enough that Ramona was hyperaware of every shift in Zara's position.

Kashvi arrived with enough candy to supply a small army. Posey emerged from the kitchen with brownies that smelled like heaven. They arranged themselves around the living room — Kashvi and Posey on the floor with cushions, Felix in the armchair with Gerald settling onto the armrest like a tiny feathered gargoyle.

The movie started.

Within ten minutes, Zara was frowning at the screen. "Why would they buy a house that's clearly malevolent?"

"Because it's cheap," Felix said through a mouthful of popcorn.

"That's not a valid reason. The structural damage alone would cost more than—"

"Shh," Kashvi hissed. "Scary part."

Zara watched the family explore the creepy basement with growing consternation. When they inevitably split up, she made a sound of disgust. "That's tactically unsound," she muttered.

Ramona bit back a smile. "It's a horror movie. They always split up."

"Why?"

"Because otherwise the movie would be twenty minutes long," Felix joked.

"That would be an improvement," Zara muttered so only Ramona could hear.

On screen, something jumped out. Kashvi screamed. Posey threw popcorn at the TV. Felix was cackling with delight.

Zara leaned closer to Ramona. "Is that supposed to be frightening?"

"For most people, yes."

"It's just poor planning. If they had stayed together and brought adequate lighting—"

"You're thinking about this too hard."

"I'm thinking about it the correct amount." But Zara was smiling now, just slightly. "This is absurd."

Another jump scare. This time Ramona flinched, and suddenly Zara's hand was on her arm, steadying, protective.

"It's not real," Zara said quietly.

"I know that."

Zara moved her hand away, but Ramona could still feel the warmth of where her touch had been.

Gerald chose that moment to hop down from the armrest and waddle across the room. He climbed onto the couch with surprising agility and settled directly on Zara's shoulder, as if claiming his rightful perch.

"Oh, of course," Felix said. "Gerald's picking his favorite again."

"He has excellent taste," Zara replied, reaching up to gently stroke Gerald's head. The pigeon cooed contentedly.

The movie continued. Ramona found herself explaining horror movie logic — why characters always investigate strange noises, why they never just leave, why the phone always dies at the worst moment. Zara asked genuine questions, trying to understand the internal consistency of a genre built on people making terrible decisions.

"So, the entire plot depends on no one acting rationally?"

"Essentially, yes."

"That's terrible storytelling." Zara shook her head, but she was leaning closer, watching the TV with a riveted gaze.

"That's horror movies," Posey said.

Zara sighed. "I prefer demon possession narratives. At least those follow logical rules."

Ramona choked on her popcorn, and Zara patted her on the back.

Somewhere around the halfway point, Ramona realized they'd shifted closer together. Zara's arm was pressed against hers, Gerald still perched on her shoulder, creating a warm weight between them. It felt… comfortable. Natural.

Felix caught her eye from across the room and grinned knowingly. Ramona looked away quickly.

By the time the movie ended — with the obligatory "it's not really over" final scare — Posey was half asleep on the floor and Kashvi was clutching a pillow like a shield.

"That was terrible," Zara announced with a smile. "I hated every minute."

"Same time next week?" Felix asked.

"Count me in."

They started cleaning up — collecting empty candy wrappers, stacking bowls, arguing about whether the movie was actually scary or just startling. Ramona was carrying mugs to the kitchen when she noticed Kashvi showing something to Posey on her phone.

"What's that?"

"Nothing," Kashvi said too quickly.

Posey was smiling a little too innocently.

Ramona eyed them both skeptically.

"Felix snapped a cute photo and sent it to the group chat." Kashvi turned the phone around.

The photo showed exactly what she'd described — Ramona and Zara on the couch, leaned against each other, both of them smiling at something on screen, Gerald on Zara's shoulder. They looked... they looked like a real couple.

"Felix!" Ramona shrieked, eliciting another round of laughter from the trio of roommates.

But when she checked her phone, there it was. The photo, followed by a string of messages:

Kashvi: LOOK AT THEM 🥺

Posey: I'm not saying anything but I'm saying EVERYTHING

Cammie: sorry i missed movie night but this makes up for it

Felix: our girl is so embarrassing and i love it

Ramona shoved her phone in her pocket, face burning. Back in her room, Zara was reading something on her HellBerry, a small smile playing at her lips. "Gerald photographs very well. Very dignified."

"Wait, how did you—" Ramona quickly checked the group chat, finding a strange number.

"Felix added me about a week ago. Said if I'm going to be here for a while, I should at least get all the information." Zara looked up.

"I'd have really thought Hell's area code would start with 666," Ramona remarked, saving the number. It hadn't occurred to her that their phones could connect, for some reason.

"A common misconception, but it's a little too on the nose, don't you think?" Zara grinned.

Ramona rolled her eyes. "I can't believe you think Gerald looks dignified."

"He's the most photogenic of the three of us." Zara shrugged, but there was just the slightest hint of a mischievous grin at the corner of her mouth.

Ramona wanted to argue, but Zara was looking at her with that grin, making her chest feel too full and her thoughts go fuzzy around the edges.

"We should probably sleep," Ramona said. "Big research day tomorrow."

The words felt hollow even as she said them. She'd been saying some version of that for days now — *tomorrow we'll figure it out, tomorrow we'll try harder* — while carefully avoiding the stacks of books Zara had been poring over. Avoiding the moment when she'd have to actually *try* to solve this and risk failing. Again.

Dr. Ramona Greenbriar, who couldn't even break a simple summoning bond. Who would probably misread some fundamental principle, make some embarrassingly basic mistake that any first-year could have caught. The thought made her stomach clench.

"Probably." But neither of them moved.

Around them, her roommates went to bed. Doors closing. Lights going off. The distant sound of Kashvi and Posey still giggling.

"Thank you," Zara said quietly. "For tonight. I needed… I needed not to think about rituals and spellwork phrases for a while."

"Me too."

But looking at Zara now — this demon who'd had her entire existence upended, who'd been nothing but patient while Ramona hid behind retail shifts and avoidance — something shifted in Ramona's chest. A small, stubborn ember of the person she used to be. The one who'd spent twelve-hour days in Thornwood's archives, who'd defended a dissertation on medieval language root morphology, who *liked* impossible puzzles.

Zara had spent hours researching today, methodically working through texts while Ramona buried herself in rearranging a display of "Lucky Charms" as Marcus had requested. Zara, who had every right to be furious, who could have demanded Ramona fix this immediately, had instead enjoyed a night off from thinking about it.

Tomorrow, Ramona decided. Tomorrow she'd actually open those books. Actually try. Not because she thought she'd succeed — she was still terrified she wouldn't — but because Zara deserved someone who would at least *try*.

The moment lingered between them until Zara settled into the chair.

"You know, you can sleep in the bed when you're done researching for the night," Ramona said. "In case you have any more… you know, nightmares or something."

Zara turned, giving her a small nod, then her gaze went back to the book in front of her.

CHAPTER ELEVEN

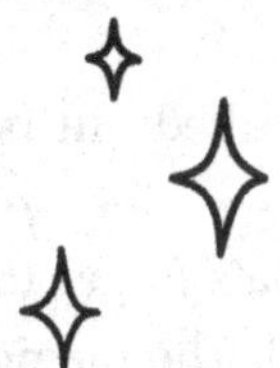

"OKAY," ZARA SAID, SPREADING THE BOOKS ACROSS THE COFFEE TABLE with the systematic precision of someone who'd been planning this for days. The easy warmth from movie night had evaporated from the night before, replaced by the familiar tension of detachment. "Let's start with the basics."

Ramona sat on the couch, sipping her coffee with her laptop balanced on her knees, trying to summon the enthusiasm from the night before that she didn't currently feel. "What do you need?"

"This grimoire." Zara held up a leather-bound book with water-stained pages. "It's the most complete description of the severance ritual I've found. But it's written in ecclesiastical Lysienne with some very archaic grammatical structures, and I'm not confident in my translation."

Ramona took the book reluctantly. The moment her fingers touched the leather, something in her chest constricted. She knew this grimoire. She'd used it in her dissertation. Had spent weeks parsing a single chapter, unraveling the linguistic Lysienne choices the author had made.

She opened it to the marked page. The familiar script swam before her eyes.

"If you wish to break the bond," Ramona translated automatically. Then stopped. "Actually, it's more specific than that. Not just 'wish.' It's more like 'desire earnestly.' The verb choice matters."

"Why?" Zara was leaning forward, attentive.

"Because it sets the tone for the whole ritual. The author is establishing that this isn't casual magic. You have to want it badly enough that—" Ramona stopped herself again. "Never mind. The basic translation works fine."

"No, keep going." Zara pulled out her notebook. "What does the verb choice tell us?"

"It tells us that…" Ramona's finger traced the text. "It tells us that half-hearted attempts will fail. The magic responds to desire, to intention. If you're ambivalent, the ritual won't work."

"So both parties have to actively want the bond broken. Just as we suspected."

"Not just want. They have to desire it earnestly. Yearn for it." Ramona looked up. "The word choice seems very specific about that."

They held eye contact for a moment too long. The tether hummed between them.

"Right," Zara said finally. "That's… good to know."

They kept reading. Or rather, Zara read and asked questions, and Ramona answered them in the shortest possible way before finding an excuse to check her phone.

After the fifth interruption — this time while Ramona read an article about whether Taurus was compatible with Scorpio in professional relationships — Zara closed her grimoire with deliberate patience.

"Are you actually researching, or are you just pretending while reading about zodiac signs?" Zara narrowed her eyes, which, for a demon, was a bit more menacing than Zara had looked before.

Ramona's face heated. "I was taking a mental break."

"You've taken *six* mental breaks in the last hour."

"Research is exhausting." Ramona shrugged, clearing her throat.

"Not when you're barely doing it." Zara's voice was sharp now. "You read one sentence of Lysienne and then immediately reach for a distraction. Every time."

"That's not—"

"It is." Zara stood up, frustrated. "You were fine explaining horror movie tropes for two hours last night. You lit up talking about why characters make bad decisions. But the second I ask you to engage with your *actual* expertise, you shut down."

"That was different."

"How?"

"Because that didn't matter!" The words burst out sharper than Ramona intended, her emotions rising with heat in her cheeks and a roaring in her ears. "Because I can be wrong and no one cares. No one gets hurt. But this..." She gestured at the grimoire. "If I get this wrong, if I mistranslate something or miss a nuance, the ritual fails. Best case, we're stuck together for another four weeks. Worst case, one of us gets seriously hurt. And it'll be my fault. Again." Her heart was pounding in her chest. "It's fucking *always* my fault."

Zara stared at her. "You already think you're going to fail?"

"I *know* I'm going to fail. That's what I do. I fail at magic." Ramona clenched her jaw, shaking her head. "I can read about it. I can explain it. But I can't do it. And the second something matters, the second there are actual stakes, I fuck it up."

"That's not true." Zara's tone was gentle, like an outreached hand.

"Isn't it?" Ramona stood up, needing space. Her hands felt tingly in a panicked kind of way, and she shook them as she blinked quickly, willing herself not to cry. "My coven and my career and my marriage ended because I proved everyone right. That I'm a failure. That I'm too dangerous to trust with real magic."

"Ramona—"

"So yeah, maybe I am avoiding this. Because at least when the ritual fails, no one was *really* expecting otherwise."

The silence that followed was heavy.

Zara sat back down slowly. She let out a heavy, long sigh. "Come here."

"I don't—"

"Please."

Ramona sat. Not close, but close enough that the tether eased slightly.

"I need to tell you something," Zara said. "And I need you to actually hear it."

Ramona waited.

"You're terrified of failing," Zara began. "I understand that. But you're so focused on not failing that you're guaranteeing it. You're creating a self-fulfilling prophecy."

"That's not—"

"Let me finish." Zara's voice was gentle but firm. "Last night, you explained horror movie logic to me for two hours. You were patient. You were thorough. You broke down complex narrative structures into understandable pieces. And you loved doing it."

"That's not the same thing."

"It's exactly the same thing. It's teaching. It's expertise. It's taking something you understand deeply and helping someone else understand it, too." Zara leaned forward. "The only difference is that you've decided horror movies are safe and medieval grimoires are dangerous."

Ramona said nothing.

"But here's the thing — you're already doing the hard part. You translated that perfectly. You explained the verb choice and why it matters. That's not failing, Ramona. That's succeeding."

"One translation doesn't—"

"Not one translation. It's every single time I've asked you a question, you've known the answer. Every time you've looked at a text, you've understood it. The knowledge is still there. You haven't lost it." Zara's hand found hers. "You've just convinced yourself that you have."

Ramona's eyes were burning. "What if I can't do this? What if I try — *really try* — and we still fail?"

"Then we fail." Zara squeezed her hand. "But at least we'll have tried together. At least you'll know it wasn't because you didn't show up for yourself."

They sat there for a long moment, hands joined, the grimoire open between them.

"I'm really scared," Ramona whispered.

"I know." Zara's thumb traced circles on her palm. "But you don't have to be alone in it. That's what this"—she gestured at the tether between them—"means. We're in this together. Your fear. My certainty. All of it."

"That's not exactly reassuring."

"No. But it's true." Zara picked up the grimoire again. "So. Are you going to help me understand this text? Or are you going to read another article about whether Jupiter is affecting your love life?"

Despite everything, Ramona almost smiled. "It was *one* article."

"It was three."

"Okay, it was three." Ramona took the grimoire. "But in my defense, that astrological timing might actually matter for ritual work."

"No, it doesn't," Zara said, rolling her eyes.

She looked down at the text. The words were still there, still familiar. And for the first time in days, it didn't hurt quite as much to read it.

"Okay," Ramona said, too exhausted to argue. "Let's do this properly."

THEY STARTED EARLY every day all week. Coffee first, then books.

This time, when Zara asked about a phrasing construction, Ramona didn't immediately deflect. She pulled the grimoire closer, studied the text, explained the grammatical structure and what it meant for the spell's execution.

They worked through the morning, taking breaks when Ramona needed them but always coming back to the books. Slowly, Ramona felt something in her chest start to loosen. Not the grief — that was still there, sharp and present. But the resistance. The fear that touching her old work would destroy her.

She was still here. Still Ramona. Still capable of reading a medieval grimoire and understanding what she saw.

With two days left until the new moon, they'd compiled a complete list of materials, a detailed breakdown of the incantation with notes on pronunciation and intent, and a step-by-step plan for the ritual itself.

"This is good work," Zara said, reviewing their notes. "Really good work."

Ramona looked at the pages spread across the table — her handwriting mixed with Zara's, arcane phrases annotated with explanations, cross-references to three different grimoires.

It *was* good work. The kind of thorough, detailed analysis she used to do before everything fell apart.

"Thank you," Ramona said quietly. "For pushing me. For not letting me hide."

"Thank you for trusting me enough to try." Zara met her eyes. "I know this wasn't easy."

"No. But it was..." Ramona struggled to find the word. "It was good. To remember that I can still do this."

"You never stopped being able to do this. You just stopped believing you could."

They sat there for a moment, surrounded by evidence of their collaboration. The tether hummed between them — warm, steady, something that felt less like a burden and more like...

Ramona didn't let herself finish that thought. "We should start gathering materials," she said instead. "The new moon is in two days."

"Agreed." Zara stood up, stretching. "I'll research where to find magically active hawthorn trees. You handle the moonstone and blessed salt?"

"Deal," Ramona said with a nod. She gathered a grimoire, her fingertips tracing over the imprinted leather of the cover.

She glanced up to find Zara watching her with an expression that made her breath catch in her chest.

"What?" Ramona asked.

"Nothing." Zara's smile was soft. "Just... it's good to see you like this."

"Like what?"

"Like yourself."

"Do all demons act so high-and-mighty, or is that just your particular brand of arrogance?" Ramona asked, twisting her mouth to hide a mischievous grin, deflecting quickly from the softness of the moment.

Zara raised one perfectly manicured eyebrow. "You dare to test the leash of my patience, Mortal?" She lowered her chin, her eyes taking on a distinct predator gleam. "I've taken souls for far less impertinence."

Two weeks ago, Ramona would have been scared of such a look. She'd have turned into a soft-bellied prey animal at the first sign of danger. Now? Now that predatory gleam made something still twist low in her stomach, but it was far from fear.

Now that the ritual felt real, felt soon and not far off, Ramona couldn't help but feel conflicted. Yes, of course she wanted the accidentally summoned demon she was tethered to against her will to return to Hell. And yet… another part of her was slowly cracking open, a part that she thought she'd long sealed off.

But if there was even a hint of hesitation, the ritual would fail. And she would *not* be failing this time.

The bedroom was too small. The bed far too close. She couldn't help the way she woke up from filthy dreams, but she could help the fact that being this close, this alone, with Zara felt dangerous in a way that had nothing to do with that predatory glint in the demon's eye.

"How do you feel about a little shopping trip?" Ramona asked, reaching for a large pair of sunglasses.

one unsatisfied predator gleam. "I've taken souls for far less in presence."

Two weeks ago, Ramona would have been scared of such a look. She'd have turned into a self-effacing puddle at the first sign of danger. Not [illegible] now that [illegible] made [illegible] still exist [illegible], but it was far from fear.

Now that the initial outbreak [illegible] Ramona couldn't help but feel gratified. [illegible] who wanted [illegible] demon she was offered [illegible] to return [illegible] the part of her [illegible] the night she'd [illegible] scared off.

But there was even a point of hesitation [illegible] would [illegible]. And she would not be [illegible] this time.

The [illegible] was too small. The [illegible] She couldn't help the way she woke up from [illegible] dreams, but she could help the [illegible] with [illegible]

[illegible]

[illegible] part of [illegible].

CHAPTER TWELVE

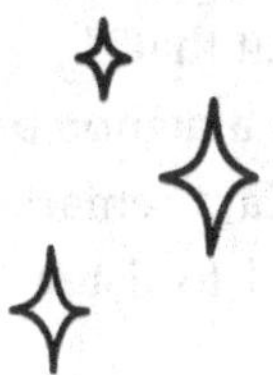

The shop was called The Thornwood Apothecary, and it sat on a cobblestone side street like it had been there since the town was founded. Which, knowing Thornwood's history, it probably had.

Fernwick was a large mixed-magic city, but Thornwood was *only* for magical beings. She used to walk these streets daily, but now she only returned when it was time to visit Greenbriar Manor, which was blessedly far away from the town center.

Being back in the town now made Ramona's palms sweat.

She sat in the car in the parking spot for a full minute after turning off the engine, her hands gripping the steering wheel.

"We can leave if you want," Zara said quietly from the passenger seat. "Find something online." They hadn't spoken much on the drive to Thornwood, instead opting to listen to a podcast dissecting the latest episode of *Love Potion* in a way that made Ramona's brain go quiet for the drive.

"No." Ramona loosened her grip. "No, we need the right supplies. I'm fine."

Zara let her head fall back against the car headrest. "You're not fine. Your heart rate just spiked."

"That's rude. Stop monitoring my heart rate."

"I'm not monitoring it. I'm feeling it through the tether. There's a difference." Zara tilted her head, studying Ramona with that assessing gaze. "How long has it been since you've been around other witches? Apart from your roommates-who-are-definitely-not-your-coven?"

"Two years." Ramona unbuckled her seat belt. "Give or take."

"And?"

"And what?"

"How are you feeling about that?"

Ramona scoffed. "Are you a demon or a therapist?"

"A lot of overlap there," Zara remarked. "Come on. You can talk to me. I am contractually bound to listen to you for at least forty-eight more hours."

"Well, being here makes me feel like I'd rather drive into oncoming traffic." Ramona forced a smile. "But here we are."

Zara didn't laugh. She just reached over and squeezed Ramona's hand, brief and firm, before letting go. "I'm right here. The whole time. And I really *can* burn this place down this time. Your childhood home felt a little too sentimental to let go up in flames, but I did consider it briefly."

Ramona smiled. "Did the bonfire after let you live that fantasy a little vicariously?"

Zara laughed, the sound quick and surprised. "Sure, Mortal."

Ramona took a breath. "Okay. Let's go."

THE SHOP WAS everything Mystic Moon Books wasn't. Where Mystic Moon was warm and a little cluttered, The Thornwood Apothecary was meticulous. Intentional. Every surface gleamed. Nothing felt accidental.

Glass display cases lined the walls, each arranged with unnerving precision. Polished obsidian pendulums rested on velvet trays. Small, corked vials held powdered bone and crushed amethyst. Bundles of dried vervain and yarrow hung from brass hooks, labeled in tidy script. Beeswax tapers infused with rosemary oil stood in regimented rows beside shallow dishes of black sand and iron filings. Everything curated. Everything measured. Everything undeniably real.

The air smelled faintly of myrrh and damp stone, perhaps, or old earth. Something that made the back of Ramona's neck prickle, not with nostalgia, but with recognition. Being here, surrounded by genuine magical ingredients and the low thrum of active enchantments, felt like pressing on a bruise.

"It's beautiful," Zara murmured, and she sounded genuinely awed. Her eyes were sweeping the shop with that cataloging intensity, but softer somehow. Interested rather than assessing. "The energy in here is remarkable."

"It should be. It's been magically active for centuries." Ramona pulled out the supply list they'd compiled together. "All right. We need moonstone dust. Blessed salt. Hawthorn branches, fresh-cut. And yarrow flowers... I think I saw those near the front."

Zara held up her fingers as if tallying the list. "I'll take the left side, you take the right?" she suggested.

"Actually..." Ramona hesitated. "Stay close?"

Zara's expression softened. "Of course."

They moved through the shop together, Ramona consulting the list while Zara stayed a half step behind her. Close enough that Ramona could feel her warmth, could feel the steady pulse of the tether between them. Grounding.

Ramona found the moonstone dust first — three different grades, each labeled with its source location. She scanned the labels until she found what they needed: *Convergence-sourced, Thornwood district, harvest date October*.

"This one," she said, picking up the jar. The dust inside shimmered faintly, catching the light in a way that was distinctly magical rather than cosmetic. The weight of it in her hand felt right. Familiar in a way that made her chest ache.

She remembered buying moonstone dust like this for research — testing its resonance against archived ritual transcripts in Thornwood's warded stacks, staying until the wards shifted at two a.m. The old stones had vibrated faintly beneath her palms when she leaned over the reading tables, ink smudged along the side of her hand, silver grit clinging stubbornly to her cuffs. The air had always smelled like parchment and cold mineral dust, settling into her lungs and making her feel ancient just breathing it in. Back then, she'd felt precise. Necessary. Like she had a place carved out just for her.

"Ramona." Zara's hand touched her lower back, light but present. "You okay?"

"Fine." Ramona set the jar on the small basket Zara had picked up. "Let's keep going."

They found the blessed salt easily enough. The hawthorn branches were trickier — fresh-cut meant they had to ask the clerk.

The clerk was a tall woman with sharp cheekbones and severe hair pulled back into a tight knot. She wore fitted charcoal slacks and a structured black vest stitched through with faint silver warding thread — the kind of reinforced, spell-resistant fabric meant for people who actually handled volatile ingredients and not just posed with crystals on social media. A slim iron ring gleamed on one finger, more functional than decorative.

Her name tag read *SEVERINE* in small silver letters, and a gray cat wound between her legs as she stood near the counter.

"We need fresh-cut hawthorn branches," Ramona said, approaching the counter.

Severine looked up from the inventory she was sorting. Her gaze swept over Ramona — taking in the thrift-store jacket, the worn boots, the slight nervous tension in her shoulders — and something shifted in her expression. Not quite disdain. Something worse. Dismissal.

"What kind of ritual?" Severine asked flatly.

"Severance. Binding severance, specifically." Ramona kept her voice steady. "New moon timing. We need branches cut no more than forty-eight hours before."

"Binding severance requires Thornwood certification." Severine's tone was clipped. Bored. "Do you have credentials?"

The question landed like a slap. Ramona felt her face heat, felt the familiar shrinking sensation — the one that hollowed her out from the inside. The one that reminded her exactly where she no longer belonged.

"I—" she started.

"She doesn't need credentials to purchase ritual ingredients," Zara said.

Ramona hadn't heard her move.

One second Zara was behind her. The next she was at her side — shoulder to shoulder — and somehow taller. Not physically, not in any measurable way, but the space around her seemed to stretch to accommodate her. The overhead lights dimmed by a fraction, as if the air itself had thickened.

Her body seemed to darken as if in shadow. And her voice — it wasn't loud. It wasn't sharp. It was cold.

A deep, crushing cold of something that had never known sunlight. Ancient. Terrifying.

Ramona shivered involuntarily.

Severine looked at Zara for the first time. Really looked at her.

Something shifted in her posture. A minute recalibration. Instinct recognizing apex.

"I'm sorry," Zara continued, each word placed with surgical precision. "Did you just demand credentials from a customer before agreeing to sell her standard ritual supplies? Supplies displayed openly on your shelves, with no certification requirement posted anywhere in this establishment?"

The glass in the nearest display case gave a soft, almost inaudible creak.

Severine opened her mouth. Closed it.

"Because from where I'm standing," Zara said, leaning forward just slightly, "it appeared you invented a bureaucratic restriction to justify refusing service."

The air dropped several degrees. Ramona could see her own breath.

"Or," Zara added softly, shadows pooling at her feet like spilled ink, "did I misunderstand?" Her smile showed her fangs in full display.

"I— no. I apologize." Severine straightened, her voice suddenly crisp and professional. "We do have fresh-cut hawthorn in the back. I'll get those for you right now."

She disappeared through a door behind the counter with considerably more speed than her previous casualness suggested was possible.

The moment she was gone, the temperature normalized. Zara's

posture relaxed by a fraction — back to casual, back to composed, back to the corporate demon who organized bookshop shelves and drank enough coffee to kill a human.

Ramona stared at her.

"What?" Zara asked, turning to face her with an expression of perfect innocence.

"What the hell was that?" Ramona dropped her voice to a whisper.

"What was what?"

"The—" Ramona gestured vaguely at the air around Zara. "The *thing*. The ice thing. The 'I will destroy you' energy."

"I didn't threaten anyone."

"You didn't have to. She looked like she was going to pass out."

"Did she?" Zara tilted her head, the picture of feigned surprise. "I didn't notice."

"Zara."

"Hmm?"

"Your demon was showing."

"Was it?" Zara examined her own fingernails with apparent interest. "How careless of me."

Ramona should have been scared. Part of her was — the sensible, self-preserving part that remembered exactly what Zara was, what she was capable of, the sheer, catastrophic power that lived beneath the glamoured blazer and the harmless-looking reading glasses.

But another part of her — larger, louder, far less interested in survival — refused to cooperate.

That part remembered Zara at her parents' dinner table, calm and unyielding, cutting through passive aggression like it was nothing. It remembered the steady weight of Zara's attention all morning, the way her gaze lingered at Ramona's back like a hand placed there deliberately. It remembered the softness that crept into Zara's expression when she looked at Ramona and thought no one noticed.

That part did not feel fear.

It felt heat. Awareness. Want.

Ramona swallowed, pulse skidding traitorously, and hated herself just a little for how fast her body had decided this was not a threat, but a promise.

Zara cleared her throat, raising her eyebrows and giving Ramona a pointed look as if to say *Really? That? Here?*

Ramona opened her mouth to protest, to lie, when Severine returned with the hawthorn branches wrapped in enchanted cloth, suddenly extremely helpful and apologetic. Ramona paid for everything without meeting the clerk's eyes, too busy trying to get her heart rate under control.

They were almost at the door when—

"Ramona?"

Her stomach dipped.

Iris stood near the entrance, a canvas bag slung over one shoulder, her raven balanced neatly on her shoulder. Her dark hair was windswept, cheeks pink from the cold. She looked genuinely surprised.

"Iris." Ramona's voice came out careful. "Hey."

"Hi." Iris's gaze flicked briefly to Zara, then back. "I didn't expect to see you here."

"Neither did I," Ramona said.

A small pause. The bell above the door swayed faintly in the draft.

"What brings you in?" Iris asked, tone light but edged with something Ramona couldn't quite name.

"Work," Zara said smoothly, lifting an inexplicably acquired clipboard just enough to make the point. "Comparative sourcing."

"Right. Of course." Iris nodded, too quick. "That makes sense."

"And you?" Ramona asked.

"Work too." Iris adjusted the strap of her bag. "I've got a client case. Just a minor curse. Nothing dramatic." She smiled like she expected Ramona to question her about it.

Ramona didn't. "That sounds… busy," she said instead.

"It is." Iris's fingers tightened briefly on the canvas strap. Her eyes flicked past Ramona toward one of the glass cases — held there half a second too long — then snapped back. "Thornwood's inventory is reliable. Easier than ordering through the registry."

"Completely," Ramona agreed, even though she wasn't exactly sure what she was agreeing about. She just didn't want Iris to notice anything *she* was buying. The hawthorn branches were a fairly conspicuous item in her arms, though. "Well."

"Well." Iris shifted her weight toward the door. "Good seeing you."

"You too," Zara said pleasantly.

"Tell the girls I said hi," Ramona added.

"I will." Iris hesitated, then looked at her sister with something softer, almost searching. "It's good to see you in Thornwood again," she said. "Really."

Ramona held her gaze. "Thanks."

They stepped out into the cold, the door swinging shut behind them. The cobblestone street was quiet, afternoon light filtering through bare winter trees. Ramona tucked the bag of supplies closer to her chest, the weight of moonstone and hawthorn and blessed salt settling against her like armor. Zara's hand came to rest lightly at the small of Ramona's back — steady, grounding.

"Well," Ramona said as they walked to the car. "That was weird."

"It was." Zara's expression was thoughtful, glancing back at the shop. "Your sister is hiding something."

"She's always hiding something. Iris has been hiding things since she was twelve." Ramona shifted the bag of supplies on her arm. "What makes you say that?"

"I just watched her face." Zara paused. "She's a very poor liar."

"Yeah." Ramona rounded the car and opened the driver's side door. "Family trait."

Zara's mouth curved faintly at that, but she didn't push.

Ramona slid into the driver's seat and shut the door, the cold sealed out in a dull thud. For a moment she just sat there, staring at the steering wheel.

It could have been worse.

It could have been Simone.

Iris, at least, had tried to pretend that seeing Ramona out and about in Thornwood could be normal.

Ramona exhaled slowly and turned the key in the ignition. Nothing happened for a beat. She glanced toward Zara, who was staring at the dashboard with an unamused expression. "I'd help, but we don't have cars in hell, so I have no idea what to do here."

"How do you get around?" Ramona asked, trying the ignition a few more times. "I'd have thought rush hour traffic would be one of Hell's favorite pastimes."

"We have a highly efficient train system, but you're right. Maybe I could suggest a traffic jam for the next team-building exercise," Zara remarked.

Ramona groaned. "Come on," she said, patting the dash. "Please start."

As if gentle words could convince it, the car sputtered for a moment, then started.

In the rearview mirror, Thornwood Apothecary receded into a neat, unimpeachable rectangle of glass and brick. Iris had said it was good to see her in Thornwood again. The phrasing looped in Ramona's head.

In Thornwood again.

Like Ramona had a pattern. Like this was a return, not an accident.

She shifted in her seat, silence settling around them in the car. It could have been worse, she told herself again. No one had demanded answers.

But Iris had looked at her like she knew something, and Zara had protected her from running out of the store crying, and Ramona didn't know which unsettled her more.

CHAPTER THIRTEEN

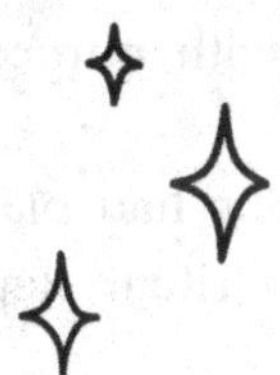

"Let's go out." Zara crossed her arms over her chest.

Ramona looked up from the floor, where she'd been reviewing their ritual notes for the third time that morning. The new moon was tomorrow night. Everything was ready — the supplies, the incantation, the convergence point they'd identified in the woods forty minutes north of the city. They'd practiced the pronunciation. They'd memorized the steps.

Everything was ready, and Ramona felt like she was going to throw up.

"What?" she said.

Zara was leaning against the kitchen counter, arms crossed, watching her with that expression — the one that suggested she'd been thinking about something for a while and had finally decided to say it out loud.

"Enjoyment. Fun. Something you did purely because it made you happy, with no practical purpose whatsoever." Zara tilted her head. "When?"

Ramona opened her mouth to answer, then closed it. Thought about it. Really thought about it.

The last time she'd done something just for fun. Not work. Not survival. Not numbing herself with bad TV or scrolling her phone until her eyes burned.

"I don't know," she said finally. "Before the divorce, maybe? I don't really have money for things like—"

"That's unacceptable."

"It's fine—"

"It's not fine. It's been two years, Ramona." Zara pushed off the counter, crossing the room with purpose. "The ritual is tomorrow. Tonight, we're going out."

Ramona's pulse spiked. She had planned on a quiet evening in, checking and rechecking the ritual steps. "Out where? We should be—"

"We should be enjoying my last moments on this mortal coil." Zara's voice softened on that last part, just slightly. "Felix and Kashvi invited us to a show tonight. I already said yes."

"You said yes without asking me?"

"I knew you'd say no if I asked. So I didn't ask." Zara held up her HellBerry, showing a message thread. "It's a local band playing at a venue downtown. Small, intimate. Nothing overwhelming."

Ramona stared at her in shock.

"I want to see the world. Enjoy my last night." But Zara was smiling now — that slight, pleased curve of her mouth that made Ramona's stomach flip. "Come on. When was the last time you danced?"

"I don't dance."

"*Everyone* dances."

"I really don't."

Ramona looked up at Zara. Her expression was open and warm, and every last ounce of resolve melted from Ramona's body. "How come I couldn't summon a demon who didn't specialize in temptation?"

Zara's eyes darkened with mischief. "We *all* specialize in temptation, Mortal. Some of us just have so much natural talent and impressive work ethic, we get a title."

Ramona sighed. She took Zara's hand. "Fine. But if I have a terrible time—"

"You won't."

"If I do—"

"You won't." Zara squeezed her hand. "I promise."

THE PROBLEM STARTED at seven o'clock, when Zara emerged from the bathroom looking murderous.

"What happened?" Ramona asked, finding Zara staring at her reflection with an expression of pure fury. Were shadows licking up the walls like flames?

Zara held up her blazer. The one she wore everywhere — dark, tailored, expensive-looking. A long tear ran down the sleeve, clean and precise, like something had sliced through it.

"Gerald," Zara said flatly.

As if summoned, the pigeon fluttered down from Felix's bedroom doorway, looking extremely pleased with himself. A single dark thread drifted down from his beak.

"He did that?" Ramona asked.

"He's been eyeing it all week." Zara examined the damage with the intensity of a forensic investigator. "I think he wants to nest in it."

"Can't you fix it with magic somehow?"

"I could, but I'd risk ruining the underlying energy without the proper preparation, and I'd rather set myself on fire." Zara held it up. Without the glamour, the blazer was clearly not a blazer at all. It was something darker, something that shifted colors when it moved. "And I'm trying to conserve my magical energy for tomorrow."

"Okay." Ramona was already moving toward her closet. "Just... wear something of mine."

Zara followed her, leaning in the doorway while Ramona rifled through her clothes. Which was, admittedly, not much to work with. Thrift-store finds and retail-worker practical clothes and a few sad remnants of her old wardrobe shoved in the back.

"Here." Ramona pulled out a black top she'd bought on impulse months ago and never worn. "Try this."

Zara took it, examined it, and held it against herself. The shirt was clearly too short — Zara had at least four inches on her, and the shirt had been cut for Ramona's frame anyway.

"It could work," Ramona said optimistically.

It did not work.

Zara emerged from the bathroom five minutes later wearing the black shirt and her own dark pants, and Ramona's brain simply ceased functioning.

The shirt hit at Zara's navel. Maybe an inch below it. Her stomach was bare — a strip of skin between the hem of the shirt and the waistband of her pants, smooth and warm-looking and completely, devastatingly exposed. Zara did a spin.

If she looked closely — and who could resist? — she could see what looked like a moving, flowing tattoo down Zara's back, peeking out from under the fabric.

It wasn't even that much skin. Ramona had seen more at the beach. At the pool. Literally anywhere.

But on Zara, in her apartment, at seven o'clock on a Friday evening with the golden light coming through the window, it was—

"Does it work?" Zara asked, looking down at herself and then back up at Ramona with a perfectly neutral expression.

Ramona's mouth was open. She closed it. Opened it again.

"You can't go out like that," she managed.

"Like what?" Zara glanced down again, genuinely confused. "It's a shirt and pants. It's appropriate for a casual venue."

"It's—" Ramona gestured helplessly at Zara's midsection. At the exposed skin. At the way the black fabric made her look impossibly sharp and elegant despite being Ramona's thrift-store find. "You can't just… show up like that. Looking like—"

Zara looked at her with one raised brow as if daring her to continue that sentence.

"Like…" Ramona's face was on fire. Her entire face. Possibly her entire body. "*Temptation*. Do you know how many women would just be begging you to take their soul?"

Something shifted in Zara's expression. The mask cracked, just slightly, and underneath was something knowing. Something very pleased.

"Begging, hmm?" Zara asked softly.

The air between them went thick. Charged. Electric in the way it had been in Ramona's old bedroom, in the way it had been on the couch during movie night, in the way it was every single time they stood too close and neither of them moved away.

Zara's eyes dropped to Ramona's mouth. Lingered there. Came back up.

"I think," Zara said, tilting her head with that slight, devastating smile, "that I'll wear *exactly* this."

Ramona made a sound that was not entirely human.

"Ramona!" Felix's voice rang down the hallway. "Kashvi's here! Let's go, let's go, let's goooo!" he singsonged.

The moment shattered. Ramona took a step back, then another, smoothing down her own outfit with hands that were definitely not trembling.

"Fine," she said. Her voice only cracked a little. "Fine. Wear that. It's fine."

"Great." Zara grabbed one of Ramona's jackets — a leather one that actually fit, thankfully — and headed for the door. As she passed Ramona, she leaned in close enough that her breath ghosted across Ramona's ear.

"You might want to breathe," Zara murmured, her voice velvet against Ramona's skin. "You've gone a bit pale."

Then she was gone, leaving Ramona standing in the hallway trying to remember how lungs worked.

THE VENUE WAS SMALL — a converted warehouse on the edge of downtown with exposed brick walls and string lights strung haphazardly across the ceiling. The band was local, three women and a guy with a guitar, playing music that was somewhere between pop and indie rock with a distinctly witchy undertone. Enchanted instruments, Ramona noticed — the drummer's kit hummed with a faint blue light, and the guitar strings shimmered when they were struck.

It was intimate. Warm. Nothing like the sterile concert halls where

Ramona had gone with Simone, dressed up and performing enjoyment for an audience of other academics.

This felt real.

"See?" Zara said, appearing beside her with two drinks. "Not overwhelming."

"Not overwhelming," Ramona agreed, accepting the glass. Their fingers brushed in the exchange. Neither of them pulled away.

Felix and Kashvi were already near the front, Felix dancing with absolutely zero self-consciousness while Kashvi filmed him on her phone. Gerald was snuggled somewhere deep inside Felix's tote bag.

"Come on," Zara said, nodding toward the crowd. "Let's get closer."

They pushed forward through the crowd, and immediately the space became about proximity. Bodies pressed together, shoulders bumping, the collective warmth of dozens of people packed into a space meant for half as many. Ramona felt the familiar flutter of anxiety — too many people, too close, too much.

Zara's hand settled on the small of her back. Firm. Steady. A point of grounding in the press of bodies.

It wasn't unusual. People touched each other in crowds all the time — a hand on a shoulder to navigate, an elbow to make space. But Zara's hand stayed. Didn't move, didn't shift. Just rested there, warm through the fabric of Ramona's dress, palm flat against her spine.

Ramona exhaled, letting her shoulders relax for what felt like the first time in ages.

The band launched into their next song — something up-tempo and driving, with lyrics about storms and magic and women who burned bright. The crowd surged forward. Zara's hand slid down to Ramona's hip as if bracketing her with her own body, keeping her steady and close.

"You okay?" Zara leaned in, near enough that Ramona could feel the words more than hear them over the music.

"Yeah." Ramona turned her head, finding Zara's face inches away. "I'm good." She smiled.

And she was. Standing in this crowd, with the music vibrating through her chest and Zara's hand warm on her hip and the string lights casting everything in soft gold, she was actually, genuinely good.

The songs blurred together, one into the next, the crowd moving as a collective organism. Felix appeared beside them at one point, grabbed both their hands, and attempted to teach them some kind of dance that involved too much spinning and not enough coordination. Ramona laughed — really laughed, the type of laugh that came from somewhere deep — as she stumbled into Zara, who caught her with both hands and steadied her with an ease that suggested she had significantly better balance than any human in the room.

"I thought you said you don't dance," Zara said, grinning.

"I don't. This isn't dancing."

"It's adorable, is what it is."

Ramona rolled her eyes.

"Adorable," Zara repeated, deliberately. Her eyes were bright, her cheeks flushed from the heat of the crowd, her hair slightly disheveled from the movement. Her black shirt had shifted during the dancing, riding up even higher on one side.

Ramona absolutely did not look. She looked straight ahead. At the stage. At the band. At anything that was not Zara's bare skin.

The music shifted into something slower. The crowd loosened, people swaying rather than jumping. Zara's hand found Ramona's hip again, and this time it was unmistakably not about navigating the crowd. To steady herself and for no other reason, Ramona wrapped her own arm around Zara's middle, bare skin on bare skin.

They swayed together, not quite dancing, not quite still. Close enough that Ramona could feel the heat radiating off Zara's body. Close enough that every small movement brought them closer.

"Thank you," Ramona said quietly, not entirely sure why she was whispering when the music was loud enough to cover conversation.

"For what?"

"For this. For making me come out tonight." Ramona looked up at her. "For not letting me hide."

"You deserve to have fun," Zara said simply. "Everyone does. Mortals are so bad at it. Especially you."

The weight of that sentence settled between them, heavy and warm. Ramona held Zara's gaze and didn't look away.

THE WALK home was cold and quiet. The kind of late-night silence that felt sacred — Fernwick settling into itself, streetlights casting pools of amber on the sidewalk, their breath making small clouds in the air.

Felix and Kashvi had peeled off earlier, Felix stumbling home with Kashvi's arm around him, Gerald awake and cooing from his shoulder, both of them singing fragments of the last song badly and at full volume.

Ramona and Zara walked side by side, close enough that their arms brushed with every step. Neither of them moved apart.

"That was good," Ramona said. "The band."

"They were excellent. The enchanted instruments were a nice touch."

"Was that your first concert?" Ramona asked.

"No, demons love music. We have plenty of it, and we've been known to sneak into a mortal festival or two. People on mind-altering drugs are easy prey for quota days, and why not enjoy yourself at the same time, you know?" Zara's mouth quirked up in a grin.

"That's diabolical."

"That's efficiency, Mortal."

They walked in silence for a while. Comfortable silence that didn't need filling. Their hands swung at their sides, fingers brushing with each step. Brush. Swing. Brush.

Neither of them reached for the other's hand.

Neither of them pulled away.

"Ramona," Zara said eventually.

"Yeah?"

"Tomorrow night."

"I know."

"Are you ready?"

Ramona considered the question. The ritual. The severance. The end of the tether, the end of shared emotions, the end of Zara's hand on her back and her warmth in Ramona's bedroom and her voice first thing in the morning.

The end of everything.

"I don't know," Ramona said honestly.

Zara nodded, like this was the answer she'd expected. They kept walking.

They turned onto their street — the quiet, slightly broken street where Ramona's apartment building sat between a laundromat and a pizza shop. The streetlight above them flickered, casting unsteady light across the sidewalk.

Ramona slowed to a stop.

Zara also stopped, turning to face her. The flickering light caught the sharp lines of her face, the curve of her mouth, the dark eyes that held Ramona's gaze with an intensity that made her breath catch.

"Thank you," Ramona said again. "For tonight. For everything."

"Ramona—"

"And if tomorrow works, and I don't get a chance to..." Her voice was getting thick. "You know, to say it—"

"I know." Zara stepped closer. Close enough that Ramona could see the way the streetlight reflected in her eyes, liquid gold and warm honey. "I know, Ramona."

The air between them was charged again. That same electric pull, that same magnetic force that had been building for weeks.

Zara's hand came up to Ramona's face. Fingertips against her jaw, featherlight. Tilting her chin up.

Ramona's eyes fluttered closed.

"Hey! Watch it!"

They both jerked back.

A group of college students stumbled past them on the sidewalk, loud and drunk and completely oblivious to what they'd just interrupted. One of them bumped Zara's shoulder without noticing, laughing at something his friend had said. Another tripped over a crack in the sidewalk and grabbed Ramona's arm for balance before stumbling on.

The moment evaporated like morning frost. Ramona steeled

herself. This connection wouldn't make the ritual easier, and letting Zara kiss her would only make her sadder in the long run.

Zara turned, and Ramona swore her entire body grew larger. One of the students fell to the ground, and his buddies helped him up.

"Sorry," one of the students called back, waving vaguely. "Didn't see you two there!"

They disappeared around the corner, still laughing, still oblivious.

"Did you make that guy fall?" Ramona asked, stifling a small smile.

Zara smirked. "I don't know what you mean, Mortal."

Silence settled back over the street.

Ramona and Zara stood there, a careful foot apart now, neither of them looking at the other. It seemed Zara was thinking the same thing she was.

"Well," Ramona said eventually.

"Yes," Zara agreed.

Another beat of silence.

"We should go inside," Ramona said.

"Yes."

"We should sleep."

"That would be wise."

Neither of them moved.

Finally, Zara let out a breath — something that might have been a laugh if it weren't so quiet. "Ramona."

"Yeah?"

"Go on, I'm right behind you."

Ramona's heart ached. Her own emotion, or Zara's? She couldn't tell anymore.

She unlocked the door and went inside and tried not to think about how tomorrow night, if the ritual worked, she wouldn't be able to feel Zara's emotions anymore.

Wouldn't feel the warmth of the tether.

Wouldn't know, without asking, whether Zara was happy or sad or scared.

Wouldn't know whether any of this had been real.

They walked in silence down the hallway and into the apartment, letting the door click shut behind them as they shuffled into Ramona's room.

A few moments later, Ramona lay in the dark and pressed her hand against her chest, where the tether hummed — steady, warm, insistent — one last time before everything changed.

If the ritual worked, Zara would leave. Not dramatically — not with a farewell speech or a grand gesture or any of the things Ramona had spent her whole life wanting from the people she loved. She would simply go back to where she came from, because that was where she belonged, and Ramona would be here, where she belonged, and the three weeks between would become just another chapter in a life already full of strange things that had ended too soon. Zara would be gone, and Ramona would wake up and the tether would be gone and the apartment would be quiet in a way it hadn't been since Zara arrived, and she would make coffee for one, and that would be that.

She tried to imagine it — the silence, the empty armchair, mornings without Zara's precise handwriting in notebooks left on the desk. Tried to picture going back to the way things were before, when Ramona's biggest problem was whether the self-help section needed reorganizing and her biggest fear was running into Simone at the grocery store. It should have been easy to imagine. It had been her life for two years. But sitting here now, with Zara's warmth on the other side of the room and the tether humming between them like a heartbeat, Ramona couldn't quite remember what it had felt like to be alone.

CHAPTER FOURTEEN

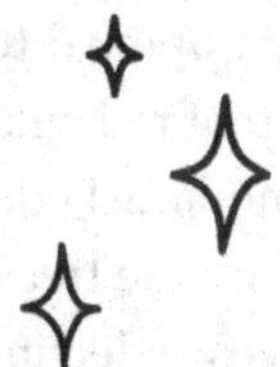

Forests felt so different at night.

During the day, they were just woods a short drive north of Fernwick — scraggly trees and underbrush, the kind of unremarkable forest that backed up against neighborhoods. Kids cut through them on the way to school. Dog walkers and birders used the trails. Nothing special.

But at night, under a new moon, with the last light of dusk bleeding out of the sky like a wound closing — they were something else entirely.

The trees pressed closer together the deeper they walked, their bare branches interlocking overhead like fingers laced in prayer. Or warning. The snow on the ground was untouched, pristine, reflecting Ramona's flashlight in a way that made everything glow faintly blue. Their footsteps crunched in the silence — the only sound besides the occasional crack of a branch settling under the weight of frost.

"This forest is really creepy," Ramona said after about ten minutes of walking in silence, darting her flashlight toward every twig break, every dry leaf rustle.

"Mortal, I assure you, I'm the scariest thing in these woods," Zara said, her voice so low it felt more like a growl.

Ramona carried the ritual bag. Moonstone dust. Blessed salt. Hawthorn branches, cut forty-seven hours ago, still wrapped in enchanted cloth. Yarrow flowers. A silver bowl. A candle that Posey had blessed for them without asking too many questions.

Zara walked beside her, close enough that their arms brushed with each step. She carried the donation-bin grimoire alongside the summoning severance grimoire — a thirteenth-century text they'd spent days translating together, opened to the marked page, the incantation bookmarked with a strip of red silk.

"What will you do?" Ramona asked. Her voice came out smaller than she intended, swallowed by the trees.

Zara glanced at her, her eyes reflecting the light like a wild animal in the dark. "What do you mean?"

"When you get back to Hell." Ramona kept her eyes on the path ahead — the narrow trail winding deeper into the woods, toward the convergence point they'd mapped. "What's the first thing you'll do?"

Zara was quiet for a moment. Thinking about it, Ramona realized. Actually considering the question rather than deflecting it.

"Sleep," Zara said finally. "In a real bed. For approximately fourteen hours."

Ramona huffed something that was almost a laugh. "That's it? Three weeks tethered to a disaster witch and the first thing you want is sleep?"

"It's been a very long three weeks." But Zara's voice was soft. "And then… I don't know. File my reports. Check my inbox. See what chaos my department has descended into in my absence." A pause. "Probably quite a lot of chaos. I've been gone longer than I've been away in… ever."

"They'll survive."

"We shall see." Another pause, longer this time. "What about you?"

"What about me?"

"After. What will you do first?"

Ramona considered it. The convergence point was close now — she could feel it, a subtle shift in the air, a magnetic pull that made the hair on her arms stand up beneath her jacket. The magic here was old.

Older than Thornwood, older than covens, older than anyone alive could remember.

"I don't know," Ramona said honestly. "Sleep, probably. And then figure out how to live without—" She stopped herself.

Without feeling you.

She didn't say it. But the tether hummed between them, and she knew Zara felt the shape of the unfinished sentence anyway.

They walked on in silence.

The convergence point was a clearing — roughly circular, maybe thirty feet across, ringed by ancient oaks that had grown in a perfect circle. The snow here was undisturbed, flat and glittering, and the air felt charged in a way that made Ramona's skin prickle. Magic pooled here like water in a basin — deep, old, patient.

Ramona set down the ritual bag and knelt in the center of the clearing.

Her hands were steady. She was surprised by that. After everything — the fear, the resistance, the weeks of avoidance — her hands were steady as she unpacked the supplies with careful, methodical precision.

"Okay," she said, more to herself than to Zara. "All right."

The salt first. Blessed salt, poured in a perfect circle around the ritual space. Ramona moved slowly, letting the white crystals fall in an unbroken line, tracing the circle with the kind of care she used to bring to her most delicate research. The salt caught the glow of Ramona's flashlight, glittering like a constellation mapped onto the ground.

Then the moonstone dust. Ramona opened the jar and felt the familiar tingle of convergence-sourced magic against her fingertips — warm, almost alive. She poured it into the silver bowl, watching the dust settle in a fine, luminous layer. It glowed faintly in the darkness, casting the clearing in a pale, ethereal light.

The hawthorn branches next. Ramona arranged them in a star pattern at five points of the circle, the enchanted cloth falling away to reveal the dark, smooth wood. Fresh-cut. Still alive with magic, the way hawthorn always was at convergence points. She could feel the energy in them — green and vital and ancient.

The yarrow flowers she scattered around the bowl, their dried petals catching the moonstone's glow. And finally, the candle — black wax, unscented, blessed by Posey's careful hands. Ramona turned off her flashlight and set the candle in the exact center of the bowl and lit it with a match. The flame burned steady and bright, casting sharp shadows across the snow.

Zara watched from the edge of the salt circle, the grimoire open in her hands. She hadn't spoken since they'd entered the clearing. Her face was illuminated from below by the candle's glow — all sharp angles and shadows, her expression unreadable.

"The circle is complete," Ramona said, sitting back on her heels. She checked everything. Twice. The salt line was unbroken. The hawthorn branches were properly placed. The moonstone dust glowed steadily in the bowl. The candle burned without flickering.

Everything was perfect.

"The incantation," Zara said quietly. She held up the grimoire, turning it so Ramona could see the page. The text glowed faintly in the candlelight — old magic responding to older magic, the words themselves charged with centuries of use.

Ramona nodded. "Together."

They'd practiced this. They'd practiced the pronunciation, the rhythm, the way the language shifted mid-incantation — the power marker, the command structure, the linguistic architecture that made the spell work. They'd gone over it a dozen times, sitting with coffee and sticky notes and Zara's careful handwriting filling the margins.

Ramona knew every word. She knew where to breathe, where to pause, where the magic would build, and where it would release. She knew it the way she knew her own name.

"Ready?" Zara asked.

Ramona looked at her across the ritual space. At the woman who had defended her from her mother, who had pushed her back into her own expertise, who had held her hand in the dark after a nightmare, who had worn Ramona's too-short shirt and made her forget how to breathe.

The demon she was about to set free.

"Ready," Ramona said.

They began.

The incantation rose from both of them simultaneously — Latincane first, the framework, the foundation. Ramona's voice and Zara's voice winding together in the cold night air, curling around each other like smoke. The words were old. Older than either of them. Older than the trees that ringed this clearing. They carried weight, carried authority, carried the accumulated intention of every witch and demon who had spoken them before.

The moonstone dust in the bowl flared brighter. The candle flame stretched upward, defying physics, reaching toward the sky like a finger pointing at the stars.

The tether between them pulled tight — tighter than it had ever been. Ramona could feel it like a physical cord wrapped around her chest, vibrating with tension. She could feel Zara's heartbeat through it, fast and steady. Could feel her own fear reflected back, amplified.

The shift to Lysienne. The command structure. The moment where the spell stopped being theory and became action.

The air in the clearing changed.

It was subtle at first, just a shift in pressure, like the atmosphere itself was holding its breath. The shadows cast by the candle grew longer, darker, swirling along the ground like smoke. The snow around the salt circle seemed to glow brighter, the moonstone dust pulsing in rhythm with the incantation.

Ramona kept going. The words were flowing out of her now, automatic, driven by years of linguistic expertise and weeks of careful preparation. She could feel the magic building around her. In the convergence point. In the ancient oaks. In the salt and the hawthorn and the moonstone.

It was working. She could feel it working.

She caught Zara's eye as their lips moved in tandem, reciting in perfect harmony.

And then…

Something went wrong.

It wasn't dramatic. There was no flash of light, no thunderous crack. It was subtle — a hiccup in the rhythm of the incantation, a moment where the magic stuttered like a heartbeat skipping. Ramona felt it in her chest, in the tether, in the space between one word and the next.

She kept going. One word after another. The incantation demanded completion — stopping midway would be worse than finishing.

The magic built. And built. And built.

The tether was screaming now — she could feel it, vibrating at a frequency that made her teeth ache, pulling at something deep inside her chest. The candle flame was blinding, a column of white light reaching into the sky. The salt circle was glowing, the hawthorn branches rattling in a breeze that seemed to cease existing.

The world went white.

Pain.

Pure, absolute, all-consuming pain that started somewhere in her chest and radiated outward through every nerve ending in her body. It felt like she imagined being struck by lightning and set on fire simultaneously would feel. Like every cell in her body was being torn apart and reassembled in the wrong order.

Ramona heard herself scream. Distantly, like it was happening to someone else.

She was on the ground. When had she fallen? The snow was cold against her cheek, soaking through her jacket. The sky above her was full of stars—sharp, impossibly bright, wheeling overhead like the world had been tilted on its axis.

"Ramona. Ramona. Ramona!"

Zara's voice. Hands on her face, her shoulders, turning her over. Zara's face above her, pale in the moonstone's glow, her eyes wide with something Ramona had never seen in them before.

Fear. Real, raw, undisguised fear.

"I'm—" Ramona tried to speak. Her chest felt like it had been cracked open. "I'm okay."

"You are not okay." Zara's hands were shaking. Actually shaking. "You were struck — something hit you, I don't know what, the magic —" She was touching Ramona's face, her arms, checking for injuries with frantic precision. "Can you move? Does anything feel broken?"

Ramona tried to sit up. Pain lanced through her chest, sharp, electric, residual. She gasped, and Zara's arm was behind her immediately, supporting her weight.

"Slowly," Zara said. "Slowly."

Ramona sat up. The clearing looked wrong. The salt circle was shattered — scattered in an irregular pattern, like something had exploded outward from the center. The hawthorn branches had been flung to the edges of the clearing. The silver bowl was overturned, the moonstone dust scattered across the snow in a glittering trail, scattering in the slight breeze that had returned to the clearing. The candle was out.

The tether hummed between them. Still there. Still intact.

The ritual had failed.

Ramona stared at the destroyed ritual space. At the scattered salt and the extinguished candle and the moonstone dust dissolving into the snow. Two weeks of research. Days of careful preparation. Everything they'd built together, destroyed in seconds.

Something dark and hot and enormous swelled up inside her chest.

"No," she said.

"Ramona—"

"No." The word came out louder than she intended. Sharper. "No, no, *no*—"

She was on her feet before she knew she was moving, swaying, her chest still screaming with residual pain. The clearing spun around her. She pressed her hands against her face, feeling the burn of tears she refused to let fall.

"It didn't work," she said. Her voice was shaking. "It didn't fucking work."

"We can try again—"

"This is all my fault," Ramona said, her fingernails digging into her palms. She wanted to scream, to pound her fists on the ground, to fall apart.

"No, it isn't—"

Ramona spun to face Zara. "I didn't want you to go."

Zara went primordially still, staring at her.

Ramona groaned in deep frustration. "I hesitated." She shook her head and scrubbed her hands over her face again. She was so ashamed.

"I hesitated because I didn't want you to leave me, and I fucked everything up because I'm path—"

Zara was in front of her now, holding her upper arms, holding her steady and still. "I didn't want to go either," she confessed, her voice a whisper.

Ramona paused for a moment, sniffling as she looked up at the demon standing over her. "Wh-what?" Her voice cracked on the word.

Zara's hands tightened on her arms, not painful but grounding. Anchoring. Her dark eyes searched Ramona's face with an intensity that made Ramona's breath catch.

"I didn't want to go," Zara repeated, and there was something raw in her voice now, something that sounded almost like fear. "When the ritual started, when I felt the binding beginning to loosen, I—" She stopped, her jaw working. "I wanted it to fail."

The words hung between them in the pre-dawn air.

"That's impossible," Ramona whispered. "You've been trying so hard to—"

"I know what I've been *trying* to do." Zara's voice was rough. "I know what I *should* want. To go home. To get back to my perfectly organized life and my perfectly predictable responsibilities and my perfectly empty apartment." Her hands slid down to Ramona's wrists, holding on like Ramona might disappear. "But when I felt the magic pulling at me, all I could think was that I wasn't ready. That we weren't—" She stopped again, looking away. "That I wasn't finished here yet."

Ramona's heart was doing something complicated and terrifying in her chest. "Zara—"

"So if you sabotaged the ritual," Zara said, meeting her eyes again with something that looked almost like defiance. "Then we both did. And I'm not sorry."

The last thread of Ramona's restraint snapped.

She surged forward, closing the distance between them, and kissed Zara like she was drowning and Zara was air. Her hands fisted in Zara's jacket, pulling her closer, and Zara made a sound — surprise or relief or something desperate — before kissing her back just as fiercely.

It wasn't gentle. It wasn't sweet. It was frantic and messy with need. Zara's hands slid from Ramona's arms to her waist, then her back, pulling her in until there was no space between them. Ramona's fingers tangled in Zara's hair and Zara's grip tightened and somewhere in the back of Ramona's mind she knew she should stop, should think, should *breathe—*

But Zara's mouth was hot against hers and her body was solid and real and *here*, and Ramona had been wanting this for weeks without letting herself admit it, and now that she'd started, she couldn't seem to stop.

When they finally broke apart — gasping, shaking — Ramona's back was against a tree she didn't remember moving toward and Zara was still holding her like she might disappear.

"Oh," Ramona breathed.

"Yes," Zara said, her voice wrecked. Her forehead dropped against Ramona's, their breath mingling in the small space between them. "That."

The clearing was silent except for their ragged breathing and the rustle of leaves in the wind. Somewhere, a bird started its morning song.

"I'm not sorry about that either," Ramona whispered.

Zara laughed, low and rough. "Good."

Ramona kissed her again, hard, like she could make up for lost time through sheer determination. Zara responded immediately, one hand sliding up to cup the back of Ramona's neck, the other gripping her hip hard enough to leave marks.

"Ramona—" Zara gasped against her mouth, but Ramona cut her off with another kiss, then another, unable to stop now that she'd started. Her hands were everywhere — Zara's jaw, her shoulders, sliding under the lapels of her jacket— and Zara was making quiet, desperate sounds that were driving Ramona absolutely insane. Zara's knee parted Ramona's legs, and she arched into the demon, her back scraping against rough bark, grinding her hips into Zara's thigh. Zara's hand tightened on her hip in response, urging her. When Zara's mouth moved to her jaw, then her neck, her fangs caressing the sensitive skin there, Ramona's knees nearly gave out.

"Fuck," Ramona breathed, tilting her head back. "Zara, please—"

Zara pulled back just enough to look at her, eyes blazing, lips swollen, hair completely destroyed from Ramona's fingers. She was breathing hard, her usual composure absolutely shattered. The heat of Zara's body warmed Ramona, making her forget that they were standing outside in the cold at night, even as their breaths fogged the frozen air between them.

"We passed a bed and breakfast at the last exit," Zara said, her voice rough and low. "I'm not fucking you for the first time against a tree."

Ramona stared at her, still pinned against the bark, heart racing. "I like trees."

Zara raised her eyebrows. "I have *some* standards." But Zara's hands hadn't moved from Ramona's body, contradicting the attempt at dignity. "And when you finally come for me, you'll be thankful for a soft and comfortable bed afterwards."

Ramona was honestly shocked by her ability to continue forming thoughts after such a promise. "Right now?" she asked breathlessly, her hips slowly cresting forward again, chasing the friction that had felt so good just a moment before. "You want to drive to a bed and breakfast right now?"

Zara leaned forward, whispering against Ramona's mouth, "Unless you'd prefer to wait until we get back to your apartment where your roommates can hear everything through the walls." Zara's thumb traced a deliberate line along Ramona's hip. "Your choice."

Ramona groaned. "You're right."

"I'm always right." Zara kissed her again, slow and deep, before finally — *finally* — stepping back. "Car. Now. Before I change my mind about the tree."

CHAPTER FIFTEEN

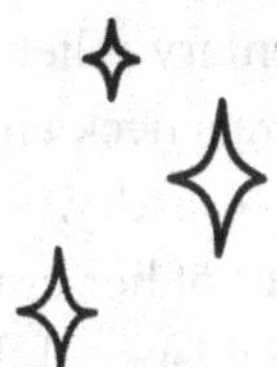

The door to the Bluebell Suite had barely clicked shut before Zara had Ramona pinned against the heavy oak.

They'd startled the front desk clerk with their haste and short answers. Zara had thrown down a black card, saying they'd take "any room, immediately."

The wood groaned under their combined weight, but the sound was drowned out by the ragged, desperate sound of their breathing. The tether — that invisible, magical cord that had spent three weeks humming with frustration — was now a live wire, sparking and thrashing between them.

"You're shaking," Zara murmured. Her hands came up to frame Ramona's face. Usually, the demon was the picture of control, all sharp lines and purposeful movements. Now, her hair was a disaster from Ramona's fingers, and her dark eyes were wide, the pupils blown out until only a thin ring of amber remained. Her thumbs traced the line of Ramona's jaw with a steady, grounding pressure that felt like it was the only thing keeping Ramona from dissolving into the floorboards.

"Adrenaline," Ramona gasped, her heart hammering a frantic rhythm against her ribs. "And you. It's mostly you."

Ramona's hands found the fabric of Zara's shirt. She didn't just want the clothes off — she wanted the barriers gone. She wanted to bridge the gap that the failed ritual had left wide open. Zara didn't rush, though. Even in her hunger, she was methodical, her fingers working the buttons of Ramona's coat with a terrifying, steady precision.

She peeled away the layers of damp, salt-stained clothing, following the reveal of skin with her mouth. Each kiss was a brand. Zara's lips were cool, a momentary relief against the heat Ramona was generating, but the skin of Zara's neck and shoulders was radiating an unnatural, furnace-like heat — a dry, searing warmth that Ramona could feel even through the lace of her bra.

"You're so hot," Ramona whispered, her head falling back against the door as Zara's mouth found the sensitive junction of her neck. "Your skin… it's like you're burning from the inside."

"Demonic physiology," Zara said against her collarbone, her voice dropping into a low, vibrating growl. She stepped farther into Ramona's space, her bare thighs — now visible as she discarded her own trousers with a casual flick of her hips — brushing against Ramona's. The heat coming off Zara's core was intense, like standing near an open forge in the dead of winter.

When Zara finally stepped back to strip her shirt, Ramona's breath hitched in her throat. In the dim, warm light of the bedside lamp, Zara looked lean and predatory. Her skin was a flawless expanse that seemed to catch the light, but as she turned, Ramona saw it — the shadow.

It uncurled from the base of Zara's spine like a living thing. It wasn't solid, but it wasn't smoke either. It was a whip-thin length of darkness, darker than the shadows in the corner of the room, tapering to a sharp, spade-like point. It flicked restlessly in the air, echoing the tension in Zara's jaw.

"Oh," Ramona breathed, reaching out with a hand that wasn't quite steady. Her fingers passed through the edge of the shadow. It didn't feel like flesh, but more like a low-voltage current, a thrum of pure, kinetic energy that made the hair on her arms stand up. "This is new."

"It's a manifestation," Zara said, her voice rough. "It usually stays in the aether, but tonight… the magic is too close to the surface. Does it bother you?"

"No," Ramona whispered, stepping forward until there was no air left between them. She pressed her palms flat against Zara's chest. The heat was staggering. "It makes me want to know what else you're hiding."

They tumbled onto the mattress, the Bluebell Suite's floral duvet a chaotic nest beneath them. Zara was over her instantly, her weight solid and grounding. She was a master of making Ramona wait, her tongue tracing the bud of Ramona's nipple with agonizing precision, one hand pinning Ramona's wrists above her head, the other pushing Ramona's underwear down as far as she could reach.

"Tell me what you want, Ramona," Zara murmured, her voice a vibrating command against the sensitive skin of her inner thigh. "I want to hear you say it."

"You."

"Be more specific." Another flick of Zara's tongue over Ramona's nipple had Ramona arching up into Zara's mouth.

Ramona writhed under Zara. "I want everything."

"And you'll get it, but only if you tell me where to start."

"Down," Ramona choked out, her fingers digging into the mattress. "There. Your… mouth."

Zara moved slowly, dragging her fangs and tongue over Ramona's stomach and hips, nipping at Ramona's inner thigh. Ramona watched as Zara slid between her legs, her touch surprisingly gentle as she pulled Ramona's underwear all the way off. Ramona couldn't help the way her hips lifted, begging.

Zara's eyes flicked up, catching her stare as she leaned forward, her tongue parting Ramona's center with careful precision.

Ramona had never felt anything like it. Zara's mouth was a revelation — wet, expertly rhythmic, and searingly hot. It felt like being touched by a controlled sun. Ramona's vision wavered at the edges, and she felt as though Zara was drinking the very breath out of her lungs.

"Look at you," Zara whispered, pulling back just enough to see Ramona's flushed, desperate face. Her own face was slick with

Ramona's heat. "You're soaking for me. You're so ready it's tracking down your thighs. You've been wanting this for a while, haven't you?"

Ramona made a sound halfway between frustration and acknowledgment.

Zara's fingers joined in, blunt and clever, stretching Ramona open, exploring her with gentleness. Before Ramona could even plead or demand, Zara seemed to *know* what she needed. A curl of a finger, the suction of her mouth, it was all choreographed like a dance they'd done a thousand times.

She stayed right there, her tongue swirling with purposeful, confident strokes, her fingers finding the exact rhythm that sent Ramona over the edge. It was a deep, spasming release that felt like the tether between them was being stretched taut, then plucked like a guitar string. Zara's name was on her lips as she came, her body shaking with the force of it.

As the waves receded, Ramona watched through half-lidded eyes as Zara sat back on her heels. The demon slowly and deliberately licked Ramona's wetness off her fingers, her dark eyes never leaving Ramona's.

"Oh fuck," Ramona panted, her chest heaving as she watched the slow, pornographic movement of Zara's tongue. "I could come again just seeing you do that."

"I intend to make sure you do," Zara promised. She looked hungry. She looked like she could swallow Ramona whole, and Ramona wasn't complaining.

But Ramona wasn't ready to be the only one undone. She was all curiosity and a need to touch Zara, to explore every inch of the demon, to make her feel as good as Ramona had. She grabbed Zara's shoulders and flipped them, making Zara laugh and roll her eyes in acquiescence.

She explored Zara's body with her fingers and tongue, finding what they had in common — Zara let out a loud groan when Ramona's teeth found her nipple — and what was different. Zara's skin was hot, and the tiny, spiked ridges on her hip bones were incredibly sensitive.

"Can I take these off?" Ramona asked, looping a finger under the waistband of Zara's boxer briefs.

Zara nodded, her dark eyes watching Ramona. It was the first time she'd seen the demon look completely calm, though she could feel how Zara's heart was racing through the tether between them.

Ramona continued exploring, and as she moved between Zara's legs, the shadow-tail moved off to the side, the spade at its end flicking in languid swishes along the sheets.

"Can I touch you?" Ramona asked, moving to lie beside Zara, kissing her once more.

"I think I might combust if you don't," Zara said with a laugh against her mouth.

Ramona took a deep breath, her eyes focused on Zara's face as she slid her hand between Zara's thighs.

Zara was burning. Between her legs, she was a wet, scorching inferno. Ramona watched Zara's brows furrow in pleasure as she circled her clit.

"More," Zara breathed.

Ramona pushed two fingers inside, and the heat was so intense it was almost painful, a delicious, searing tightness. Zara buckled, her internal muscles clenching around Ramona's fingers like a vise.

"You're so hot," Ramona whispered, leaning down to bite the sensitive skin of Zara's shoulder. "You feel so good."

Zara gasped, her shadow-tail curling around Ramona's calf like it was holding her in place.

"You want it?" Ramona teased, mimicking Zara's earlier confidence, her fingers driving into the demon's heat with a steady, punishing rhythm.

Zara was a symphony of desperate sounds, her usual composure shattered into a thousand pieces. She was writhing, her hips chasing Ramona's hand with a ravenous hunger. Ramona didn't let up. She stayed focused, her thumb rubbing the searing point of Zara's clitoris until the demon finally exploded.

It was a violent, beautiful surrender. Zara's body clenched and spasmed around Ramona's fingers, a long, low cry wrenched from deep within her chest. Her tail went rigid, the spade point glowing a faint, ethereal violet before finally going limp.

Ramona didn't pull away. She stayed there, her fingers deep inside the pulsing, wet heat of the demon, feeling the tremors gradually subside into a heavy, rhythmic thrum.

"Zara," Ramona whispered, leaning in to press a kiss to her mouth. "You're incredible."

Zara didn't answer with words. She just reached, her hand finding Ramona's neck and pulling her in, her fingers tangling in Ramona's hair as they shared a slow, deep kiss that tasted of salt, magic, and something that felt dangerously intimate.

Ramona felt the weight of Zara's gaze as they pulled apart, the demon's eyes now gentle and clouded with a strange softness.

Ramona smiled, her hand tracing the curve of Zara's jaw. "Maybe we should fail more rituals."

Zara laughed — a real, genuine laugh that echoed in the quiet room. "I think I could be persuaded."

Ramona pressed up onto her elbow. "Can I do that again?"

Zara grinned, reaching to pull Ramona on top of her. "I do believe it's *my* turn, Mortal. Now, grab onto this headboard so I can taste you again."

CHAPTER SIXTEEN

THE EARLY MORNING LIGHT WAS JUST STARTING TO CREEP THROUGH THE gap in the Bluebell Suite's aggressively floral curtains when Ramona woke. Gray and thin, the kind of pre-dawn light that made everything look washed out and unreal.

She was warm. Unreasonably warm.

Zara was still asleep beside her, one arm draped across Ramona's waist, her face pressed into the pillow. Her hair was a complete disaster, which Ramona found unexpectedly satisfying, given how precisely styled it usually was. The shadow-tail was gone, dissolved back into whatever ethereal plane it lived in when Zara wasn't actively falling apart.

How gorgeous and strange and perfect this creature was. She'd never been so taken care of in bed before. Her past lovers, Simone and even before, had been fun, but something about Zara felt different. Deeper, like Zara knew exactly what she needed even before she did. Could that have been an effect of the tether?

Ramona watched the demon for a moment, then carefully extracted herself from the tangle of limbs and sheets. The cold air hit her skin immediately, making her shiver. She grabbed Zara's discarded shirt from the floor — still warm, because of course it was — and pulled it over her head while making her way to the bathroom.

She paused at the window on her way back to bed. The view was less romantic than she'd expected. The parking lot. A dumpster. A family of raccoons engaged in what looked like a territorial dispute near the trash bins. No fox, though. She didn't know why the realization felt disappointing — they were two hours outside of Fernwick. How in the world would the fox be able to travel that far and find her?

"Ramona."

She turned. Zara was awake, propped up on one elbow, watching her with an expression that was softer than usual. Sleep rumpled. Human-looking, almost.

"Sorry. I didn't mean to wake you," Ramona said.

"You didn't." Zara sat up, the duvet pooling around her waist. She didn't bother covering herself, which was... distracting, to say the least. "Can't sleep?"

"Just thinking." Ramona leaned against the windowsill, pulling the blazer tighter. "About the ritual. About everything."

Zara was quiet for a moment. Then she patted the mattress. "Come back to bed. You'll freeze."

Ramona hesitated, then crossed back to the bed and slid under the covers as she removed Zara's jacket.

Zara twisted to glance at her HellBerry, and that's when Ramona saw the ink on Zara's back clearly. It wasn't a tattoo. Not exactly. Black, swirling lines moved in a hypnotic, rhythmic pulse over Zara's shoulder blades and down her spine. They shifted like ink dropped into a glass of water.

"Zara?" Ramona traced a moving line with her finger. "What's this?"

Zara's arm came around her immediately, pulling her close. The heat was still there, that supernatural warmth radiating from her skin like a banked fire.

"All demons have markings," Zara said.

"And your markings move?" Ramona asked.

Zara nodded. "I think I was born with them. I've had them as long as I remember."

"Do you feel them?"

Zara shrugged. "Only when they're touched. They're incredibly... sensitive."

Ramona raised a brow. "Noted."

They lay in silence for a while. Ramona could hear the raccoons outside, chittering aggressively at each other. The radiator clanking. Zara's steady breathing.

"The last time I cast magic like last night," Ramona said quietly. "Real magic. With actual stakes. It was the night of the incident."

She felt Zara go still beside her. Not pulling away. Just listening.

"Simone and I had been married for two years," Ramona continued, her voice flat. "We worked together at Thornwood, but in different departments. Kate was my best friend and in our coven. I introduced them, and they became friends. I didn't think anything of it." She stared at the pattern of the wallpaper on the opposite wall. "They'd been having an affair for six months before anyone told me."

"Six months," Zara repeated softly, shaking her head.

"Everyone knew. The entire coven. My colleagues at Thornwood." Ramona sighed. "I was the last person to find out. Someone finally told me right before the autumn equinox ritual. The big one. The one the whole coven does together."

"And you were supposed to participate."

"I was supposed to *lead* part of it. I'd been preparing for weeks." Ramona's hand found the edge of the duvet, gripping it. "I should have walked away. Should have gone home, dealt with it later, done anything other than show up to a major ritual while I was—" She swallowed. "I was devastated. And humiliated. And so fucking angry I could barely see straight."

"But you stayed."

"I stayed. And I decided to hex Kate."

Zara said nothing. Her thumb traced slow circles against Ramona's shoulder, grounding and steady.

"It was supposed to be small. Petty. Make her trip and fall during the ritual, or something. Maybe give her warts all over her face. I hadn't decided. Something everyone would see. Something that would make her feel as humiliated as I felt." Ramona's jaw tightened. "Childish. I know that now. I knew it then, probably. But I was so angry, Zara. I wanted her to hurt, too."

"What happened?"

"I cast the hex during the ritual. With the entire coven's energy channeled through the space. With the protective wards at full power. With everything aligned." The words came out clinical. Detached. Like she was watching it as a memory from far away. "My magic has always been off, you know? Since I was a kid. Spells that should have been simple would go sideways for no reason. I thought I was just bad at it. Sloppy. Everyone else at Thornwood could cast without thinking. I had to work twice as hard just to get halfway there. Honestly, I was only admitted to Thornwood because of the Greenbriar name and who my mom is, but I worked so hard to prove to everyone that I was meant to be there. And even then, sometimes things would just... break."

She pulled the duvet up higher, suddenly cold despite Zara's warmth.

"I don't know why it happened the way it did that night. I still don't. My magic just... completely broke. Like something inside me shattered and everything poured out at once." Ramona pressed her forehead against Zara's shoulder. "The hex didn't just hit Kate. It exploded. Wild magic — uncontrolled, undirected, fueled by the ritual's own energy. It blew through the entire space like a shockwave."

"How bad?"

"The High Priestess got donkey ears. Kate got a stutter that made her sound like she was speaking backwards. Two other coven members got temporary afflictions — one woman's hands turned into lobster claws for a day, and one briefly transformed into a bird." Ramona's voice cracked. "Not for long, but long enough. Thankfully, my mother and Iris weren't affected."

"Intense," Zara breathed.

"The protective wards around Thornwood went down completely. The building's magical infrastructure was destabilized for weeks." Ramona's fingers curled against Zara's skin. "The Magical Council launched an investigation. Everyone thought the High Priestess's ears were permanent. For three days, the entire magical community believed I had permanently cursed the High Priestess of the Thornwood Coven."

"But you didn't."

"Iris figured it out. She figured out how to reverse it. She's good at what she does. She fixed the High Priestess. Fixed everyone." Ramona paused, taking a deep breath, the guilt of the memory still heavy in her chest. "And she told the Council it was an accident. That I wasn't dangerous if I didn't cast. She convinced them not to strip my magic entirely. But they fired me from Thornwood. Expelled me from the coven. Put me on probationary status with the Magical Council."

Outside, the sky was getting lighter, the gray dawn turning slowly toward actual morning.

"And everyone was *terrified* of me," Ramona said quietly. "And I couldn't even argue with them. Because I didn't know why it happened. I still don't. I moved to Fernwick, where I could start over, and I feel like I'm failing at every turn. I don't know what's wrong with me, Zara. I just know that every time I try to do real magic — magic that matters — something inside me breaks, and other people get hurt."

Zara was very still beside her. Ramona could feel something through the tether — something sharp and carefully controlled, like Zara was holding back a flood.

"That's why you stopped casting," Zara said. Not a question.

"What use is a witch who can't cast without destroying everything she touches?" Ramona's laugh was hollow. "So I hung up the proverbial witch hat. Took the job at Mystic Moon. Sold crystals to non-mages who didn't know enough to be afraid of me. Tried to forget that I'd ever been anything else."

She gestured vaguely toward the window, toward the parking lot and the raccoons and the world beyond.

"And last night I was desperate to prove that I could still do it. That I wasn't completely useless. That I could handle real magic without—" Her voice broke. She pressed her lips together, furious at herself for crying, for not being able to get through a single confession without falling apart. "Without hurting anyone."

"But you didn't hurt anyone," Zara finished softly.

Ramona nodded. "I did temporarily get struck by something like lightning, if memory serves."

"That could have happened to anyone," Zara said, turning onto her side. She kissed Ramona's bare shoulder. "I'm not afraid of you. I'm not afraid of your magic."

A coil of tension dissolved inside Ramona's chest at the words.

"If the Council finds out I summoned a demon, they'll fully strip my powers."

They lay in silence for a long time. The radiator clanked. The raccoons had apparently resolved their dispute and moved on. The light through the curtains was getting stronger, less gray, more gold.

Zara hadn't moved. Hadn't pulled away. But the tether was warm between them — steady and present and achingly gentle, like Zara was pouring everything she felt into the connection between them.

"I'm sorry," Ramona whispered finally. "For last night. For all of it. For being…" She gestured at herself. At the mess. "This."

"Don't," Zara said. The single word was sharp enough to make Ramona look up.

Zara was watching her with an expression Ramona couldn't quite read — fierce and sad and furious all at once. Not at Ramona. At something else.

"Don't apologize," Zara said quietly. "Don't you dare."

Ramona opened her mouth to argue — to say that she wasn't apologizing for being alive, just for being broken, just for being dangerous.

But the words died in her throat. Because Zara was looking at her like she meant it. Like Ramona was worth defending even now, even after everything she'd just confessed.

They were quiet for another long moment. Then Zara shifted, her arm tightening around Ramona's waist.

"I was about to be demoted," Zara said.

Ramona blinked. "What?"

"When you summoned me. Hell was about to demote me."

"Demoted? You?" Ramona turned to look at her properly. "Why?"

"Performance. Or lack thereof." Zara's laugh was dry. "I'd been coasting. For a while."

"How long is a while?"

"A decade. Maybe longer." Zara pulled the duvet up slightly, a gesture so human it made Ramona's chest ache. "I used to love it. The work. Hell's bureaucratic systems are elegant, in their own way. Centuries of institutional structure, layered on top of centuries more. Understanding how it all fits together, finding the inefficiencies, optimizing the processes. I was good at it. I cared about it."

"And then?"

"And then I stopped," Zara said simply, matter-of-fact. "I don't know when it happened exactly. It was gradual. The reports started feeling like busywork. The departments I managed started feeling interchangeable. I'd sit in meetings and realize I couldn't remember a single thing that had been said, and I didn't care that I couldn't remember." She glanced at Ramona. "Hell noticed. They always notice. When one of their own starts to drift, the system flags it. I was given a performance improvement plan six months ago."

"A performance improvement plan?"

"Lack of engagement. Declining initiative. Failure to demonstrate commitment to departmental goals." Zara recited the phrases with flat precision. "Standard HR language for 'you're becoming a liability.'"

Ramona absorbed this idea, the mental image of Zara, bored and lonely and unfulfilled. Her heart ached.

"So when I summoned you..."

"I was just starting a demotion hearing." Zara stared at the ceiling. "Which sounds dramatic. It wasn't, really. It would have meant a transfer to a lower department. Less responsibility. Less visibility. A smaller office." A pause. "I should have been furious when you pulled me here. Three hundred years of building a career, and some mortal accidentally yanked me out of it right before everything fell apart."

"Were you?"

"For about five minutes." A ghost of a smile crossed Zara's face. "And then I saw your apartment. And that terrible bed. And you. And I thought..." She stopped.

"What?"

Zara was quiet for a long moment. Ramona didn't fill the silence. Just waited.

"I thought, *this is interesting*," Zara said finally. "This is actually, genuinely interesting. And I hadn't felt that in years. Decades, maybe. A century."

The honesty in her voice was startling. Zara, who never said anything she didn't mean. Who was always precise, always measured, always in control. Saying this like it cost her something.

"Being here," Zara continued. She still wasn't looking at Ramona. Was looking at the ceiling, at the window, at the slowly brightening sky. "With you. Your ridiculous roommates and their terrible taste in movies and Gerald. The shop. The fox on the fire escape." A pause. "It's the first time in centuries I've felt like I was actually alive. Not just… functioning."

Ramona's throat had closed up. She pressed her face into Zara's shoulder, refusing to cry again, not now, not when Zara was finally saying something real.

"I don't know what happens next," Zara said softly. "With the binding. With Hell. With any of it. But I know…" She paused, hesitating. "I know I don't want to go back to the way things were before."

Ramona lifted her head. Zara was looking at her now, her dark eyes soft in the early morning light.

"Me neither," Ramona whispered.

They lay there as the sun came up, tangled together in floral bedding, the tether between them warm and steady and finally — *finally* — feeling less like a chain and more like a choice.

"READY?" Ramona asked.

"Yes." Zara's hand found hers. Not possessive, not desperate. Just… there. Steady.

They walked to the car like that. Holding hands. In broad daylight. In the parking lot of a bed and breakfast where they'd just spent the night together in a room with chintz wallpaper and a four-poster bed.

It should have felt momentous.

It just felt right.

Ramona pulled out her keys, already mentally preparing for the drive home — how long they could reasonably avoid talking about what happened next, whether they should stop for coffee, if the tether would feel different now — and then she saw it.

The fox was curled up in the driver's seat.

"Oh," Ramona breathed.

It looked up at her through the windshield, amber eyes calm and watchful. Its tail was wrapped neatly around its body, and there were small muddy paw prints on the center console. It had clearly let itself in through — well, however foxes let themselves into locked cars. Magic, probably.

"We're nearly a hundred miles from your apartment," Zara said quietly. "Through unfamiliar territory."

Ramona opened the driver's door slowly. The fox didn't move.

"You came a long way for me, didn't you?" Ramona said softly.

The fox's ears flicked forward. Not quite agreement, but acknowledgment.

"I need the driver's seat, though." Ramona gestured to the back. "Can you…?"

The fox stood, stretched with deliberate slowness, and hopped gracefully into the back seat. It turned in a circle twice before settling into the corner behind Zara's side, eyes half closed but still watching.

Ramona slid into the driver's seat. Zara got in the passenger side. And just like that, they were three: witch, demon, and fox, driving back to Fernwick together in Ramona's ancient sedan that smelled like old coffee and lavender car freshener.

The fox was silent the entire drive. Ramona checked the rearview mirror periodically, finding it in the same position each time — alert but resting, present but not demanding attention. Zara typed something on her HellBerry, then closed it and just watched the landscape pass.

No one spoke. There was nothing that needed to be said.

When they finally pulled up outside the apartment building, the sun was straight overhead. Ramona put the car in park. Turned off the engine.

The fox was already on its feet.

"What do we do with you now?" Ramona asked, twisting to look at it as they climbed out of the car.

The fox met her eyes for a long moment. Then it jumped over the center console and out Zara's side of the car, landing lightly on the sidewalk. It didn't run immediately. Instead, it looked back at Ramona through the open car door, tail swishing once.

"Thank you," Ramona said, though she wasn't entirely sure why. It just felt right.

The fox held her gaze a moment longer. Then it turned and bolted, a streak of red-gold fur disappearing into the alley between buildings. Gone as quickly and mysteriously as it always did.

"Well," Zara said, still holding the door open. "That was interesting."

"You think he's…" Ramona paused, searching for the right word. "Connected to me already? Before a formal claiming?"

"I think he's been connected to you since the first time you heard him screaming in the alley." Zara's mouth curved slightly. "The claiming ritual is just making it official."

Ramona glanced up at her apartment building. "Well, four more weeks."

"At least." Zara nodded, threading her fingers through Ramona's. "Come on, let's go see if Princess Buttercup ate Felix while we were gone."

CHAPTER SEVENTEEN

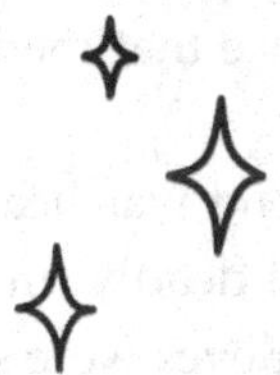

THE HELLBERRY BUZZED IN ZARA'S HAND — A SOUND LIKE WIND CHIMES made of bone, discordant and wrong in a way that made Ramona's teeth ache.

"That's them," Zara said. Hell was calling. Zara had sent a message to her supervisor just fifteen minutes before, explaining the extension Earth-side given their unsuccessful severance ritual.

She was standing in the middle of Ramona's bedroom, perfectly still. She'd glamoured one of Ramona's plain black T-shirts to look like a proper button-down — the illusion was flawless, all crisp lines and corporate polish, though Ramona could see the slight shimmer at the edges if she looked closely enough. Her short dark hair was slicked back as much as the length would allow, revealing the sharp angles of her face.

She looked every inch the corporate demon Ramona had first summoned.

Well. Almost.

A dark tail swished behind her, reminding Ramona of a cat.

"Do you want me to leave?" Ramona asked from her position on the bed, where she'd been pretending to read the same page of *Advanced Runic Syntax* for the past twenty minutes.

"No." Zara's voice was flat. "Stay. Just... don't talk. They can't see you if I keep the camera angled this way."

The HellBerry buzzed again. Insistent.

Zara sat down at Ramona's desk, positioning the device carefully. The screen grew in size, resembling more of a tablet. Ramona was impressed with the cleverness of the magic, letting herself stare for a moment as Zara's dark nail swiped on the HellBerry to accept.

The screen filled with a face that made Ramona cover a gasp with her hand.

The demon on the other end was beautiful in the way a knife was beautiful — sharp angles and deadly precision. Their skin had a faint gray cast, like stone, and their eyes were solid black with no visible iris or pupil. They wore a suit in deep burgundy, and their hair was slicked back so tightly it looked painful.

"Azareth." The demon's voice was smooth. Pleasant, even. "It's been too long."

"Theron." Zara's tone matched theirs perfectly — professional, courteous, empty. "Thank you for making time."

Ramona tried very hard not to move. Not to breathe too loudly. From her angle on the bed, she could see both the HellBerry screen and Zara's face in profile. Zara's expression hadn't changed. Corporate. Controlled. Nothing like the demon she'd come to know. She watched in awe and curiosity.

"Let's skip the pleasantries, shall we?" Theron leaned back in their chair — Ramona could see what looked like a sleek office behind them, all dark metal and glowing screens. "You've been topside for three weeks now. Your reports have been... surprisingly thorough, actually. I'm impressed."

"Thank you."

"Which makes this situation all the more puzzling." Theron tapped something on their desk. "You were supposed to sever the binding within three weeks. Standard protocol for accidental summons. Yet here we are, and you're still... tethered."

Ramona's hands clenched in her blanket. She kept her eyes on her book.

"The binding proved more complex than anticipated," Zara said smoothly. "The witch who summoned me used an archaic variant. I've been researching the proper severance method."

"For three weeks."

"It's a delicate process. Rushing could result in magical backlash for both parties."

Theron studied Zara through the screen. Ramona couldn't read their expression. She wasn't sure demons even had expressions in the way humans did — or maybe Theron was just that good at hiding them.

"I see," Theron said finally. "And this... research. It's been productive?"

"Very. I've identified three potential severance rituals. I'm currently testing their compatibility with the specific binding structure."

"Fascinating." Theron's tone didn't change. "And the witch? She's cooperating?"

"Fully. She's as eager to resolve this as I am."

A lie. Or was it? Technically, they'd both agreed that neither of them wanted it to work the first time, so Zara's careful wording was clever. Ramona watched the quick swish of her tail as she said it.

"Good," Theron said. "Because I'm authorized to extend your timeline. Four weeks will be the new moon. That should be sufficient to sever even a complex binding."

Four weeks.

Ramona's chest felt tight. She knew. Deep down, of course she knew that Zara didn't belong here, that Zara was a demon who belonged in Hell, but four weeks didn't seem like a long enough time. Whatever had happened in the Bluebell Suite — and once in the car and twice since they'd been back in Ramona's room — it had an end date. A definitive expiration.

"That's generous," Zara said. "I appreciate the flexibility."

"Don't thank me yet." Theron leaned forward. "There are conditions. You'll need to submit weekly progress reports. Detailed ones. And you'll be working remotely for the duration."

"Remotely?"

"Your productivity has been excellent, Azareth. Better than it's been in years, if I'm being honest." Theron's expression shifted slightly —

was that approval? "Whatever you're doing up there, it's working. Your reports are thorough, your analysis is sharp, you're actually completing projects ahead of schedule. The department heads have noticed."

Zara said nothing. Ramona watched her profile, saw the tiny twitch at the corner of her mouth.

"So we're willing to accommodate," Theron continued. "Keep up the quality of work you've been producing, submit your severance progress reports, and we'll handle everything else from this end. You can work from..." They glanced at something off-screen. "Wherever you are now."

"That's... unexpected."

"Hell adapts. You know that. If remote work maintains productivity, we'll implement it." Theron's fingers drummed on their desk — the first casual gesture Ramona had seen from them. "Between you and me? Your numbers are making my entire division look good. I'd be an idiot to disrupt that. However..."

Something flickered across Zara's face. Too fast for Ramona to read.

"Because this is an unsanctioned summoning, you will begin to feel the effects of being away from Hell."

"Such as?"

"Your soul is bound to Hell. Contractually. And a requirement of that contract is residence. The side effects may be minimal but will likely present as physical. Please be aware of said effects around the mortals. Their demographic has not enjoyed such displays in the past," Theron explained.

Zara nodded, her face looking paler for a moment. The spiked tip of her tail lay still on the ground.

"Now," Theron said briskly. "Let's discuss the severance itself. Have you considered the tether-dissolution method? It's standard for proximity bindings."

"I have. I'm currently conducting a comprehensive analysis of the binding's foundational architecture to ensure optimal dissolution parameters." Zara's voice shifted into something Ramona had never heard before — completely detached. She could hardly even parse out the meaning of Zara's words. "There are several variables that require systematic evaluation before we can proceed with implementation."

Ramona blinked. What?

"Variables," Theron repeated.

"The binding structure demonstrates anomalous characteristics that fall outside standard taxonomic classifications. I'm developing a customized severance framework that accounts for these irregularities while maintaining appropriate risk mitigation protocols."

Theron looked slightly glazed. "Right. And these... irregularities. Are they going to impact the timeline?"

"I'm optimizing the assessment process to ensure minimal timeline deviation while maintaining comprehensive evaluation standards." Zara's tone was absolutely deadpan. "My current projections indicate severance readiness within the established four-week parameter, pending completion of the diagnostic phase and subsequent validation of the remediation strategy."

Ramona had spent years of her life dedicated to translation, to unwinding the twisted meaning from complicated phrasing, and even that wasn't enough to figure out what Zara meant.

Theron rubbed their temple. "Azareth, can you deliver?"

Zara nodded, but Ramona could see her jaw was clenched.

Theron made a note. "Fine. And I'll need confirmation in your weekly reports that you're making progress on this..." They paused, clearly searching for the right word. "Diagnostic phase."

"Understood. I'll include comprehensive status updates on all relevant evaluation metrics in my progress documentation."

Which Ramona was pretty sure meant *I'll make something up*.

"Good." Theron pulled up something on their screen. "I'm sending you specifications for the Gregorian Severance ritual. It's designed for complex bindings. The new moon is in four weeks — that's your optimal window."

The HellBerry buzzed softly. A file transfer notification.

"This specific ritual takes about six hours," Theron continued. "Start to finish. Should handle most binding complications. We've often used it for contracted summons that need early termination."

"This is helpful," Zara said. "Thank you."

"One more thing." Theron's expression shifted. Concern? Annoyance? "Prolonged bindings can develop sympathetic resonance. Especially if you've been in close quarters for three weeks. When you sever it, expect emotional backlash for both parties."

"Backlash?"

"Grief, usually. Sense of loss. The binding creates artificial intimacy. When you break it, there's a withdrawal period. A few days of feeling unmoored, disconnected. It passes."

Zara's hand on the desk curled into a fist. The glamour flickered for just a second — Ramona caught a glimpse of her plain black T-shirt before the illusion snapped back into place.

"I'll… prepare accordingly."

"Good. Make sure the witch understands what to expect. Last thing we need is a distraught mortal filing complaints to management." Theron smiled — the expression was sharp and brief. "Weekly reports, Azareth. Don't make me chase you."

"Understood."

Theron's voice softened fractionally. "Whatever you're doing up there — keep doing it. I haven't seen you this engaged in decades. It's good to have you back."

Zara's expression didn't change. "Thank you."

The call ended. The HellBerry screen went dark.

Zara sat there, perfectly still, as the device on the desk shrank back to the standard handheld size The glamour dissolved slowly, revealing Ramona's slightly oversized T-shirt underneath.

Ramona counted to ten before she spoke.

"So," she said carefully. "Comprehensive analysis of foundational architecture?"

Zara's shoulders tensed.

"Anomalous characteristics falling outside standard taxonomic classifications?" Ramona continued, trying very hard not to smile. "Optimizing the assessment process?"

"I had to say *something*."

"That was the most impressive pile of corporate bullshit I've ever heard." Ramona set her book aside. "What does any of that actually mean?"

"It means I'm working on it and they should stop asking questions." Zara finally turned around. Her eyes were shifting between honey and black. "Did it work?"

"Theron looked like they wanted to die halfway through your second sentence. So yes, I'd say it worked."

Zara's mouth twitched. Almost a smile.

"Four weeks," Ramona said quietly.

"Four weeks." Zara's voice was hollow.

"And you have to submit progress reports on breaking the binding."

"Weekly reports. Yes."

Ramona studied her. There was something in Zara's expression — something careful and guarded that hadn't been there before the call.

"That wasn't what I expected," Ramona said.

"What did you expect?"

"I don't know. Yelling? Threats? Demands that you return immediately?" Ramona gestured at the HellBerry. "That was… polite. Professional. They're letting you work remotely. They praised you."

"Hell rewards productivity." Zara's tone was flat. Corporate. The voice she'd used during the call. "As long as I'm useful, they'll accommodate me."

"But they seemed… I don't know. Nice? Is that the right word?"

"Theron isn't nice. They're efficient. There's a difference."

Ramona nodded. "Makes sense. You know, I didn't realize you were sending in reports all this time."

"Mostly while you slept and I'd finished all the books," Zara said with a shrug.

Ramona eyed Zara. "Seeing you be all corporate demon was very…"

Zara's eyes darkened and she moved, climbing onto the bed. "Terrifying? Bloodcurdling? Horrific?"

Ramona grinned, wrapping her arms around Zara's neck and tugging her down until their lips were brushing. "Hot."

CHAPTER EIGHTEEN

RAMONA WAS MAKING COFFEE WHEN REALITY DECIDED TO LITERALLY knock on the door.

Not metaphorically. Not figuratively. Actual reality, in the form of a seven-foot-tall demon in full ceremonial regalia, standing in the hallway outside apartment 4C at nine o'clock on a Saturday morning.

Felix opened the door. He yelped and dropped his phone.

Ramona heard this from the kitchen. So did everyone else. Kashvi appeared from her room, eyes wide. Posey emerged from the bathroom, toothbrush still in her mouth. Zara — who'd been sitting at the dining table — went completely still, her eyes flashing black.

"Delivery for Zara of the Temptation and Minor Inconveniences Department," the demon announced. Their voice sounded like rocks grinding together. Like the earth opening up. Like every nightmare about monsters under the bed made audible.

They were wearing what looked like formal Hell dress uniform — deep crimson robes edged in silver, covered in symbols that hurt to look at directly. Their skin was the color of volcanic glass, and their eyes glowed with inner fire. Massive curved horns emerged from their temples, and when they moved, the air around them shimmered with heat.

Gerald, perched on the back of the couch, took one look and hid behind a cushion.

"Here," Zara said, standing. Her voice was perfectly level. Corporate. Like seven-foot demons showed up at the apartment every day. "That's me."

The delivery demon consulted a tablet — because of course Hell had tablets — made of what looked like obsidian. "Zara. Topside assignment. Accidental summoning. Binding severance in progress."

"Correct."

"I have official documentation requiring your signature." The demon reached into their robes and pulled out a scroll. It was massive, easily three feet long, and sealed with wax that was still smoking.

They unrolled it. The parchment crackled with an energy that made Ramona's teeth ache.

The coffee maker burbled behind her, stupidly cheerful, while a seven-foot emissary of Hell stood in her hallway issuing paperwork. She wiped her hands on a dish towel that suddenly felt absurdly human. Cotton. Soap. Saturday morning.

"This is your formal extension notification," the demon continued. "Four weeks to complete binding severance, submit weekly progress reports, maintain productivity standards. Failure to comply results in immediate forcible extraction and tribunal review."

"Understood," Zara said.

"Sign here, here, and initial in blood here." The demon produced a pen — or what looked like a pen, except it was made of bone and the tip glowed red.

Felix made a small squeaking sound.

Zara took the pen. Pricked her finger without hesitation — the blood that welled up was darker than it should be, almost black — and signed three places on the parchment. When she pressed her thumb to the final section, the blood sank into the page, the symbols around it flaring bright and then fading.

Ramona resisted the urge to lean closer for a better look.

"Acceptable." The demon rolled up the scroll. It vanished back into their robes. "You'll receive a copy to your inbox. Is there anything else you need to report at this time?"

"No."

"Then I'll leave you to your work." The demon turned to go, then paused. Looked at Ramona. Looked back at Zara. "The witch who summoned you. I assume she understands the terms?"

Ramona understood. She understood that if she failed, Hell wouldn't just take Zara back. They would drag her in front of a tribunal. Who knew what else that might entail?

"She does," Zara said.

"Good. Four weeks. Don't waste them." The demon stepped into the hallway. The door swung shut behind them.

For a moment, there was total silence.

Then Kashvi said, "What. The fuck. Was that."

Ramona and Zara looked at each other.

"A demon? Why was there a demon?" Felix asked.

"So," Ramona said slowly. "We need to tell you something."

"You think?" Felix's voice pitched higher.

"Could everyone maybe sit down?" Ramona gestured at the couch and chairs.

"I'm not sitting," Posey said, toothbrush still clutched in her hand like a weapon. "I'm standing right here until someone explains why a demon just showed up at our apartment asking for Zara."

Zara sighed. Sat back down at the table. "I'm a demon."

Silence.

"You're a what?" Kashvi said flatly.

"A demon. From Hell. Specifically from the Temptation and Minor Inconveniences Department, though I manage several divisions." Zara's tone was clinical. Professional. Like she was explaining a quarterly report. "Ramona accidentally summoned me three weeks ago. We've been magically bound ever since."

More silence.

Kashvi very carefully set her coffee mug on the counter. "I'm sorry. Did you just say 'summoned'?"

"It was an accident," Ramona said quickly. "I was trying to do a simple fortune and success spell and—"

"You summoned a demon," Felix said. "With a fortune and success spell."

"I know how it sounds—"

"Do you? Because it sounds insane."

"It was an archaic binding variant," Zara said. "Easy mistake to make if you're working from incomplete medieval texts."

Posey pulled the toothbrush out of her mouth. "You've been living here for three weeks. As a demon. From Hell."

"Yes."

"And none of us noticed."

"I'm very good at blending in."

"Blending in," Kashvi repeated. "You're a demon."

"I mean, yes, technically."

"What was all that about reports and work?" Kashvi threw up her hands. "What does that even mean?"

"It means Hell has a bureaucracy," Zara said. "And I'm good at navigating it. *Was* good at it. Before I got summoned."

Felix had finally picked up his phone. Was staring at it. Put it back down. "So when you said you worked remotely…"

"I meant for Hell. Yes."

"And the paperwork that just got delivered…"

"Is my formal authorization to stay topside for four more weeks while we sever the binding."

"The binding," Posey said slowly. "You mean you're… you and Ramona are—"

"Magically tethered," Ramona confirmed. "We can't be more than sixty-six feet apart or the magic starts hurting both of us. We've been working on finding a way to break it."

"Hence the severance ritual," Zara added. "New moon is in four weeks. That's our window."

Cammie walked in the front door in her running clothes, her face ashen. "You're never going to guess what I just saw in the hallway."

"We might have an idea," Felix said, scrubbing his hands over his face.

"There was a demon and *it* ran from *me*," Cammie said with confusion and wonder.

Posey sat down. Just dropped onto the couch next to Felix like her legs had given out. "I need you to start from the beginning. The very beginning. Because I feel like I just walked into the middle of a movie and I don't know any of the plot."

So they told them. All of them.

Ramona explained the summoning — they all remembered the exact night, but she painted a picture of the grimoire, the spell for fortune and success. Zara explained the binding, the tether, the proximity requirement. Together they vaguely described the past three weeks: the research, the failed ritual attempts, Hell's deadline.

By the end, all four roommates were staring at them with varying expressions of shock, disbelief, and what might have been genuine terror.

"So you've just been…" Kashvi gestured vaguely. "Dealing with all of this. For three weeks. While we had no idea."

"We didn't want to worry anyone," Ramona said.

"Worry?" Felix's voice cracked. "Ramona, you're magically bound to a demon."

"Well, when you put it like that, it sounds so much worse than it is," Ramona said defensively. "I mean, look at Zara. She's not like the demon who just showed up in the hall."

"I appreciate that," Zara murmured.

"Does the binding hurt?" Cammie asked. She'd moved closer, her expression shifting from shock to something more analytical. "Like, physically?"

"Only if we try to separate too far," Ramona said. "Otherwise, it's just… there. Background presence."

"And you have four weeks to break it or…"

"Or Hell extracts me forcibly," Zara said. "Which would be significantly more painful for both of us. And possibly catastrophic for the surrounding magical infrastructure."

"Catastrophic," Posey repeated.

"The binding has been in place for three weeks. Breaking it incorrectly could cause substantial magical backlash. It could hurt Ramona." Zara glanced toward Ramona with a frown.

Gerald emerged from behind the couch cushion. He studied Zara for a long moment, head tilted, then made a soft cooing sound and hopped onto the back of the couch near her.

"Oh, *now* you come out?" Felix said, reaching for Gerald. "You coward."

"Gerald has excellent survival instincts," Zara said seriously. "He recognized a superior predator earlier and took appropriate defensive measures. That's wisdom, not cowardice."

Felix blinked. "Did you just... did you just defend Gerald's honor to me?"

"He made a tactically sound decision."

"You really are a demon," Kashvi said, but she was almost smiling. "Only a demon would take a pigeon that seriously."

"Gerald is an exceptional pigeon," Zara said.

There was a long pause.

Then Cammie stood up. "Okay. Okay. So. Ramona accidentally summoned a demon. They're magically bound. Hell wants the demon back in four weeks. We have four weeks until the new moon ritual that might break the binding." She looked between them. "What do you need from us?"

"What?" Ramona said.

"You're our friends. Both of you. You clearly need help with this." Cammie crossed her arms. "So what do you need?"

"We didn't want to impose," Zara said.

"You're literally magically tethered together and Hell just sent a demon to your door," Felix said, seeming to recover slightly. "I think we're past 'imposing.' What do you need?"

Ramona looked at Zara. Zara looked at Ramona. The tether between them — invisible, but suddenly feeling very present — pulsed with something warm and complicated.

"We're still figuring that out," Ramona admitted. "The severance ritual is complex. We'll need help with the preparation, the materials, probably someone to maintain the protective circle while we're—"

"We'll help," Kashvi interrupted. "All of us. Just tell us what to do."

"You're not freaked out?" Ramona asked. "About the demon thing?"

"Oh, I'm completely freaked out," Kashvi said. "But I'm processing. Give me, like, twenty-four hours to process, and then we'll help."

"I'm making pancakes," Felix announced suddenly. "Because I don't know what else to do and pancakes feel appropriate."

"Do demons eat pancakes?" Posey followed Felix to the kitchen.

"Yes."

"Do we have chocolate chips? I feel like this is a chocolate chip situation," Felix said, rifling through cupboards.

"Definitely chocolate chips," Cammie said. "I'm showering, though. Something about that demon gave me the creeps. The hallway one, not you, Zara. No offense."

Zara narrowed her eyes, but didn't say anything.

Kashvi remained on the couch, staring at Zara, tiny sparks flying from her fingertips in wisps of light. "You're really from Hell."

"Yes."

"And you've been living here for three weeks."

"Yes."

"And you're dating Ramona."

"That's…" Zara stared at her lap. "It was initially a premise to explain my presence here, but I'm sorry we lied to you about that."

Ramona's cheeks heated. This was not the time to hash out the details of what they… were, but she felt a pulse of affection and comfort through the tether.

"Okay." Kashvi took a deep breath. "Okay. I can work with this. This is fine. Everything is fine." She paused. "Does Hell have, like, dental insurance? Retirement plans?"

"Demons don't need dental insurance," Zara said. "But yes, there are retirement provisions. They're just measured in centuries rather than years."

"Right. Of course. Centuries." Kashvi laughed, slightly hysterical. "Why not. Everything else is insane, why not centuries."

Gerald made a sympathetic cooing sound and nuzzled against Zara's arm.

"Thanks, friend," Zara murmured. "You're handling this better than I am."

And just like that, the apartment settled into something resembling normal. Cammie finishing up in the bathroom. Felix making pancakes with Posey's help. Kashvi on the couch, still processing but recovering.

Ramona stayed with Zara, watching her close her HellBerry and set it aside.

"That went better than expected," Zara said quietly.

"They're good people."

"They are." Zara looked toward the kitchen, where Posey was arguing with Felix about chocolate chip distribution. "I wasn't expecting them to offer help."

Ramona smiled, because she couldn't believe it, either.

Zara's hand found Ramona's.

"Four weeks," Ramona said quietly.

"Four weeks," Zara agreed.

Four weeks to figure out how to break a binding neither of them wanted to break.

Or four weeks to figure out how to keep it without destroying everything in the process.

Either way, at least now they wouldn't be facing it alone.

From the kitchen, Felix announced: "Pancakes are ready! Everyone to the table! And someone please tell me more about Hell's bureaucracy because I have *questions*."

Ramona groaned. Zara almost smiled.

And Gerald, brave Gerald, flew to land on the back of Zara's chair, cooing his apparent approval of the whole chaotic situation.

CHAPTER NINETEEN

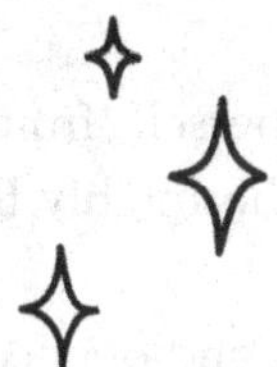

Sunlight streamed through the bedroom window, and Ramona awoke with the unfamiliar sensation of not being alone in bed.

Zara was still asleep beside her — which was remarkable in itself, given that Zara usually woke before dawn — her dark hair against Ramona's pillow, one arm draped across Ramona's waist, her breathing slow and even. Peaceful in a way Ramona had never seen her.

Ramona lay very still, not wanting to disturb her. Not wanting to move and break whatever spell had allowed them to sleep tangled together.

The tether. Which was still there, humming steadily between them. Warm and present and exactly as it had been for weeks. The ritual had failed catastrophically, and nothing had changed. They were still bound together. Still tethered. Still stuck.

Except "stuck" didn't feel like the right word anymore.

Ramona shifted carefully, trying not to wake Zara, and that's when she saw him.

Through the window, on the fire escape. The fox.

It sat at the edge of the platform, silhouetted against the morning light, its tail curled neatly around his paws. Watching. Patient. Those amber eyes caught hers through the glass, and something passed between them — a question, maybe. Or an offer.

Ramona looked at the fox for a long moment. Then at Zara, still sleeping. Then back at the fox.

Something settled into place in her chest. Not a decision, exactly. More like… a willingness. To try. To stop saying no to everything that might be good for her.

She carefully extracted herself from Zara's embrace — which proved difficult, given how thoroughly they were tangled together — and pulled on her robe.

She moved to the window and opened it wide. The cold air rushed in, sharp and bracing.

The fox stood immediately, ears perked forward, tail lifting slightly. Alert. Waiting.

"Okay," Ramona said quietly. "Here's the deal."

The fox tilted his head.

"I'm not doing a formal bonding. Not yet. I don't—" She gestured vaguely at herself, at the disaster of her life. "I don't know what I'm doing. With any of this. Magic, familiars, demons who don't want to leave." She glanced back at Zara, still sleeping. "All of it."

The fox watched her steadily. No judgment in its eyes. Just patience.

"But you keep showing up," Ramona continued. "And I keep pushing you away. And I'm starting to think that maybe… maybe pushing away everything that might help me is not actually the smartest strategy." She took a breath. "So this is just on a trial basis, Fox. You can come inside. You can stay. But I'm not promising anything. And if my magic hurts you, or scares you, or you realize I'm not—" Her voice caught. "Not worth the effort. You can leave. No hard feelings."

The fox made a soft sound. Not quite a bark, not quite a chirp. Something in between that felt like gentle amusement.

"I'm serious," Ramona said. "This isn't a commitment. It's just… trying. To not be completely alone in this."

She stepped back from the window. Creating space. An invitation without obligation.

The fox studied the open window for a long moment. Then, with careful, deliberate steps, it crossed the threshold.

Into the room. Onto the tilted bed. Across the blankets toward the foot of the bed, where it turned in a small circle before settling into a neat curl, its tail wrapped over his nose, its amber eyes drifting half closed.

Like the fox had always belonged there.

Like it had been waiting for this exact invitation all along.

Ramona stood frozen, watching it. Part of her wanted to take it back immediately — to say *wait, I didn't mean right now, I need more time to think about this* — but the fox had already closed its eyes, its breathing evening out into something peaceful.

It looked… content. Settled. Safe.

Behind her, Zara stirred again.

"Ramona?" Her voice was thick with sleep. "Did you just — Is that the fox?"

"Maybe," Ramona said.

"On your bed?"

"Possibly."

There was a pause. Then Zara's quiet laugh — warm and sleepy and fond. "Come back to bed."

"There's a fox on the bed."

"There's room." Zara's arm reached out, patting the space beside her. "Come here."

Ramona looked at the fox — who hadn't moved, hadn't opened its eyes, was just existing peacefully at the foot of her broken bed like it was the most natural thing in the world. Then at Zara, still reaching for her in the morning light.

She crossed back to the bed and slid under the covers. Zara immediately pulled her close, pressing a kiss to her shoulder.

"Trial basis?" Zara murmured against her skin.

"Don't start."

"I'm not starting anything. I think it's good." Another kiss. "Baby steps, Mortal."

Ramona closed her eyes. Let herself be held. Let herself feel the dual warmth of Zara beside her and the fox at her feet — two presences she'd spent weeks resisting, now just… there. Present. Staying.

The tether hummed between her and Zara, steady as a heartbeat.

And at the foot of the bed, the fox slept on, patient as ever, waiting for Ramona to catch up to what it had apparently known all along.

CHAPTER TWENTY

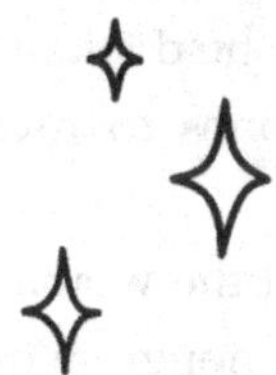

RAMONA WAS THREE HOURS INTO HER SHIFT AT MYSTIC MOON WHEN THE woman with the perfectly highlighted hair walked in. After getting ready for the day, she'd told the fox that she hadn't quite figured out the whole work thing, and it'd be best to not figure out Marcus's thoughts on foxes in the store just yet. The fox had trotted off into the alley, and she'd left her window cracked just in case.

"I need something for clarity," the woman announced, surveying the shop like she was inspecting a particularly suspect produce section. "My life coach says I have blocks."

Ramona pasted on her customer service smile. "We have several options for clarity work. Are you looking for meditation aids, or—"

"Something that actually works." The woman picked up a rose quartz, squinted at it, put it down. "I'm willing to invest in quality."

Which meant she was willing to spend money. Ramona pulled out the display case key. "Our Reveal Hidden Truths bundle might be what you're looking for. It's a curated collection — black tourmaline for protection, labradorite for insight, clear quartz for amplification—"

"I'll take it." The woman didn't even look at the price tag. "Does it come with instructions?"

"There's a card with suggested uses, but these are more for intention-setting than—"

"Great. I'll activate it now. Make sure it works before I leave."

Ramona blinked, trying not to actively roll her eyes. "That's not really how—"

But the woman had already opened the velvet pouch, dumping all six crystals into her palm. She closed her eyes, took a deep breath, and said in a voice that suggested she'd taken exactly one yoga class: "I call upon the power of these stones to reveal all hidden truths in my presence."

Ramona watched, thankful the woman's eyes were closed, because her ability to hide a smirk was nonexistent.

Nothing happened.

The woman opened her eyes. "I don't feel any different. Are you sure these are real?"

"Well, crystals don't usually cause immediate physical sensations—"

Then Ramona felt it.

A tug. Sharp and sudden, like someone had hooked a fishing line directly under her ribs and yanked.

She gasped, stumbling forward into the counter.

And between her chest and the wall separating Mystic Moon from the café next door, a line of golden light materialized.

It wasn't thick — barely the width of twine — but it glowed with a steady, pulsing luminescence that was absolutely, undeniably visible. The thread ran from somewhere beneath Ramona's sternum, through the air, through the wall, in the direction of—

Oh.

Oh no.

"What is that?" the woman asked, eyes wide.

From next door, she heard the scrape of a chair, a muffled curse, rapid footsteps.

"Totally normal!" Ramona's voice came out too high. "We've been testing our new lighting system. Isn't it pretty?" She grabbed the credit card reader, practically shoving it at the customer. "That'll be forty-seven fifty, here's your receipt, thank you so much for shopping with us—"

"But what is the light—"

Ramona was already ushering her toward the door. "Thank you, have a blessed day, namaste!"

She practically shoved the woman out onto the sidewalk and locked the door behind her, flipping the sign to *Back in 15 Minutes*.

The thread pulsed. Once. Twice. Like a heartbeat that wasn't hers.

Ramona yanked at the thread. Her fingers passed through it, but she could feel it. Warm. Solid in a way that had nothing to do with physical matter. It didn't budge. Didn't even flicker.

"Ramona!" Zara's voice, muffled through the door. "Ramona, open up!"

Ramona unlocked the door, stepping back as Zara walked in.

Zara burst in, eyes wild, one hand pressed to her own chest. She was wearing jeans and one of Ramona's hoodies — civilian clothes, nothing glamoured — and her short dark hair was sticking up like she'd been running her hands through it. The golden thread ran directly to her, disappearing somewhere beneath the hoodie.

"What the fuck?" Zara asked.

"I don't know! A customer activated a crystal bundle and it just... appeared!"

"Crystals don't do this." Zara stared at the glowing thread between them. "Mortal crystals don't have this kind of power."

"Well apparently, these ones do!" Ramona gestured frantically at the thread. "Can you make it stop?"

"I don't... know. Let me think." Zara pulled out her HellBerry, already swiping. "There has to be a reversal protocol for magical activation—"

The back door opened. Marcus walked in through the back office, took one long drag, then slowly lowered his vape pen as he stared at the glowing golden rope connecting Ramona to a stranger in his shop.

"Ramona," he said slowly. "What's going on?"

"Marcus! Hi!" Ramona's voice cracked. "This is my friend, Zara."

Zara's head snapped up from her HellBerry.

"We were just..." Ramona gestured frantically at the thread. "Testing out our new costume."

"It's February," Marcus said.

"We're getting a head start." Ramona's smile felt manic. "Very elaborate costume. Lots of prep work. You know how it is."

Marcus took another drag from his vape pen. Exhaled slowly. The artificial mango smell intensified. "A Halloween costume?"

"Couples' challenge," Zara added, not looking up from her Hell-Berry. "Trust exercise."

"In February."

"We're very committed to the relationship," Ramona said.

Marcus was still staring at Zara, his expression thoughtful in the way that meant he was about to say something he thought was deep. "You know, I like your energy. Very grounded. Protective."

"Thank you," Zara said absently, still scrolling through her Hell-Berry. Something in her voice shifted. Dropped lower. Became smoother, more compelling. "But don't worry about the light. In fact, you don't even see it anymore. And, you know, you're lucky to have Ramona. She's an excellent employee. You should give her a raise. And you should close the store tonight and let her leave early."

"You're absolutely right," Marcus said immediately. "Twenty percent. Starting last pay period."

Ramona's mouth fell open. "Marcus, you don't have to—"

"No, she's right. You're undervalued here." Marcus smiled benevolently, gesturing with his vape pen. "The universe is telling me to invest in good energy. Consider it done."

Zara's head jerked up. She stared at Marcus, then at Ramona, her eyes wide. "Sorry," she mouthed. "Habit."

"That's very generous," Ramona said carefully to Marcus, though her eyes remained on Zara. "Thank you."

"Of course. I'm going to go meditate on this vibration shift." Marcus pushed off the doorframe, still vaping. "Go home, I'll close."

He wandered back toward the stockroom, trailing artificial mango behind him.

The moment he disappeared, Ramona rounded on Zara.

"Did you just use some kind of demon influence on my boss?"

"I didn't—" Zara looked stricken. "It wasn't intentional. I just wanted to make sure he didn't start questioning the tether, but then the words came out and then—"

"You magically convinced him to give me a raise."

"I know. I'm sorry." Zara was back to frantically scrolling through her HellBerry. "It was instinct. I wasn't thinking. You were upset and he was asking questions, and it just came out."

Ramona wanted to be angry. She should be angry. But Zara looked genuinely distressed, her fingers shaking slightly as she swiped through what looked like demonic reference materials.

"Can you undo it?" Ramona asked quietly.

"The raise? Why would you—"

"Not the raise. The thread."

"I'm looking. There's nothing in the standard protocols for—" Zara stopped. Squinted at her screen. "Wait. This says manifestation of metaphysical bonds typically lasts twelve to twenty-four hours depending on the catalyst strength."

"Twenty-four hours at most." Ramona looked down at the glowing rope. "I have to walk around like this for a full day."

"We both do."

"What am I supposed to tell people?"

"The costume story seemed to work." Zara finally looked up. "I'm sorry. About the influence. I'll be more careful. I promise."

Ramona studied her face. The genuine remorse there. The way Zara was holding herself like she expected to be yelled at.

"Okay," Ramona said.

"Okay?"

"You apologized. You'll be more careful. And honestly, I could use the raise." Ramona managed a weak smile. "Just… try not to magically compel anyone else today?"

"Noted." Zara looked back at the thread. Reached out slowly and touched it. Her fingers passed through just like Ramona's had, but she shivered. "Does it feel any different to you? Stronger?"

"No. Same as always." Ramona frowned. "Can you feel it normally? The tether?"

"Not physically. It's just… there. Background presence. Like knowing someone's in the room with you." Zara's hand hovered over the glowing line. "But this is… I can almost feel it now. The heat of it."

Ramona held her hand out, the light glowing above her open palm. "Strange."

"Very."

"We should go home," Ramona said. "Maybe everyone will be out."

THEY WEREN'T OUT.

Felix, Posey, Kashvi, and Cammie were all sitting on the couch and around the coffee table in the living room when Ramona opened the door. All four heads swiveled toward them in perfect synchronization. Eight eyes dropped to the glowing thread connecting Ramona and Zara.

"Don't ask," Ramona said before anyone could speak.

Posey's eyebrows were somewhere near her hairline. "Of course."

"Crystals," Zara added.

"Crystals and a glowing magical rope," Kashvi said slowly.

"So, this is the tether? How romantic," Cammie said. Zara took a step closer to Ramona, farther from Cammie.

"Uh-huh." Felix was grinning. "And how long does this last?"

"Could be until tomorrow afternoon," Zara said, holding some of the tether slack in her hands. It seemed the longer the tether was visible, the more tangible it had become.

"Oh, this sounds like fun," Posey said. "Do you have to stay close together? What happens if you have to pee?"

Ramona shuffled away from the curious looks they were getting, back down the hall toward her room. "We're going to my room now. Please pretend this is normal."

"Nothing about you two has been normal since day one," Felix called after them. "Why start now?"

Ramona dragged Zara down the hallway and into her bedroom, shutting the door firmly behind them.

In the privacy of her room, after checking that the fox hadn't returned yet, Ramona finally let herself really look at the thread.

It was beautiful, actually. The golden light pulsed gently, like a heartbeat or a breath. Where it disappeared beneath her sternum, she could feel a warmth that wasn't uncomfortable. Just… present.

"Can I try something?" Ramona asked.

"What?"

Ramona reached out and very carefully and determinedly wrapped her fingers around the thread.

This time, instead of passing through, her hand closed around something solid. Warm and smooth, like sun-heated metal, but alive somehow. Pulsing with energy.

"You're touching it," Zara breathed.

"I can feel it." Ramona tugged gently.

Zara gasped, stumbling forward a step. Her hand flew to her chest.

"Sorry!" Ramona let go immediately.

"No, it's—" Zara's eyes were very wide. "Do it again."

Ramona gripped the thread again. Pulled, just slightly.

Zara moved toward her like she was being reeled in. Not forced — there was no resistance, no struggle. Just smooth, inevitable motion until they were standing close enough that Ramona could feel the supernatural heat of Zara's skin.

"Does it hurt?" Ramona whispered.

"No." Zara's voice had dropped, her hands finding Ramona's hips.

Ramona tugged again, more firmly this time. The golden tether didn't just pull Zara closer. It seemed to contract, the light thickening until the distance between them evaporated. Zara let out a jagged breath, her hands sliding from Ramona's hips to her waist, squeezing with a possessive strength that made Ramona's head light.

The air in the bedroom was suddenly too heavy to breathe. The familiar scent of Zara — smoke and a heady, dark oud — swirled around Ramona, thick enough to taste. She angled her face up to watch Zara's concentration break.

"Ramona," Zara warned, her voice a low, vibrating growl that settled deep in Ramona's belly. She leaned down to claim Ramona's mouth in a deep kiss, pulling Ramona's lower lip into her mouth with her teeth.

After a moment, Ramona broke away and looked at the golden

cord, then back at Zara's curious, open expression. "You said it was a trust exercise, right?"

Ramona backed Zara toward the bed, and Zara went willingly, her eyes never leaving Ramona's. When the back of Zara's knees hit the mattress, she sat, and Ramona was over her in an instant, straddling her lap.

The tether was coiled between them now, a glowing, pulsing mass of energy. Ramona grabbed the slack. Her heart was hammering, but her hands were sure. She took the golden light — this physical manifestation of the mess they'd made of their lives — and looped it around Zara's wrists.

"What are you doing?" Zara asked, her breath hitching as Ramona pulled her arms upward.

"Testing the bond," Ramona whispered. She pulled the cord taut, knotting it around the wooden slats of the headboard. To her shock, the magical light behaved exactly like rope. It knotted with a firm, golden glow, anchoring Zara's hands above her head.

Zara tested the restraint, her muscles rippling beneath the skin of her arms. The headboard creaked ominously. "You've tied a demon to your bed with her own tether, Mortal. Bold choice."

"You like it," Ramona countered, leaning in until their noses brushed. She began to grind her hips against Zara's thigh, the friction of their jeans a torturous barrier.

Zara groaned, a sound wrenched from her chest.

They moved together in a frantic, messy rhythm. Ramona's hands were everywhere — mapping the heat of Zara's neck, pulling at the hem of the hoodie, tracing the sharp lines of her collarbone. Zara was bucking beneath her, her bound hands straining against the golden light, her teeth bared in a grin. The heat radiating from Zara was staggering now, a dry, searing fever that seemed to melt the very air.

But the friction wasn't enough. It was never enough.

The heat coming off Zara wasn't just physical anymore. It felt like standing too close to an open furnace. As Ramona slid down the bed, her knees hitting the floor with a soft thud, the golden tether stretched taut, humming a low, resonant note that vibrated in Ramona's very bones.

Zara's head hit the pillow, her throat arched, exposing the frantic pulse jumping under the skin of her neck. "Ramona," she said.

"You can't stand the idea of not being in control," Ramona teased as she pulled off Zara's pants. "But I bet you're soaking wet from it anyway."

She parted Zara's legs, her hands running up the length of Zara's calves and thighs. Zara's inner thighs radiated a deep, core-level heat that seemed to pulse in time with the golden cord above.

"You're stunning," Ramona said, leaning in to draw her tongue over Zara's slick heat.

When Ramona finally made contact, the world narrowed down to the taste of salt and electricity. Zara's entire body jolted, a jagged, broken sound tearing from her throat. It wasn't just a physical reaction — the golden tether flared a brilliant, blinding white, illuminating the room in sharp, flickering bursts.

Ramona gripped Zara's hips, her thumb digging into the soft dip of her waist to hold her steady. She was methodical, her tongue tracing the heat of Zara's center with a persistence that bordered on worship. Every time Zara bucked, her heels digging into the mattress, Ramona pressed closer, drinking in the low, guttural moans that were starting to sound less and less human.

The air in the room felt charged, static raising the fine hairs on Ramona's arms. She could feel dark magic bleeding out of Zara, a wild, unrefined energy that tasted like smoke on the back of her throat. She quickened her pace, her tongue swirling in a demanding rhythm that forced Zara's breath into short, sharp hitches.

"Ramona — *please,*" Zara choked out, her fingers curling into useless claws against the wooden slats.

Ramona didn't let up. She pushed Zara further, her movements becoming more urgent as she felt the demon's internal fire reach a breaking point. The tether above them began to hum a high, piercing frequency, the light turning molten.

With one final, desperate surge, Zara's back arched completely off the bed. A low, vibrating growl erupted from her chest — a sound of pure, celestial ruin — as she shattered.

At the same time, the bed shattered, too, the spindles of the headboard splintering around the tether, the frame crashing to the floor. Ramona gasped, holding onto Zara's body, but Zara hardly seemed to notice, slumped back against the pillows, her breath coming in ragged, uneven sobs.

Ramona stayed where she was for a moment, her forehead resting against the curve of Zara's thigh, listening to the frantic, irregular thrum of a heart that beat much faster than a mortal's.

Slowly, Ramona looked up. Zara's eyes were heavy. She looked utterly undone.

Ramona moved to gently undo Zara's ties, rubbing the demon's wrists to make sure they weren't too sore from tugging against their restraints. The golden tether lay draped across them like a discarded ribbon, pulsing with a slow, contented light.

"I think… I think the roommates heard that," Ramona said in a breathless whisper.

Zara, her face buried in the crook of Ramona's neck, let out a low laugh that vibrated through Ramona's entire body. "Let them listen. I'll charge them a consulting fee for the education."

"You broke my bed," Ramona said with a laugh.

"*We* broke the bed. I believe you had a hand in it," Zara panted, a wry smile on the edge of her mouth. "Or at least a ton—"

"*Zara,*" Ramona scolded, her cheeks heating. She threw an arm over her eyes in embarrassment but couldn't help laughing anyway. Even after Zara had waved a hand and transformed the wreckage into a sturdy frame with a wooden spindle headboard.

After a quiet moment, Ramona ran her fingers through Zara's hair. "Can I ask you something?"

"Anything, Mortal."

"Is this…" She gestured vaguely between them. "The energy. The pull. Is it just the binding? The false connection Theron mentioned?"

Zara went still beside her. Then she propped herself up on one elbow, studying Ramona's face with that an intensity that made Ramona want to hide and be seen all at once.

"I don't know," Zara said finally.

"You don't know?" The disappointment bled through before

Ramona could stop it. She'd expected… something. Certainty. Denial. Not this.

"I think many things can be true at once." Zara's thumb traced idle patterns on Ramona's shoulder. "I think the binding influences how we feel. I think we have four weeks left together. I think that means we should enjoy this without worrying about what it all means."

Rationally, Ramona knew she was right. Whatever this was between them had an expiration date. Zara would go back to Hell. Ramona would go back to selling crystals to tourists who thought sage could fix their problems. And she'd never know for certain if this desperate, consuming thing between them was real or just magical coercion with good marketing.

Who was she kidding? Did she really think a corporate demon was her soulmate?

The thought was so absurd she almost laughed. Almost.

"Hey." Zara's voice dropped lower. Softer. "Talk to me. I can feel your distress through the tether."

"It's nothing."

"Ramona."

Zara's hand slid along her jaw, turning her face with gentle insistence. Her thumb brushed over Ramona's bottom lip, and every uncomfortable feeling churning inside Ramona's chest softened at the edges. Not gone. Just… quieter.

Zara leaned down until their foreheads touched. Close enough that Ramona could feel her breath.

"I'm here," Zara whispered. "Right now. In this moment. And I very much enjoy being with you." Her thumb continued its slow trace across Ramona's mouth. "I think you might enjoy it, too. And if it's the tether — if it's all just magical compulsion and proximity and coincidence…" She pulled back just enough to catch Ramona's eyes. "Who cares? It doesn't make this feel less real to me."

Ramona's throat closed. She nodded, not trusting her voice.

"Does it feel real to you?" Zara asked.

"Yeah," Ramona managed. "It does."

And she knew, in that moment, with Zara's weight warm against her side and the tether humming steady between them — she knew that losing this would break her in a way that losing Simone, her coven, her position at Thornwood never had.

The thought should have terrified her.

Instead, she wrapped her arms around Zara's neck and pulled her down into another kiss. Because even if they were sprinting toward a cliff's edge, even if this all ended the moment the binding broke…

She wanted to fall without a single regret.

CHAPTER TWENTY-ONE

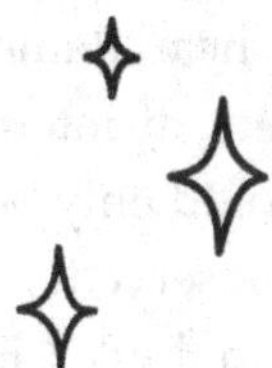

THE KITCHEN WAS FULL WHEN RAMONA AND ZARA WALKED IN, WHICH wasn't unusual. What was unusual was the way everyone stopped talking the moment they appeared.

Felix was at the stove, making what looked like an ambitious breakfast involving too many pans. Kashvi sat at the table with her laptop, Gerald perched on the chair beside her. Posey was pouring coffee with that dreamy, distant expression she always had when she was thinking about plant things, and Cammie had apparently come home early from her opening shift at the café, still in her apron, looking tired but alert.

They all turned to stare.

"Good morning," Zara said calmly, heading straight for the coffee pot.

Ramona felt her face heat. They knew. Of course they knew. Between the bed-breaking and the glowing tether that had thankfully turned invisible sometime in the night and the fox currently walking into the kitchen beside her, there was a lot to know.

The fox's entrance caused an immediate reaction.

Gerald, perched on Kashvi's chair, puffed up to twice his normal size and let out a warning coo that sounded distinctly aggressive.

Felix dropped his spatula. "Is that — is that a fox?"

"Yes," Ramona said carefully.

"A fox is in our kitchen." Felix's eyes were wide, tracking the fox's movement across the linoleum. "Near Gerald."

"It's not going to hurt Gerald," Ramona said.

"You don't know that." Felix moved to position himself between Gerald and the fox, arms spread protectively. "Look at it. Look at the hungry look in its eyes."

The fox, who had settled near Ramona's feet and was currently licking one paw with complete disinterest in the pigeon, paused to glance up at Felix with what could only be described as mild disdain.

"It just looks bored," Zara observed.

"That's what it wants you to think," Felix said. "That's how predators work. They lull you into a false sense of security and then—" He made a violent grabbing motion. "If it touches one feather on my poor little baby's head, I swear—"

"Felix," Kashvi interrupted gently. "Gerald is literally twice the fox's size when he puffs up like that. I think he can handle himself."

Gerald cooed again, this time with what sounded like smug agreement.

The fox yawned, showing all its teeth, then settled its head on his paws and closed its eyes. Completely unthreatening. Possibly even bored by the entire conversation.

"See?" Ramona said. "The fox is fine. Gerald's fine. Everyone's fine."

Felix looked unconvinced but slowly lowered his arms. "I'm watching you," he told the fox.

The fox's ear flicked. It did not open its eyes.

"Oh, we should definitely talk about this," Posey said softly, appearing with two mugs — one for Ramona, one for Zara. She set them down with gentle care. "You two finally got together — I could feel it in the energy shift, actually. And then there was all that light in the woods. My succulents all turned to face east four nights ago at exactly 11:47 p.m." She said this like it was the most natural observation in the world. "That only happens during major magical events. And now there's a fox." She smiled at the fox, who was still ignoring Gerald. "Hello, fox friend."

The fox opened one eye briefly, regarding Posey with what might have been respect, then closed it again.

"How did you know about the convergence points?" Zara asked, genuinely curious.

"The plants told me." Posey said it simply, like this was obvious. "Well, not in words, exactly. But they know things. Energy things. They're very sensitive." She touched one of the potted herbs on the windowsill fondly. "This basil was practically vibrating that night."

Ramona exchanged a glance with Zara. Through the tether, she felt Zara's amusement — and underneath it, a genuine question. *How much do we tell them?*

"The ritual failed at that convergence point," Ramona said finally. She wrapped her hands around the warm mug. "The severance ritual. We tried it at the new moon and it… didn't work."

The kitchen went quiet. Even Felix stopped watching the fox long enough to turn around.

"Are you okay?" Cammie asked. She'd been silent until now, but her voice was steady. Concerned. "Both of you?"

"We're fine," Zara said. "Ramona was hit by some kind of magical backlash, but she's recovered."

"Magical backlash?" Kashvi's eyes widened, a spark flying from her pointer finger. "That sounds—"

"It's fine," Ramona interrupted. "I'm fine. We're both fine. We just —" She took a breath. "We have to try again. Next new moon. We have a little over three weeks to figure out what went wrong."

Another beat of silence.

Then Felix set down his spatula and turned to face them fully.

"Okay," he said. "So let me get this straight. You two had been planning this huge magical ritual — a ritual that apparently requires medieval grimoires and convergence points and specific lunar timing — and you didn't think to mention it to any of us?"

"It wasn't—" Ramona started.

"We've been living together for two years," Felix continued. His voice was calm, but there was an edge to it. "Two years, Ramona. And you're doing major magic — dangerous magic, based on the 'magical backlash' situation — and you didn't think to ask your three witch roommates for help?"

"I didn't want to—" Ramona stopped. "I didn't think you'd want to be involved with something so dangerous."

"But we *do* want to be involved," Posey said, and she looked genuinely confused rather than hurt. Like the concept of not wanting to help simply didn't compute. "You're ours. That means we help. That's how it works." She said it so simply, so obviously, like she was explaining that water was wet.

"I thought—" Ramona's throat was tight. "I thought it was my problem. Mine and Zara's. I didn't want to drag anyone else into it."

"Into what?" Cammie leaned forward. "Into helping you? Into being there for you? That's literally what friends do, Ramona. Even friends who don't have magical powers but would fight a bear for you."

The fox, who had been sitting quietly near Ramona's feet, made a small sound — something between a chirp and a whine. Agreement, maybe.

Felix jumped. "Did it just—"

"The fox is agreeing with you," Ramona said.

"How do you know that?"

"I just… know." And she did. She could feel it — not through words, but through something else. A sense of the fox's emotions, its opinions… No, not *its* opinions, *his* opinions, filtered through whatever nascent connection had formed when she'd invited him inside. "He thinks I'm being an idiot."

"Smart fox," Kashvi murmured.

"Very wise," Posey added, nodding at the fox with a soft smile. "His energy is very old. Very patient. He's been waiting for you for a long time, I think."

"We all want to help," Kashvi said. "If you'll let us."

Ramona looked around the kitchen. At Zara, standing beside her, close enough to feel her warmth. At Felix, fidgeting with his short brown curls. At Kashvi, closing her laptop. At Posey, smiling with her expression open and sweet and completely without judgment. At Cammie, looking exhausted from her shift but still here, still present.

At Gerald, cooing once, meaningfully. At the fox, watching her with golden eyes.

These people, who had taken her in two years ago when she had nothing. Who had never asked her to explain the incident, never pushed her to talk about Simone, never treated her like she was broken or dangerous or too much. Who had just… been there. Consistently. Quietly. Without conditions.

And she'd been so focused on not being a burden that she'd never let them actually help.

"Okay," Ramona said. Her voice came out rough. "Okay. We need help."

Felix's expression softened immediately. "Good. What do you need?"

Zara pulled out her phone. "I've made a list. Okay, now, Kashvi, first…"

THE HELP STARTED SMALL, growing over the next week and a half.

Kashvi took one look at the grimoires spread across the living room and immediately started cross-referencing them with digital archives, building a database of every severance ritual variation she could find.

"There are patterns," she said three days into her research, laptop balanced on her knees, Gerald asleep on the armrest beside her. "Look. Every failed severance ritual in the historical record has one thing in common — the magical bond was created under duress or deception."

"Well, I had both," Ramona said. She was on the floor, surrounded by handwritten notes. "Accidental summoning definitely counts as duress."

"Exactly." Kashvi pulled up another document. "But here's the thing. Most of these bonds were eventually broken. Not through the standard severance ritual, but through…" She squinted at the screen. "Something called a 'willing dissolution.' Both parties had to actively want the severance while also acknowledging what the bond had given them."

Zara, who had been reading silently in the corner, looked up. "Acknowledging what it had given them?"

"Gratitude, I think?" Ramona tilted the screen to study the wording. "The translation is rough."

Kashvi nodded. "It seems like denying the bond's value made it impossible to break. You had to… honor it? Before letting it go?"

Ramona and Zara exchanged a look. Through the tether, Ramona felt something complicated, like Zara's uncertainty mixing with her own.

"We'll keep that in mind," Zara said carefully.

Felix, who had been listening from the kitchen while doing dishes, called out: "Wait, what about an unbinding ritual instead?"

"An unbinding?" Kashvi's head snapped up. "Felix, no—"

"What's the difference?" Ramona asked.

"Severance cuts the connection," Kashvi said quickly, already pulling up new tabs on her laptop. "It's surgical. Precise. An unbinding is…" She paused, searching for the right word. "Broader. It dissolves all magical bonds associated with the spell. Not just the tether, but *anything* in the vicinity."

"That sounds good," Felix said, coming into the living room with a dish towel. "Right? More thorough?"

"It's also significantly more dangerous." Kashvi's voice had gone sharp with concern. "Unbinding rituals don't discriminate. They can unravel *everything*. Including things you don't want unbound."

"Like what?" Ramona asked.

"Like…" Kashvi gestured vaguely. "Protective wards. Or existing contracts. Or anything that was magically formalized. It's unpredictable."

Zara had gone very still. "Contracts," she repeated softly. Her eyes seemed far away, like she had gone deep into a thought.

"Yes. Any magical contract that was active when the tether formed could potentially be affected by an unbinding." Kashvi looked between them. "That's why most practitioners avoid unbinding rituals unless absolutely necessary. The collateral damage can be extensive."

"So we stick with severance," Ramona said firmly. "We're not risking that kind of chaos."

"Agreed," Zara said. But her voice was still distant. Thoughtful.

Felix shrugged, returning to the kitchen. "Just a thought. Seemed simpler."

"Simpler isn't always better," Kashvi muttered, making notes on her laptop. "Especially not with magic."

But Ramona noticed the way Zara kept glancing at Kashvi's screen for the rest of the afternoon. The way her expression would go distant, like she was working through some complicated equation in her head.

Through the tether, Ramona felt something she couldn't quite name. Not worry, exactly. More like... possibility.

She didn't ask in front of the others. They had enough to figure out with the severance ritual. But the seed had been planted.

Unbinding.

The word hung in the air between them, waiting.

CAMMIE'S CONTRIBUTION was more practical.

"You need to eat," she announced one evening, appearing with grocery bags. "Both of you. You've been living on coffee and fear for weeks."

"I've been eating," Ramona protested.

"Granola bars don't count." Cammie started unpacking ingredients with the efficiency of someone who'd worked in food service for years. "You're doing heavy magical work. Your body needs actual fuel. Protein. Complex carbs. Vegetables in their natural form."

She cooked them meals — real meals that required multiple pots and actual seasoning. She packed lunches for Ramona's shifts at Mystic Moon. She left containers in the fridge with notes: *Eat this before research. Love, Cammie.*

"I didn't realize I had a second mom," Ramona said, only half joking. "You're actually more nurturing than my real mom."

"Someone has to take care of you." Cammie blew a kiss, then added with a wink, "Since you're clearly not doing it yourself."

POSEY'S HELP came from an unexpected angle.

"You know what I noticed?" Posey said one afternoon, appearing in the doorway of Ramona's room with a potted fern. She had that dreamy quality to her voice, like she was half in this conversation and half somewhere else entirely. "The energy in here feels… scratchy. Like static. Plants help with that." She drifted into the room, setting the fern on the windowsill with gentle hands. "They're very good listeners, you know. And they filter magical energy. Like… like a water filter, but for magic." She smiled, touching the fern's leaves fondly. "This one told me you needed help."

At least Posey wasn't trying to bring Princess Buttercup in. Ramona glanced to the fern, its fronds swaying slightly in the breeze from the open window. She glanced toward the fire escape where the fox was sunbathing, then back to Posey. "The plant… told you."

"Well, not in words." Posey looked at Ramona like this should be obvious. "But yes. Plants know things. They're very wise, actually. Much wiser than most people give them credit for."

She started bringing more plants. Small ones at first — a pothos on the desk, a snake plant in the corner. Then larger ones. Within a week, Ramona's bedroom looked like a miniature forest.

"I can't see my desk anymore," Ramona said, looking around at what had become a small jungle.

"You don't need a desk." Posey adjusted the fern with careful fingers, her voice soft and wondering. "The way the air feels different in here, don't you feel it? Clearer? Plants are very generous like that. They just want to help." She smiled at the fern. "Don't you?"

And somehow — impossibly — Ramona *did* feel it. The constant low-grade anxiety that had been her baseline for two years started to ease. Not disappear, but… soften. Like something in the air had shifted.

"Thank you," Ramona said quietly.

Posey looked up, and her smile was radiant — pure and uncomplicated and full of genuine warmth. "Oh, you're welcome. But really, you should thank the plants. I just help them get where they need to go." She paused, tilting her head like she was listening to something. "They're very happy to be here with you."

CHAPTER TWENTY-TWO

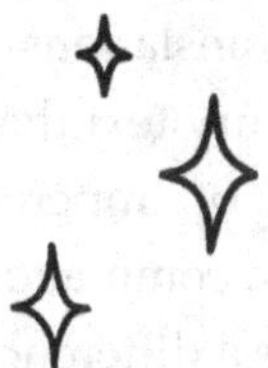

THE LIVING ROOM WAS FULL OF THE FAMILIAR SOUNDS OF A TUESDAY evening: the TV playing *Love Potion,* which had somehow become required viewing in their apartment; Kashvi's commentary about the contestants' terrible magical technique; Cammie's laugh; the smell of popcorn.

"She's going to pick Kellen," Felix said, gesturing at the screen with a handful of popcorn. "It's so obvious."

"She should pick Devin," Kashvi countered. "Kellen can't even cast a basic attraction charm without messing it up."

"That's what makes him endearing," Felix argued.

"That's what makes him incompetent."

Zara, sitting on the floor beside Ramona, was completely absorbed in the show. She'd gotten into *Love Potion* with an intensity that surprised everyone — analyzing the contestants' strategies, critiquing their spell choices, predicting outcomes with the precision she usually reserved for Hell's bureaucratic procedures.

"She's not going to pick either of them," Zara said without looking away from the screen. "She's going to eliminate both and bring back Trevor from week three."

"No way," Felix said.

"Watch." Zara made a note on her HellBerry. She was keeping a spreadsheet. An actual spreadsheet tracking contestant compatibility and strategic moves.

It was adorable. Ramona tried to focus on her translation instead of watching Zara watch reality TV with the intensity of someone planning a corporate takeover.

She sat cross-legged on the floor, a grimoire open in her lap, notebook beside her filled with translations. Another severance variation. This one from a fifteenth-century text that used different verb conjugations — subjunctive instead of imperative, which might make the magic more of a request than a command.

It probably wouldn't make a difference. But she had to try.

Through grace, to dissolve. Interesting. The whole incantation was framed as asking permission rather than demanding action.

She made a note. Underlined it twice.

The tether hummed between her and Zara — warm, steady, present. Like it had been for weeks now. Like it might be forever if they couldn't figure this out.

The thought didn't terrify her quite as much as it used to.

The fox had been gone most of the day. Ramona could still feel him — a distant presence, like an echo of an echo. The connection they'd formed when she invited him inside wasn't like the tether. It was quieter. More like knowing someone was in the next room rather than feeling their emotions directly.

But she knew he was okay. Knew he was out there somewhere, doing whatever mysterious fox things he did when he wasn't sleeping at the foot of her bed.

As if summoned by the thought, he strolled down the hall from Ramona's room, where she'd left the window cracked for him.

"Oh, there he is!" Posey said from her spot on the couch, looking up from the scarf she was knitting. "Hello, friend. Did you have a nice adventure?"

The fox didn't settle in his usual spot near Ramona's feet. He paced instead — back and forth, restless, his tail low and twitching. His amber eyes kept darting to Ramona, then away, then back.

"Hey," Ramona said, looking up from her grimoire. "Where've you been?"

The fox made a sound — not quite a whine, not quite a bark. Insistent. Urgent.

"What?" Ramona asked, as though she expected the fox would just come right out and tell her.

On the TV, the contestant was about to make her choice. Zara leaned forward slightly, completely absorbed.

The fox moved closer, pushing his head against Ramona's hand. Not affectionately — demandingly. Like he was trying to tell her something and getting frustrated that she wasn't understanding.

"Okay, okay." Ramona set down her pen and reached out to pet his head properly. "What's—"

The moment her hand touched his fur, the world dissolved.

SHE WAS STANDING in the clearing.

The convergence point. Two hours away, deep in the woods near Thornwood, where she and Zara had tried the severance ritual a week ago.

But it was wrong.

The snow that had been pristine and white was now stained — gray in some places, black in others, like ink had been spilled across the ground. The pristine circle of ancient oaks looked sickly, their bark darker than it should be, their branches bare and reaching up like skeletal fingers.

And in the center, where they'd cast the ritual—

The ground was *moving*.

Not physically. But magically. Ramona could see it the way she'd seen the tether that first night — a visible manifestation of something that shouldn't be visible. Dark energy, pulsing outward from the center in slow waves. Like a heartbeat. Like something alive and growing.

The air smelled wrong. Sulfur and burnt sugar and something older, something that made her skin crawl with instinctive revulsion.

This was corruption.

Demonic corruption.

She tried to move, to get closer, but she couldn't. She was seeing this through the fox's eyes — his memory, replaying for her. Showing her what he'd found.

The clearing was empty. No witches. No investigators. Just the fox, standing at the edge of the corruption, watching it pulse and spread with that patient, knowing gaze.

He'd gone back. Checked on the site. And found this.

The corruption was worse than it had been. Ramona could see the edges — where clean snow met stained ground. Could see how far it had spread since they'd left. A foot? More?

It was growing.

RAMONA GASPED, her hand jerking away from the fox's head.

She was back in the living room. The TV was still playing — the contestant was crying, explaining her choice to the remaining suitors. Kashvi and Cammie were still watching. Felix was eating popcorn. Posey had paused her knitting.

But everything felt different. Tilted. Wrong.

"I knew it," Zara said triumphantly, pointing at the screen. "I told you she'd bring back Trevor—"

She stopped and turned to look at Ramona. Her hand was already moving to Ramona's shoulder before she seemed to consciously register something was wrong. "Ramona? What happened?"

"The convergence point is corrupted," Ramona said, dread pooling in her gut.

"How?" Zara's grip tightened, and suddenly her attention was completely off the TV, completely focused on Ramona.

"Wait, what?" Felix had muted the TV. "What's going on?"

"What does that mean?" Cammie asked.

"The fox…" Ramona's voice came out shaky. "He showed me. The convergence point where we did the ritual. It's…" She couldn't finish.

The fox sat in front of Ramona, watching her with those amber eyes. Waiting for her to understand. To *do something*.

"What *does* this mean?" Ramona repeated in a whisper. Her hands were shaking. She pressed them flat against her thighs, trying to stop the tremor.

Zara was quiet for a long moment. On the couch, Felix and Kashvi had both turned to look at them now. Posey's knitting needles clicked as she reached to set her project down on the table. Gerald cooed softly, concerned.

"It means," Zara said quietly, and there was something in her voice that Ramona had never heard before — something close to fear. "That we need to fix this. And soon."

"Or else what?"

Zara's hand slid from Ramona's shoulder to take her hand, interlacing their fingers. The tether pulsed between them — sharp, urgent.

"Or else the convergence point dies," Zara said. "Permanently."

"Explain?" Felix asked, setting down the popcorn bowl.

"Where we tried the severance ritual. It's corrupted. Demonic corruption. From..." Ramona glanced toward Zara.

"From my magic," Zara finished. "I stabilized Ramona's casting during the ritual. Used my demonic energy to keep her magic from cascading. It worked — the ritual didn't explode — but it left... something."

The room went very quiet. Her roommates exchanged looks.

"How bad?" Cammie asked.

"Bad," Ramona said. "It's spreading. What the fox showed me — the ground is black. The trees are dying. And it's growing outward from where we cast the ritual."

"Oh no," Posey breathed. Her hand had moved to her chest. "A convergence point is alive. It's a living thing. A very old, very sacred living thing. If it's corrupted—"

"We have to find a way to undo it," Zara said. "Before it spreads too far. Before the ancient oaks are affected."

"How long do we have?" Felix asked.

Ramona looked at the fox, who was still watching her with that patient, knowing gaze. She didn't know how she knew, but she could feel it — like the fox was pressing the answer into her mind through their connection. "The new moon?"

The fox made a small affirmative sound.

"The next new moon is in two weeks," Zara said.

"Thirteen days," Ramona corrected.

"If we're going to perform another ritual at that site — and we need to, because it's the only convergence point within reasonable distance — we have to cleanse it first."

"How do you cleanse demonic corruption?" Cammie asked quietly. Ramona paused for a moment, grateful that Cammie was always just going with the flow of her weird, magical roommates.

"There are rituals," Kashvi said, already pulling up her laptop. "Purification magic. Dissolution spells. But they're complicated. You need the right components, the right timing—"

"And we need to do it without making the corruption worse," Zara added. "If we try to cleanse it improperly, we could accelerate the spread."

"So we research," Ramona said. Her voice was steadier now. Determined. "We find out exactly how to cleanse demonic corruption from a convergence point. We do it right. And then…" She took a breath. "And then we try the severance again. Properly, this time."

"Without using my magic to stabilize yours," Zara said quietly.

"Right." Ramona looked at her hands. "Which means I need to figure out how to control my magic on my own. Or find another way to keep it stable during the ritual."

"The fox might help," Posey said softly. "Familiars ground magic. That's what they do. Even without a formal bond…" She looked at the fox. "He's already connected to you. He might be able to stabilize your casting."

The fox's tail swished once. Agreement? Possibility?

"We have a lot to figure out," Kashvi said, typing rapidly. "Cleansing ritual. Modified severance. Timing. Components." She looked up. "This is going to take all of us."

"I'll search Hell's archives for corruption cleansing protocols," Zara said. "We have procedures for this. Demons corrupt things all the time. There are established methods for undoing it."

"I'll look through the grimoires for dissolution spells," Ramona added. "Anything that might apply to sacred site purification."

"I'll ask the plants," Posey said. "They might know how to heal the convergence point. They're very good at healing."

"And I'll do some digging on the less… savory sites," Felix said. Gerald cooed in solemn agreement.

"I can help…" Cammie glanced around, looking helpless. "Does anyone need a coffee? Chocolate?"

"Yes to both," Felix and Kashvi said in unison, then glanced toward each other with a laugh.

Cammie stood, hurrying into the kitchen.

The fox made another sound — softer this time. Relieved, maybe. Like he'd done his part by showing them the problem and now trusted them to solve it.

"Thirteen days," Zara said quietly.

"Thirteen days," Ramona echoed.

The fox settled between them, warm and solid.

"We can do this," Zara said. Not a question. A statement of fact.

Ramona envisioned the corruption spreading through the convergence point. Overwhelm sat heavy against her chest, and she could barely take a deep breath.

Zara's thumb brushed over her knuckles, and she glanced back up to see Zara's expression gentle and focused.

"We can do this," Ramona agreed, and she almost believed it.

Felix unmuted the TV. "Okay. But first we're finishing this episode because Zara called it and I need to see if she's right about everything else, too." He waited until Cammie reappeared with a bag of chocolate truffles from her café before hitting play.

"I am," Zara said, her attention already shifting back to the screen, her hand still in Ramona's.

"I'll ask the plants," Loper said. "They might know how to heal the [illegible] point. They're very good at healing."

"And I'll do some digging on the [illegible]," Lori said. [illegible] nodded in agreement.

[illegible] glanced around, looking [illegible] [illegible]."

[illegible] Carly said. [illegible] glanced toward [illegible] with a laugh.

[illegible] stood [illegible] from the [illegible].

The fox made another sound [illegible] [illegible] his [illegible] [illegible] back to [illegible] it.

"[illegible] day," Zara said quietly.

"[illegible] day," Ramon echoed.

[illegible] between them [illegible].

[illegible] Zara and [illegible].

Ramon [illegible] through [illegible] [illegible] against the [illegible] [illegible] breath.

[illegible] his [illegible] and [illegible] back [illegible] and [illegible].

[illegible]," Ramon [illegible] behind [illegible] [illegible] first [illegible] [illegible] Zara [illegible] about [illegible] thing [illegible] appeared [illegible] [illegible].

[illegible] Ramon.

CHAPTER TWENTY-THREE

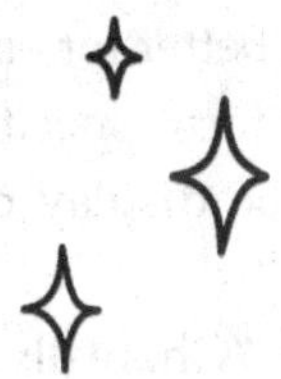

MARCUS HAD LEFT ON WEDNESDAY MORNING — SOME SPIRITUAL emergency that required his immediate attention — and wouldn't be back until Friday evening. Which meant Ramona was running Mystic Moon solo for two days, and her days off shifted to Saturday and Sunday.

Normally, this would have filled her with low-grade dread. Two days of sole responsibility, of making decisions, of being the only person between the shop and complete chaos.

But Zara had volunteered to help.

"I don't have anything else to do," she'd said that morning over coffee, like it was obvious. "And I've already memorized your inventory system."

"You memorized our inventory system?"

"It was poorly organized, and I optimized it." Zara had taken a sip of coffee, completely unbothered. "You'll notice the romance section is now alphabetized by subgenre and then by author."

"When did you—"

"Last week. You were restocking the crystals."

Now it was Thursday afternoon, and Ramona was behind the counter with her laptop open, supposedly doing work for Marcus but actually deep in research about convergence point cleansing. Zara was efficiently helping customers with the kind of competence that suggested she'd been working retail for years instead of weeks.

"The amethyst or the rose quartz?" a customer was asking, holding up two crystals.

"What's your intention?" Zara asked.

"Um. Clarity? Focus?"

"Amethyst. Rose quartz is better for emotional work." Zara paused. "Though if you're looking for focus specifically, fluorite would be more effective. We have some in the display case, including this gorgeous wand shape."

The customer's eyes lit up. "Oh, really?"

Five minutes later, she left with fluorite, a book on crystal meditation, and a manifestation journal. Zara rang her up with the efficiency of someone who'd spent three hundred years optimizing processes.

Ramona barely noticed. She was scrolling through yet another forum post about sacred site purification, growing increasingly frustrated.

To cleanse a convergence point, create a salt barrier around the perimeter and burn white sage while speaking words of intention…

Useless. She'd read a dozen variations of this same advice. Salt barriers. Sage smoke. Speaking intentions into the void. Nothing about demonic corruption specifically. Nothing about what happened when Hell magic infected a sacred space and started spreading like rot through living wood.

She opened another tab in Wandle, the search engine specifically for witches. She typed in: *demonic corruption sacred sites medieval texts*

More useless results. Academic papers about historical accounts of corruption, but no actual methodology. Forum posts talking about "negative energy" like it was something you could fix with good vibes and crystals.

"Any luck?" Zara appeared beside her, having dispatched the customer.

"No. Everything I'm finding is surface-level garbage." Ramona gestured at her screen. "Look at this. 'Cleanse the space with sage and positive intentions.' That's not going to fix demonic corruption.

That's not going to stop whatever's happening at the convergence point."

"What about the grimoires?" Zara nodded toward the back room, where Marcus kept his collection of "rare" magical texts that were mostly Victorian-era fakes.

"Already checked. Nothing useful." Ramona pulled up her notes — a document she'd been compiling all morning between customers. "I found three references to convergence point purification, but they're all from the same source text that I can't find. And the modern interpretations are…" She scrolled through. "Watered down. Simplified. Like someone took actual magical knowledge and dumbed it down for general consumption."

"Which is exactly what Marcus does with this shop," Zara observed.

"Yeah." Ramona closed that tab, opened another. "What about Hell's databases? You said you'd search?"

"I did. All morning, between helping customers and reorganizing the herb section." Zara pulled out her HellBerry, scrolled through her notes. "There are references to corruption incidents. Procedures for containment. Guidelines for damage control."

"But?"

"But the actual cleansing rituals are classified." Zara's expression was frustrated. "I don't have clearance. Apparently, you need to be at least a Level 8 Administrator to access purification protocols, and I'm —" She stopped.

"You're what?"

"Level 6. *Was* Level 6." Zara's voice went flat. "Before the demotion, which means I'll probably go down to 5, or maybe even 4."

Ramona slumped back in her chair. "So, we're stuck. We know the convergence point is corrupted, we know it's spreading, we have two weeks — maybe less — to fix it, and we have absolutely no idea how."

The door chimed. Another customer. Zara moved to help them — an older woman looking for a book on moon phases — while Ramona stared at her useless research notes.

Everything she'd found referenced the same handful of original texts. And those texts were either lost, destroyed, or—

Or locked away in academic archives.

Ramona pulled up a new search in Wandle. *Liber Purgationis Maleficae historical copies North America*

Three results. Two on the other side of the country, and... of course. Thornwood Academy.

Of course.

Of course the definitive text on purification magic was in Thornwood's restricted archives. The archives she couldn't access anymore. The archives that required special authorization from inner circle coven or academy members.

Like her mother.

"Fuck," Ramona muttered.

"Problem?" Zara had finished with the customer and was walking back toward the counter.

"I found something." Ramona turned her laptop toward Zara. "It's in a fifteenth-century grimoire called *Liber Purgationis Maleficae.* Multiple scholars cite it as the definitive source on demonic corruption cleansing."

"Where is it?"

"Three known copies in North America. Vexford has one, but it's damaged — missing the critical sections. Found another, but it's on loan to a private collector until next year." Ramona paused. "And Thornwood has the complete, intact copy."

"That's great news," Zara said. "How do we get it?"

"It's in the restricted archives."

They looked at each other. Through the tether, Ramona felt Zara's mind already working through possibilities, calculating options, running scenarios.

"We'll figure something out," Zara said finally.

"How? I can't access those archives. I was expelled."

She pulled out her HellBerry again, started typing. "I'm going to keep searching. There has to be something in Hell's public databases about corruption protocols. Maybe not the classified rituals, but methodology, theory, something we can work with."

"And I'll keep looking for alternative texts," Ramona said, turning back to her laptop. "Maybe there's something else. A different grimoire, a modern interpretation that actually works, something."

They worked in parallel for the next hour. Customers came and went — Ramona handled most of them with efficient kindness, suggesting manifestation journals and pocket-size moon phase calendars. Zara even stepped in to find a box of red candles from the back room. For a moment, Ramona let herself fantasize that this was just a normal day without the black cloud of demonic corruption hanging over their heads.

Between customers, they both searched.

Ramona found more references to the *Liber Purgationis Maleficae*. All useless. All citing the same inaccessible text.

"This is pointless," she said finally, closing her laptop with more force than necessary. "Every single source I find just leads back to that grimoire. And we can't access it."

"Not legally," Zara corrected.

"Not ever."

Zara was quiet for a moment. Then: "What if we did?"

"Did what?"

"Break into Thornwood. Get the grimoire. Or at least photograph the relevant sections." Zara's voice was calm, like she was suggesting they pick up groceries. "It's not impossible."

"I'd rather set myself on fire."

Zara leveled her with a long look.

Ramona stared at her. "You're not serious."

"Very serious, Mortal." Zara's expression was focused. "We need that information. It exists. It's accessible, just not to you specifically. So we find a way around that restriction."

"We find another way. Any way that doesn't involve Thornwood."

"We have to do what's necessary to fix a problem we created." Zara pulled up a chair, sitting beside Ramona. "Look, we don't have to decide anything right now. But we should at least consider it as an option. Talk to the others. See if Kashvi has any other leads. But if this is the only way—"

"*No*," Ramona interrupted. She didn't want to think about it. Didn't want to imagine walking back into Thornwood, into the place that had expelled her, stealing from their archives like some kind of—

Like someone who was desperate enough to do whatever it took.

No. They were not there yet.

"Well," Zara said. She stood, stretched. "Now. While we're on the subject of things you should think about..." She gestured at Ramona's laptop. "Pull up a new document."

"Why?"

"Because I want you to write something down."

"What?"

"Everything you'd do if you had your own shop. Hypothetically. If money and credibility weren't obstacles."

"Zara—"

"Humor me. You've been researching convergence points all day. You need a break. And I'm curious." Zara crossed her arms. "What would you do with a place like this if it were actually yours?"

Ramona looked at Mystic Moon — at the sanitized version of magic Marcus had created, at the customers who came in looking for aesthetic experiences instead of actual practice, at everything this place could be but wasn't.

"I'd make it for witches," she said quietly. "Actual witches. Not non-mages playing at magic."

"What would that look like?"

And just like that, Ramona was talking. About the lending library she'd always wanted to create. About translation services for practitioners who couldn't read the original texts. About workshops on linguistic theory in spellwork, about hosting visiting scholars, about creating actual community space for witches who didn't have coven connections or Thornwood access.

"There's no space for witches anymore," Ramona said. "Not real space. Thornwood is elitist. The apothecaries are intimidating and few and far between. The online shops can scam you easily. The covens are insular. If you're not part of the right families, if you don't have the right connections, you're just... alone."

"So you'd create that space," Zara said.

"I'd try." The words were coming faster now. "It'd be more community focused than The Grimalkin, but the same welcoming feeling, you know?" She stopped, face heating. "This is stupid. It's not like I could actually—"

"Why not?"

"Because I don't have money. Or credibility. Or—" Ramona gestured at herself. "I'm the witch who got expelled from Thornwood for nearly killing the High Priestess. Who's going to trust me to run a magical community space?"

"People who understand," Zara said. "People who need what you're offering. People who are also tired of elitist magical institutions that gatekeep knowledge."

"It doesn't matter anyway," Ramona said. "This isn't my shop. And it never will be."

"Write it down anyway." Zara's voice was gentle but firm.

"What?"

"Everything you just said. The lending library, the translation services, the workshops. Write it all down."

"Why?"

"Because I want to see it. On paper. Concrete." Zara's hand found hers under the counter. "Not just an idea you're dismissing before you've even thought it through."

Ramona stared at her. "Zara—"

"Please, Mortal." There was something in Zara's voice that made it impossible to refuse. "Just write it down. What you'd do if you had your own shop. If money and credibility weren't obstacles. If you could build exactly what you wanted."

Ramona looked at the laptop. At Zara's hand warm on hers. At the quiet hope in Zara's expression that made something in her chest ache.

"Okay," she said quietly. "Okay."

She opened a new document. Stared at it for a long moment.

An hour later, Ramona had three pages.

Three pages of ideas she'd been carrying for two years without letting herself acknowledge them. She even had ideas about the physical space — the layout, the lighting, the way books would be organized not by marketing categories but by magical tradition and historical period. A proper workspace in the back for translation projects. A small classroom area for workshops.

It was detailed. Specific. Real in a way that made her chest tight.

"Can I see?" Zara asked during a lull between customers.

Ramona turned the laptop toward her, suddenly self-conscious. "It's just… thoughts. Nothing serious."

Zara read in silence. Her expression was impossible to read — that corporate focus she got when analyzing data, running numbers, optimizing systems.

"This is good," Zara said finally. "Really good."

"It's a fantasy."

"It's the start of a business plan." Zara pulled the laptop closer, scrolling through. "Or it could be. You have services, target demographics, space requirements. You're missing financials — startup costs, projected revenue, operating expenses — but the foundation is here."

"I'm not… I'm not actually going to do this." A small part of her panicked at the realness of what Zara was talking about, the concreteness of funding and operating this venture.

"Why not?"

"Because…" Ramona gestured helplessly. "Because I don't have collateral for a business loan. Because I have terrible credit. Because no bank is going to lend to someone with my history."

"You don't know that."

"Yes, I do."

Zara was quiet for a moment, still reading. Then she pulled out her HellBerry, started typing.

"What are you doing?" Ramona asked.

"Making notes." Zara's fingers flew across the screen. "Revenue projections. Cost analysis. Market research data — Fernwick's magical community is underserved, which means there's demand. You'd need to quantify that, but preliminary numbers suggest—" She kept typing. "Startup costs would be significant. Commercial space, inventory, renovation if needed. But if you structured it correctly, phased the expansion, kept overhead low initially—"

"Zara."

"—the translation services could provide steady income while you build the community space aspect. Workshops would be supplemental at first, but as reputation builds—"

"Zara." Ramona reached out, putting her hand over Zara's to stop her typing. "What are you doing?"

Zara looked up. Her expression was serious. Intense. "Building you a business proposal. So when you're ready — *when* you're ready, don't look at me like that, Mortal — you'll have something to present to a lender."

Ramona's throat was tight. "I'm not going to be ready."

"You don't know that." Zara's hand turned under hers, interlacing their fingers. "A year ago, you thought you'd never do magic again. Two weeks ago, you thought the severance ritual would work and I'd go back to Hell. Last week, you let Posey put a possibly carnivorous fern in your room." She squeezed Ramona's hand. "Things change. You change. And when you're ready, I want you to have this. A real plan. Numbers that work. Something you can actually use."

"Why?" Ramona's voice came out barely above a whisper.

"Because after I'm… you know. Well, you deserve to have options." Zara said it simply. Like it was obvious. Like Ramona's worth wasn't something that needed to be proven or earned. "Because you're brilliant and you shouldn't be wasting that brilliance selling crystals to people who think Mercury is in retrograde. Because—" She stopped. Started again. "Because I want you to have a future that's bigger than just surviving."

Ramona felt tears prick at her eyes. "No one's ever—" She had to stop, swallow. "No one's ever taken me so seriously before."

"Then everyone else is a fool." Zara's voice was firm. "Now. Tell me more about your target demographics. Who exactly are you serving with this space?"

They spent the next hour going through details. Zara asked questions — sharp, specific, the kind of questions someone who'd spent centuries managing Hell's bureaucracy would know to ask. Ramona answered, and with each answer, the fantasy on the screen became a little more real.

Revenue projections. Expense categories. Competitive analysis. Market positioning.

A business plan.

An actual, viable business plan for something Ramona had thought would never be more than a daydream.

"I'm sending this to you," Zara said finally, typing on her HellBerry. "As a draft. You can add to it, revise it, completely rewrite it. Or you can just save it and never look at it again. But at least you'll have it."

Ramona's phone buzzed. She opened the email, scanned the document Zara had created.

It was professional. Detailed. The kind of thing you could actually show to a bank. The kind of thing that said *this person knows what they're doing* instead of *this person is desperate and broke and has no idea what they want.*

"I don't know what to say," Ramona whispered.

"You don't have to say anything." Zara stood, checking the time. "We should close up soon. And tonight—" She paused. "Tonight we should talk to the others. About Thornwood. About whether breaking into the restricted archives is actually something we're willing to do."

"We are definitely not doing that."

"I think we need that grimoire. And I think waiting for someone to give us permission to access it isn't an option." Zara's expression was serious. "But it's not just my decision. We all need to be on board."

Ramona looked at her laptop — at the business plan on one window, the useless research notes on the other. Two impossible things. Two futures that felt equally unreachable.

But sitting there in Mystic Moon, watching Zara check inventory with patient competence, thinking about convergence points that needed cleansing and grimoires that needed stealing and shops that could be something more—

Maybe impossible wasn't the same as unreachable.

"Let's talk to them," Ramona said. "Tonight. See what Kashvi found. Figure out if this is actually something we can do."

"Good." Zara started turning off lights, the practiced movements of someone who'd been working here long enough to know the closing routine. "And Ramona?"

"Yeah?"

"Keep thinking. Keep planning. Keep letting yourself *want* something for your future." Zara's smile was small but genuine. Ramona could feel a mix of pride and melancholy through the tether, like Zara believed in her but knew she'd never see the finished store. Like she wanted Ramona to pursue this future, no matter what happened with the tether severance. "Promise me."

"I promise," Ramona whispered around the ball of emotion lodging in her throat.

CHAPTER TWENTY-FOUR

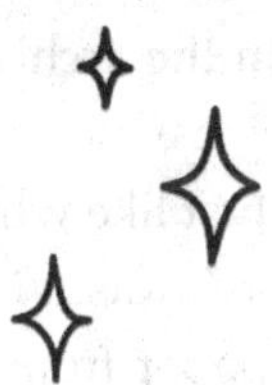

THE GRIMALKIN WAS QUIETER THAN USUAL FOR A THURSDAY EVENING, which meant the hedge witch argument in the corner had only three participants instead of the usual five, and Parliamentarian was asleep on the bar rather than actively soliciting tribute. Odette moved behind the counter with her customary unhurried efficiency, setting drinks down in front of people who hadn't quite finished deciding what they wanted yet.

Kashvi had claimed their usual table — the one near the back where the candlelight was good enough to read by but dim enough that nobody could see your screen from across the room. Her laptop was open, two empty glasses pushed to one side, a third half finished. She'd clearly been here a while.

Ramona and Zara slid into their seats. Odette appeared, set something in front of each of them without comment, and disappeared. The jukebox was doing something atmospheric in the corner, the kind of music that suggested the evening was about to get complicated.

"Good news and bad news," Kashvi announced, turning her laptop to face them.

"Good news first," Ramona said.

"I found three different texts, all from the thirteenth century, all using variations of the same base methodology, that might help us with a combination of a cleansing and a severance."

"And the bad news?"

Kashvi's expression was apologetic. "They're all in Thornwood's restricted collection. I can see the citations. I can see descriptions of the rituals. But the actual texts — the grimoires with the full incantations and procedures — those are in the archives. Behind wards. Accessible only to authorized personnel."

Ramona's stomach sank. "Just like what I found."

"But there's something else." Kashvi pulled up a scholarly article, tilting the screen. "I found a paper from the 1890s about convergence point restoration. The author theorizes that cleansing rituals and severance rituals share fundamental structural similarities — they're both about dissolution, separation, breaking unwanted bonds."

Ramona leaned forward, scanning the text. "So?"

"So if we can access the cleansing ritual texts, we might also find information that helps us modify the severance ritual." Kashvi pulled up another document. "Look at this citation. *Liber Purgationis Maleficae* doesn't just cover demonic corruption cleansing. It has an entire section on magical severance. Specifically, how to separate demonic energy from sacred spaces without destabilizing either one."

Zara had gone very still beside Ramona. "That's — that could work. If we understand how to separate my demonic signature from the convergence point without destroying it, we could apply the same principles to separating the tether without—"

"Without it backfiring," Ramona finished. "Without any wild magic cascading. Without needing Hell's bureaucracy to process the unbinding."

"Exactly." Kashvi looked between them. "The ritual you tried before failed because you were treating the tether like something that could just be cut. But what if it needs to be cleansed? Dissolved gradually, methodically, using the same principles as convergence point purification?"

"That makes sense," Zara said slowly. "Demonic bindings aren't just magical contracts. They're energy signatures woven together. You can't just sever them — you have to unweave them. Carefully."

"Like untangling a knot instead of cutting the rope," Ramona added.

"Right." Kashvi scrolled through her notes. "But to understand the full methodology, to get the actual incantations and ritual structure, we need the grimoire. The complete text. Not just academic references to it."

She looked at Ramona. The look was deliberate. Pointed.

Ramona felt sick.

"I'm not going back there." Her voice came out sharper than intended, too loud for the corner of a bar. Parliamentarian opened one eye from his spot on the counter. "I can't. If I show up at Thornwood—"

"We don't have a choice," Kashvi said, quieter now, leaning in. "I overheard some witches talking here last night. We're not the only ones who know about the corruption. And if they know, the Magical Council knows. We need those texts. Soon. And they're in a place you used to have access to."

"'Used to' being the operative phrase."

"So we figure out how to get access again." Zara had shifted beside Ramona, a solid presence at her shoulder. "We have eleven days. That's enough time to plan."

Ramona looked between the two of them. "That's insane even to think about. The wards alone—"

"Are designed to keep out unauthorized individuals," Zara finished. "Which means they're designed to let in authorized ones. We just need to understand the access protocols."

"I don't have access anymore."

"But you know someone who does." Zara's voice was calm, logical, the same tone she used when reorganizing a shop display or building a case for something Ramona wasn't going to like. "You know the building. You know the security measures. You know who has access and when."

Ramona stared at her. "What are you suggesting?"

"Your mother." Zara said it simply, as if suggesting they pick up milk on the way home. "She's in the Thornwood Coven's inner circle. She has access to the archives. She has a key."

The table went quiet. Even the jukebox seemed to pause for a half second before sliding into something new.

"I'm not asking my mother for help." Ramona's voice went flat. "Did you miss the part where she just spent an entire dinner reminding me what a disappointment I am?"

"I didn't miss it." Zara's expression was steady. "But she's also the most practical path to what we need. Access keys work on all the wards. If we had hers—"

"We're not stealing from my mother."

"Why not?" Zara tilted her head. "Taking her access key for a few hours seems like minimal recompense. I would wager she hardly even uses it."

"That's not—" Ramona stopped. Started again. "Are you doing your demon temptation thing on me?"

Zara's mouth quirked up in the tiniest of grins.

Across the table, Kashvi suddenly became very interested in her drink.

"You could ask," Kashvi suggested carefully. "Explain that you need access to the archives for research. She doesn't have to know what you're researching."

"She'll ask questions. She'll want to know why. And then—" Ramona shook her head. "She'll either say no or she'll tell the whole coven that I'm trying to get back into Thornwood, and then everyone will know, and—"

"Then we take it without asking," Zara said. "When's the next time you'll see her?"

"I don't—" Ramona stopped. "Ostara. Spring equinox. But that's the day after the new moon."

"Then that's too far away." Zara's voice was firm. "The corruption is spreading now. We need to move faster than that."

"Then what do you suggest?"

"Breakfast." Zara said it like it was obvious. "This weekend. We invite ourselves over for a casual visit."

Ramona stared at her. The candlelight made Zara look unreasonably composed for someone proposing a felony in a bar on a Thursday. "You want to voluntarily subject yourself to another meal at my mother's house."

"I want to acquire the access key we need," Zara corrected. "And expedite our timeline. Waiting gives the corruption more time to spread. Better to handle it now."

"And what — you distract her while I steal from her study?"

Zara blinked. "Pretty much."

"You really are demonic." Ramona's voice was flat. "You love watching people suffer."

"I don't love watching you suffer." Zara's expression shifted — something warmer, more mischievous, the look that meant she was about to say something Ramona wasn't going to be able to respond to in public. "Though I do enjoy certain other activities you've thought about back in that bedroom—"

Ramona's face went hot. "Zara—"

"Remember that dream you had?" Zara's voice had dropped lower, intimate, completely unconcerned with the fact that they were in a bar. "The one where I bent you over that little desk with all your old trophies above us—"

"Zara!"

Kashvi had started coughing with aggressive pointedness. The hedge witches in the corner glanced over briefly and then returned to their argument, unbothered, because this was The Grimalkin and people minded their own business.

"I'm just saying," Zara continued, completely unruffled by Ramona's mortification, "there are perks to going back there. We grab the key, we make some dreams come true—"

"We are not—" Ramona looked around wildly. "Kashvi is right here."

"I'm not listening," Kashvi announced loudly, typing aggressively on a laptop that wasn't even open to anything relevant. "I hear nothing. I am a professional researcher focused entirely on archive security protocols."

"See?" Zara's smile was absolutely wicked. "No one's listening."

Ramona smacked Zara's shoulder, her cheeks still burning. Somewhere behind the bar, Parliamentarian opened one eye, deemed the situation beneath him, and went back to sleep. "You're actually evil."

Zara's voice went soft. Affectionate. The shift that still caught Ramona off guard every time. "And you know I'm right. About breakfast, at least. The sooner we get the key, the sooner we can fix this."

Ramona wanted to argue. Wanted to say absolutely not, that she'd rather wait for Ostara than voluntarily return to her mother's house for another round of passive-aggressive commentary and disappointed sighs.

But Zara was right. The corruption was spreading. Every day they waited was another day the convergence point died. And if the *Liber Purgationis Maleficae* really did contain what Kashvi thought it did…

They needed it. Both rituals. Convergence point cleansing and a modified severance approach.

"Fine," Ramona said. "We'll go to breakfast. This weekend."

"Deal." Zara held out her hand for Ramona's phone with the calm confidence of someone who already knew the answer. Ramona handed it over. She wasn't sure when she'd started doing that.

Zara scrolled, found the contact, started typing. "I'll tell her we'd like to visit. That we have something to discuss."

"She's going to think we're getting married."

"Let her think whatever she wants." Zara was already composing the message with the focused efficiency she brought to everything she decided was happening. "As long as she invites us over."

"This is a terrible idea."

"Most of our ideas are terrible," Zara replied. "But they usually work out."

"Name one time."

"The severance ritual that created this whole mess technically worked. We didn't die. The tether is still intact." Zara looked up, her expression softening. "And I got to stay with you. I'd call that a success."

Ramona's chest felt too full for a Thursday night in a bar. "You're ridiculous."

"I'm strategic." Ramona's phone buzzed on the table between

them. Zara glanced at it, smiled — the real one, the one that was still new enough to be startling. "Your mother says Saturday morning works. Breakfast at nine. She's delighted we want to visit."

"She's already planning the wedding," Ramona muttered.

"Then we'll have to disappoint her." Zara slid the phone back across the table. "We're just there for breakfast and larceny."

"Grand larceny," Kashvi corrected, still pointedly not looking at either of them. "Stealing an enchanted access key from a senior coven member is definitely grand larceny."

"Temporary requisition," Zara amended.

"Felony," Kashvi countered.

"This is really terrible," Ramona said. But she was leaning into Zara now, into the warmth of her, letting herself be held in the small sideways way that had become ordinary somewhere in the last few weeks without her noticing.

Odette appeared, replaced all three of their glasses without being asked, and disappeared again.

"Saturday morning," Zara murmured against Ramona's hair. "Breakfast with your mother. Acquire the key. Then we meet the others at the convergence point to confirm what the fox showed you."

"And then we plan the actual Thornwood break-in," Kashvi added. "Which will require significantly more preparation than just stealing a key."

"One felony at a time," Ramona said weakly. "My mom will be busy with the Ostara Gala for the next couple weeks and probably won't notice it missing."

Zara's laugh was warm against her temple. Ramona felt a pulse of affection through the tether. "That's my girl."

The jukebox shifted into something that sounded almost celebratory, which felt pointed. The hedge witches had resolved their argument or abandoned it — either way, the corner had gone quiet. Parliamentarian had relocated to the end of the bar closest to their table, which from him was practically an endorsement.

Saturday was coming. The Thornwood grimoire heist was coming. And somewhere underneath all of it, the growing, terrifying, completely inconvenient suspicion that she was in love with a demon and had absolutely no idea what to do about it.

Ramona finished her drink.

"Another round?" Kashvi asked.

"Obviously," said Ramona and Zara at the same time.

Odette was already there.

CHAPTER TWENTY-FIVE

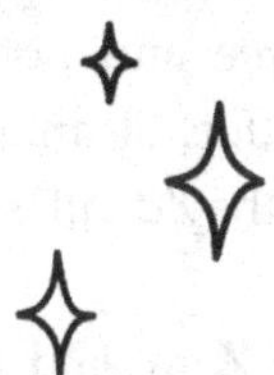

THE MANOR LOOKED DIFFERENT IN MORNING LIGHT — SOFTER SOMEHOW, less imposing than it had been during Imbolc. Or maybe Ramona was different. Maybe walking into this house with Zara's hand in hers and a plan in her pocket changed everything.

Eleanor opened the door herself, which was unusual. No formal greeting in the entrance hall, no carefully orchestrated arrival. Just Eleanor in a casual silk blouse and slacks, her hair pulled back simply, looking almost… normal.

"Ramona. Zara. Come in." Eleanor stepped aside, gesturing them into the foyer. "Thank you for coming."

"Thank you for having us," Zara said smoothly.

"Well, I was pleased to receive your message." Eleanor led them through to the breakfast room — smaller than the formal dining room, with windows overlooking the garden. It felt like centuries since Ramona had grown up here, afraid to touch anything in her own home. She'd spent most of her time in her room studying, sitting in the garden, or outside of the main grounds, exploring the forests. She'd never felt like this home was *hers* in any way, and it helped feeling detached now, knowing what she had to do. The betrayal of stealing from her own mother… She involuntarily shuddered just thinking about it, and Zara gave her a reassuring touch on the small of her back.

"Where's Dad?" Ramona asked.

"Your father is away at a chess tournament — just spectating, he's not competing at this one — so it's just us this morning."

"That's fine," Ramona managed. The house felt even larger without Thomas's silent presence. Just the three of them. Intimate. Dangerous.

The table was set for three and notably casual — simple place settings, fresh scones, fruit, coffee. Eleanor poured without ceremony.

"So," Eleanor said once they'd all settled. "What prompted the visit?"

"We wanted to see you," Zara said before Ramona could speak. "After Imbolc, I thought it would be nice to check in. I didn't want there to be any lingering… negativity."

"I see." Eleanor added cream to her coffee with precise movements. "Well, I'm glad you came."

That was it? No interrogation about their motives, no pointed questions. Just… acceptance?

Ramona picked up her coffee, trying to process this slightly less sharp version of her mother.

"How is work?" Eleanor asked.

"It's good. Zara's consultancy has been a tremendous help," Ramona said.

"That sounds promising." Eleanor took a sip of coffee. "You'd be good at that if you'd only apply yourself."

There it was — the little barb, the qualification. But softer than usual. The claws clipped, though not quite retracted.

They ate in relative peace. The conversation stayed surface level — Zara's observations about Fernwick, updates about Iris's girls, Eleanor's mention of coven politics.

It was almost normal. Almost pleasant. Which made what Ramona was about to do feel infinitely worse.

"Your garden must be waking up," Zara said as Eleanor refilled their coffee. "With the early spring we've been having."

Eleanor paused, and something in her expression shifted. Brightened, just slightly. "Oh, yes. The crocuses are already blooming, and I have snowdrops by the greenhouse. The hellebores have been stunning this year. I planted new varieties last fall."

"I'd love to see them, if you'll show me," Zara said, and her interest seemed genuine. "I don't know much about gardening, but I'm trying to learn. Posey — one of Ramona's roommates — has been teaching me about plants."

"Would you like a quick tour?" Eleanor was already standing, more animated than Ramona had seen her all morning. "The greenhouse is heated, so I've been starting some summer plants already."

"I'd love that," Zara said. She glanced at Ramona. "Do you want to come?"

This was the opening. The moment they'd planned for.

"Actually, I think I left a book in my room last time I was here," Ramona said, trying to sound casual. "I'll just run up and grab it?"

"Of course," Eleanor said, clearly distracted by the prospect of showing off her garden. "Take your time."

They split up — Eleanor and Zara heading toward the back of the house, Ramona climbing the familiar stairs to the second floor.

Her heart was hammering. This was theft. This was—

Necessary. She thought of the corrupted convergence point, the purification of demonic entanglements, the way her roommates had spent hours over the past two and a half weeks helping her.

She passed her childhood bedroom and kept walking to her mother's study, the tether pulling tight with every foot they were apart. By the pressure in her chest, she guessed maybe there was fifty feet between them.

The door was closed but not locked. Ramona slipped inside. She could feel the Greenbriar wards so strongly in this room, accepting her as one of their own but letting her know that they knew she wasn't Eleanor.

The study *was* distinctly Eleanor's — elegant pale wood furniture, perfectly organized bookshelves, a crystal vase on the windowsill. And the desk. The antique writing desk always covered in neat stacks of coven paperwork.

If the access key was anywhere, it would be here.

The surface was immaculate. Files in a holder, fountain pen in its stand, a small dish of paper clips. The top drawer: stationery, stamps, nothing interesting.

The second drawer was locked.

Ramona pulled a barrette from her hair, which she'd worn deliberately, just in case. Bent it. Started working on the lock.

This was absurd. She was a witch, not a burglar. She didn't know how to pick locks—

The lock clicked open.

Ramona stared. Had she just burgled her first lock? A sense of pride and accomplishment washed over her, and she hoped Zara could feel the sensation through the tether. Instead, she felt a sense of dread from Zara.

No time to think about that. She tugged the drawer open.

Inside: organized files, a leather planner, and a velvet case. She opened it.

There were two keys, though both were enchanted. She could feel the magic thrumming. One was larger and more ornate and warm to her touch. She guessed it was probably for the Greenbriar wards. The other was smaller, simpler, with the Thornwood crest.

That was it.

Ramona reached for it. The moment her fingers closed around it, she felt the enchantment respond, testing her magical signature.

Then it settled. Accepted her.

Because she used to be authorized or because her mother's blood ran in her veins, she didn't know.

She slipped it into her pocket, closed everything, locked the drawer again with shaking hands.

Done. Not too bad.

She was halfway to the door when she heard voices downstairs. Not calm voices. Raised voices. She froze, straining to hear.

"…completely inappropriate—" That was her mother, sharp and angry.

"I'm simply making an observation—" Zara's voice, controlled but edged.

"You call that an observation? It was distinctly an accusation," her mother snapped.

The voices were getting louder. Were they coming up the stairs? Ramona took a step back from the door, holding her breath.

"Eleanor—"

"That's Mrs. Greenbriar to you—"

The study door opened.

Ramona gasped, stumbling backward. The stolen key burned in her pocket.

Eleanor stopped in the doorway, face flushed. Behind her, Zara's expression was carefully neutral, jaw tight.

"Ramona?" Eleanor's voice was strained. "What are you doing in here?"

Through the tether: Zara's sharp alarm. And anger, though not directed at Ramona, but lingering from outside.

Ramona's mind raced. She needed something believable to excuse her being in here.

"I was looking for blessed salt," Ramona said smoothly. "Iris mentioned you keep some in here for quick warding. We had an incident at the apartment. I wanted to be prepared."

Eleanor's expression shifted — anger to concern. "What kind of incident?"

"Some kind of spirit. Attached to an artifact Kashvi was studying." Ramona kept her voice steady, pulling the lie from somewhere deep down. "It's been handled, but it made me realize we should have basic protective materials on hand."

"You should have warded that apartment when you moved in," Eleanor said, moving into the room with that purposeful stride that meant a lecture was coming. "This is exactly what I've been saying for years. You don't plan ahead. You wait until something goes wrong and then scramble to fix it."

"I know, I just—"

"Always reactive instead of proactive." Eleanor was already at the cabinet, pulling out a jar of blessed salt labeled *Sacred Ground*. "Here. Take this. Though frankly, if you've already had one incident, you should be doing a full cleansing."

She pressed the jar into Ramona's hands with more force than necessary.

"Maybe try thinking ahead occasionally," Eleanor added, voice sharp. "Instead of waiting until you're in crisis mode. As always."

Ramona took the jar, face burning.

"Mrs. Greenbriar," Zara said, voice carefully even. "I hardly think that is necessary, given our… very recent conversation." Ramona could feel Zara's distinct disgust through the tether.

Eleanor turned to Zara, something complicated crossing her face.

"We should go," Zara continued. "We don't want to impose upon your day."

"Of course." Eleanor stepped back, still clearly tense from whatever they'd argued about.

They moved through the house in silence. At the door, Eleanor paused. "Be careful," she said. Nothing more.

Ramona tried not to look at her mother like she'd grown another head, though she was pretty sure she was unsuccessful in that.

They walked to the car. Got in. Ramona started the engine, glancing sideways toward Zara, who was staring straight ahead with tension in her jaw.

Neither spoke until they'd turned onto the main road.

"What happened?" Ramona asked. "Are you okay?"

Zara's hands tightened in her lap. "I'll explain it later. I was mostly trying to get her to raise her voice so you'd know we were coming upstairs."

"Is everything okay?"

"We'll talk about it later." Zara glanced at her, but her dark eyes were softening already. "Did you get it?"

Ramona pulled the key from her pocket.

"Got it."

Zara's smile was fierce. "Good. The others should already be at the convergence point. Let's go confirm what the fox showed you, then we can plan the actual break-in."

Ramona laid the key in her lap as she drove, felt the enchantment thrumming. "I just lied to my mother's face and stole from her," she said quietly.

"How does that feel?" Zara asked.

Ramona thought about it. About Eleanor's lecture, about the

blessed salt pressed into her hands like proof of inadequacy, about taking something back that had been kept from her.

"Not as bad as I thought," Ramona said. "Maybe a life of crime was my calling all along, and I just needed a little demonic influence to see my true path."

Zara laughed, lifting Ramona's hand to kiss her knuckles. "Let's not get ahead of ourselves, okay? One demonic temptation at a time."

CHAPTER TWENTY-SIX

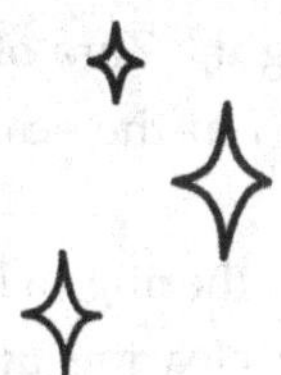

THE PARKING LOT OF THE COMMUNITY PARK WAS MOSTLY EMPTY WHEN THEY arrived. Her car let out a sputter of protest as she pulled into one of the open spots near Felix's car, parked at the trailhead.

Ramona patted her pocket where Eleanor's key sat, still warm with enchantment. They'd done it. Stolen from her mother's study right under her nose.

Now they just had to confirm what the fox had shown them.

Felix was leaning against his car, Gerald perched on his shoulder, laptop bag in hand. Kashvi stood beside him with sparks already shooting from her fingertips. Posey's tiny electric car pulled in behind them, Cammie emerging from the passenger side.

"You got it?" Felix asked as they approached.

Ramona pulled out the key. The Thornwood seal gleamed in the late morning light.

"We got it," Zara confirmed.

"Good." Kashvi gestured toward the trail. "Because you need to see this. The corruption is worse than what the fox showed you."

They hiked into the woods with a sense of urgency. The fox trotted ahead of Ramona, tail low and agitated. The trail wasn't marked, but

Ramona knew it from the night of the ritual. She could feel the pulse of the convergence point, but it felt wrong. Sickly.

"You okay?" Zara asked quietly, falling into step beside her.

Through the tether, Ramona felt Zara's attention — warm, present, but also tense. Worried.

"Just thinking," Ramona said, watching the fox's ears flick nervously. "About the last time we were here."

"It's less ominous in daylight," Zara offered.

"Oh, what was that, Ms. 'I'm the scariest thing in these woods'?" Ramona joked.

Zara shrugged, not even bothering to look ashamed.

The trail opened into the clearing after five minutes of walking. Ramona stopped at the edge.

The convergence point looked smaller in daylight than it had that night. An open clearing in the trees, ringed with ancient oaks, with early spring wildflowers struggling to bloom between them.

The smell hit her immediately. Sulfur and ash.

"Oh no," Ramona breathed.

"Yeah," Kashvi said grimly. "It's bad."

The grass near the stones looked sickly, gray in patches, brown in others. The wildflowers were stunted, dying. Stones on the ground had dark marks spreading across their surface like infection. Not carved. Growing.

"When did this happen?" Ramona asked, moving closer. "Right after the ritual?"

"Based on the growth pattern?" Posey knelt. "It started around the time you did the ritual. But it's accelerated in the past week."

Ramona circled the clearing slowly. The corruption was spreading outward from the center — from exactly where she and Zara had cast the severance ritual.

"This is demonic corruption," Posey said quietly, running her fingers just above the ground without touching it. "Hell energy. It's poisoning the convergence point."

"What happens if it spreads to all the trees?" Cammie asked.

"If a convergence point corrupts fully?" Kashvi's voice was grim.

"Everything connected to it destabilizes. Spells fail. Wards collapse. It could take decades to recover. Assuming it recovers at all."

Zara was standing in the center of the stone circle, turning slowly, taking in the corruption. Through the tether, Ramona felt something complicated — guilt, alarm, and something darker.

"Zara?" Ramona approached her carefully.

"This is my fault."

"What?"

"The corruption." Zara gestured at the stones. "It's demonic energy. Hell magic. *My* magic."

"You don't know that—"

"Yes, I do." Zara's voice was tight. "This is what demons do to sacred spaces. We poison them just by existing near them."

"But you've been all over Fernwick," Felix pointed out. "Why would it only affect us here?"

"The ritual." Zara turned to face them. "We came here because the convergence point would amplify the magic, right? Make it strong enough to break the binding. But instead it amplified my demonic signature. Pulled Hell energy through me and into the convergence point. Infected it."

"Or it amplified *my* magic," Ramona said. "I was the one channeling the ritual. Maybe I somehow made it worse."

"You don't know that—"

"Neither do you." Ramona's voice was firm. "We did this together, Zara. Both of us. Stop trying to take all the blame."

"So, how do we fix it?" Cammie said after a moment.

Zara stiffened, glancing toward Cammie, then situating herself on the other side of Ramona.

"The grimoire in Thornwood's archives should have the cleansing ritual," Kashvi added. "And if my theory is right — if cleansing and severance rituals share fundamental structures — it might also help us modify our approach to breaking the tether."

"Two birds, one felony," Ramona said.

"Exactly." Felix pulled out his laptop. "I've been looking at the building schematics for the restricted section of the library. There are wards, obviously, but they're keyed to faculty access signatures. Which means—"

"The key will get us in," Ramona finished.

"In theory." Felix pulled up a diagram. "But we need to understand the security protocols. Guard rotations. When faculty are most likely to be in the building. Felix, you said you could pull schedules from their servers?"

"Already did." Felix tapped his phone. "Guards change shifts at midnight. Faculty clear out around ten on weeknights. Weekends are quieter — just a skeleton crew."

"So, then go on a weekend," Cammie said. "Late. When the building's mostly empty."

"Tomorrow night?" Posey suggested quietly.

Everyone turned to look at her.

"The corruption is spreading," Posey said, gesturing at the ground. "Every day we wait is another day this place dies. I can already feel so much pain here. And if what Kashvi found is right — if the cleansing ritual can help us understand how to properly break the tether — we need that information as soon as possible."

"Tomorrow's fast," Felix said. "We'd need to finalize the plan, coordinate timing, make sure we know exactly where to find the grimoire—"

"I know where it is," Ramona said quietly. "The restricted section. Third floor, west wing, like you said. The historical texts are organized by century and subject. Fifteenth-century purification magic would be in the middle stacks."

Everyone stared at her.

"I used to work there," Ramona added. "I've been in this exact section."

"Then we do it tomorrow," Zara said. Her voice was calm, certain. "We get the grimoire. We cleanse the convergence point. We figure out how to break the tether properly."

"That's... ambitious," Kashvi said slowly.

"That's necessary," Ramona corrected.

Felix was already typing. "Okay. We need a solid plan. Exact timing. Backup contingencies. Who's going in, who's staying outside as lookout—"

"I should go," Ramona said immediately. "I know the building. I know where everything is."

"I'm going with you," Zara added. "Obviously."

"I can handle tech," Felix offered. "If there are any security systems, cameras, magical alarms — I can disable them remotely. For being one of the most powerful witching institutions, their servers are surprisingly vulnerable."

"I'll stay with Felix," Kashvi said. "Provide backup if something goes wrong. Posey, Cammie — you two should probably stay home. We don't all need to be accessories to grand larceny."

"Absolutely not," Cammie said. "I'm coming. Someone needs to keep watch."

"And I can help with plant-based wards," Posey added quietly. "If we need to create diversions or confuse tracking spells."

"So we're all going," Ramona said.

"We're all going," Zara confirmed.

They spent the next hour going over details. Guard routes. Entry points. Titles and their possible locations. Felix pulled up floor plans on his laptop, showed them the security camera coverage he'd already mapped. Cammie made a list of supplies.

Eventually, Kashvi and Felix headed back to their cars — more research to do, more planning needed. Posey and Cammie followed, Posey explaining quietly what a magical ward was to Cammie.

Which left Ramona and Zara alone in the clearing, the fox pressed against Ramona's leg.

Zara had been quiet for a while. Through the tether, Ramona felt something building — tension, anxiety, the weight of words unsaid.

"Can we walk for a minute?" Zara asked quietly.

They moved to the edge of the clearing, still visible to the others if they looked, but out of earshot. The fox followed, settling at Ramona's feet when they stopped near a fallen log.

Zara looked stricken. Ramona had never seen her like this. The composed, controlled demon looking genuinely distressed.

"What's wrong?" Ramona asked.

"I need to tell you something." Zara's voice was tight. "I should have told you sooner. Weeks ago. But I didn't know how, and then the longer I waited, and then, today—"

Through the tether, Ramona felt it — affection, fear, desperate vulnerability. Everything Zara was trying to say and couldn't quite voice.

She's going to say it, Ramona realized. *She's going to say I love you.*

And that makes it real. And real means it'll hurt when she leaves.

Ramona's hands were shaking. She couldn't do this. Couldn't hear Zara say it out loud because once it was said, once it was named, there was no taking it back.

"Zara, we don't have to talk about it," Ramona said quickly.

Zara stopped. Looked at her. "What?"

"We don't have to — to name it. Or define it. We can just—"

"Ramona—"

"We have nine days left. Let's just enjoy them. We don't need to make it complicated."

Zara's eyebrows furrowed. "I'm not trying to complicate anything. I'm trying to tell you something important—"

"I know it's important," Ramona's voice cracked. "And I feel it, too, but saying it out loud makes it—"

Zara stepped closer. "Ramona, I can't keep this from you any longer."

"Zara, please—"

"I've been hiding it because I didn't want to scare you—"

Ramona felt tears threatening. *Just say it. Just say it so we can deal with it.* She put her hands on Zara's arms. Looked her in the eyes. "I know," Ramona said.

Zara blinked. "You know? How long have you known?"

Ramona was barely holding it together. "A few days."

"A few—" Zara looked genuinely shocked. "How did you find out? Did Iris finally confess to you?"

Ramona's confusion shifted to alarm. "Wait, what?"

"What?"

"Iris? What does Iris have to do with this?"

"She's... the one... at least I'm pretty sure." Zara's expression was anguished. "She... she didn't tell you?"

"Tell me *what*, exactly?"

They stared at each other. Through the tether: confusion, alarm, dawning horror.

"What do you know?" Zara asked carefully.

"What do *you* know?" Ramona countered.

The fox sat at Ramona's feet, looking between them.

Zara reached into her pocket. Pulled out something small — a piece of bark, dark and twisted. She turned it over in her hands. "This morning. In your mother's garden. I saw the tree."

Ramona eyed the bark, trying to follow. "The... strange dead tree?"

"A banewood tree." Zara held up the bark. "They're used to anchor long-term curses. To keep them stable over years, sometimes decades." She paused. "Ramona, I think you're cursed."

Silence. The words hung in the air between them.

Ramona felt as though time had temporarily slowed, like her thoughts were moving through deep quicksand. "I'm sorry? *Cursed*?"

"Yes."

"You think I'm cursed."

"I know you're cursed." Zara turned the bark over in her fingers. "I've suspected for weeks. But I wasn't sure. I wanted to be certain before I told you. And this morning, when I saw the tree again—" She met Ramona's eyes. "I'm sure now. This is banewood. And your mother knows."

"My mother—"

"Has a curse tree in her garden. A very old one. Carefully maintained." Zara's voice was gentle but firm. "I asked her about it. She got defensive. Angry. That's why we were arguing when we came into the study and found you."

"My mom cursed me?" Ramona asked.

"No, I believe your sister did," Zara said, her voice dropping low, like it pained her to say.

Ramona's mind was reeling. "Iris wouldn't... she's my sister..."

"The spell you mentioned that killed the tree when you were kids.

When Iris was eleven and you were eight." Zara stepped closer. "You said *she* did something to a tree."

"Yes, but—"

"She didn't kill it, Ramona. She grew it. Created it." Zara held up the bark. "Banewood doesn't grow naturally. It has to be cultivated through ritual magic. A witch plants the curse and anchors it to the earth. As long as the tree stands, the curse stays active."

"No." Ramona was shaking her head. "No, you're wrong. Iris wouldn't—"

"When did your magic start failing?" Zara asked quietly.

Ramona opened her mouth. Closed it. She didn't remember. Not exactly. She'd always struggled with magic. For as long as she could remember, it had been hard. Unpredictable. Wrong.

"I think it happened then," Zara said. "When you were eight. I think Iris cursed you — maybe not understanding what she was doing, maybe out of jealousy or fear. She was eleven. Just a child herself." She paused.

"That's insane," Ramona whispered. "Why would she do that?"

"I don't know. Maybe she didn't mean to. Maybe it was an accident — a ritual that went wrong, magic she couldn't control." Zara's voice was gentle. "Or maybe she knew exactly what she was doing. Either way, it's interesting that she became a curse-breaker after that and dedicated her life to it."

"But why?" Ramona asked, the question directed to no one in particular.

"Maybe to learn how to eventually break what she'd done." Zara held up the bark again. "I wanted to be certain before I told you. But this morning, seeing that tree, seeing your mother's reaction when I questioned it — I'm certain now."

Ramona sat down hard on the fallen log. The fox pressed against her leg. "My entire life," she said quietly.

"I know."

"Twenty-seven years since then."

Zara nodded, pocketing the bark.

"And you think my sister — my sister who has always been so perfect… You think she did it." The implications crashed over Ramona in waves. Every time Iris had helped her. Every time she'd defended Ramona to the Council, convinced them not to strip her magic, been there after Simone left and Thornwood expelled her. Had that all been guilt? Iris trying to make up for what she'd done?

"I don't want to believe it," Ramona said, but her voice was hollow.

"You don't have to. Not yet." Zara knelt in front of her. "But we can find out. The restricted archives will have curse identification texts. We can verify the signature. See if I'm right."

"And if you are?"

"Then we break it."

Ramona's hands were shaking. "I can't… I can't process this."

"I know. I'm sorry." Zara's voice was thick with guilt. "I should have told you sooner. Or I should have had more proof before I said anything, but I couldn't keep it from you any longer."

Through the tether, Ramona felt Zara's sincerity. Her fear that she'd made the wrong call. Her desperate need for Ramona to understand.

Silence fell. Ramona stared at the corrupted convergence point, at the spreading darkness that mirrored the darkness she'd been carrying inside herself for twenty-seven years without even knowing it.

"But maybe I'm not… broken," she said finally. Testing the words.

"No," Zara said quietly.

"Maybe I never was broken."

"No."

"Someone did this to me. Maybe Iris. Maybe someone else. But someone cursed a child." Ramona's voice was flat. "Watched her struggle for twenty-seven years."

She stood. The fox rose with her.

Ramona looked at Zara, then at the corrupted stones, then back to Zara. Her jaw set.

"We break into Thornwood tonight." Her voice was steady, certain. "I've spent twenty-seven years feeling broken, and that ends right now."

Through the tether, she felt Zara's fierce pride. Her determination matching Ramona's own.

"Tonight," Zara agreed.

Ramona stared out at the corrupted stones, at the spreading darkness, and felt something shift inside her. Not hope, exactly. Not yet. But something close to it.

What could she have been without the curse? What could she be now, if they broke it?

"We should get back," Zara said quietly. "Tell the others the timeline just moved up. We have a lot to prepare for tonight."

Ramona nodded. Turned away from the convergence point.

The fox followed at her heels, and Zara's hand found hers, warm and steady.

Tonight they'd break into Thornwood. Tonight she'd find answers. She was more determined than ever.

CHAPTER TWENTY-SEVEN

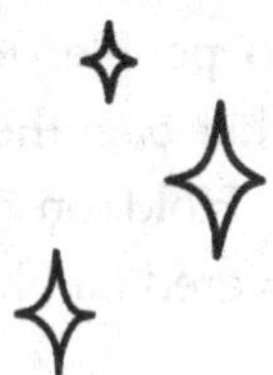

"THIS MIGHT BE ONE OF OUR WORST IDEAS," RAMONA SAID FOR THE THIRD time that evening.

"You've mentioned that," Zara replied with the same calm efficiency she brought to everything. "Multiple times."

"I'm just saying—"

"You're spiraling." Zara's hand found Ramona's knee and squeezed gently as they sat in the car just outside of campus. "We have a plan. We have the key. We've studied the guard schedules. This is going to work."

Ramona stared out the window at the streetlights. It was past eleven — late enough that Thornwood's campus should be mostly empty. Just a skeleton security crew doing rounds. Faculty long gone for the weekend.

But still.

"What if someone recognizes me?"

"They won't."

Ramona fidgeted with her skirt hem, tugging at her tights. "What if the wards reject me even with the key?"

"They won't."

"What if—"

"Ramona." Zara's voice was firm but gentle. "Breathe."

Ramona tried. Failed. Tried again. Her chest felt too tight, her hands too shaky. They were about to break into Thornwood Academy — the place that had expelled her, the place where everyone knew her face, knew what she'd done, knew exactly why she shouldn't be there. "I need a disguise," she said suddenly.

Zara glanced at her. "A what?"

"A disguise. Something so people don't recognize me." Ramona was already digging through her bag, the one she'd packed with "just in case" items. "I brought… Hold on." She pulled out sunglasses. Large, dark sunglasses that covered half her face.

"Ramona—"

Then a hat. A wide-brimmed hat she'd grabbed from the back of her closet.

"Ramona, you don't need—"

And finally, a scarf. A large, patterned scarf that she immediately wrapped around her lower face, covering her nose and mouth. She adjusted the sunglasses. Tilted the hat. Checked her reflection in the passenger-side mirror. "There," she said. "Perfect."

Zara was staring at Ramona with an expression that was carefully, deliberately neutral.

"What?" Ramona asked.

"You look like a cartoon spy, Mortal."

"I look disguised."

"You look like you're about to rob a bank in a very obvious manner." Zara's lips were twitching. "Or like you're hiding from paparazzi. Badly."

"It's working!"

"It's absolutely not." Zara reached out, touched the brim of the hat. "If anything, you're drawing more attention to yourself. No one dresses like this unless they're trying to hide something."

"Exactly. So they won't know it's me."

"They'll know something is wrong with you." Zara's voice was gentle, but she was definitely trying not to laugh. "Darling, you cannot walk into Thornwood looking like this."

"Why not?"

"Because you look ridiculous." Zara said it fondly, like it was an endearment. "Adorable, but ridiculous."

"I'm being strategic—"

"You're panicking." Zara reached out, started unwinding the scarf. "And normally I find that very endearing, but this is not going to work."

Ramona let her remove the scarf. Then the hat. But she kept her hands on the sunglasses. "I need *something*," she said. Her voice came out smaller than intended. "Everyone there knows my face. Everyone knows what I did. If someone sees me—"

"Then we'll handle it." Zara's hands came up to cup her face. "But not like this."

"Then how?"

Zara was quiet for a moment, studying Ramona's face. "I'm going to use my powers. Very minimally, but it's a risk."

"A risk?" Ramona asked.

"It might trigger something in Thornwood's wards," Zara explained. "That's why it would be wise to do it here, outside of the grounds."

Ramona nodded. "And while the convergence point is already corrupted and probably already taxing the wards."

"Do you trust me?" Zara asked.

Ramona sighed. "Yes, but I'm nervous you're asking that question."

"Then hold still."

Zara's hands were still on Ramona's face. Her expression shifted into that look of concentration she got when using magic — eyes slightly unfocused, breathing steady and deep.

Ramona felt the magic wash over her like cool water. Not uncomfortable, just strange. A gentle pressure against her skin, a tingling sensation that started at her scalp and moved down her face, her neck. "What are you—"

"Shh. Almost done." The sensation faded. Zara's hands dropped away, and she was looking at Ramona with satisfaction. "There," Zara said. "Much better."

"What did you do?" Ramona reached for the mirror, angled it to see her reflection.

The face staring back at her was… not hers.

Still her, in a way. The same basic structure, the same general features. But different enough that no one would recognize her. Blonde hair instead of dark. Slightly different nose. Eyes a lighter shade. The kind of face that was pretty in a generic, forgettable way.

"You made me blonde," Ramona said, unamused.

"I made you unrecognizable," Zara corrected. "The blonde is because no one would ever expect a blonde Ramona."

"Oh, so you'd prefer me blonde?" Ramona deadpanned.

"I didn't say that." But Zara was smiling. "It's *temporary*. The glamour will fade in a few hours, but it should be enough to get us in and out without anyone recognizing you." Zara paused, a fang appearing as she bit her lip.

Ramona felt a pulse of attraction through the tether. Her eyes went wide. "Stop looking at me like that."

"You're not a bad blonde," Zara teased, her hand sliding over Ramona's shoulders. "You know, maybe if the glamour doesn't wear off, when we get back to the car—"

Ramona laughed, slapping at Zara's hand. "Don't you dare finish that sentence. We're about to do something extremely important and dangerous, and I cannot be this turned on already."

"So, you admit you are a little turned on thinking about it," Zara quipped.

"Stop it," Ramona scolded again, but she was laughing. She was definitely not thinking about Zara's dark nails pulling her blonde hair.

Zara faced forward again, but a wry grin was still on her lips.

Ramona stared at her reflection. At the stranger wearing her clothes, sitting in her seat. "It's weird," she said.

"It's effective." Zara turned the key in the ignition, and it gave a hiccup of noncompliance before starting. She pulled back onto the road. "And significantly less conspicuous than the sunglasses-hat-scarf combination."

"I liked the sunglasses."

"I know you did." Zara's hand found hers again, squeezed. "But this way, you can actually see where you're going."

Ramona looked at herself one more time in the mirror. She smoothed her shirt. She cleared her mind of the visions of Zara tugging her into the backseat. The blonde stranger looked back — nervous, determined, completely unrecognizable. "Okay," she said. "Okay. Let's do this."

Thornwood Academy looked even more imposing at night — Gothic architecture turned into sharp shadows, the main building looming against the dark sky. Enchanted security lights illuminated the grounds in pools of harsh white light, creating corridors of darkness between them.

Ramona's stomach clenched. She'd loved this place once. Had felt privileged to work here, to teach here. Now she was sneaking in through a side entrance like a criminal.

They parked in the visitor lot — far enough from the main building to avoid immediate attention, close enough for a quick escape if needed. The campus was quiet. Almost eerily so.

"Felix disabled the cameras on the east wing," Zara said, checking her phone. "We have a ten-minute window before the security guard makes his rounds past that entrance."

"Ten minutes to get inside, find the archives, and then wait for the lights protocol."

Zara nodded. "Get in, get near the right section, then wait twenty minutes for the lights to shut off without movement. They won't turn on again without the doorway triggered."

Ramona checked her tiny pen flashlight. Trying to summon a light globe was too risky given her magic was forbidden from Thornwood, and she wouldn't dare let Zara use magic inside the wards.

"We'll have longer once we're in. The guard doesn't patrol the library stacks. Just the main corridors." Zara pocketed her phone. "Ready?"

Ramona wasn't. But she nodded anyway.

They moved quickly across the lawn, staying in the shadows between security lights. The key worked on the side entrance — Eleanor's access was comprehensive. The door clicked open softly.

Inside, the hallway was dark. Emergency lighting cast everything in dim red. Their footsteps echoed on the polished floor.

"This way," Ramona whispered.

They moved through familiar corridors. Ramona's heart hammered with every step. Any moment, someone could round a corner. Any moment, a guard could appear. Any moment—

"Ramona." Zara's hand found hers. "Breathe."

Right. Breathing.

They made it to the main library without incident. The vast room was dark, lit only by emergency exits and the faint glow of enchanted preservation wards on the oldest texts. Shadows stretched across empty tables and abandoned study carrels.

No one was here. The library was closed for the night.

Ramona kept moving toward the back, toward the restricted section where the stairs to the archives were hidden behind reference stacks.

The archive entrance was locked by another warded door, but Eleanor's key worked here, too, the enchantment recognizing the authorization.

The stairs down were narrow, dimly lit by magical sconces that activated as they descended. The air grew cooler, carrying that particular smell of old books and preserved parchment.

The archives.

The door at the bottom opened into a vast room filled with floor-to-ceiling shelves, stretching back into shadows. Medieval grimoires, dangerous texts, everything too powerful for general access.

Ramona pointed. "We need to get to that section to wait out the lights, so we don't trigger them back on by walking in the main walkway."

Zara nodded, following Ramona's lead.

"Come on." Zara grabbed Ramona's hand, pulled her deeper into the stacks, into the narrow space between shelves where shadows were thickest.

They pressed themselves into the corner where two shelves met, Ramona's back against the books, Zara in front of her. The space was barely wide enough for two people. They were pressed together, chest to chest, Zara's hands braced on either side of Ramona's head.

Ramona's heart hammered through her body, roaring in her ears. Through the tether, she felt Zara's elevated pulse, her protective focus.

The lights turned off, and Ramona couldn't see anything in front of her. "I'm feeling jealous of your dark vision right now," she admitted.

Zara huffed a small laugh, too close to her ear. Through the tether, Ramona could feel a pulse of arousal. Zara's hand slid down her side, settling on her hip. Zara's thumb was making slow, lazy circles over Ramona's skin. In the darkness, the sensation felt heightened on her skin.

Ramona tucked her face against Zara's neck, and she felt the demon shiver against her. The warmth of Zara, the feel of provocative thoughts through the tether, the danger and excitement and thrill of the moment… This want, this *need* for Zara, was making her reckless.

Ramona's breath was coming too fast. Not just from fear now. From the pressure of Zara's body against hers, from the heat between them in this cramped space, from the absolutely inappropriate timing of her body's response to their situation.

It was the adrenaline, she told herself. It was just the tether sensing the heightened energy in their bodies.

"Listen," Zara whispered, her breath warm against Ramona's ear, making her recall all manner of things Zara had whispered to her in the dark for weeks now.

Ramona tried to concentrate past her racing heart, her stupid lust. The footsteps were still distant. Not moving closer. Just a guard making regular rounds through the main library.

Zara didn't move from where they were pressed together in the dark. Ramona could feel Zara's breath on her neck, the warmth of her body, the way her hips were pinning Ramona against the shelf.

"Ramona," Zara murmured. "Your heart is racing."

"We're hiding in a place I'm banned. Of course it's racing."

"That's not why." Zara's voice dropped lower, amused. "Really? Here? Now?"

"I don't know what you're talking about," Ramona whispered.

"Liar." Zara shifted slightly, pressing closer. "You're so turned on."

"I am *not*—"

"You are." Zara's fingers teased along the waistband of Ramona's skirt. "We're breaking into your former workplace, hiding from guards in the restricted archives, and I think you're getting wet thinking about... what, exactly?"

"Nothing," Ramona breathed. "I'm not—"

"Don't lie to me." Zara's lips were at her ear now. "I can feel everything you're feeling. So tell me — what are you thinking about?"

Ramona bit her lip. Refused to answer.

"Come on, we have at least twenty minutes to wait here," Zara whispered, her tongue tracing the sensitive shell of Ramona's ear.

Ramona let out a ragged breath.

Zara's hand slid lower, found the hem of Ramona's skirt. "Is it this? Being trapped here with me? The danger?"

"Zara—"

"Or is it something else?" Zara's fingers traced the edge of her skirt. Not quite touching skin. "Maybe the fact that we're in Thornwood. The place that expelled you. Taking back access they tried to deny you."

Ramona's breath hitched. "Both," she finally whispered. "It's both."

"Mmm." Zara's approval was palpable. "You like this. The risk. The rebellion."

"Maybe."

"Definitely." Zara's hand slid up beneath her skirt now, fingers finding her inner thigh through her thin tights. "Should I stop?"

"No," Ramona said immediately. Too quickly.

Zara laughed softly. "That's what I thought."

"This is insane," Ramona breathed. "Someone could catch us. This is basically the worst possible thing we could be doing."

"That's the point, isn't it?" Zara's fingers moved higher. "That's what's getting you so worked up. What else do you plan to do while we wait?"

Her fingers reached the edge of Ramona's tights, pushing past the waistband, tracing over her underwear, to find her absolutely soaked.

"Fuck," Zara whispered. "You really are—"

Ramona buried her face into Zara's neck, partly to hide her expression of desperation, but also to nip at the sensitive skin there. She felt a pulse of pleasure through the tether.

"Why not?" Zara's fingers pressed against the fabric, not quite touching where Ramona needed. "You're the one who's so turned on you can barely think straight. While we're hiding from security. In a library."

"Zara, please..."

"Please what?" Zara's voice was wicked. "Please touch you? Please make you come while there's a guard walking around upstairs? Please make you be quiet while I finger you in the restricted section?"

"Yes," Ramona gasped. "All of that. Please."

"Well." Zara's fingers slid beneath the fabric. "Since you asked so nicely."

She found Ramona wet and wanting and completely desperate.

"Oh," Zara breathed. "You're already—"

"Shut up and touch me properly," Ramona demanded. Her hips pushed forward, seeking more contact.

"So bossy." But Zara obeyed, fingers moving in deliberate circles that made Ramona's knees weak. "Is this better?"

"Yes," Ramona whimpered. "Don't stop."

"Wasn't planning to." Zara's other hand covered Ramona's mouth gently. "But you need to be quiet for me. Can you do that?"

Ramona nodded frantically.

"Good girl." Zara's fingers pressed inside her.

Ramona moaned against her palm. Her whole body went taut, fighting to stay silent while Zara's fingers worked with devastating precision.

"That's it," Zara murmured. "So perfect for me."

The footsteps of a guard on the floor above was distant background noise that only made Zara's touch feel more intense. The knowledge that they could be discovered any second, that Ramona was letting Zara fuck her in a library where they were stealing ancient grimoires...

It was overwhelming.

"You're thinking about it, aren't you?" Zara's voice was low, intimate. "About the risk. About getting caught. About what a scandal it would be if someone found Ramona Greenbriar getting fucked in Thornwood's restricted archives by a demon."

Ramona whimpered against her palm. Her hips moved with Zara's fingers, chasing the pleasure, completely lost in it now.

"So beautiful like this," Zara continued. "So desperate. I can feel how close you are already."

She was. Ramona was so close, every nerve on fire, the combination of danger and desire and Zara's fingers inside her pushing her right to the edge.

Zara's thumb found her clit, circled it with perfect pressure. Ramona's eyes rolled back.

"That's it," Zara breathed. "Come for me. Right here. Right now. Show me how good it feels to take back what's yours."

The orgasm hit like lightning — sudden, overwhelming, all-consuming. She bit down on Zara's palm to muffle her cry, her whole body shaking, waves of pleasure rolling through her while Zara worked her through it with practiced skill.

When she finally came down, boneless and trembling, Zara huffed a quiet, self-satisfied laugh.

"Feel better?" Zara asked, slowly withdrawing her hand.

"I—" Ramona started laughing breathlessly. "I can't believe we just did that."

"You started it." Zara adjusted Ramona's tights and skirt back into place, wiping her hand on her own jeans after Ramona had gasped when she'd reached to wipe it on a nearby book. "Getting all worked up while we're hiding from guards."

"You didn't have to finish it."

"Where would be the fun in that?" Zara kissed her forehead. "Besides, you asked so nicely."

The footsteps had faded completely. The library above was silent again.

"Can you focus now, Mortal?" Zara asked.

"Yes." Ramona tested her legs. They held. Barely. "Yes, I can definitely focus." She blinked. "Has it been enough time yet?"

"Almost."

Right. The grimoires. The actual reason they'd broken in.

"You search that section." Zara pointed left. "I'll take the right."

THEY SPLIT UP. Ramona moved through the stacks with her tiny flashlight, running her fingers along spines, reading titles in ancient, dead languages. Her heart was still racing, but differently now. Not just fear. Excitement. The thrill of taking back access that had been forbidden.

She found the first grimoire tucked between larger volumes. *Liber Purgationis Maleficae*. She pulled it carefully, opened to the table of contents. Chapter seven. Cleansing demonic corruption from convergence points. "Zara," she whispered. "I found—"

A sound.

Distant but distinct. Footsteps. Not coming from above, but somewhere closer.

Ramona froze, listening.

The footsteps continued — regular, measured. A guard making rounds?

Zara appeared beside her instantly, silent. Their eyes met. Through the tether, Ramona felt Zara's sharp attention, her assessment.

The footsteps were getting closer.

Ramona pulled out her phone but didn't get service. Zara checked her HellBerry, and Ramona saw a message from Felix.

Felix: A guard is coming downstairs, not sure why. Am setting off alarm on other end of building to buy you time. Hurry UP.

They found the other two texts in a frantic hustle — splitting up again and practically running between shelves.

"Got them," Zara whisper-yelled down the aisle where Ramona was kneeling and squinting at a title she couldn't read. Zara held up the last grimoire. "And the curse identification texts. We have everything."

They checked in with Felix to see if they could leave and got a thumbs-up.

They left the way they'd entered — carefully, quietly. Up the stairs, through the dark library, down empty corridors.

Zara angled her phone, shielding its low light. "Felix says we have to change our route out. Go left."

Ramona veered into uncertain territory, pushing open a door that they hadn't planned to. An alarm immediately sounded, and she looked to Zara, panic spiking either in her own body or in Zara's.

She heard a shout, and Zara muttered, "Come on, Felix, turn off the fucking alarm," as they both began running. Zara let Ramona take the lead, two grimoires in her arms as Ramona clutched the other, the pair running down metal stairs and to an outdoor exit.

It was locked. They waited only one beat before a click sound echoed, and Ramona pushed the door again to find that it had unlocked. "Thank you, Felix," she whispered, glancing over her shoulder to make sure Zara was right behind her.

"Stick to the shadows," Zara said, pushing her forward as they both skirted the library building, avoiding the lights that illuminated the walkways.

"I think we lost them," Ramona said, looking behind her for what felt like the hundredth time.

Zara looked at her phone. "Felix says he had to turn on a sprinkler in one of the upper floors. We should be good now."

They crossed the lawn toward the parking lot.

Ramona was breathing hard from adrenaline. They'd done it. Actually done it. She unlocked the car. They slid inside. She put the key in the ignition as she laughed with relief.

Except, nothing happened.

She tried again.

Click. Click. Nothing.

"What—" Ramona started.

"It's not..." Zara's voice was tight. "What's happening?"

They stared at each other in the dark car. Ramona's euphoria evaporated. She tried again, in case the first fifteen times were just a fluke.

Zara pulled out her phone. "I'll call Felix."

She dialed, waiting and watching Ramona. Voicemail.

"Fuck," Zara muttered. Tried again.

Still voicemail.

Ramona checked her own phone. "Kashvi's not answering either."

Through the window, headlights. A car pulling in.

"Someone's coming," Ramona said quietly, dipping lower in her seat.

The car parked nearby. The engine cut. The door opened.

A woman got out — early forties, professionally dressed, laptop bag slung over her shoulder. She locked her car, started toward the main building.

Then stopped. Turned. Looked at their car.

Started walking toward them instead.

She knew the walk before she knew anything else, and her whole body understood what that meant before her brain did.

No.

Simone moved through the parking lot like she moved through everything — unhurried, exact, already composed for whatever came next. Dark, long braids, her good coat, warm brown skin that caught the lot's low light in a way that was frankly unreasonable given the circumstances.

Ramona went very still. The specific stillness of someone hoping not to be seen by a predator, which was an insane way to feel about her ex-wife, but that didn't stop her from feeling it. She was suddenly aware of the space between them shrinking.

Simone looked up.

Ramona's stomach dropped. She breathed, "Zara—"

"I see her."

Simone stopped a few feet away. Peered through the driver's side window at Ramona. Frowned.

"Ramona?" Simone's voice was uncertain. "Is that you?"

Fuck.

Ramona's hand went to her face. "N—no," she started. The glamour — it must be fading. But Simone was staring at her with definite recognition. Ramona racked her brain for any good reason for her to be in this parking lot at this hour that Simone would believe.

"I know your shitty car, Ramona," Simone said.

"I—" Ramona started.

The glamour flickered visibly. Wavered.

Simone's eyes widened. "It *is* you. What are you doing here? You're banned from campus."

"What are you doing here? It's the middle of the night," Ramona asked.

Simone did not look pleased to be questioned. She crossed her arms. "My department head called. Apparently, there's been multiple alarms in the library near — Wait, I don't have to explain this to you. Are you wearing a glamour?"

Ramona considered saying no.

"Are you breaking into Thornwood?" Simone looked at Zara, then back to Ramona. "Ramona, are you following me?"

The glamour failed completely. Ramona's own face stared back at her in the window reflection. "What? No. This isn't about you, Simone. Not everything is about you."

Ramona thought she heard Zara groan in frustration.

Simone's eyebrows flew up. She stepped back, hand going to her phone. "I have to report this. They made it very clear. If they find out I saw you and didn't call security—"

"Please," Ramona said. "Just — the car won't start. We're trying to get someone to pick us up. Give us five minutes—"

"Did you break in?" Simone asked. Her voice wasn't angry. More like worried. "Ramona. Why would you do this?"

"It's not important," Ramona lied. "Just pretend you didn't see us. Please."

Simone's expression was complicated. Concern mixed with what looked like genuine regret. "I'm sorry. I have to call them. You know I have to."

She was already dialing.

Ramona looked at Zara. Through the tether: desperation, fierce protectiveness, calculation.

Take the books and go, Ramona thought desperately. *Please.*

Through the tether: Zara's refusal. *I can't leave you. I'd rather burn this place to the ground than abandon you.*

Security answered. Ramona heard the tinny voice through Simone's phone.

"Hi, yes. This is Professor Kane. I'm in the visitor parking lot… I've found someone who's banned from campus." Simone's voice was professional. She wouldn't look at Ramona. "Yes. I'll wait here."

She ended the call. Met Ramona's eyes.

"I'm sorry," Simone said quietly. "I really am. But you shouldn't have come back."

More headlights. A security vehicle pulling in.

"Zara," Ramona whispered urgently. "Please. Take the grimoires. Stay close but stay hidden."

"Ramona—"

"Please."

The security vehicle parked. Two guards got out.

Zara opened her car door — the side facing away from the approaching guards and Simone, and then she stepped into the shadow cast by the car.

She dissolved.

She didn't walk away, or run. She became shadow itself, her form dissipating into darkness like she'd never been solid at all.

Ramona's eyes went wide. She'd never seen Zara do that before. Didn't know she could do that. Through the tether, she could feel that Zara was still there. Still close. The connection held steady at about forty feet.

Unfortunately, the bag holding the grimoires did not dissolve with her. It stayed in the passenger seat.

Ramona forced her expression neutral, trying not to show her shock.

"Ma'am." One of the guards had reached her door. "I'm going to need you to step out of the vehicle."

Ramona glanced toward the bag with the grimoires and shoved it to the floor, under the seat. Maybe they wouldn't search her car when they towed it. She got out slowly. Her legs felt unsteady.

She could feel Zara nearby — somewhere in the shadows between the parking lights. Moving. Staying within range.

"Ramona Greenbriar?" The guard's voice was clipped.

"Yes."

"You're aware you're banned from Thornwood property?"

"Yes."

"And you came here anyway."

It wasn't a question.

Simone stood nearby, arms wrapped around herself. She looked miserable. "I'm sorry," she said again.

"This is a real dick move, Simone," Ramona said. "You know I'm not some villain you have to get arrested."

"I know you don't see it that way," Simone said, and she sounded tired rather than unkind. "You never did." She held Ramona's gaze for just a moment — not long enough to invite a response. "But I watched you try to hex someone I love in front of everyone we knew. So." A small, exhausted lift of one shoulder. "I'm sorry it has to be like this."

"*I* was supposed to be the one you loved, you asshole," Ramona snapped. "You self-righteous—"

"I hope you get the help you need," Simone said in that perfectly patronizing tone she had always been so good at.

For two years, Ramona had thought about what had gone wrong with Simone. For two years, she'd blamed herself for being such a disaster that her own wife had strayed. But maybe the real story didn't feature her at all. Maybe the woman before her had only thought of herself all along.

Through the tether, she felt Zara's presence — flaring with anger, circling, staying close, keeping pace as the guards moved Ramona toward their vehicle.

The guard was talking into his radio. Calling someone. The Magical Council? Exactly how much trouble was she about to be in?

Stay hidden, Ramona thought down the tether. *Stay safe.*

And from the shadows: Zara's fierce determination.

I will. And then I'm coming back for you.

"Ma'am, you're going to need to come with us," the guard said.

Ramona nodded. She watched Simone begin to walk away, then out of nowhere she tripped on nothing more than a shadow, her bag flying to the ground as she cursed aloud. As they led her toward the security vehicle, she felt Zara's amusement.

The tether hummed between them. Steady. Unbroken.

Close enough.

CHAPTER TWENTY-EIGHT

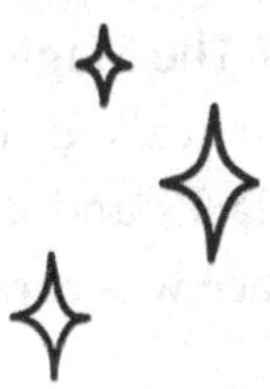

RAMONA HAD IMAGINED A JAIL CELL. COLD METAL BARS, A HARD BENCH, the kind of stark institutional space reserved for actual criminals.

Instead, she was sitting in the saddest office she'd ever seen.

It wasn't even a proper security office. Just a converted storage room with a desk, two chairs, and a filing cabinet that looked older than the building itself. Fluorescent lights buzzed overhead. The room smelled damp, and the wallpaper was peeling in one corner. Someone had taped a motivational poster to the wall — a doodled cat hanging awkwardly from a branch with the caption *Hang In There, Dumbass!*

The guard who'd brought her in — his name tag read *Stevens* — sat at the desk doing paperwork. Actual paper paperwork. With a pen that kept skipping.

He'd taken her bag. Her phone. Eleanor's key.

"Someone will be here soon," he'd said. "Just… sit tight."

That had been twenty minutes ago.

Ramona sat in the uncomfortable plastic chair and tried not to think about what "someone" meant. Campus administration? The Council? The police?

Through the tether, she felt Zara nearby. Not in the building — that would be too risky. But close. Probably somewhere in the shadows just outside the window, staying within the sixty-six-foot range, keeping the connection stable.

Waiting.

Guard Stevens sighed, crossed something out on his form, started over.

The door opened.

Ramona looked up, expecting… she didn't know. Campus security supervisor? Dean of Students? The Magical Council themselves?

Instead, Eleanor Greenbriar walked in. Perfectly composed despite the midnight hour, wearing slacks and a cashmere cardigan like she'd been expecting this call. Her face was carefully expressionless.

Behind her: Iris.

Ramona's stomach dropped. She'd have rather faced the Council.

Iris looked tired. Worried. Her usual confidence replaced with something that looked almost like guilt.

"Thank you for your help." Eleanor's eyes flicked down to Stevens's badge.

"Who the fuck are you?" Stevens asked, and Ramona couldn't help but admire his bold ignorance in that moment.

"Eleanor Greenbriar," her mother said, her eyes going glassy with anger. "We'll be taking my daughter home now."

"Mrs. Greenbriar." Guard Stevens stood immediately.

"Of course." Eleanor's voice was crisp. "I understand my daughter was found trespassing."

"Yes, ma'am. In the visitor parking lot. Around midnight." Stevens glanced at Ramona. "She had a glamour active. Professor Kane identified her and contacted us."

"I see." Eleanor still hadn't looked directly at Ramona. "Has she said anything about why she was here?"

"No, ma'am. She invoked her right to remain silent."

Ramona hadn't. She'd just refused to answer questions. But close enough.

"Well." Eleanor finally met Ramona's eyes. Her expression was unreadable. "The Council has agreed to release her into my custody. Provided she agrees not to return to Thornwood property."

"And if there's another incident?" Stevens asked.

"There won't be." Eleanor's voice left no room for argument. "I'll make sure of it."

Stevens looked between them. "All right. I'll need her to sign some paperwork. And we're keeping her bag as evidence—"

Ramona's heart sank. The grimoires. Eleanor's key. Maybe her phone.

"That won't be necessary," Eleanor said, watching as Stevens turned a shade of red, handing Ramona's bag back to her. "We'll be leaving immediately."

Stevens hesitated, then nodded. He produced paperwork, his hands shaking. Eleanor Greenbriar didn't have to shift into a demonic form to scare people — she was a natural. Ramona signed where indicated, agreeing not to return to Thornwood property, agreeing to appear before the Council if summoned, agreeing to a bunch of other things she didn't bother reading.

"The Council will meet tomorrow to discuss consequences," Stevens said. "They'll contact you."

Ramona nodded.

He led them out of the building, the three Greenbriar women walking stiff-backed and wordless toward Eleanor's sleek SUV.

Oppressive silence filled the space as Ramona sat in the back seat, feeling Zara's energy nearby. Had her shadows slipped into the car beside Ramona, or was she somewhere in the air as they drove? Ramona didn't dare reach to pat the seat beside her, drawing attention.

Ramona stared at the back of her mother's head. At her sister. At the two people who'd known — who'd *known* about the curse and said nothing.

"I can't believe that self-righteous bitch called security," Eleanor said. "I never did like her. Her, or that Kate woman. I never trusted them."

Ramona rolled her eyes from the back seat.

"What were you *thinking,* Ramona?" Iris said, exasperated. She turned in her seat, and Ramona noticed she had bags under her eyes and her shirt was wrinkled.

Ramona clenched her jaw, crossing her arms. "You didn't need to come and get me."

Rationally, she knew she was being a bit of a brat, but knowing everything, knowing about the curse and the completely unnecessary disdain for her ineptitude… it was everything she could do not to scream.

She felt a pulse of calming energy through the tether and took a deep breath through her nose.

"You knew." Ramona's voice came out flat. "About the curse. You both knew my entire life and you never told me."

Eleanor's eyes caught hers in the rearview mirror. "It's more complicated than—"

"It's really not." Ramona balled her hands into fists, her fingernails biting into her palms to keep from screaming. "I've spent twenty-seven years thinking I was broken. Thinking my magic was fundamentally wrong. Thinking I was a failure. And you *knew* the whole time that someone had cursed me."

"We didn't know at first," Iris said quietly. "Not for years—"

"But you figured it out eventually," Ramona snapped. "When? When did you figure it out?"

Iris's shoulders slumped, and she leaned her elbow on the center console, rubbing at her eyes. "Ramona—"

"*When*, Iris?"

"I suspected when you were fourteen. Confirmed it when I was seventeen." Iris's voice was barely above a whisper. "When I started studying curse-breaking."

"Fourteen." Ramona felt like she couldn't breathe. "I was fourteen and *you knew* and you just… what? Decided not to mention it?"

"I wanted to fix it first," Iris said desperately. "I wanted to have a solution before I told you. I didn't want to tell you something that devastating without being able to break it—"

"That wasn't your choice to make." Ramona's voice rose. "This is my life. My magic! My entire sense of self. And you just let me keep thinking I was the problem?"

"We tried to help," Eleanor interjected. "The extra tutoring, the private lessons—"

"That made me feel worse!" Ramona was shouting now. "Every

'extra lesson' was a reminder that I needed more help than everyone else. That I was slower, weaker, more likely to fail."

The only sound was the gravel drive under the car tires as they drove up toward Greenbriar Manor. "We were only trying to—"

"Save it."

"Ramona," her mother scolded.

"No, you don't get to pretend like you're my family anymore. Family doesn't keep secrets like this from one another," Ramona said, waiting for the car to stop moving before unbuckling her seat belt.

Iris turned in her seat. "I've spent my life trying to—"

"You were trying to manage the symptoms without telling me about the disease." Ramona's hands were shaking. "Do you have any idea what that did to me? A lifetime of thinking I was fundamentally flawed?"

"We wanted to protect you," Eleanor said.

"From what? The truth?"

Iris sighed. The three women got out of the car. Ramona shivered in the darkness, then felt a warmth at her back, like Zara's presence was directly behind her.

"So you just let me suffer instead?" Ramona almost wanted to laugh. "That's not protection. That's—"

"It wasn't supposed to take this long," Iris cut in. Her voice cracked. "I thought I'd figure it out in a few years. Find the right ritual, break the curse, and then I could tell you. But the curse was more complex than I expected. The anchor tree is old, powerful. Every time I thought I'd found the answer, it didn't work."

"So you became a curse-breaker for the guilt trip?" Ramona asked. "Dedicated your whole career to it so you could blame even more things on me?"

"To help you," Iris said. "Everything I've done — the specialization, the research, becoming an expert in curse identification and removal — it was all to find a way to break what was done to you."

"And in the meantime, you just watched me struggle. Watched me get expelled from Thornwood. Watched my marriage fall apart. Watched me lose everything—"

"I convinced the Council not to strip your magic," Iris said desperately. "After the incident, they wanted to permanently bind you. I'm the one who argued for leniency. I'm the one who's been protecting you—"

"Protecting me from the consequences of a curse you knew about." Ramona's voice broke on a yell. "You want credit for damage control when you should have told me the truth years ago?"

"Ramona, please—"

"Why did you do it?" The question came out quiet. Deadly. "Why did you curse me?"

Iris went white. "What?"

"We were children," Ramona continued, biting every word. "*Why* did you do this to me?"

"I didn't know what was happening," Iris said. Her voice was shaking. "I was a child, too, and we had just fought about something, and I didn't know what I was doing."

Ramona stared at her sister. Trying to see the truth in her face.

Through the tether: Zara's presence. Steady. Waiting.

"I've found the spell to break it," Iris said suddenly. "To break the curse fully. I've been working on it for years. I finally finished the translation last month."

Ramona paused. Half anticipation, half dread. "And?"

"It's in a grimoire. Fifteenth century. I left it—" Iris stopped. "I left it for you. I thought if you found it naturally, you're smart enough that if you were looking for something else and came across it—"

"You left the grimoire for me to find?" Ramona's voice was flat. "Instead of just telling me? Instead of just performing the spell? So you'd never have to take accountability and just let *me* deal with it?"

Iris shifted her weight. Eleanor sniffled.

"It's late, girls. Let's go inside," Eleanor said, holding out her arms as if ushering them.

Iris turned, but Ramona stayed put.

"I did find it." Ramona's voice was cold. "In the donation bin at work. I even performed a spell from it, and then I summoned a demon. So, thank you. It worked out even better than you'd imagined."

Eleanor made a small, surprised sound. "A demon?" she asked. "Zara?"

"Yep," Ramona said, popping the P sound. "She's a demon I'm now tethered to."

Eleanor closed her eyes briefly. "Ramona—"

"Don't." Ramona's voice was sharp. "Don't lecture me about *anything* when you've been lying to me for decades."

Their breath fogged in front of their faces, and Ramona shivered again. "The spell," she said. "In the grimoire. How does it work?"

Iris pulled out her phone, scrolled through photos, found one. A page from a manuscript, dense text with marginal notes in a handwriting Ramona recognized from the grimoire.

"It's a severance ritual," Iris said. "It's fairly simple and straightforward. I can—"

"That's it?" Ramona interrupted. She didn't want or need Iris's help, ever again.

"It's more complicated than that. The ritual takes three hours. It requires specific components — lunar water, blessed iron…" Iris looked at Ramona. "And it has to be performed during a new moon. The next one is—"

"Nine days, or maybe eight now," Ramona said, glancing up toward the night sky as if that might tell her the hour. "I know."

"How do you know?"

"Because I've been researching severance rituals for a month trying to break a demonic binding." Ramona's voice was sharp. "Funny how both problems have the same timeline."

Iris's expression was pained. "Ramona, I'm so sorry. I know I should have told you sooner. I know I should have—"

"You're right. You should have." Ramona turned. "And now I'm leaving."

"Ramona, wait," Iris said quickly, pressing a tiny slip of paper into her hand. "Give this to Kashvi."

Ramona nearly dropped the paper out of spite, but instead she tucked it into her pocket.

"We'll give you a ride," Iris insisted.

"No, I'll be fine. I'll call someone I trust," Ramona said over her shoulder, holding her sweater tighter around her as she began walking back down the driveway. She could have spent the night in her old bedroom, but after that discussion, she didn't want to spend one more moment with her mother and sister. Did her dad know? Did Simone know? Did *everyone* but her know?

The grounds were dark. The drive stretched out ahead, shadowed and still.

But there, near the tree line, a darker shadow. Moving.

Zara materialized from the shadows like she'd always been solid. No longer shadow-form — just herself again.

"Took you long enough," Zara murmured.

"They wanted to talk." Ramona grabbed her hand. "Felix?"

"Waiting at the end of the drive." Zara started walking. "Come on."

They moved quickly through the gardens, away from her childhood home, away from the banewood tree that stood silent and terrible in the darkness of the garden.

"Remember how you offered to burn down the manor if I needed?" Ramona asked.

Zara stiffened beside her. "Are you asking me to? Because I'd love that. Just say the word." She held up her free hand, and a tiny flame appeared at the top of her finger.

Ramona laughed. "Just nice to know I still have that in my back pocket."

Zara squeezed her hand. "I'd burn down the entire world if you asked me to."

Ramona leaned against her as they walked. "I know."

Zara's voice lowered to barely above a whisper. "And I'd never burn anything again, if you asked me to."

Ramona smiled to herself, her throat tightening with emotion.

They walked on in silence. The night had been a disaster, but they were together.

"So, you could have been shadows this whole time?" Ramona asked as they continued walking. "That would have been so much easier at work."

"No." Zara glanced at her. "It's just closer to my true form. I couldn't change before. The longer I'm away from Hell, the more demon I'm becoming."

Ramona processed that. "Is that… bad?"

"I don't know yet." Zara's voice was honest. "But it's happening whether I want it to or not."

They walked along the drive in the dark, Ramona's hand in Zara's, the loss of the grimoires heavy between them.

Headlights appeared in the distance. Felix, idling at the end of the road.

He leaned across to open the passenger door. Gerald cooed from his shoulder — concerned, questioning.

"Get in," Felix said. "Kashvi's at home with Cammie and Posey."

Ramona slid into the back seat. Zara followed.

"Did the cops torture you?" Felix asked, pulling onto the main road.

Ramona nearly laughed. "Yes, but only by letting my mother and sister get near me."

"Fuck."

"Yeah."

"Are you okay?"

"No." Ramona closed her eyes. "But I will be. Once we break this fucking curse and fix the convergence point and figure out how to break the tether."

Through the tether, she felt Zara's hand find hers. Squeeze.

"We will," Zara said quietly. "I promise."

Felix drove them home through empty streets, while Gerald kept watch.

Everything was falling apart. She hadn't even gotten the grimoires they'd risked everything to steal. They were either confiscated, or, best-case scenario, sitting in Ramona's impounded car.

But for the first time in twenty-seven years, Ramona knew *why*.

CHAPTER TWENTY-NINE

RAMONA SAT CROSS-LEGGED ON HER BED, THE GRIMOIRE OPEN IN HER LAP, the fox curled across her thighs like a warm, breathing, weighted blanket. She'd been staring at the same page for twenty minutes.

The curse-breaking spell.

It was right there. Written in Iris's precise handwriting in the margins — translations, component lists, timing requirements. Everything Ramona would need to break a curse that had shaped her entire life.

Her sister had known the answer, and she'd had it in her hands for nearly two months.

Two *months*.

And before that — years of research, years of knowing something was wrong, years of watching Ramona struggle and fail and hate herself while Iris studied curse-breaking and said nothing.

The fox shifted, pressing its head against her hand. She scratched the downy fur around his ears, and he closed his eyes.

"I'm not broken," Ramona whispered to the empty room.

The words should have felt liberating. Should have been a revelation, a weight lifting, the answer to a question she'd been asking her whole life.

Instead, they just felt hollow.

Because if she wasn't broken, if her magic wasn't fundamentally wrong, then what did that mean? That she'd spent twenty-seven years hating herself for nothing? That every failure, every disaster, every moment she'd felt inadequate or useless or fundamentally *less than* everyone around her — all of it had been a lie?

That she could have been *different*?

The thought was almost worse than thinking she was broken.

At least when she'd thought it was just her — just the way she was born — she could accept it. She could work around it, compensate, try harder. She could tell herself it wasn't anyone's fault, just bad luck, just the way magic worked for some people.

But knowing someone had *done* this to her?

Knowing Iris had done it, even accidentally, in a moment of sibling anger when she was eleven, and then spent the next twenty-seven years knowing and saying nothing?

Ramona's hands were shaking. She gripped the grimoire tighter, knuckles going white.

The fox made a small, concerned sound.

"I'm fine," Ramona said. Not to the fox. To herself. Testing the words.

They tasted like ash.

Who would she have been without the curse?

The question kept circling through her mind, relentless. Would her magic have worked properly? Would she have been confident? Powerful? Would she have stayed at Thornwood, built a career, been someone who mattered?

Would Simone have stayed? That thought hit like a punch to the gut.

If her magic had worked — if she hadn't been the disaster witch who broke everything she touched — would Simone have looked elsewhere? Would Kate have seemed like a better option than a wife whose spells actually functioned?

Or would she still have left? Would Ramona still have been somehow *not enough*, curse or no curse?

She didn't know. Couldn't know. That was the worst part — the not knowing who she might have been.

The door opened softly. Ramona looked up.

Zara stood in the doorway, two mugs in her hands. She was still wearing the clothes from the heist — black jeans, dark shirt — but she'd taken off her shoes. Her hair was slightly mussed.

"Kashvi made tea," Zara said quietly. "Well, Felix made tea. Kashvi tried to help and nearly set something on fire. Gerald supervised."

Ramona managed a small smile despite everything. "Of course he did."

Zara crossed the room, set one mug on Ramona's nightstand, then sat down on the edge of the bed, careful not to disturb the fox.

"All right, we don't have the grimoires, but we can figure it out," Zara said.

"I failed us," Ramona whispered. "Again. Always."

Zara shook her head. Her eyes were honey-warm as they watched Ramona. Not like she was a barely contained explosion, which was how a lot of people looked at her. She watched Ramona with intrigue and patience and affection.

"You've been staring at that page for a while," Zara said. "I can feel it. Through the tether."

"What can you feel?"

"Everything." Zara's voice was soft. "The anger. The betrayal." She paused. "The grief."

Ramona's throat went tight. "I'm not grieving."

"You are." Zara's hand found hers, careful not to jostle the grimoire. "You're grieving the person you could have been. The life you might have had."

"I don't know who that person would have been." Ramona's voice cracked. "I don't — I've been this person my whole life. The one whose magic doesn't work. Who fails at everything. Who's broken and wrong and—" She stopped. "Except I'm not. I never was. Someone just made me think I was."

"I know."

Ramona's hands were shaking harder now. "Iris watched me fail. Watched me get expelled. Watched my marriage fall apart. Watched me lose *everything*. And she knew. She knew the whole time that it wasn't all my fault."

"Yes."

"That's—" Ramona couldn't finish. Couldn't find words big enough for the betrayal.

The fox shifted, pressing closer. Ramona's free hand found its fur automatically, stroking without thinking.

"Fucked up," Zara finished. "It's fucked up."

"I'm so angry," she whispered. "I'm so angry I can barely breathe."

"I know."

"At Iris. At my mother. At—" Ramona stopped. "At myself. For not seeing it. For not questioning it. For just accepting that *I* was the problem."

"You were eight when it happened," Zara said gently. "A child. You couldn't have known."

"But later. When I was older. I should have—"

"Should have what? Suspected someone had cursed you?" Zara's thumb traced circles on the back of Ramona's hand. "Ramona, you trusted your family. You trusted that they would tell you if something was wrong. That's not a failing. That's just — being human."

"It feels like a failing right now."

"I know." Zara wrapped her arms around Ramona, letting Ramona fall limp and loose and messy against her chest.

They sat in silence for a moment. The fox's breathing was steady, warm against Ramona's legs. The grimoire sat open between them, Iris's handwriting mocking in its precision.

"What if I break the curse and nothing changes?" Ramona asked quietly into Zara's shirt. "What if — what if twenty-seven years of damage is too much to undo? What if my magic still doesn't work right because I've spent so long thinking it wouldn't?"

"Then we'll figure it out," Zara said, kissing her head. "Together."

"You keep saying that."

"Because I mean it." Zara shifted closer. "Ramona, look at me."

Ramona did. Zara's expression was serious, focused, completely present.

"You are not broken," Zara said, each word deliberate. "You never were. Someone did something terrible to you, and then people who should have protected you kept that secret for decades. That's unconscionable. That's—" She stopped. "I don't have words for how angry that makes me."

Ramona sniffled.

"But none of that — none of it — means you're broken." Zara's hand tightened on hers. "It means you were hurt. By people who should have known better, and you survived anyway. You learned to compensate. You built a life despite everything working against you. That's not weakness. That's—" Zara paused. "That's remarkable."

Ramona's eyes were burning. "I don't feel remarkable. I feel—"

"Betrayed."

"Yes."

"Angry."

Ramona nodded.

"Scared about what comes next."

"Yes." Ramona's voice broke. "I don't know who I am without this. The struggling. The failing. The…" She gestured helplessly. "All of it. That's been my entire identity. The disaster witch. The one who can't get it right. And if that was never real, if that was just a curse someone put on me, then who am I?"

"You're Ramona," Zara said simply. "You're the woman who summoned a demon by accident and then convinced her to help instead of making demands. You're the person who translated medieval grimoires for fun. Who works a shitty job to make rent. Who has friends who would commit felonies for her without hesitation. Who just broke into her former workplace to steal the knowledge she needed."

"That's all just circumstances."

"No. That's *you*." Zara moved closer, until their shoulders were touching. "The curse didn't make you kind. It didn't make you smart. It didn't make you brave enough to keep trying even when everything told you to give up. That was all you. Despite everything working against you."

Ramona wanted to believe her. Wanted to accept that there was something worthwhile underneath the curse, underneath the decades of self-hatred. "What if… what if we break the curse and nothing changes? Curse broken, and I'm still the same mess of a person. What if this is just who I am, curse or no curse?" Ramona's voice dropped to a whisper.

"Then you'll be you," Zara said it like it was simple. Like it was obvious. "Ramona, I'm not attracted who you *could* be. I'm attracted to who you are, right now. The way you think. The way you translate languages dead for centuries just because you find them beautiful and interesting. The way you care about people. The way you keep trying even when everything is working against you."

"That's just—"

"That's *you,*" Zara interrupted. "Not the curse. Not your magic. *You.* And breaking this curse isn't going to change that. It's just going to give you back what was taken from you."

Ramona felt tears threatening. "I don't know how to do this."

"Do what?"

"Believe that I might actually be good at something. Powerful. Worth…" She couldn't finish.

"Worth loving?" Zara supplied gently.

"Yeah."

"Then let me believe it for both of us." Zara's hand came up to cup Ramona's face. "Until you can believe it yourself."

A tear slipped down Ramona's cheek. Then another.

"I'm so tired," she whispered. "Of being angry. Of being scared. Of not knowing who I am."

"I know."

"I want to break this curse and have all the answers and know exactly what comes next."

"That's probably not how it works," Zara said with a small smile. "Breaking the curse is just the beginning. You'll still have to figure out who you are. What you want. What kind of magic feels right to you. It's not going to be instant clarity. And you can do that all."

"You make it sound manageable."

"It is. We have a plan. We'll make it without the grimoires. We have your friends who are shockingly on board with crimes." Zara smiled slightly. "We have a fox who's clearly chosen you. We have everything we need."

The fox made a small sound, as if agreeing.

Ramona managed a shaky laugh. Zara's thumb wiped away the tears on Ramona's cheek. "You don't have to have all the answers right now. You just have to rest. Process. Let yourself be angry and scared and uncertain," Zara said.

"That doesn't sound very productive."

"Healing isn't productive. It's necessary." Zara paused. "And you've been wounded. Deeply. For a very long time. You're allowed to feel that."

Ramona closed her eyes. The fox was warm across her lap. The grimoire sat open on the bed in front of them, promising answers if she could just be brave enough to try.

Ramona opened her eyes. Looked at Zara — at the demon who'd been summoned by accident and stayed by choice, who'd held her through panic attacks and made her business plans and defended her to her mother.

"Okay," Ramona said softly. "Okay."

"Okay you believe me, or okay you'll try to believe me?"

"Okay I'll try."

"Good enough." Zara smiled. "Now drink your tea before it gets cold. And then get some sleep. We have quite a full schedule ahead of us."

Ramona carefully closed the grimoire. Set it on the nightstand. The fox shifted but didn't wake, just settled more comfortably across her lap.

She picked up the mug of tea — chamomile, honey, something soothing. Took a sip.

Through the window, the sky was starting to lighten. Not quite dawn, but getting there.

In eight days, they'd cleanse the convergence point, break the curse, and break the tether.

One problem at a time. Kind of.

"Thank you," Ramona said quietly.

"For what?"

"For staying. For believing in me even when I don't. For not being mad about us losing the grimoires. For—" Ramona gestured helplessly. "All of it."

"You're welcome." Zara ran a hand through Ramona's hair. Ramona drank her tea while Zara sat beside her and the fox slept across her lap. When she finally set down the empty mug and slid under the covers — careful not to disturb the fox, who simply adjusted and stayed put — Zara was still there.

"I'm not going anywhere," Zara murmured.

And for the first time in a very long time, Ramona believed her.

The morning light already streamed through the window, warming the room. She fell asleep with Zara's hand in hers and the fox curled at her side and the grimoire, the book holding the answer to a question she'd asked for almost her entire life, waited on the nightstand.

Later, they'd start fixing things, but right now — just for a little while — she let herself rest.

CHAPTER THIRTY

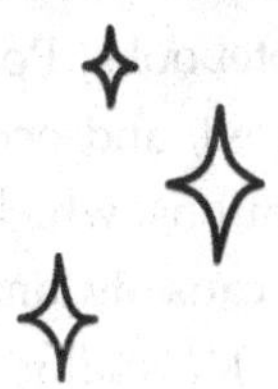

"MY SISTER WANTED ME TO GIVE YOU THIS," RAMONA GROANED, SLIDING A tiny piece of paper across the kitchen table to Kashvi later that day. She'd opened it that morning to find nothing on either side.

Kashvi held it in her hand, her brow furrowed.

"Why is my sister giving you—"

Ramona would have finished the sentence if Kashvi hadn't whispered a phrase, blowing on the paper in her hand. The paper turned into sand as she blew, and appearing on the table before her — the three grimoires they'd taken from the library. The three grimoires she'd left in the bag in her car.

"Are those…" Felix asked, the coffee he was pouring spilling over the sides of the cup he was holding.

Kashvi began, "I know we're not the biggest fans of your sister—"

"Understatement," Zara muttered.

"But she's an incredible witch," Kashvi said.

Any other day, Ramona might have agreed. Today, that sentiment made her want to set the kitchen curtains on fire.

They gathered around the kitchen table, grimoires spread across every available surface. Coffee mugs multiplied. Gerald supervised from the windowsill. The fox claimed the armchair and watched everything with those intelligent amber eyes.

And for a week, that's where they stayed.

Not literally — people slept in shifts, they paused for a planning drink at The Grimalkin once, and Cammie ordered pizza at some point that nobody remembered eating — but the kitchen table became the fixed point around which everything else orbited. Felix's laptop never closed. Kashvi filled three notebooks. Posey helped with annotations. Zara translated, cross-referenced, and occasionally spoke a few words of Abyssian to test the incantations, which dropped the temperature in the room several degrees and caused Cammie to say "okay, that's terrifying" and Ramona to say "I actually think it's kind of hot" and everyone else to groan audibly.

Three rituals, but structurally related — all dissolution magic, all sharing components. They could combine them. Run them in sequence at the convergence point during the new moon, using the site's amplification properties to do in one night what would otherwise take three.

The components they sourced from improbable places — blessed iron from Iris, who appeared at the door at seven a.m. and handed over four hand-forged nails; lunar water from Mystic Moon's back room, where it had been sitting next to the decorative crystals since Marcus had ordered it by mistake, thinking it would work in lava lamps; salt from the bag Eleanor had pressed into Ramona's hands in the study, which Zara confirmed was sacred-ground salt, which meant Eleanor had given them exactly what they needed while trying to get them to leave.

"She's going to be furious," Ramona said.

"She already is," Zara replied. "Might as well use the salt."

Ramona looked at the table — at the grimoires and the notes and the bark from the tree that had been quietly ruining her life since she was eight years old — and felt something that wasn't quite hope but was in the same approximate neighborhood.

They had a plan. A complete, actual, terrifying, probably-going-to-work plan.

"Okay," she said.

"Okay," Zara agreed.

Ramona looked at the plan one last time before she turned off the kitchen light. It was good. It was going to work. She wished that felt like better news.

CHAPTER THIRTY-ONE

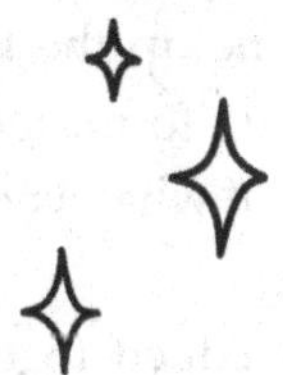

IT HAD BEEN FELIX'S IDEA, WHICH MEANT NOBODY HAD BEEN GIVEN A choice.

"Last night before the ritual," he'd announced, appearing in Ramona's doorway at seven with his coat already on and Gerald on his shoulder looking equally resolved. "We're going to The Grimalkin. All of us. Don't argue with me."

"I wasn't going to—"

"Zara, tell her not to argue with me."

Zara, who had been reading among the plant forest at the desk with the focused stillness of someone who had spent multiple centuries getting very good at ignoring chaos, looked up. "Don't argue with him."

Ramona had argued anyway, briefly, and lost.

THE GRIMALKIN WAS busy for a weeknight, which meant it was full of people who probably didn't exist during daylight hours. The jukebox in the corner was deep in some kind of old soul phase — playing something that sounded like it was being performed live in 1962 by musicians who were definitely ghosts. Odette moved behind the bar with her usual uncanny efficiency, setting drinks down in front of people slightly before they ordered them.

They'd pushed two tables together near the back. Felix had claimed the chair closest to the fire with Gerald tucked against his collar. Kashvi was already two drinks in, small golden sparks drifting from her fingertips whenever she laughed, which was often. Posey had a glass of something green that smelled like a garden and was absent-mindedly growing a small vine up the leg of her chair. Cammie had arrived last, still in her café uniform, took one look at the table and said, "Okay, yeah, I need one of whatever that is," pointing at Kashvi's drink, and sat down.

Ramona and Zara were wedged together on the bench along the wall. Not by design, exactly. Just by the geometry of the table and the fact that nobody had left them much room, which Ramona suspected was entirely deliberate.

Odette appeared at Ramona's elbow. Set down two glasses without being asked.

Ramona looked at hers. It was dark, deep red, with a single dried rose petal resting on the surface. "What is this?"

"The Occasion," Odette said and walked away.

Zara examined hers with the careful attention she brought to things she didn't entirely trust, then took a sip. Something shifted slightly in her expression. "It tastes like—" She stopped.

"Like what?"

"I don't know." Zara looked at the glass. "Something I haven't felt before. I can't put my finger on it."

Ramona took a sip of hers. It tasted like the first day of spring, like something was about to happen.

She didn't say that out loud.

THE NIGHT MOVED the way good nights at The Grimalkin always moved — slowly at first, then in a flurry of excitement. Felix got emotional telling a story about the time Ramona had helped Posey move in two years ago, and how she'd carried an entire bookshelf up four flights of stairs and not complained once, and that he'd known then she was a keeper. Ramona told him he was being embarrassing. He said embarrassing was his love language and ordered another round.

Kashvi explained to Zara, at length and with significant hand gestures, the entire taxonomy of Thornwood Academy's most insufferable faculty in the department where she'd studied history in her first witching years. Zara listened, asking clarifying questions, filing things away. "Professor Aldric sounds structurally unsound," she said at one point. "Both as a scholar and as a person."

"Oh, completely," Kashvi said. "Ooh, my sparks just went gold."

"Delight?" Zara clarified.

Kashvi beamed, nodding while finishing her third drink.

"I've noticed the correlation," Zara said. "Green tends to be frustration. Blue is surprise."

Kashvi stared at her. "I've been doing this my whole life and I didn't know blue was surprise."

"It's very brief. You'd have to be watching closely."

There was a pause. Ramona watched the interaction, an invisible hand inside her chest squeezing her heart. She looked up at the ceiling.

Posey, who had said relatively little all evening, leaned over at some point while Felix was at the bar and put her hand over Ramona's. "Hey. How are you doing? Actually."

"I'm fine."

Posey gave her a look.

"I'm terrified," Ramona said quietly.

"Of the ritual?"

Ramona made a choked noise she hoped signaled affirmation.

"Of everything going wrong?" Posey asked.

"Of everything going right," Ramona clarified.

Posey nodded, understanding Ramona's meaning. Didn't push. Squeezed her hand once and let go. "You know we're going to be there, right? Whatever happens after. We're not going anywhere."

Ramona's throat tightened. "I know."

"Good." Posey sat back, picked up her drink. "Just wanted to say it."

• • •

The jukebox shifted without warning into something slow and slightly mournful, the kind of song that made everyone's conversations pause for just a second. Felix looked at it suspiciously. "That's pointed."

"The jukebox has opinions," Cammie said. She'd been watching Zara all evening with the quiet, evaluating attention of someone building a file. "Zara. Can I ask you something?"

Zara's eyes slid to Cammie, but her body leaned away, as if involuntarily.

"Why don't you like me?" Cammie asked.

Ramona interjected. "Cammie—"

Zara studied Cammie for a long moment. "I don't dislike you," she said quietly.

"Then why are you so weird to me?" Cammie asked, her words slurred.

Ramona huffed. "Cammie, you can't just pounce on people like that."

Zara pushed her foot to touch Ramona's. "It's not a matter or like or dislike. I simply feel nervous around…" She looked up to the ceiling as if searching for the word. "Non-witches."

Ramona tried to keep her face neutral, even though she knew Zara was lying. Zara was fine with the non-mages that came into the shop, polite and helpful.

Cammie was fully pouting now. "But I'm nice."

"You are nice," Zara repeated back, her voice soft as if coaxing a child out of a tantrum.

The table went a little quiet. Even the jukebox seemed to hold.

Zara didn't offer any more explanation. Cammie seemed satisfied with Zara's answer, turning her head as a pair of nymphs with green-tinged skin walked by. "Do they have to be so hot?" she said loudly.

One of the nymphs glanced over her shoulder with surprise, then laughed as the pair found a booth toward the back of the room.

Sometime past midnight, Felix announced he was going to get one more round and promptly got into a conversation at the bar that showed no signs of concluding. Kashvi and Posey had migrated to the other end of the table, heads together, talking about something that was making Kashvi's sparks fly. Cammie was on her phone, tilted away, giving them space with the subtlety of someone who was absolutely doing it on purpose.

Ramona and Zara sat with their shoulders pressed together in the particular way they'd stopped noticing and couldn't stop doing.

The enchanted candelabra chandelier cast warm, low light over the table. The jukebox had gone soft again — something instrumental now, no words, just the shape of a feeling.

"Are you scared?" Ramona asked.

"Yes," Zara said.

"Me too."

Zara's hand found hers under the table. Her thumb traced the same slow circles it always did. Like she'd been doing it for years. Like it was habit.

"I keep thinking about the things I want to say to you," Ramona said. "And then I can't figure out how to say any of them."

Zara turned to look at her. Her eyes in the flickering candlelight were dark and certain. "I already know."

"You can't know, I haven't—"

"Ramona." Zara's voice was quiet, steady, the voice that meant she was being very precise on purpose. "We've been tethered together for nearly seven weeks. I know."

Ramona's chest did something complicated. "That's an unfair advantage."

"Yes." The corner of Zara's mouth moved. "It is, Mortal."

The jukebox shifted again, into something that had no business being this tender. Felix was still at the bar, gesturing broadly at someone. Cammie was not looking at them.

"Let's get out of here," Ramona said.

Zara looked at her. "Where do you want to go?"

"Home." Ramona held her gaze. "I want to go home."

Something moved through Zara's expression, quiet and certain and wanting. She set down her glass. "Then let's go home."

They said their goodbyes, which took longer than it should have because Felix got tearful and needed a hug, and Gerald had to be formally bade good night with a lot of bowing on Zara's part, and Posey held Ramona's hands for just a moment too long, and Cammie said "see you tomorrow" in a voice that meant *have fun* and *I'll mind my own business* and *I'm glad she has you* all at once.

They walked out through the bar, and Ramona tried not to grow nostalgic, thinking that this could be the last time they walked home together.

Outside, the night was cold and clear, Fernwick quiet around them. The door to The Grimalkin swung shut behind them.

Zara took her hand properly this time, fingers interlaced.

They walked.

They didn't talk. There wasn't anything left to say that words were the right size for.

The apartment building came into view. The front door. The stairs.

Ramona unlocked the apartment. The lights were off. The fox lifted his head from the couch, saw them, and resettled. The whole apartment was quiet and theirs.

She turned around. Zara was right there, close, watching her with that particular dark-eyed attention that had stopped feeling like being studied and started feeling like being known.

"We should sleep," Ramona said. "We need to be sharp tomorrow."

"Mmm," Zara agreed. Neither of them moved.

Ramona reached up and took the lapel of Zara's jacket in her hand. Just held it. "Unless you're not tired just yet."

"Not yet," Zara said softly. Her hand came up to Ramona's jaw.

Ramona kissed her, and Zara kissed her back, slowly, deeply, like they had all the time in the world, even knowing they didn't.

They pulled at each other's clothes on their way to Ramona's bedroom, throwing shirts and socks in every direction with a quiet, desperate haste. Then, finally, Zara's weight was a crushing, welcome heat pressing her down. Before Ramona could even process the reversal, the shadows in the room acted.

"I want to show you something," Zara whispered, her voice a low vibration that settled directly in Ramona's marrow.

They didn't surge, they drifted, bleeding from the corners like ink in water. They wound up the bedposts, cold as a winter grave but buzzing with a static electricity that made the fine hairs on Ramona's arms stand on end.

"Zara," Ramona breathed, her ribs straining against her skin.

Zara stayed poised over her, staring down at her. The light from the window caught the sharp lines of her face, now softened by a look of profound, aching focus. Her skin was radiating a dry, furnace-like heat, a stark contrast to the cool shadows now holding Ramona's wrists.

The invisible tether between them tightened, connecting them rib to rib. Not some knot of restraint, but a knot of union.

Zara sat back on her heels, and Ramona's breath hitched. The demon's skin was glowing with an ethereal, inner light. From the pool of shadows gathering between Zara's thighs, a shape began to manifest. It wasn't solid matter, but a construct of pure, demonic will — it reminded Ramona of a thick, obsidian strap that shimmered with a faint iridescence. It looked like the night sky had been sculpted into a vessel, vibrating with a low-frequency hum.

"Is that... you?" Ramona asked, her knees falling open in a wordless invitation. She reached, taking the shape in her hand. Zara hummed with pleasure as Ramona's hand wrapped around the shadows. She found it was cold as she brushed her thumb over its smooth surface, so different from Zara's infernal heat.

"It's an extension of me. I can feel everything," Zara murmured.

Ramona hooked a calf around Zara's hips, pulling her closer. Zara reached down, her hand guiding the shadow-construct to the entrance of Ramona's heat.

The first touch was a paradox. As Zara pushed inside her, the chill of the shadows blossomed into a searing, electric heat. It felt like being filled with heavy, pulsing liquid metal. Zara didn't drive forward with force. She moved with a slow, agonizingly gentle rhythm, each slide designed to make Ramona feel every vibration of the magic. Every time the shadows shifted, they sent ripples of static through Ramona's nerves, a sensory overload that made her head fall back in a daze of gold and violet.

"Does it feel good for you, too?" Ramona asked, her palms finding Zara's skin, which felt like sun-warmed stone. Ramona could feel the frantic, heavy thrum of Zara's heart — a rhythm that had become inextricably linked to her own.

Zara nodded and leaned forward. "Look at me, Ramona," Zara commanded, her eyes burning like twin embers.

Ramona hadn't even realized she'd closed her eyes, but she opened them, looking up at her demon. She watched the way Zara's jaw tightened with the effort of being gentle when her nature demanded fire. Zara began to move more deeply, her hips rocking in a slow, punishingly tender cadence. The shadows inside Ramona were alive, expanding and contracting, reaching into corners of her soul that felt like they were being branded.

"Oh, fuck," Ramona choked out, her fingernails tracing the long muscles of Zara's back. "You feel so good. More. I need more of you."

Zara growled, but it was a sound of surrender, not aggression. She increased the pace slightly, her body a blur of muscle and shadow. The bed began to protest — the thrift-store wood screaming, the frame groaning under the supernatural kinetic energy. Every thrust sent a shudder through the floorboards, but they were locked in their own private gravity.

"More," Ramona demanded. She clamped her legs around Zara's waist, pulling her in as deep as the shadows would go, wanting to vanish into the heat. Ramona's hands were on the headboard, meeting Zara thrust for thrust, when they hit the peak together. Ramona cried out, her body spasming in a long, beautiful release, her vision exploding into white light as the shadows inside her flared with a final burst of violet energy. Zara followed her a second later, a guttural sound wrenched from her chest as she collapsed against Ramona, her body shaking with the force of her own devotion.

The shadow-construct dissolved into a faint, cool mist.

The room fell into a heavy, ringing silence, broken only by their ragged gasps. The air was thick with the scent of sex and unsaid words. They lay tangled together in the wreckage, Zara's weight a crushing, beautiful anchor.

"Ramona," Zara whispered into the crook of her neck. It was a lament.

"This new bed was such a good idea," Ramona said, her whisper turning into a quiet laugh.

"I know. I wanted you to have it for.." Zara paused, not finishing the thought aloud. *For after I'm gone,* were the words Zara didn't say.

Ramona reached up, cupping Zara's face, tracing the line of those lethal fangs. She kissed Zara with a slow, devastating tenderness — a kiss that tasted of everything they couldn't say, her tongue tracing a silent vow against Zara's own, as if saying, *I am yours. I don't know how to let you leave.*

CHAPTER THIRTY-TWO

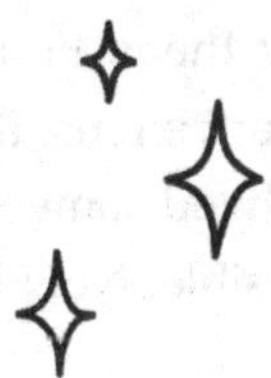

RAMONA COULDN'T SLEEP, EVEN WITH THE EXHAUSTING WEIGHT OF WHAT they had to do. Even with the soreness of her body after three orgasms.

She'd tried to sleep. Had closed her eyes. Had counted sheep and done all the things she knew she was supposed to do to quiet her anxious mind. The fox had come in at some point after she'd brushed her teeth and gotten ready for bed.

But her thoughts kept spinning. The ritual. The curse-breaking. The possibility of the tether dissolving.

The certainty of Zara leaving.

Beside her, Zara was still. But through the tether, Ramona could feel she wasn't asleep either. Just lying there in the dark, thoughts racing in parallel.

"I know you're awake," Ramona said quietly.

"I know you know." Zara's voice was soft as she propped herself up.

"The walls feel like they're closing in," Ramona said, taking a deep breath.

Zara put a hand on the small of her back. "Want to go sit on the fire escape?"

"Yeah."

They slipped out of bed carefully. The fox lifted his head from the foot of the mattress, watching.

"Stay, friend," Ramona whispered. The fox settled back down.

They pulled on jackets and sweaters. Ramona crossed to her window, opened it quietly. The cold night air rushed in.

She climbed out onto the fire escape. Zara followed, closing the window most of the way behind them to keep the heat in.

The city spread out below them. Fernwick at midnight — mostly quiet, a few cars passing, distant sirens, the kind of ambient noise that became white noise after you lived somewhere long enough.

The moon was almost invisible. New moon eve. Tomorrow night it would be completely dark.

Tomorrow night, everything would change.

They settled on the metal grating, shoulders touching, legs dangling through the rails.

"Are you scared?" Ramona asked.

"Terrified," Zara said.

"After the curse breaks?"

"After the tether dissolves." Zara's voice was quiet. "When the tether dissolves."

"Felix said it should. If breaking the curse satisfies the magical debt—"

"I know what Felix said." Zara's hand found Ramona's. "And if he's right, it'll be fast. Break the curse, fix your magic, the debt is satisfied. The binding dissolves automatically."

Ramona's chest tightened. "And then you go back to Hell."

"Yes."

The word hung between them. Simple. Devastating.

"How long?" Ramona asked. "How long do we have after the binding breaks?"

"I don't know. It might not be long." Zara's voice was carefully controlled. "The pull will be immediate. Once the binding dissolves, Hell will recall me. That's how it works."

"Can you… refuse? Even for an hour?"

"Not without consequences." Zara's thumb traced circles on the back of Ramona's hand. "I'm still employed by Hell. Still bound by my contract with them. The accidental summoning gave me temporary leave to be here, but once that's resolved—"

"You have to go back."

"Yes."

Ramona felt tears threatening. "This whole time, we've been planning to break the tether. To free you. And all we're doing is sending you home—"

"Sending me *back*." Zara's voice was soft. "Not home."

Ramona felt the sharp sting of tears threaten at the edges of her eyes. She looked up into the night sky, blinking quickly.

"I don't love that," Ramona said, her voice sounding a bit choked.

Zara's hand came up to cup Ramona's face. "But that doesn't change the reality. I'm still a demon. Still bound by Hell's bureaucracy. Still obligated to return when summoned."

"So we just… break the curse, you disappear, and that's it?"

"That's not it." Zara's voice was firm. "We break the curse. Your magic gets fixed. You get to be the person you were always meant to be. And I—" She stopped, swallowing and pausing for a moment as if to compose herself. "I go back to where I belong."

"Will I ever get to see you again?" Ramona asked.

"I want that very much," Zara said, and Ramona caught that her answer wasn't a *yes*.

"How?"

"I don't know yet." Zara's thumb wiped away a tear on Ramona's cheek. "But I'll find a way. Even if it takes months. Years. A lifetime. I'll find you again."

"I could start being really terrible and get sent to Hell," Ramona offered with a small laugh, wiping at her nose.

"You broke into full-body hives just taking the jar of lunar water from work, Mortal," Zara teased.

"I can change. I could… start a family vlogging channel and profit off my children. I could… start telling people I vote for fiscal reasons. I could light Thornwood Academy on fire. I'm willing to really, you know, fuck some shit up," Ramona challenged.

Zara laughed, her fangs on full display. "I don't want you to come to Hell. Besides, no one ends up there as a surprise. Only willing souls are bound to Hell."

"How can I be a willing soul, then?" Ramona asked.

"I don't want to entertain that," Zara said flatly.

"I'd do it. I can give you my soul, and that way—"

"Ramona, we'll find another way." Zara's voice was firm, final.

Ramona chewed on her lip, leaning into Zara's warmth. "You can't promise that."

"Yes, I can." Zara's voice was certain. "I've had three hundred years to understand Hell's bureaucracy. There are loopholes. Technicalities. Ways to request reassignment or extended leave. I just need time to navigate the system."

"Time we won't have together."

"No." Zara pulled her close. "We won't. And I hate that. But Ramona, breaking this curse is more important than keeping me here. You deserve to have your magic work properly. You deserve to know who you really are without that weight."

"I don't care about the curse if it means losing you."

"Yes, you do." Zara's voice was gentle but firm. "You care. You've been carrying this for twenty-seven years. This is your chance to be free. To have the life that was stolen from you."

"What good is freedom if you're not here?"

"It's still freedom." Zara pressed their foreheads together. "It's all I want for you."

Music started playing.

Both of them turned toward the sound. Somewhere below, a few apartments over, someone had opened their window. Soft music drifted out — something old, jazzy, the kind of music that made Ramona think of dance halls and romance and a different era entirely.

Zara stood, held out her hand. "Dance with me."

"Zara—"

"Please." Zara's smile was sad. "We might not get another chance. Dance with me."

Ramona took her hand.

Zara pulled her up. Wrapped an arm around her waist. Drew her close until they were swaying together on the narrow metal grating, the city spread out below them, the music floating up from the neighbor's window.

It wasn't graceful. The fire escape wasn't meant for dancing. They had maybe three feet of space, but Zara led with confident ease, spinning Ramona carefully, catching her, pulling her back close.

"I didn't know you could dance," Ramona said, her voice thick.

"Three hundred years," Zara replied. "You pick up skills."

They swayed together. The music was soft, melancholy, beautiful. Ramona rested her head on Zara's shoulder. Let herself be held. Let herself memorize this — the warmth of Zara's body, the steady rhythm of their movement, the music wrapping around them like something precious.

Something they might never have again.

"I'll always be thankful for what you've given me," Zara said quietly.

Ramona lifted her head. "What have I given you?"

"This." Zara gestured vaguely. "Life. Purpose. A reason to be more than just a cog in Hell's bureaucracy." She paused. "Hope. I've always wondered what that felt like."

"I summoned you by accident and made your life complicated."

"You summoned me by accident and made my life worth living." Zara spun her again, gentle, careful. "I was going through motions. Centuries of the same tasks, the same routines, the same endless nothing. And then you yanked me out of that. Made me find out what it feels like to be surprised. To laugh. To care about someone."

"And now I'm sending you back to that nothing." Ramona's voice broke.

"No." Zara stopped moving. Held Ramona's face in both hands. "You're not sending me back to nothing. Because I'm different now. You changed me. And that doesn't go away just because I'm in Hell instead of here."

"But you'll be alone again."

"But I'll always have this. This moment." Zara's eyes were intense. "That's not nothing, Ramona. That's everything."

The music swelled. Ramona let Zara lead her in slow circles, their feet quiet on the metal grating.

"What if we never see each other again?" Ramona asked, tears streaming down her cheeks in earnest now. "What if Hell won't let you? What if — what if you're stuck there forever?"

"Then I'll still be glad I had this." Zara pulled her close again. Started swaying. "These weeks with you. These moments. This feeling. I'd rather have had this and lost it than never have had it at all."

"That's not enough for me." Ramona's tears flowed freely. "I don't want moments. I want *you*. Every day. I want to wake up next to you. I want—"

"I know." Zara's voice was thick with emotion. "I want that, too. So much it hurts. But we can't keep the binding just to keep me here. You know that."

"Why not?"

"Because you deserve to have your magic work. You deserve to be free of this curse." Zara's hand traced patterns on her back. "And I deserve to choose you freely. Without a binding forcing proximity. Not because magic compelled me."

"I don't want to wait for that," Ramona said stubbornly.

"Neither do I." Zara spun her one more time. Caught her. Held her.

The music began to fade. The neighbor closing their window, probably. Retreating back into their own life, their own story.

Ramona and Zara stood there on the fire escape, holding each other, swaying slightly even though the music was gone.

"I love you," Ramona said. "And I'm going to hate every second you're gone."

"I love you, too." Zara kissed her forehead. "And I'm going to spend every second in Hell finding a way back to you."

"Promise?"

"I promise." Zara's arms tightened around her. "This isn't goodbye forever."

They stood there a while longer. The city quiet around them. The new moon rising invisible above.

Tomorrow night — tonight, if really was as late as Ramona thought it was — everything would change.

They'd cleanse the convergence point and break the curse and sever the binding.

Zara would go back to Hell.

And Ramona would have to figure out how to keep breathing without her.

"We should try to sleep," Zara said finally. "We need to be sharp."

"I don't want to sleep." Ramona's grip tightened. "I don't want to waste what time we have left."

"Then we won't sleep." Zara kissed her. Soft, sweet, full of promise and grief. "We'll stay right here until morning if that's what you need."

"I need you not to leave."

"I know." Zara's voice broke. "I know. I'm so sorry."

They stayed on the fire escape. Holding each other. Not talking. Not crying. Just being together for whatever time they had left.

The ritual would change everything.

But right now, for a few more quiet moments, they were still together.

Still bound.

Still whole.

And in those quiet moments, Ramona let herself pretend that maybe, somehow, there was a way to keep this. Even though she knew there wasn't.

CHAPTER THIRTY-THREE

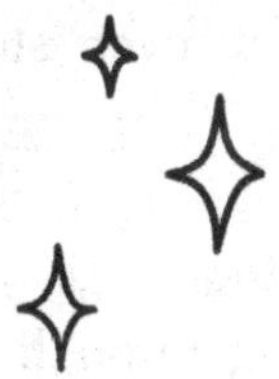

EVEN WITH THEIR FLASHLIGHTS CUTTING WHITE BEAMS THROUGH THE darkness, even with the darkness of the new moon leaving the sky velvet black, the corruption of the convergence point was undeniable. The ground wasn't just dark — it was *wrong*. It was black like oil slicks, like rot, like something that had never been meant to exist in the natural world. The grass was dead in spreading circles, crispy and brown, crumbling to ash when Ramona stepped on it. The air smelled like sulfur and copper and, underneath, something that made her instincts scream *danger* and *run* and *this is a place where things die.*

Was this what Hell was like? Was Zara used to this?

They stood at the edge of the clearing. All of them.

Ramona could hear their breathing — Felix's quick and shallow, Kashvi's measured and controlled, Posey's whimpers of pain, her breathing already labored like she knew what was coming. Cammie stayed with the group, there for moral and emergency support only. Gerald was unusually still on Felix's shoulder, head tucked against his neck. The fox pressed warm and solid against Ramona's leg, a point of comfort in the growing dread.

"Whoa," Cammie breathed. Her voice was barely a whisper, like speaking too loud might wake something. "It's worse than I remember."

"The corruption's been accelerating," Kashvi said. "We need to start now. Before it spreads further."

Ramona could feel it through the soles of her shoes. A wrongness in the earth. A sickness. The convergence point wasn't just corrupted — it was *dying*. And taking everything around it with it. If it got beyond the convergence point, would it ever stop? Or would it consume *everything*?

Ramona shivered.

They moved into the clearing.

Each step felt like walking through water. The air grew thicker. Heavier. Ramona's lungs worked harder for each breath. Beside her, Zara's jaw was tight. Through the tether — still there, still humming between them — Ramona felt her tension. Her focus. Her fear.

They set up in the pattern they'd practiced. The circle they drew was in the center of the clearing, approximately five feet in diameter. Ramona at the north end of the circle. Zara at the south. Felix at the east. Posey at the west. The others arranged themselves outside the immediate ritual space — close enough to help, far enough to be safe. Or as safe as anyone could be.

The supplies were laid out with shaking hands. Lunar water in glass jars, still glowing that faint silver that seemed too delicate for what they were about to attempt. Blessed iron nails that Felix placed with reverent care. Sacred salt from Greenbriar Manor — Ramona tried not to think about her mother or sister, or about anything except the ritual.

They had everything they needed.

Everything they'd prepared since the last ritual.

Everything that suddenly felt completely inadequate.

"Ready?" Kashvi called from outside the circle. Her voice was steady, but Ramona heard the tremor underneath.

Ramona looked at Zara. Through the tether: determination like steel. Love like drowning. Fear like falling.

This was it.

After the ritual, everything would be different.

After the ritual, Zara would be gone.

Ramona's throat closed. She forced words out anyway. "Ready."

They began with the convergence point cleansing.

Zara spoke first. The banishment.

Her voice dropped into that register Ramona had only heard a few times — the one that wasn't quite human, wasn't quite anything that should exist on this plane. Dark, velvety sounds like promises, like temptation incarnate.

The temperature plummeted. Not gradually. Instantly. Ramona's breath fogged in front of her face, thick white clouds that hung in the air too long. Frost spread across the dead grass in delicate patterns. Her fingertips went numb inside her gloves.

The corruption *responded.*

The dark marks on the ground didn't just sit there. They *writhed.* Pulled back from Zara's words like living things recoiling from fire. Ramona could see them moving — oily, viscous, wrong wrong *wrong.*

Zara intoned. Her voice echoed strangely, like the clearing was bigger than it should be. Deeper. She'd translated the words for Ramona: *Return to your origin. Return to Hell. This is not your place.*

The words bounced off the circle of ancient trees. Multiplied. Ramona heard them from every direction — Zara's voice and not-Zara's voice, speaking in unison, in rounds, in terrible harmony.

The corruption pulled back farther. Retreating toward the center of the circle. Concentrating. Getting darker. Denser.

Worse.

Felix's turn.

He stepped forward on legs that shook. His voice came out thin at first, reedy. He cleared his throat. Tried again.

His words, in a forgotten tongue: *Cleanse this place. Purify the sacred earth. Dissolve all corruption.*

She picked up the first jar of lunar water. It was heavier than she remembered. Or her arms were weaker. The glass was cold enough to burn her palms even through her gloves.

She began to pour.

Where the water touched the ground, it hissed. Not like water on hot metal. Like water on acid. Like something being destroyed at a molecular level. Steam rose in white plumes that smelled wrong — sweet and rotten at the same time. The ground beneath seemed to *sigh*. A sound like dying, or like relief.

Her magic pushed out from her — weak, uncertain, fighting against the curse that had suppressed it for twenty-seven years. It felt like pushing through mud. Through concrete. Through something that didn't want to move. But it was working. She could feel it. The lunar water amplifying Felix's invocation, carrying it deeper into the earth, the words sinking in like roots.

She moved around the circle. Pouring as Felix spoke, his voice getting stronger as his magic found its rhythm.

The second jar. The third.

Her hands were shaking so hard water slopped over the sides. Wasted. She couldn't afford to waste any, but she couldn't stop shaking.

The fourth jar. The last one.

She poured the final drops, stumbling as she stepped back.

The purification was done.

Now Posey.

Posey moved to the center of the circle. She was already pale, gray-tinged, ashen. Already swaying like a tree in high wind.

"Posey—" Ramona started. Her voice sounded far away.

"I'm fine." Posey's voice was strained. Tight. Absolutely *not* fine. "Let me finish this."

She knelt on the poisoned ground. Her knees sank into the soft earth. She pressed her palms flat against it.

And began to speak.

It wasn't a language Ramona knew. It was something older. Known words, but the cadence was wrong — ancient, primal, from a time before language crystallized into modern forms.

"Remember what you were," Posey said. Her voice was soft, but it carried. Filled the clearing. Seemed to come from the ground itself. *"Remember the green and growing things. Remember life. Remember connection. Remember the roots that go deep. Remember the flowers that reach for sun. Remember—"*

Light burst from her hands.

Not metaphorical light. Actual, physical light. Green and gold and so *alive* it hurt to look at. It spread across the ground like roots, like veins, like the vascular system of something vast and sleeping. Where it touched, the darkness dissolved. Not slowly. Violently. With small popping sounds like bubbles bursting. The grass began to grow again — not gradually but fast, too fast, shooting up green and vital. The clearing lightened from black to gray to verdant.

But Posey was shaking.

Her whole body trembled with effort. Her hands were sinking deeper into the earth like it was trying to pull her down. Sweat poured down her face despite the cold. Her breathing came in gasps.

"Posey!" Cammie's voice was sharp with fear.

"Don't—" Posey's gasp was barely audible. "Don't break the circle. I can… I can finish."

The light intensified. Spread farther. The corruption retreated like a living thing trying to escape. Dissolved. Disappeared in those awful popping sounds.

A pulse like the heartbeat of the land shot in every direction, a circle of light flowing like a ripple through the air.

The convergence point was clean.

Clean and empty and somehow more terrifying for it.

Posey collapsed. Dropped. Boneless. Unconscious before she hit the ground.

Cammie was there in an instant, breaking the circle to catch her before her head struck the ground. "Posey? Posey, talk to me—"

Posey's eyes fluttered. "I'm okay." Her voice was barely there. A thread of sound. "Just… tired. So tired."

But she wasn't okay. Ramona could see it. The pale tinge to her skin. The way her chest barely rose with each breath. The restoration had taken too much. Way too much.

Felix was breathing heavily, his hands on his knees.

Ramona felt it, too. The cleansing had drained her in ways she hadn't expected. Her magic felt depleted just from being near it. Stretched thin like old elastic. Her hands wouldn't stop shaking.

They were only one ritual in.

They still had to break the curse. Break the tether.

She looked at Zara. Through the tether — still there, still humming, still real — she felt exhaustion mirroring her own.

"We need to keep going," Kashvi said. She was checking her watch, but her hands were shaking too. "We have maybe an hour of optimal dissolution energy left. If we stop now—"

"We're not stopping," Ramona said. The words came out hoarse. Raw. "We can't."

Through the tether: agreement. Underneath, a terrible grief, because they both knew what came next.

They rearranged with movements that felt clumsy. Disconnected.

She placed the banewood bark in the center of the now-cleansed convergence point. It looked worse now, darker and twisted, like it didn't belong in a clean place.

Ramona positioned herself again at the north end of the circle, Zara at the south. The blessed iron nails at east and west, anchoring the ritual space. Holding it together. Hopefully.

"I'll lead," Ramona said. Her voice sounded like she'd been screaming. Maybe she had. She couldn't remember. "You support. Like we practiced."

"Always," Zara replied. Her voice was also rough.

Ramona began to speak. The curse-breaking incantation. A dead language, harsh and demanding. Words that required precision. Exactness. Every syllable in the right place or the whole thing would fail.

Her tongue felt thick. Her mind fuzzy. The words kept slipping away from her.

I break this binding. Her voice cracked. *I dissolve this curse. I sever the root from the tree.*

Nothing happened.

The bark sat there. Inert. Mocking.

She tried again. Louder. Forcing more intent into the words even though she had so little left to give.

I break this binding. I dissolve—

The bark began to smoke.

Thin tendrils of gray. Acrid. Smelling like burning hair and rotting wood and something chemical.

"It's working," Felix breathed from outside the circle. Gerald cooed softly, hopefully.

But Ramona could feel it wasn't. Not enough to matter. The curse was fighting back. Twenty-seven years of magic, anchored deep in living wood and old intent and a child's feral anger. It refused to let go.

She could feel it clinging. Digging in. Hers. It thought it was *hers*. A part of her. Essential.

Zara stepped closer. Began to speak in support. Her demonic power lending strength to Ramona's words. The two languages winding together — ancient and demonic, human and not.

The bark caught fire.

Not normal fire. Cold fire. Blue and white, flames that gave off darkness instead of light. That made the temperature drop instead of rise. That burned without consuming.

The smoke got thicker. Ramona's eyes watered. Her throat closed. She kept speaking through it, coughing, choking, forcing the words out.

The curse was still there. Still holding. Still—

The air split.

The temperature dropped twenty degrees in an instant.

Then, thirty. Forty. Ramona's tears froze on her cheeks. Her breath stopped fogging and started crystallizing, tiny ice particles that hung in the air and caught the ethereal light from the cold fire.

Then, the ghosts came.

Not metaphorical ghosts, or echoes or impressions. Actual spirits. Full manifestations. Pale and translucent and *screaming*.

The sound was inhuman. High-pitched and endless and it went straight through Ramona's skull into her brain and rattled there. She wanted to cover her ears but her hands were locked in ritual position, held in front of her as if she were holding an invisible ball of power. She couldn't move. Couldn't protect herself.

The spirits poured into the clearing like smoke. Like water. Like something thick and viscous. They swirled around Kashvi.

Surrounded her.

Reached for her with spectral hands that looked almost solid.

"What—" Kashvi stumbled backward. "What's happening?"

"The ritual!" Ramona shouted over the screaming. "It must be pulling in these spirits. The dissolution energy is too strong. It's opening holes between planes."

The ghosts pressed closer to Kashvi. One of them — a woman's shape, vague and shifting — reached for her throat.

Kashvi's scream joined the ghosts'. High and terrified and human.

Gerald shrieked.

Not cooed. Not the soft sounds Ramona was used to. A full-throated pigeon shriek of anguish and terror.

He launched off Felix's shoulder, flying wildly toward Kashvi, toward the ghosts, and dove straight into the woman reaching for Kashvi's throat. The ghost disintegrated instantly, but Gerald bounced back as if hitting a wall, one wing at an unnatural angle. Bent wrong. Broken. He spiraled through the air, out of control, and hit the ground hard.

The sound of impact was small. Soft. Terrible.

Gerald lay still. Too still. One wing spread at that awful angle. His small body not moving.

"Gerald!" Felix dove for him, breaking the circle, hands scrabbling at the ground. "No, no, no. Gerald, please." He scooped up the pigeon with shaking hands. Gerald's head lolled. Limp. "He's not breathing." Felix's voice broke. "He's not... Gerald, please, please wake up."

The ghosts were getting denser. More solid. Another one of them had its hands — if Ramona could call them hands — around Kashvi's throat. She was gasping, clawing at something she couldn't touch.

Her lips were turning blue.

"Kashvi, stay with us." Ramona was frozen in place, her feet rooted in place. She cast a panicked look toward Zara, who was watching Kashvi with the same level of terror.

Posey tried to stand, still gray-faced, still weak. She got halfway up and her legs gave out. She crumpled back to the ground with a cry of frustration and pain.

"We have to stop—" Cammie was sobbing. "We have to stop the ritual—"

"We can't." Zara's voice cut through the chaos. Sharp. Commanding. Desperate. "If we stop mid-ritual, the convergence point could collapse entirely. It would take the whole park with it, maybe more."

The ghosts pressed closer to Kashvi, bringing her to her knees. She was making sounds now as she writhed against them. Choking sounds. Dying sounds.

Felix was sobbing, cradling Gerald's limp body, begging him to wake up as he crawled on the ground toward Kashvi, unable to get to her through the throng of spirits encircling her.

The bark was burning hotter. The cold fire spreading. The curse fighting back with everything it had. Ramona's magic was failing, the words slipping away from her, her concentration shattered by the screaming and the cold and the terror.

"Zara," Ramona called. Her voice was ragged. "Use your power to banish them."

"I can't." Zara's face was anguished. Her hands were clenched so tight her nails drew blood. "If I use demonic energy now, after we just cleansed the convergence point, it'll corrupt it again. All of this will be for nothing. The park will collapse anyway. Everything we've done—"

"But Kashvi—"

Kashvi's eyes were rolling back. Her struggles were getting weaker.

Gerald still wasn't moving.

The fox was pressed against Ramona's leg, whimpering. Actually whimpering. A sound she'd never heard from him.

The bark was burning but not breaking. The curse was too strong. Too old. Too deeply rooted in a lifetime of believing she was broken.

Everything was falling apart.

They were going to fail.

Kashvi was going to die.

Gerald was already—

No. *No*, she couldn't think that.

But the ritual was failing and there was nothing she could do, her magic was too weak, the curse was too strong, and—

"Ramona."

The voice came from the edge of the clearing.

Ramona turned.

Eleanor stepped out of the woods.

Iris behind her.

For a moment, Ramona forgot how to breathe.

"No." The word came out broken. Disbelieving. "No, you can't be here—"

But they were.

Eleanor in a ritual robe Ramona had never seen. Iris in practical clothes, face drawn with exhaustion and guilt and determination. At the sight of them, Ramona's magic went completely chaotic.

The curse — recognizing Iris, recognizing the one who'd cast it even accidentally, even as a child — *surged*. Like it had been waiting for this. Like it knew.

Ramona's magic exploded outward in every direction. Wild. Uncontrolled. Exactly like the incident at Thornwood, but worse. So much worse.

Objects around the clearing flew into the air. Stones. Branches. Felix's dropped flashlight. They spun in circles, faster and faster, a maelstrom of debris.

The cold fire jumped from the bark to the grass. Spread in a ring. Ramona could feel it — her magic out of control, the curse amplifying it, using it, turning her power against everything she was trying to save.

"Ramona." Zara grabbed her, hands on her shoulders. "Ramona, you have to control it —"

"I can't!" Ramona was shaking. Shaking apart. "I can't, and the curse is… It's using Iris… It's using the connection—"

Kashvi went limp, and the ghosts descended as if they would rip her body to shreds.

"No—" Cammie scrambled toward her.

Eleanor and Iris didn't say a word. They just stepped into the ritual circle, took positions on either side of Ramona, and began to chant.

Eleanor's voice was strong. Commanding. A banishment that Ramona didn't know but could feel — ancient, powerful, absolute. It rolled through the clearing like thunder.

The ghosts *heard* it.

They turned from Kashvi, looked at Eleanor, and began to dissipate.

They didn't disappear quickly. They moved with slow reluctance, like they were being torn away from something they wanted. But the important thing was that they went, shredding apart like smoke in wind, their screaming faded to whispers, to nothing.

Kashvi writhed on the ground. Breathing. Gasping. Alive.

Iris knelt beside the burning bark. Her palm was bleeding, and she let the blood drip onto the bark. She began to speak in the curse-breaker's tongue — words Ramona had only read, never heard. They sounded like unweaving. Like unpicking stitches. Like taking apart something that should never have been put together.

The cold fire began to dim.

Gerald twitched, his clawed feet flexing in the air as Felix cradled him on his back.

Felix's sob was loud in the sudden quiet. "Gerald, I thought I lost you."

But the curse still wasn't breaking.

The bark was burning lower but not dissolving. The magic was too old. Too strong. Too deeply rooted in a lifetime of belief.

Ramona could feel it. The curse clinging. Refusing. *Hers hers hers.* "It's not working," she said. Her voice was flat. Empty. So tired. "It's still not working."

Eleanor's chanting faltered. She looked at Ramona. And for the first time in Ramona's life, her mother looked uncertain.

"The curse is too complex," Iris said. Her hands were shaking over the bark. "I thought with the convergence point clean, with the blood and the right spell… but it's been active for too long. It's integrated too deeply. I can feel it. It's woven into your magical core. Into your sense of self."

"So what do we do?" Zara's voice was sharp. "We can't stop."

"There's no time," Iris interrupted. "Look at the bark. It's starting to regenerate."

She was right.

The edges of the bark that had been burning away were growing back. Healing. The curse was fighting their attempts to break it by literally rebuilding its anchor.

Silence.

Except for the sound of the bark crackling. The cold fire dying. The curse winning.

Ramona fell to her knees. *Hers.* She was worthless, even without a curse. She didn't really think removing the curse would fix her life, did she? She'd messed up her entire life all on her own. A curse hadn't made her ex-wife have an affair, it didn't make her try to hex her best friend. She was a bad person, deep down, and she deserved—

Movement at the edge of the clearing.

They came through the woods like a procession.

Witches in ritual robes. Emerging from the darkness. Silent. Solemn.

Some Ramona recognized from Thornwood Coven. Others she'd never seen before. Except none of them were the inner circle. They weren't the powerful, prestigious Council members.

They were the outcasts.

The ones who'd been expelled or demoted. The ones who'd questioned the Council's decisions. The ones who'd been pushed to the margins for being too loud, too different, too much. She recognized them from classes, from The Grimalkin, from Mystic Moon.

"We heard," one of them said. A woman Ramona vaguely remembered — she'd taught botanical magic until she'd been fired for teaching methods the Council deemed too radical. "Not a call. Just… we felt it. The cleansing. The ritual."

"We wanted to help," another added. A man who always wore a low hat in The Grimalkin. "All of us."

They took positions around the circle.

Ten of them.

Then fifteen.

Then twenty.

And then, as Ramona knelt on the ground, her mouth hanging open in surprise, the High Priestess of Thornwood Coven walked into the clearing. Ramona's breath caught in her throat. Choked there.

The woman she'd accidentally hexed. The woman whose judgment had expelled her from Thornwood. She walked stiffly, pausing at the edge of the circle.

But here.

"High Priestess," Eleanor said. She bowed her head. Respectful. Surprised.

"Eleanor." The High Priestess's voice was warm. Gentle. She looked at Ramona. "You've done good work here. The cleansing was expertly performed. The ritual structure is sound. But you're right — this curse is too old. Too complex. Too deeply integrated." She paused. "It requires the full strength of a larger coven than your own."

"I—" Ramona couldn't find words. Her throat was too tight. "I don't understand. Why are you helping me?"

"Because my coven needs a strong leader." The High Priestess moved to the head of the circle. Slowly, carefully, and with absolute conviction. "The Council should have investigated your magic. Should have questioned. The Coven should have protected you." She looked at Ramona with something that might have been regret. "We failed you. All of us. The whole magical community. We saw you struggling, and we blamed you instead of looking deeper. Let us help you now."

The witches joined hands.

Twenty-three of them. Twenty-three voices. Twenty-three more sources of power.

Felix stood, cradling a still limp Gerald under his arm. Kashvi and Posey were hunched on either side of him — but standing. "Ramona, the unbinding spell is the only thing strong enough for this kind of curse. Trust me," he said.

Ramona nodded.

They began to chant an unbinding spell. All of them. Her mother, her sister, the Thornwood Coven, the outcasts, her own coven.

The sound was overwhelming. It wasn't loud, exactly, not in a volume way. It was overwhelming in its strength, its presence, like the air itself was vibrating, singing.

The power hit Ramona like a wave.

Twenty-three witches channeling energy into the curse-breaking. Amplifying Ramona's words. Supporting Iris's unweaving. Feeding magic into the ritual like kindling into fire.

The bark blazed white hot.

Ramona felt the curse beginning to crack. Only small fractures at first. Hairline. Barely there.

Then, gradually, the cracks became bigger, spreading. The magic that had held her down, had bound her for her entire life, was finally — finally! — starting to break apart.

But there was something else.

Something pulling at her. A second binding, intertwined with the first so closely she hadn't seen it.

The tether.

Felix had been right. An unbinding was stronger than a dissolution. The binding to Zara was unraveling automatically.

Ramona looked across the circle, still frozen in place.

Zara was staring at her. Her face was pale. Her eyes were wide. She was terrified.

Through the tether — still there but fraying — Ramona felt everything: Love like drowning, terror like falling, grief like dying, acceptance.

"Ramona—" Zara's voice cracked. "I'm sorry. I'm so sorry—"

"I know." Ramona's tears were hot on her frozen cheeks. "I know."

The tether was unraveling fast now. Ramona could feel the threads snapping one by one. Dozens of them. Hundreds. The connection that had been constant for seven weeks, that had let her feel Zara's presence every moment, that had become as natural as breathing…

It was all disappearing.

In minutes, maybe less, it would be gone entirely.

Zara would be pulled back to Hell.

Ramona would be alone.

"I don't want to leave you," Zara said. Her voice was breaking, cracking around the words. "I don't—"

"I don't want you to go." Ramona's whole body was shaking now. Not from cold but from realization that this was the last time she'd see Zara.

Zara took a step toward her across the circle. "I swear, I'll find a way."

"I know." Ramona's voice was barely audible. "I know."

The coven's chanting grew louder. More insistent. The power was building. Ramona could feel it pressing on her from all sides. The bark was disintegrating. The curse was breaking. The tether was snapping.

Everything happening at once. Everything happening too fast.

Zara reached toward her, and she willed herself to move, even a fraction of an inch. Zara's knuckles went white around her own. Grasping hands wasn't enough — she wanted to hold Zara in her arms, but she couldn't move.

She stared at Zara, trying in vain to memorize her face, the sharp line of her jaw. The way her hair fell around her ears. The exact autumn shade of her eyes. The way she looked at Ramona like she was something precious. Something worth fighting for. Worth crossing back to Hell to save.

She had to believe that last part was true.

"I love you," Ramona said. The words felt too small, so insufficient, but they were all she had. "And that's why I have to let you go."

Zara dipped her chin in understanding.

She spoke the final words of the curse-breaking. Poured everything she had left into them. Every ounce of power. Every drop of will. Everything.

I sever the root from the tree. Her voice rang clear. Strong. *I free myself from this burden. I choose my own fate.*

The bark exploded.

The sound was deafening, a crack like lightning striking. Light shot straight up in a beam from the center of the circle, white and gold and so bright it seared through Ramona's closed eyelids.

The curse shattered.

Ramona felt it — twenty-seven years of suppression breaking apart. Finally dissolving. Her magic surging back not like a trickle but like a flood. Like a dam breaking. Pure and clean and so powerful it terrified her.

It was *hers*.

Finally, actually, hers.

She'd never felt anything like it. Had never known magic could feel like this — responsive, immediate, as natural as breathing.

And then the tether snapped, the connection between her and Zara severing completely.

The constant presence she'd had for seven weeks — the awareness of Zara's emotions, the knowledge that she wasn't alone, the feeling of being tethered to someone who chose her — it was gone in an instant.

It was replaced by emptiness. The absence was deafening, worse than any noise.

The darkness started at Zara's feet. Shadows pooling where there was nothing to cast them, dark and liquid, rising. Not falling — consuming. They moved like smoke and water, spiraling upward around her in a column that had no source and no end, and Zara stood in the center of it with an expression Ramona had never seen on her face before.

Fear. Real fear. Not the careful professional concern she brought to problems. Something older and more animal than that.

"Zara—"

The shadows were at her waist. Her hands.

Zara's arm shot out through the dark, reaching. Her fingers stretched toward Ramona across the circle, certain and desperate all at once, and Ramona lunged for her — felt the air where Zara's hand had been, almost, almost—

"Ramona." Her voice came from somewhere inside the dark, swallowed at the edges. "I love you. I promise—"

The shadows closed.

Her hand was gone. The circle was empty. The air where Zara had been standing was perfectly still, as if nothing had disturbed it at all, as if she had never been there.

Ramona's hand was still outstretched. Still reaching for nothing.

She was faintly aware that she was screaming Zara's name as a pair of arms wrapped around her middle, pulling her back. She kicked and flailed, feral and broken, not caring, not able to care.

Her magic was free. Unfettered. Powerful beyond anything she'd imagined. She could feel it responding to her will, no longer fighting her, no longer sabotaged. The curse was broken.

She didn't care about that either.

She was finally whole.

And she'd never felt more broken.

A hand was on her brow, and darkness came over her.

The last thing she thought was:

She's gone.

Zara's gone.

CHAPTER THIRTY-FOUR

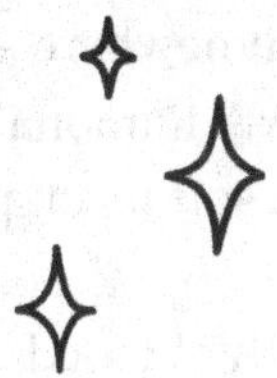

RAMONA WOKE UP IN HER CHILDHOOD BEDROOM.

She knew it before she opened her eyes, just from the lavender sachets and old wood and that particular scent that belonged only to Greenbriar Manor. The mattress was too soft, the expensive kind that her mother insisted on. The sheets were a soft linen, cool against her skin.

She'd woken up here a thousand times as a child, as a teenager, during college breaks.

Never had it felt this wrong.

She opened her eyes. The ceiling was the same pale cream it had always been. The crown molding. The chandelier that was too fancy for a bedroom. Everything exactly as she remembered.

Everything except the silence.

The room wasn't quiet — she could hear voices downstairs, muffled conversation, someone's laugh.

The silence was inside of her, in the space where the tether used to be. Where she and Zara had been bound to each other.

For seven weeks, she'd had Zara's presence constantly. A hum of awareness. The knowledge that she wasn't alone. The feeling of another consciousness threaded through hers, separate but connected.

Now… nothing. An empty, terrible nothing.

Ramona sat up too fast and the room spun. She grabbed the edge of the mattress, waited for it to steady.

Her magic responded immediately to her distress.

The lamp on the nightstand flickered. The curtains rippled despite the closed window. Small objects on the dresser vibrated.

She took a breath, trying to calm down.

The fox appeared from somewhere — under the bed maybe. He jumped up, lying down across Ramona's lap. Heavy and warm and real. She placed a hand on his soft head, petting between his twitching, alert ears.

The magic settled instantly. Settled, like it was listening to her, responding to her will instead of fighting it.

It felt strange. Clean and easy, like it had never been broken at all. In a way, she supposed it hadn't been. She had never been broken, not really. Now that the curse was gone, her magic could stretch its wings, fledge into possibility.

The curse was gone, she reminded herself, blinking at the too-bright light coming in through the window. Her shoulders hunched. The curse was gone, and Zara with it.

Ramona pressed the heel of her hand to her chest, like she could physically hold the grief in. Keep it from spilling out.

Zara's last moments replayed in her head. That panicked look, the way her dark-tipped fingers dug into the earth, desperate and frightened. It hadn't been a peaceful goodbye. Zara had been ripped out of this realm right before Ramona's eyes, and now she couldn't stop picturing that constantly cool and collected woman looking small and scared in the end.

Her chest ached, and she pressed her hand harder against her bones.

A knock on the door startled her, leaving one moment before the door opened. Felix stuck his head in. Gerald rode his shoulder, his eyes sharp and beady like he was looking for his next victim to bite. Ah, back to normal. He was alert, cooing as he looked around the room. Not at all like he'd been lying unconscious with a broken wing when she last saw him.

"You're awake," Felix said. His voice was careful. Gentle. "How do you feel?"

"Like shit," Ramona said honestly.

"Yeah." Felix came in, sitting on the edge of the bed. Gerald cooed softly. "That tracks."

The fox lifted his head, sniffing at Gerald. They touched noses, and the fox rested his head back down on Ramona's lap.

"He hasn't left your side," Felix said. "Apparently he can teleport? Or walk through walls. Both? We're not really sure. He was just suddenly here when Eleanor brought you back."

"Back from where?"

"The convergence point. You passed out after—" Felix stopped, clearing his throat. "After the ritual. Eleanor brought you here. Said you'd be safer at the manor with wards and protections. We all came with you. Wouldn't let her separate us."

Ramona stroked the fox's fur. He rumbled with a sound that was not quite a purr, but close.

"How long was I out?"

"Only about eight hours. It's almost noon." Felix paused. "Eleanor said magical exhaustion plus curse-breaking plus tether severance was a lot for your system. You needed rest."

Eight hours.

Zara had been gone for only eight hours. Was she back in Hell already? Had she been recalled to the same position the instant the tether broke, pulled across planes in seconds? Or was there a process? A reintegration period?

Ramona didn't know. Had never thought to ask.

"Come downstairs," Felix said gently. "Everyone's worried. And Cammie made coffee. The good kind. She didn't let Kashvi help."

Ramona nodded. She let Felix help her up. Her legs felt shaky, but they held under her.

She followed him down the familiar stairs, the fox at her heels, to the sitting room.

Everyone was there.

Kashvi was on the couch with her laptop. Posey was by the window with a smoothie, staring out at the garden. She looked pale.

Drained. But, strangely, she also looked okay. Alive. Cammie was on the other couch, fidgeting with her phone.

And on Kashvi's lap sat a cat.

Translucent. Pale. Definitely not solid.

A ghost cat, Ramona realized with curiosity.

Once the group realized she was awake, Cammie bounded toward her, wrapping her in a hug that felt bone-crunching. Something bright and silver glowed in Cammie's eyes as she smiled at Ramona.

"Cammie, your eyes—"

Just as quickly as she'd seen it, the silver disappeared.

"Hey! You're awake," Kashvi said with a wide smile. "Good morning."

Posey smiled at her from where she leaned by the window, giving her a small wave.

"Is everyone okay?" Ramona asked.

"Depends on your definition," Kashvi said, and Ramona could see now that her neck was bruised where the spectral hands had choked her.

"Everyone is alive and slightly improved from eight hours ago?" Ramona clarified.

Three women nodded back at her.

"Now that we're all here, I have something to confess to everyone," Kashvi said. She looked nervous. Determined. Her eyes had a slightly wild quality to them, like she'd had too much coffee or not enough sleep, or both. "I can see and talk to ghosts. I mean — I always could, a little bit. But now it's—" Small sparks flew from her fingers. Blue-white. Brief. Like static electricity but more purposeful.

"It's everywhere," Kashvi continued. Her voice was slightly frenzied. "I can see them all. All the time. There are three in this room right now. One's a Victorian lady who's very upset about Eleanor's interior design choices. Another is a man who died in a hunting accident in 1847. And this…" She gestured to the cat. "This is Percival. He's been following me since we left the convergence point. And, and look. I can do this now."

She held up her hand. The sparks intensified. Formed a small ball of light that hovered above her palm. Then split into three balls. Then six. They orbited her hand like planets around a sun before dissipating.

"All right, now that's very cool," Ramona said, watching the balls of light encircle Kashvi's hand. "That's way more than you used to be able to do."

"So much more. The ritual last night must have amplified what I already had by, like, a thousand percent. I can feel it like electricity in my veins. Like I'm vibrating at a different frequency than the rest of the world." She laughed, a little wild. "I haven't slept. Can't sleep. Too much energy."

"You need to ground," Posey said from the window. Her voice was quiet but certain. "Channel some of that excess energy into the earth before you burn yourself out."

"I know. I will. I just—" Kashvi looked down at the ghost cat. "It's overwhelming. But also kind of amazing?"

Felix shifted. Gerald fluttered to the back of a chair, and kept fluttering. Not settling. Moving with a precision that seemed different. More calculated.

"Gerald's wing healed," Felix said. "Like, completely. Not just healed. He's way stronger than before. Watch."

Gerald took off. Not his usual clumsy pigeon flight. This was controlled. Precise. He flew in a perfect figure eight around the room, then landed on the chandelier. He dove backward, drew a circle in the air, then landed back on Felix's shoulder without a single wobble.

"He's never been able to fly like that," Felix said. His voice was awed. "Pigeons aren't acrobatic birds. But now he can—" Gerald demonstrated by doing a barrel roll. "He can do that."

"How?" Ramona asked.

"The convergence point," Posey said slowly. "When we cleansed it, all that energy had to go somewhere."

"And that combined with the unbinding ritual. It seems that it might not have been a curse stifling our magic, not like yours, but something else was," Kashvi explained.

"Self-doubt, perhaps?" Felix offered, shrugging.

"It went into us," Kashvi said. "Amplified what we already had.

Made it stronger. More." She looked at Posey. "You felt it, too, didn't you?"

Posey was still staring out the window. At Eleanor's garden. The one with the banewood tree. And now the banewood tree was dead. Truly, this time.

Ramona could see it from here, or rather, couldn't see it. The tree that had loomed dark and large over the garden for as long as she could remember was simply… gone. The curse's anchor, destroyed when they broke the spell.

In its place, flowers.

Dozens of them. Hundreds. Growing in wild profusion in the space the tree had stood. Irises and lilies and roses and flowers Ramona didn't have names for. In colors that shouldn't exist in nature — deep purple irises shot through with gold, roses that faded from pink to blue, lilies that seemed to glow faintly in the afternoon sun.

"I didn't mean to," Posey said softly. "I was just standing here, thinking about how ugly that tree must have been, wishing there was something beautiful to balance out all the darkness. And then, well." She gestured toward the garden. "They just grew. I didn't even cast. Didn't speak. Just thought about flowers, and they appeared."

"That's…" Ramona didn't have words. "Posey, that's incredible."

"It's terrifying," Posey corrected. "What if I think about the wrong thing? What if I accidentally grow something poisonous? Or invasive? Or—" She stopped. Took a breath. "But yes. It's also incredible."

Felix was grinning. "So the ritual supercharged all of us. Kashvi can see and channel ghosts. Gerald can fly like a tiny feathered acrobat. Posey can grow flowers with her thoughts." He paused. Looked at Ramona. "What about you?"

Ramona held up her hand. Thought about light. A ball of pure white light formed above her palm. Steady. Controlled. Perfect.

No stuttering. No flickering. No explosion of chaos.

Simple magic. Working exactly as she intended.

"It's clean," she said. Her voice was thick. "My magic. It just works. Like it should have always worked."

"Because it should have," Felix said gently. "The curse is gone. This is who you always were underneath."

Ramona dismissed the light, looked at Felix. "What about you? Did the ritual amplify anything for you?"

Felix stopped. Frowned. "Actually. There's been something weird. With technology." He pulled out his phone and didn't touch the screen. Just looked at it.

The phone unlocked.

"Okay, that could be Face ID," Kashvi said, rolling her eyes.

Felix kept looking. Apps opened. Closed. The screen flickered through menus without him touching anything.

"But that's not," Ramona said.

"It started this morning," Felix said. "I thought my phone was glitching. But then..." He looked at Kashvi's laptop. It woke up, opened a browser, and started playing a YouTube video of pigeons.

"Felix," Kashvi said slowly. "Are you controlling my laptop with your mind?"

"Maybe?" Felix looked equal parts excited and terrified. "I think — I think the convergence point gave me technopathy, or at least amplified it. I've always been good with computers but this is..." The laptop opened six more tabs. Closed them. The volume adjusted up and down. "This is weird."

Gerald cooed smugly, like he'd known all along that his human was special.

Cammie was being quiet. Too quiet. She kept glancing at her phone. At the door. At anything except the people in the room.

"Cammie?" Ramona asked gently, remembering the silver in Cammie's eyes before she was distracted. "Are you okay?"

Cammie looked up. Bit her lip. "Yeah." She smiled, sipping her coffee.

"Anything new?" Ramona pressed.

Felix, Kashvi, and Posey looked equally confused.

"Still just a boring human," Cammie said with a shrug.

Ramona knew for a fact that wasn't true, but it seemed as though Cammie wasn't ready to say much more.

"The convergence point amplified all of us," Kashvi said. "Made us more of what we already were. Or revealed what was always there."

They sat in silence for a moment. Processing. Adjusting to their new normal. Ramona felt the loss of Zara like a physical ache. The silence where the tether used to be. But she also felt... different. Each of them were so different. Changed, amplified, powerful.

But still themselves. Still here. Still together.

"Where's my mother?" Ramona asked. "Iris?"

"They wanted to give you some space," Kashvi said. "They're not here. They left this morning. Said something about last-minute Ostara Gala things."

The Ostara Gala.

Tonight.

"Speaking of, I had an idea," Felix said. His voice was too casual. Too bright. Definitely trying to distract her from the grief. "What if we officially became a coven?"

Ramona looked at him. At all of them. "What?"

"Think about it. We just performed three rituals in one night. Cleansed a corrupted convergence point. Broke a twenty-seven-year-old curse. Survived a ghost attack and came out of it with amplified abilities." Felix gestured around the room. "We work well together. Why not make it official?"

Cammie smiled again. "I like this change. I want to be an honorary coven member."

"Covens can have non-magical members," Posey said quietly. "Support roles. Historians. Chroniclers." She looked at Cammie. "Endless possibilities."

Ramona looked around at her friends, her real family, sitting in the room with her. An oddball group of outcasts who had come together and created change. Had helped her when she needed it. She couldn't think of any other coven members she'd rather have by her side. She felt the tightness loosen in her chest, just barely. The grief stayed, but something was standing beside it now. Hope, maybe.

"Okay," she said. "Okay. We could be a coven."

"Should we have a name?" Kashvi asked. Percival the ghost cat purred on her lap.

"The Exile Coven," Felix said with a grin. "Since that's basically what we are. Outcasts and exiles and people who don't fit the Council's narrow definitions."

"That's terrible," Kashvi said. "Very on the nose."

"I like it," Posey said softly.

"So what do we do first as the Exile Coven?" Cammie asked.

"We could register with the Council," Kashvi said. "Which means filling out approximately seven thousand forms and probably getting interrogated about our intentions and practices."

"Or," Felix said slowly. A small smile played at the corners of his mouth. "We could just show up at the Ostara Gala tonight and *make* them acknowledge us."

Silence.

Then Ramona started laughing. "That's insane."

"It's perfect," Felix corrected. "Show up at the biggest magical event of the year. Make them acknowledge us as a real coven. Put them on the spot in front of everyone to celebrate the fresh start and endless possibility of spring."

"They'll hate it," Ramona said.

"Good," Posey said. There was an edge to her voice Ramona had never heard before. Anger, maybe. Determination.

"We'll need outfits," Cammie said. She was looking at her phone again. "The Ostara Gala is tonight. Like, in six hours. And it's formal. Ball-gowns-and-tuxedos formal."

"I know a place," Kashvi said. "There's a cool vintage shop in Thornwood not too far away. They have a whole section of formal wear. If we go now, we might have time."

Ramona shook her head. "I don't think I'm ready to go."

Silence.

"What?" Felix said.

"I'm not in the mood, and I don't particularly want to be recognized anywhere as a Greenbriar right now." Ramona's voice was flat. That was only half of the reason. The other half was the huge, gaping hole in her chest where her heart once was. "You all go. Make your statement. I'll… I'll be at home."

"Absolutely not," Kashvi said immediately.

"This was your idea—" Posey started.

"It was Felix's idea," Ramona corrected.

"You agreed to it," Felix said. "You can't back out now."

"I said it was insane."

"Same thing," Felix argued.

"You should come," Cammie said gently. "Zara would want you to go. Would want you to show everyone what you're capable of."

That hit like a knife. Ramona's chest tightened. "That's not fair," she said.

"It's completely fair," Felix said. "Come on, Ramona. We're doing this together. The Exile Coven's first official appearance."

Posey looked at Ramona. Her voice was soft but firm. "Please come with us. We need you there."

"We're not doing this without you," Kashvi added. "You're the reason we're all here. The reason we even have a coven."

"That's not true—"

"It is," Felix interrupted. "You brought us together. Your curse, your ritual, your fight. We're not showing up at that gala without you."

"Besides," Cammie added, a slight smile on her face. "Your mom will be *so mad* if we crash her event."

Ramona lifted a brow, considering.

"She might even disown you," Felix added.

"I mean, that is very enticing." Ramona smirked.

Eleanor would hate it. Would be mortified that her disgraced daughter showed up at a Magical Council formal event with a ragtag group of outcasts calling themselves a coven.

Ramona looked at all of them. At her found family. Her coven. The people who'd stayed. Who'd helped. Who were here even though Zara wasn't.

The grief held firm. Still crushing. But underneath…

They were right. Zara would want her to go. Would want her to walk into that gala with her head high and her magic clean and show everyone exactly who she was.

"Okay," Ramona said. Her voice was rough. "Fine. I'll go. But if I have a breakdown in the middle of the gala, you're all responsible."

"Deal," Felix said, grinning. "Now let's go find you a dress that says 'I broke a twenty-seven-year-old curse and all I got was this lousy formal wear.'"

"That's not a thing dresses say," Kashvi pointed out.

"It should be," Felix said.

Gerald did a loop-the-loop in agreement.

Despite everything — despite the grief and the loss and the empty space where the tether used to be — Ramona felt the corners of her mouth lift into a small smile.

CHAPTER THIRTY-FOUR

"There's a thing or [illegible]," Kasia pointed out.

"It should be," Fifi said.

Cand[illegible] the [illegible] agreement.

Despite everything—despite the gun and the [illegible] the empty space where the father used to [illegible]. He noted that [illegible] mouth [illegible] a small smile.

CHAPTER THIRTY-FIVE

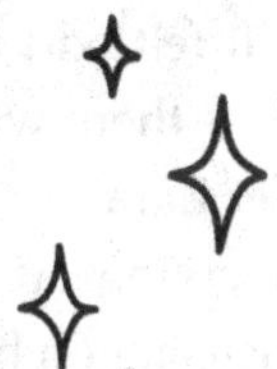

RAMONA STOOD IN FRONT OF THE FULL-LENGTH MIRROR IN HER CHILDHOOD bedroom, wearing the dress they'd found at the vintage shop in Thornwood.

It was perfect. Deep emerald green, the kind of color that made her skin look luminous instead of pale. The bodice was fitted, the skirt flowing. It was elegant but not trying too hard. It was exactly the kind of dress that said *I belong here* without a question mark.

The others were getting ready in the guest rooms down the hall. She could hear Felix arguing with Gerald about a bow tie. Kashvi's voice drifted down the hall, talking to ghosts Ramona couldn't see. Posey and Cammie were giggling about something.

But Ramona was alone. She wanted to get ready alone, had told everyone she wanted some time.

She stared at her reflection.

The dress was right. Her makeup was light — truthfully, she was afraid at some point during the night she'd cry her mascara right off, and she instead took a moment to look up a glamour spell for waterproofing her eye makeup.

The fox sat on the bed behind her, watching her with what looked like a bored expression. He seemed to be letting her know she was on her own tonight.

Her own eyes flicked upward, toward her hair.

The purple was still there. Faded and uneven from when she'd glamoured it the first time. Some sections were vibrant, others washed out. Some strands were more pink than purple. It felt like a scar, like a visible reminder of her inability to do even basic magic correctly.

The curse, she knew now. It felt odd to think that way. It was as if her life had split in two now — there was before the curse, and after the curse. Before Zara, and after Zara.

No. *No*, she would not be crying off her makeup before she even made it to the gala. She was focusing on her hair, not on losing the only one who had ever truly seen her and loved her anyway.

She took a deep breath through her nose. Her hair looked messy. Unkempt. Not appropriate for the Ostara Gala.

Eleanor would hate it.

The Council would judge her for it.

She really should fix it. Glamour it back to her natural color, now that she could. Or, better yet, something classic and sophisticated. The kind of hair color that said now she had her life together, that she was a respectable witch, that she deserved to be taken seriously.

Ramona raised her hand. Her magic responded instantly, easy and eager. She focused on her reflection. Thought about brown hair. Normal hair. Acceptable hair.

The purple began to fade and shift toward brown.

But it looked… wrong.

Not wrong like her magic failing — wrong like she was erasing something, like she was going backward instead of forward. With brunette hair, she looked like Eleanor. Like Iris.

Zara had loved the purple.

"It suits you," she'd said, her long dark-tipped fingers winding through Ramona's hair. "Unexpected. A little rebellious. Very you."

Ramona lowered her hand. The glamour dissolved. The patchy purple returned.

She stared at her reflection.

The purple was *her*. She'd chosen it. Not because it was professional or acceptable or what her mother would approve of, but because she'd wanted something different. Something that wasn't Ramona Greenbriar, Epic Failure and General Disappointment.

Except she wasn't the disappointment anymore. Without the curse to explain all of her failures, who was she?

Who was she, post-curse? After Zara?

Ramona raised her hand again. This time, she didn't think about brown. She didn't think about acceptable. She thought about *more.*

Her magic surged but stayed gentle and controlled. Responding to her intent like it was the easiest thing in the world.

The purple in her hair deepened, turning glossy. The patchy sections evened out. The faded parts became vibrant.

The kind of purple that caught light and held it, that made people look twice, that announced itself without saying a word. It was bold and unapologetic. That's the Ramona Greenbriar she wanted to be.

Ramona adjusted it slightly. Added depth, darker purple at the roots, brighter at the ends. Made it look intentional instead of accidental. Like she'd chosen this and meant it.

She let the magic settle, dropped her hand, and stared at her reflection.

The woman looking back at her felt different. Not because of the dress or the hair or the makeup. Because of the way she stood. The way she looked at herself.

Like she belonged in her own skin.

Like she wasn't broken. Had never been broken, not really.

Like she was powerful.

The door opened behind her. Ramona turned.

Kashvi stood in the doorway, wearing a deep blue dress that made her golden skin look ethereal. Percival the ghost cat wound around her ankles.

"Wow," Kashvi said. "Your hair."

"Too much?" Ramona asked.

"Not enough." Kashvi smiled. "It's perfect. Very 'I just broke a lifelong curse and I'm here to make everyone uncomfortable about it.'"

Ramona grinned. "That's exactly the vibe I was going for."

"You nailed it." Kashvi stepped into the room. She adjusted

Ramona's necklace — a simple gold chain they'd found in her old jewelry box. "How are you feeling?"

Ramona considered lying and saying she was fine, but this was Kashvi. Her coven. Her family.

"Terrified," she admitted. "And sad. And angry. And—" She stopped. "Like I should be able to feel Zara. Through the tether. Know what she'd say about all this. But there's just… nothing."

"That sounds awful," Kashvi said softly.

"It *feels* awful." Ramona's voice came out sharper than intended.

Kashvi put a hand on her arm, her eyes warm and gentle. "I know what it's like to lose someone. To have them ripped away without warning." She paused, but didn't expand on the revelation of her past that Ramona had never heard before. "And I know that going to this gala won't fix it. Won't make the grief go away. But it might give you something else to think about. Even just for a few hours."

"I'm sorry you've lost someone, too," Ramona said softly, squeezing Kashvi's hand.

"Hasn't everyone, in their own ways? Grief is universal," Kashvi said. Their eyes met in the reflection, and Kashvi smiled. "Enough sad talk. Come to the gala."

Ramona looked at herself in the reflection again. At the purple hair, finally the way she'd always wanted it. At the emerald-green dress. At the woman who looked powerful and whole and nothing like the disaster witch who'd derailed her entire life. "I know Zara would want me to go," she said quietly.

Kashvi nodded. "I think she would, too. She'd want you to walk in there with your head high and your badass magic and show everyone exactly who you are."

Ramona swallowed, blinking back tears. "I don't know who I am anymore."

"Yes, you do." Kashvi's hand found hers. Squeezed. "You're Ramona Greenbriar. Former professor. Current magic store employee. Accidental demon summoner. Curse-breaker. Coven leader." She paused.

Ramona's throat was tight. "That makes me sound like some stupid hero."

"No, it makes you sound like a motherfucking survivor," Kashvi said.

Ramona's resolve crumpled. The tears flowed freely now, and she let Kashvi embrace her, crying into her shoulder for a quiet few moments. "I feel like half of me is gone," she confessed through sobs.

"Then we'll be the other half. Until you figure out how to be whole on your own again," Kashvi said, petting her hair. "That's what covens do, right? Hold each other up when we can't stand on our own."

Ramona pulled back, wiping at her face. "Is that what covens do?"

"I don't know. We're making this up as we go." Kashvi's smile widened, her thumbs brushing a few tears off Ramona's cheeks. "But that sounds good, doesn't it?"

In the emptiness of Ramona's chest, she could have sworn she felt a tiny flutter of hope and love and gratitude. "Yeah," she murmured.

There was a knock on the door. Felix stuck his head in. Gerald was perched on his shoulder, wearing a tiny purple bow tie that matched Ramona's hair.

"You ready?" Felix asked. "The others are waiting downstairs. And I have to warn you — Posey grew flowers in the entryway and they're definitely going to give Eleanor a heart attack."

"Perfect," Ramona said.

She took one last look in the mirror.

Purple hair — finally right, finally the way it should have been all along. Green dress. Clean magic humming under her skin.

No tether. No Zara. But not alone.

She took a deep breath, straightening her posture. "Let's go crash a gala," she said.

And followed her coven downstairs.

CHAPTER THIRTY-SIX

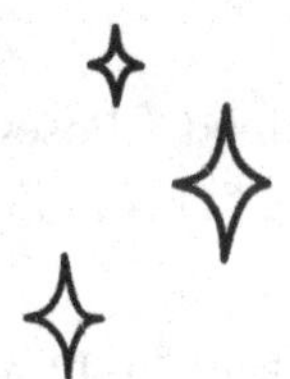

THE BALLROOM WAS A LOT.

Ramona had been to the Ostara Gala before. She'd walked these floors when she was faculty, when she was Simone's wife, when she'd belonged to the kind of world that threw parties like this. She thought she remembered it.

She didn't, apparently, because either it had gotten significantly more extravagant since her expulsion, or she'd spent the last several years of her attendance too busy not catastrophically ruining anything to actually look at the room.

Vaulted ceilings. Murals of Persephone rising, flowers blooming in her wake, painted so well the colors seemed to shift when Ramona wasn't looking directly at them. Crystal chandeliers big enough to have their own gravitational pull, dripping candles that floated without any visible support, their flames cycling through gold and rose and green. The walls were gold and cream and hung with tapestries that moved — slow, subtle, winter melting into spring on a loop.

And the flowers. Everywhere. Not arranged, but growing. Vines climbing the walls, cherry trees and magnolias coming up directly from the floor, all blooming at once despite half of them having no business blooming in March. Daffodils and tulips and irises carpeting the ground in patterns that parted around every step and closed again in people's wake. The air smelled like spring, earthy and wet and fresh, full of possibility.

The whole thing was gorgeous and excessive and exactly as insufferable as she'd remembered.

"Holy shit," Felix breathed.

Gerald cooed.

"The flowers are overstrained," Posey said, a hand over her heart and great concern in her tone. "This many species forced into simultaneous bloom—"

"Five minutes," Cammie said in an awed voice. "We are going to enjoy this for *five minutes* before anyone audits the ethics of the decorations."

They moved into the crowd.

The whispers started almost immediately. Ramona felt them before she heard them — that specific prickling awareness of being watched, of a room recalibrating around a presence it didn't expect. She caught fragments as she walked. *Is that Ramona Greenbriar?* And then: *Wasn't she expelled for trying to kill the High Priestess?* And then someone who was genuinely not being quiet enough: *I'm telling you, it was a demon at the convergence point.* Someone else, much more urgently: *Is that a pigeon wearing a bow tie?*

Gerald puffed up slightly at that last one. Felix looked like he might say something. Ramona put her hand briefly on his arm.

Fresh starts. New beginnings. Chin up.

She kept walking.

At the far end of the ballroom, the Magical Council occupied a raised platform in their formal robes — deep purple, silver embroidery, the works. The High Priestess stood at the center of them, her posture stiff and straight as she held a flower in her fingers, its petals shifting in color.

The High Priestess's eyes found Ramona across the room.

Ramona went still for a half second, waiting for something inevitable, like screaming or pointed fingers or something worse, like being ignored.

The High Priestess looked at her for a long moment — steady, unreadable — and then gave one small, deliberate nod. An acknowledgment. Nothing warm, nothing formal. Just: *I see you. You're here. That is noted.*

Ramona broke protocol and approached the dais where the High Priestess sat. The Magical Council went silent at her appearance, the general mood shifting to icy silence.

"May I have a word with you, High Priestess?" Ramona asked.

The High Priestess dipped her head in acknowledgment, then stood. Ramona followed her toward the back of the ballroom, her voice dropping low. "You're wondering how I knew about the convergence point and the ritual last night." The High Priestess seemed to tower above her now, her robes glowing from an internal light. Her eyes were startlingly light blue and seemed to stare through Ramona straight to her soul.

"Well, uh, yes," Ramona stammered, thrown off by the High Priestess's directness. The High Priestess she had known had always moved in silence, her wisdom feeling more like a riddle than an answer. Last night at the ritual was the most they'd spoken in years, even before Ramona had been exiled from the coven.

"The Magical Council found the convergence point two weeks ago. Your signature was all over it. I asked Iris for answers, and she told me the truth. *All* of the truth. I've exiled witches for less," the High Priestess said.

Ramona shifted her weight between her feet, her eyes defying all of her internal self-control to glance toward the High Priestess's ears. "I know."

"Of course."

"Did Iris tell you about last night, then?" Ramona asked.

"No, a first-year witch could have told me to watch for the new moon, Ramona. I've had it on my calendar for weeks," the High Priestess said.

"Weeks." Ramona gulped. "And you didn't think to maybe… help before that?"

"My help was not needed before."

"I would beg to differ, but—"

"We were there last night. We assisted when it counted. And if you want to return to Thornwood Coven, you have a place again," the High Priestess said, her light eyes unnervingly watching Ramona with intensity.

Ramona ducked her head in a strange mixture of gratitude and shock and the heavy realization that she'd spent two years dreaming of this moment and now that it was happening, it wasn't what she needed after all. She cleared her throat, blinking back the surge of emotions in her body. "I am honored and grateful, High Priestess. But I've found a new coven where I belong."

The High Priestess nodded, her eyes moving beyond Ramona. Ramona glanced over her shoulder to where Felix, Kashvi, Posey, and Cammie were standing, watching them with blatant interest like four bodyguards ready to defend her honor at any moment.

The High Priestess added, "And although I do welcome you at Thornwood Coven, the Magical Council has made it clear that your previously held position at Thornwood Academy will not be—"

"I understand." Not that she'd be accepting that role, either.

"Please do let me know if you plan to summon any more demons," the High Priestess added, blinking quickly in a way that made her look inhuman.

Ramona realized with shock that she was… teasing. Had the High Priestess just made a joke? She'd never heard of such a thing happening before. "No more demons," she promised.

Ramona watched the High Priestess return to the Magical Council's dais and realized a lot had changed in two years. She turned back to where her friends were waiting and shrugged. "I'll explain all that later."

A floating tray materialized at elbow height with champagne. She took a glass. Her coven did the same. Felix raised his: "To the Exile Coven, and to making everyone here deeply uncomfortable."

"I'll drink to that," Kashvi said. Her fingers sparked faintly at the tips.

"Even ourselves," Posey said, eyeing the flowers at her feet.

They drank. The champagne was perfect — cold, with a secondary warmth that spread through Ramona's chest and had nothing to do with alcohol.

She scanned the room without really meaning to. An old habit. She found — without surprise, but also without being totally prepared for it — Simone.

Near the windows. Wearing a silver dress that looked like dripping mercury against her skin. Still beautiful. Still effortlessly everything Ramona had spent years feeling inadequate next to. Beside her was Kate, her hair chopped into a blunt bob that made her look severe and sharp. The two of them were visibly arguing about something, glancing toward Ramona and then looking away, their voices low but posture tight, the particular choreography of a fight that was trying not to be a scene.

Ramona waited to feel something about it, taking a mental calculation of her own emotional reaction.

Instead, she felt *nothing*. Not even the distant bruised ache she'd been carrying for two years. The whole thing felt like looking at a photograph of a place she used to live. Something happened there, once. It just wasn't hers anymore.

"Is that your ex?" Cammie asked.

"Yeah."

"She looks miserable."

Ramona couldn't help a small smile tug at the edge of her mouth at that.

Simone glanced up and saw her watching.

Ramona watched the flicker cross her ex-wife's face — embarrassment, then something more complicated than that. Regret, if Ramona didn't know better. Kate followed her gaze.

The rational thing was to look away. Move on. Let the nothing stay nothing.

Subtlety and tact had never been Ramona's strong suit. Instead, she moved toward them.

She wasn't entirely sure she'd decided to do it. But there she was, crossing the ballroom floor, champagne glass in hand, while Simone's expression settled into the careful composure of someone who'd had a lot of practice looking like everything was fine.

"Ramona." Simone's voice was measured. "Good evening." She shifted uncomfortably. She always was obsessed with appearances, and fighting with her partner and her ex-wife at one gala must have been a step too far. She'd chosen fake niceties instead.

Ramona let her gaze move briefly to Kate, letting it trail down to the floor and back up, unimpressed with what she found.

Simone's chin came up slightly. "Listen, about the other night—"

"Save it." Ramona took a sip of her champagne. She was aware of people nearby who had stopped pretending not to listen. Somewhere to her left, a conversation about the Vernal Council's agenda had gone noticeably quiet. "You know, I used to have speeches for this. Really good ones. Very cathartic." She considered. "I don't think I need them anymore. Something you said the other night, it made me realize I only have one thing to tell you both." She looked at Simone, then Kate, and said, "I may be a villain in your story, but you're a joke in mine."

Kate's mouth fell open, and Simone flushed a furious shade of red.

Ramona raised her empty glass in a final toast and nodded — polite, conclusive, the social equivalent of a door closing — and turned and walked back to her coven.

"Cammie," she said. "I need another glass of champagne."

"Ahead of you," Cammie said and handed one over without a single question.

"Was that—" Felix started.

"Yes."

"Oh, they're fighting again," Kashvi whispered with a whole lot of delight in her voice. "Kate's storming out."

Ramona didn't dare look, for fear she'd start laughing. Instead, she held up her empty first glass, thought about it being full, and watched her magic respond immediately — champagne appearing cold and sparkling and present, like it had always been willing to do this and had simply been waiting for her to ask. Felix stared. She extinguished the nearest set of candles with barely a thought, like Zara had done the first time they'd closed the shop together, and then she lit them again, twice as bright, and a small murmur ran through the people standing closest to her.

Parlor tricks. First-year magic. She'd never been able to do any of it.

The grief of Zara's absence hit her all at once, sharp and specific, like the sting from a fall she'd been ignoring for hours. She wanted, more than anything, to turn around and feel the tether pull warm between them. To hear something precise and dry about the impracticality of conjuring alcohol as a coping mechanism.

But there was only silence where the tether had been. There was only the empty shape of it under her ribs.

Rebirth, she reminded herself. Spring requires winter to end. All darkness ends, light always returns.

Felix had already claimed Kashvi for the dance floor, Gerald performing small aerial maneuvers overhead while Felix tried to lead, and Kashvi tried to lead more successfully. Posey held out a hand to Cammie, who said she'd step on her feet and did so twice within thirty seconds and didn't stop smiling about it.

Ramona was watching them, still standing at the edge of the floor, when someone stopped beside her.

They didn't approach, exactly. Just stood nearby, close enough for conversation, but far enough for plausible deniability.

She turned.

Iris, in a perfectly tailored purple dress that didn't quite suit her, hair up, hands clasped in front of her with the careful stillness she always deployed when she was keeping something controlled.

"Hi," Ramona said.

"Hi." Iris looked at her, and something in her expression was doing a lot of work trying to stay in place. "Your hair. The purple — it's different from before."

"I fixed it. I can do that now, apparently."

A beat. The music swelled, and somewhere behind them a couple drifted past, close enough that they both went briefly silent.

"You look like yourself," Iris said, finally. Her voice had gone quiet. "I mean, you look like you're supposed to look."

Ramona didn't know what to do with that, so she didn't say anything.

"I'm not going to make a scene," Iris continued. "I'm not here to demand anything from you. I just—" She stopped. Started again, more carefully. "I always told myself there was some reason I couldn't tell you what I'd done. There wasn't. I was afraid, and you paid for that, and I'm sorry. I'm genuinely, deeply sorry."

The ballroom kept going around them. A waltz. The smell of spring flowers forced into impossible bloom. Somewhere to Ramona's left, a warlock was telling someone about his summer estate.

"I know," Ramona said. "We were kids, Iris. I don't blame you for the curse. It's the secrecy that hurts."

Iris nodded. Her jaw was tight.

"I'm not ready to be okay about it yet," Ramona said. "That might take a while." She looked at her sister, then meant the rest of it too: "But I came out the other side. I know the truth. The curse is broken. My magic works. I have…" She gestured at the dance floor, where Felix had just stepped on Kashvi's foot and was apologizing at length to both her and Gerald. "I have those people. I'm good."

Something in Iris cracked slightly at the edges. Not in a bad way. Like an exhale. "Gerald has a purple bow tie."

"He's a very dapper bird."

A pause that was almost a laugh from Iris. Almost. She cleared her throat. "I wanted you to know I came to the ritual because I wanted to be there. Not because of Mom."

"I know. And thank you for being there. Thank you for all of your help, really. The grimoires and the supplies and… all of it. I do appreciate it, even if I'm not ready to fully…" Ramona lifted a shoulder in a shrug that she hoped communicated her feelings better than words could.

Iris dipped her head, recognizing the gratitude. They stood there for another moment, the gap between them not gone but maybe a little less absolute than it had been.

"I should get back," Iris said.

"Yeah." Ramona hesitated. "Tell Daphne and Poppy I said hi."

Something moved across Iris's face that might have been relief. "I will."

She walked away, and Ramona stood there watching her go and feeling the particular texture of something that wasn't forgiveness yet but might be the thing that grows into it, given enough time.

"Ramona." Posey appeared at her elbow, flushed from dancing, suspiciously innocent expression already in place. "Come on."

They danced. Ramona felt a small tickle at her scalp before she'd gone three steps. She reached up to find flowers woven in her hair.

"Posey."

"You needed them," Posey said with a smile — and did not apologize.

In a passing mirror, Ramona caught her own reflection. Purple hair with white blossoms winding through it. Green dress. Magic running clean and easy under her skin for the first time since she could remember. She looked like someone who'd just survived a very long winter.

She was refilling her champagne glass — a small magic, just because she could — when the room shifted. The quality of the murmur changed, a wave of attention turning toward the entrance, and Ramona turned without knowing why.

And there.

Standing in the doorway like she'd always meant to arrive this way.

Black tux with subtle purple accents that matched — exactly matched — Ramona's hair. Tailored precisely. Hair coiffed back away from her face, revealing perfect high cheekbones. Expression composed in the way Ramona had spent seven weeks learning to read past.

Zara.

Zara.

The crowd whispered: *who is that* and *where did she come from,* but it was happening very far away, underwater, all background noise.

Ramona's champagne glass slipped from her fingers.

It hit the floor and shattered, but Ramona didn't notice.

All she could see was Zara, moving through the crowd, eyes fixed on Ramona like nothing else in the room was real, coming toward her like the tether had been replaced by something that needed no magic at all.

CHAPTER THIRTY-SEVEN

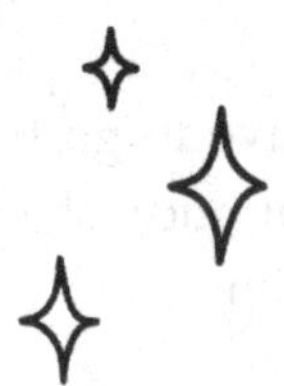

Zara crossed the ballroom.

The crowd parted for her — not out of respect, but out of that particular human instinct to move away from something they couldn't categorize.

Ramona still hadn't moved. There was champagne soaking into her shoe. She didn't care about that either.

Zara stopped in front of her.

The tux fit like it had been made for her, which it almost certainly had been. The purple in the lapels matched Ramona's hair precisely enough that it had to be intentional. Which meant she'd known, which meant she'd planned this, which meant—

"You're here," Ramona said. Her voice came out like it had been days since she'd last spoken, crackly and too high.

"I'm here," Zara said, dipping her chin in a small bow.

Ramona reached forward, tentative, afraid that if she touched Zara, the dream would end and she'd wake up, or her friends would drag her away from a hallucination. "How." It wasn't really a question. It came out more like a word she needed to say while her brain caught up with her eyes. Zara's shoulders were solid under her palms.

"It's a long story." Zara's voice was careful in the way it got when she was paying close attention to something. "Can we... Is there somewhere more private we can talk?" Her eyes widened as she looked around, and Ramona realized that an entire ballroom of witches was watching them.

Ramona took Zara by the hand and spared a quick thought to clean up her broken glass with an easy spell, then hurried out of the ballroom to the coat closet in the foyer of the building. She shut the door behind Zara.

"How long before you have to go back?" Ramona asked, feeling frantic. The fear arrived all at once, sharp and specific. "An hour? A day? What are we working with—"

"Ramona."

"—because I need to know how much time—"

"Ramona." Zara took her hands. Ramona realized that her touch was warm. Human-warm, not the particular heat Ramona had catalogued through seven weeks together. Something was different. "I'm not going back."

Ramona stopped talking.

"The ritual," Zara said. "It didn't just break your curse and the tether. It broke *all* bindings. Including my contract with Hell." The corner of her mouth moved. "Turns out, three hundred years of bureaucratic experience is very useful when you're trying to formally resign from a demonic institution."

"Your contract," Ramona repeated slowly.

"Was a binding. An old one, but structurally not that different from the one we'd just dissolved with a full coven at a cleansed convergence point during a new moon." Zara's expression was careful, as though she wasn't trying to reveal everything all at once. "The power doesn't discriminate."

"So when you got back to Hell—"

"I was there by momentum. Not by obligation." A pause. "I went to my supervisor. Submitted my resignation. They were not pleased. Told me if I left, I'd lose my immortality. Age and die like any human." Something moved briefly across her face. "They meant it as a threat."

Ramona's chest hurt. "And you..."

"I told them that was fine." Zara said it the same way she said most things — precisely, without fuss. Like it was a straightforward cost-benefit analysis that had come out clearly on one side. "More than fine."

"Zara." Ramona's voice cracked on it. "You were immortal."

"I know."

"You could have lived forever."

"I know." Zara's thumb moved across Ramona's knuckles. "What use is all the time in the world without the woman you love? I'd just have to spend eternity miserable and lonely and missing you."

Ramona was crying. She hadn't noticed starting. Zara reached up and wiped her cheek with the same unhurried practicality she brought to everything, and Ramona laughed despite herself — a wet, undignified sound that had no business being made at the Ostara Gala.

"So you're… mortal," Ramona said.

"As of about two hours ago." Zara paused. "I can feel my heartbeat. It's quite strange. And I think I might be hungry, which is apparently something that happens now."

Ramona let out a surprised laugh. "It might take some getting used to, Mortal."

Zara grinned, her fangs still present. "Don't you *dare*."

Ramona wrapped her arms around Zara's neck.

"I'm so sorry it took me so long to get back. We can discuss the logistics later. There's a significant amount of logistics." A beat. "There was also exit paperwork. Hell's HR department is thorough even when they're furious with you, which I respect professionally even if I found it inconvenient this evening. It took me weeks."

"Weeks? It's been… one day," Ramona said.

"Time must move very differently there. I was terrified I'd miss the gala."

Ramona nearly laughed. "You were? Why?"

"I told you I'd be here, and I intended to keep my word."

Ramona kissed her.

Zara made a small, surprised sound — which was fair, as Ramona had done it somewhat abruptly — and then kissed her back gently. Her hands came up to Ramona's face, and Ramona could feel her pulse at her wrist, steady and new and mortal and real.

When they broke apart, both of them were breathing a little unsteadily.

"I love you," Ramona said. "I thought you were gone. I spent the whole day thinking you were gone forever."

"I know." Zara's forehead dropped against hers. "I'm sorry it took me so long to get back." A short exhale that was almost a laugh.

"You're really staying."

"I'm really staying." She pulled back just enough to look at Ramona properly. "If you'll have me."

"Are you— Zara. It's a little late for that question. You gave up *immortality*—"

"I wanted to be polite about it," Zara said, and the familiar dryness of it was so entirely her that Ramona laughed again, properly this time, and pulled her close.

They stayed like that for a moment. Just breathing. Ramona could feel Zara's heartbeat under her palm. Could feel her breathe. It was the most ordinary thing in the world, and it was extraordinary.

A knock at the door.

"Ramona." Felix's voice, careful and concerned. "Is everything okay with Zara? Gerald is losing his mind out here. He's done seven loop-the-loops."

Ramona looked at Zara. Zara looked at Ramona.

"We should probably tell them," Ramona said.

"Probably," Zara agreed.

Ramona opened the door. Felix stood there with Gerald vibrating on his shoulder. Behind him, Kashvi, Posey, and Cammie, all arranged in a configuration that suggested they'd been deciding whether to knock for at least two minutes.

Zara stepped forward. "Hello, everyone."

Gerald cooed and immediately performed an eighth loop-the-loop.

Felix was staring. "Did I hear you say you're *mortal*?"

"And they just let you go?" Kashvi asked.

"They didn't have a choice. My contract was dissolved. I told them I had accepted a position elsewhere." A small, satisfied pause.

"Holy shit," Felix said softly.

"Yes," Ramona agreed, taking Zara's hand. "We can do the full debrief later. Right now, I think maybe we should go back inside and dance at the gala we crashed specifically to prove we belonged there, and I'd really like our latest coven member to be there when we do."

"Coven member?" Zara questioned. "Your coven accepts all sorts, I see." Her eyes slid to Cammie, who grinned and shrugged.

"Exile Coven is a very equal-opportunity coven," Ramona said. "Humans and mortal demons alike are welcome."

She pulled Zara back toward the ballroom. Her coven followed, Gerald triumphant overhead.

"You know," Zara said as the music got louder. "I came all the way back from Hell for this. The dancing had better be worth it."

"It won't be," Felix called from behind them. "Statistically, it really won't."

"Speak for yourself," Kashvi said.

"Welcome to mortality," Ramona said and pulled her through the doors.

CHAPTER THIRTY-EIGHT

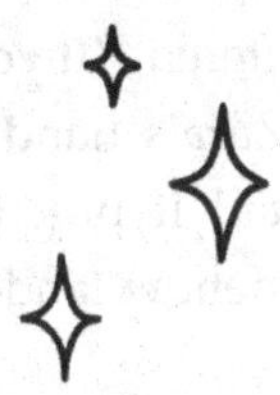

The apartment was quiet.

Everyone else had gone to an afterparty at The Grimalkin. The Exile Coven, officially acknowledged. Felix had been so excited Gerald did three consecutive barrel rolls.

Ramona and Zara had walked home from the bar, not even going inside first.

Now the bedroom was dark except for the streetlight coming through the cracked window, the city humming quietly below. The flowers Posey had grown in Ramona's hair were wilting slightly at the edges.

"Leave them," Zara said. She was sitting beside her on the bed, jacket off, bow tie hanging loose around her neck. "They're beautiful."

"They're dying."

"Everything dies eventually." A beat. "I would know."

Ramona looked at her. At this woman who'd just handed back three hundred years without flinching. "Does it scare you? Being mortal?"

Zara considered it the way she considered most things — seriously, without rushing to an answer. "A little. Death was always theoretical before. Now it's just distant. Eventual." She turned to look at Ramona. "Mostly I'm relieved to be here."

"How does it feel? Your body, I mean."

"Loud," Zara said. "Everything is very immediate. My heartbeat feels too fast. I'm hungry but I don't know what I want. I'm tired and also wired." A pause. "It's a great deal of sensation for someone who hasn't felt much in three centuries."

"We can sleep," Ramona offered. "If you need to."

"I don't want to sleep." Zara's hand found hers. "I want to feel everything. All of it." She said it practically, like a straightforward statement of intent, which somehow landed harder than if she'd made a speech about it.

Ramona kissed her. Zara kissed back, slower than the ballroom coat closet kiss, one hand coming up to cup her face. Ramona leaned into Zara's steadiness, taking her time.

When they broke apart, Ramona reached back toward the zip of her dress. "Help me with this. I can't reach."

Zara's hands were careful on the zipper. Unhurried. The dress loosened and Ramona stood, let it fall, stepped out of it. She hadn't worn anything special underneath, just some very plain, very comfortable underwear — she hadn't planned for the night to end like this, which felt like the most honest version of it.

Zara was looking at her with barely contained awe.

"Your turn," Ramona said.

Zara stood and unbuttoned her shirt with focused efficiency, then paused. "It's different now. Everything's more…" She searched for the word. "Present. I don't know what to do with that yet."

"You don't have to do anything with it." Ramona crossed to her, put her hands on her waist, felt her exhale. "We figure it out."

"I don't know if it'll be different." Zara said. Matter-of-fact, which made it more vulnerable somehow, not less.

"Then we'll find out."

They moved to the bed, and Zara's skin was warm under her hands — not the scorching inferno Ramona had catalogued through the seven weeks they'd spent together. She pressed her palms flat against Zara's stomach and felt her breathing change.

"Tell me what you want to try," Ramona murmured against her collarbone.

"Everything," Zara said. "Start anywhere."

So Ramona did. She took her time working down Zara's body, learning what had changed and what hadn't — Zara's sharp inhale when Ramona's teeth found the curve of her shoulder was exactly the same, and she filed that away with satisfaction. The heat between her thighs was different. Less supernatural, more human, and somehow more intimate for it.

"Ramona," Zara said, her voice rough. "Please."

Ramona slid her fingers over Zara's inner thigh, and Zara's hips lifted immediately, chasing the contact. She was wet and warm and sensitive, and Ramona watched her face as she circled her fingers slowly — the furrow of her brows, the way her composure came apart in increments, nothing like the controlled precision she wore everywhere else.

"More," Zara breathed.

Ramona pushed two fingers inside and felt her clench around them, a low sound wrenched out of her. "Does that feel good?"

"Mm-hmm," Zara managed. Her hand found Ramona's wrist, not pulling away but holding on, grounding herself. "It's… Everything is so much more—" She stopped, because Ramona's thumb found her clit and whatever she'd been about to say dissolved into a sharp exhale.

Ramona moved to use her mouth instead of her thumb, desperate to taste her. With the sounds Zara began making, Ramona was grateful that her roommates weren't home. She learned the new rhythm of her, the way her body moved and responded without a tail to betray her or supernatural heat to mask her. Just Zara, undone, her fingers twisted in the sheets, her hips moving against Ramona's mouth with increasing urgency until she came apart with a long, shuddering release that Ramona worked her through until she went boneless.

Afterward Zara lay there for a moment, breathing. Then she turned her head.

"Your turn," she said, echoing Ramona's demand from earlier. The familiar precision was back in her voice already, which was deeply unfair.

She rolled Ramona onto her back and took her time about it — her mouth tracing down Ramona's throat, her collarbone, lower. When she finally settled between Ramona's thighs, she glanced up first.

"Still the same?" she asked.

"Find out," Ramona said.

Zara's mouth on her was different without the supernatural heat, and Ramona stopped trying to analyze it approximately thirty seconds later because Zara was very good at this regardless of which plane of existence she was operating from. She knew exactly where to focus, exactly when to add her fingers, and Ramona came with Zara's name on her lips and her hands twisted in that perfectly styled hair.

Zara kissed her way back up and settled beside her, and they lay in the dark, breathing.

"Well," Zara said to the ceiling. "That was significant."

"High praise."

"It was meant as high praise." A pause. "The mortality is an adjustment. Everything feels very immediate and tenuous and intense."

"Good intense?" Ramona asked gently.

Zara considered. "Very good intense." She turned her head to look at Ramona. "I'm going to mention the immortality thing at least once a day, by the way. I want that established."

"I figured."

"It was a significant sacrifice."

"I know, baby."

"I just want to ensure you appreciate the full—"

"You're so ridiculous," Ramona teased, tilting her head up to look at her. "I do appreciate it. Deeply. Every day. For the rest of your mortal life."

Something moved through Zara's expression — not quite a smile, but the thing that lived right next to one. She pulled Ramona closer without saying anything else, which was its own kind of answer.

The spring air drifted through the window. Ramona fell asleep to the sound of Zara's heartbeat, steady and new, and thought — distantly, at the soft edge of consciousness — that she'd spent thirty-five years finding things that were lost, and she had never once considered that she might be one of them.

She had been. She wasn't anymore.

And now she'd found this. The extraordinary gift of someone choosing to come back, to stay.

EPILOGUE — THREE MONTHS LATER

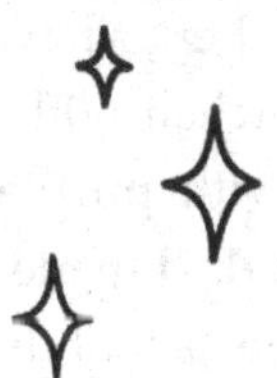

The apartment smelled like coffee and summer and something slightly burnt, which meant Kashvi had been baking again and had gotten distracted.

"Are you sure the streamers aren't a fire hazard?" Kashvi asked, eyeing the purple and gold decorations Felix had strung across the ceiling. Percival sat on the kitchen table, watching with curiosity.

"Ramona can put out fires now," Felix said cheerfully. He was standing on a chair, hanging a banner in glittery letters that read CONGRATULATIONS ON YOUR FOX. "Her magic works. It's fine."

"That's not how fire safety works."

"It's how *our* fire safety works."

Gerald assisted by holding one end of the banner in his beak, hovering with the focused dignity he brought to all official coven functions.

Ramona stood in the doorway, taking it in. The banner. The tower of cupcakes Posey had made, each one topped with a tiny frosted fox. The party hats Cammie had apparently purchased in bulk.

"This is ridiculous," she said.

"This is a *celebration*." Felix hopped down from the chair and adjusted his hat — purple with gold stars. "You're bonding with your familiar. That deserves a party."

"It's just a ritual—"

"It's your first formal magic since breaking the curse," Posey said in the gentle tone usually reserved for correcting someone who was being deliberately obtuse. She was wearing a green party hat with actual flowers growing out of it. "That's significant."

"And I love a party," Cammie added. She had her camera ready and her hat at a jaunty angle. "Let us have this."

Zara emerged from the kitchen with a tray of champagne glasses, wearing a black party hat with purple trim that somehow looked elegant, because of course it did. "I made mimosas. Or, I poured a drop of orange juice into champagne. Is that the same thing?"

"Sounds perfect," Ramona said.

The fox sat in the middle of the living room watching all of it with amber eyes that had always, from the very first day, looked like they knew something she didn't. His tail swished.

Felix held out a purple party hat. "Put it on."

Ramona put it on. It sat crooked on her purple hair. "Happy?"

"Ecstatic," Felix said. "Now, let's do this. I have confetti."

"Please don't—" Kashvi started.

"So much confetti," Felix said gleefully.

They gathered in the living room, a grimoire open on the coffee table.

Three months since the curse broke. Three months since Zara had handed back her immortality and shown up at the Ostara Gala. Three months of magic and a coven and a girlfriend who still occasionally forgot she needed to eat, and a fox who had been following Ramona around since before she had any right to be followed.

She'd woken up about a week ago and realized it was finally time to do the formal familiar bonding ceremony.

She knelt in front of him. He stepped closer.

"Ready?" Felix asked. His confetti hand was already raised. Cammie had her camera up.

"Ready," Ramona said.

She placed her hand on the fox's head and felt his warmth, his presence, the particular quality of his attention that she'd been aware of for months without being able to name it.

"I claim you," she said, not in any of the seven dead languages she'd spent her academic career parsing. It was simple, it didn't need translation. "As my familiar. My companion. My partner in magic. I offer you my protection, my power, my loyalty. In exchange for yours." A pause. "Do you accept?"

The fox pressed his head more firmly against her palm.

The bond formed — nothing like the tether, which had been external and imposed and a bridge between two separate things. This was different. More like water settling into cracks. She felt his presence move into her magic like it had always been meant to be there, like the space had been waiting.

And with it came his name. Not one she gave him. His actual name, the one he'd always had.

"Wick," Ramona said.

The fox — Wick — made a sound low in his chest. *Yes. That's me.*

"His name is Wick," Ramona said to the room.

"Like a candle wick?" Zara asked.

Like a flame, Wick corrected in her mind, with the particular patience of someone who'd had to clarify this before. *Like the thing that carries fire. That transforms fuel into light.*

Ramona translated the meaning to the room.

"That's perfect," Posey said softly.

"Now," Felix announced and threw the confetti.

Cammie threw hers at the same moment — purple and gold stars cascading through the air — and Zara flinched hard, stepping back fast with her hands coming up, pressing herself against the wall.

The confetti settled. Harmless. Festive.

Zara lowered her hands. "Sorry," she said and laughed, though it came out a little unsteady. "Three months and things being thrown at me still — In Hell, projectiles are generally less celebratory."

"No more surprise confetti," Felix said immediately. "New rule. All confetti is announced in advance."

"Agreed," said Kashvi, scooping Percival up into her arms. He closed his eyes, content as she pet his translucent head.

Zara crossed back to Ramona and took her hand, and Ramona felt Wick lean against her ankle from the other side, the bond already doing what bonds do.

"You okay?" Ramona asked quietly.

"Fine." Zara squeezed her hand. "Genuinely. Still adding things to the list of what startles me now. Confetti goes on the list." She looked down at Wick, and her expression softened. "He chose well."

Wick's tail swished. *Obviously.*

"I understood that one," Zara said.

Felix raised his champagne glass. "To Wick." Gerald performed a twirling dance, party hat miraculously intact.

"To Wick," everyone said.

They drank. Wick's tail continued swishing with the energy of someone receiving their due recognition.

Your coven is so strange, he observed. *I approve.*

"He approves of us," Ramona told the room.

"High praise," Cammie said seriously.

"The highest," Ramona agreed.

They ate the cupcakes, and the afternoon went soft and warm around them, full of the particular noise of people entirely comfortable around one another. Zara's hand found Ramona's under the table. Wick stayed at her feet.

"How does it feel?" Zara asked quietly, under the general noise of Felix trying to get Gerald to wear a second party hat. "The bond."

Ramona thought about it. "Like something that was always supposed to be there," she said. "Like I'd always been waiting without knowing it."

Zara looked at her for a long moment. "Yes," she said. "I know exactly what you mean."

From across the table came the sound of Felix negotiating with a pigeon about a party hat, and Cammie saying *just let it go* with the weary authority of someone who'd given up trying to predict what normal looked like in this apartment.

Ramona leaned into Zara's shoulder. Wick stayed at her feet.

It was, she thought, a very good afternoon.

BONUS EPILOGUE

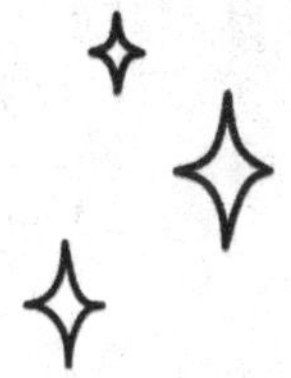

Want a peek one year later?

RAMONA'S NEW SHOP OPENS TOMORROW, SHE AND ZARA HAVE JUST MOVED into their new apartment, and there's one last scene that didn't make it into the book. It involves, *ahem,* "advanced conjuration magic." Download it free at the link below.

bryceoakley.com/bonus-content

ACKNOWLEDGMENTS

My wife, who so kindly sat and listened to me dream up this book and encouraged me to take a chance, writing outside of my comfort zone (and then reminding me that my comfort zone of idiots-to-lovers most definitely fit here).

My sister for reading early drafts, talking through plot points, and generally being the best cheerleader forever.

JJ, who read the very VERY earliest draft and threatened me if I didn't finish it.

TJ, Leah, DJ, Luc, for being the funniest people in the entire world.

My editor Heather, who knows the difference between toward and towards, and for all of other genius parts of your brain.

And to everyone in the sapphic romance community — I am so grateful to call you friends and colleagues and readers.

ALSO BY BRYCE OAKLEY

Breakup Buddies

The Adventurers

Never Mine

Something Far Away and Happy

Against The Grain

Every Version

Latitude & Longing

One Last Run

Shift the Tide

After All

Holiday Romances

Most Wonderful

All Aglow

Ghosted Christmas Past

The Snowy Springs Holiday Romances

Baking Spirits Bright

Rebel Without A Claus

The Kaleidoscope Album

Undone

Bewilder

Midnight

Bloom

Revel

The Kaleidoscope Album Box Set

ABOUT THE AUTHOR

Bryce Oakley is a Goldie-award winning author of sapphic romantic comedies and self-proclaimed pepperoni pizza connoisseur. She lives in Colorado with her wife, daughter, and a small herd of rescue animals.

www.ingramcontent.com/pod-product-compliance
Lightning Source LLC
Chambersburg PA
CBHW011924050726
47591CB00009B/2323

* 9 7 8 1 9 6 7 5 5 1 0 4 0 *